Dear Reader,

Is your *Scarlet* collection complete?

Each week I receive so many letters from devoted readers asking for back copies of books to be sent to them. Therefore, we want to give you all the opportunity to order copies of books that you might have missed the first time round. If you are interested, please write and send a stamped-addressed envelope. In return I will send you a list of available titles and an order form.

Hurry and send your order in – first come, first served!

This month, we present the exciting sequel to *The Name of the Game* by Julie Garratt – *The Trouble with Tamsin*. Tamsin must finally decide which man she loves! Is it the faithless Patric Faulkener, lost love Vaughn Herrick or the attractively menacing Craig Andrews? Then there is Mark Langham – the only person she can truly rely on – and it is only when she begins to lose him that she realizes just where her true happiness lies! In *Find Her, Keep Her* by Judy Jackson, Daniel St Clair is everything Jess Philips should avoid. She's a career woman – fighting to make a living in a man's world. He thinks she's fun to be with and sexy as hell . . . though definitely not wife material. When Jess accepts Daniel's help, she gives in to the physical attraction between them, but Jess should have remembered that romance plays by its own rules and it plays to win.

As always, each of our authors has brought something special to the telling of her romance, and choosing these new and exciting *Scarlet* novels for you was a great pleasure for me. Let me know if you enjoyed them.

Till next month,

Sally Cooper

SALLY COOPER,
Editor-in-Chief – *Scarlet*

About the Author

Judy Jackson's first *Scarlet* novel, *The Marriage Plan*, was published early in 1997 and we are now delighted to bring you her third compelling romance.

Judy spent her childhood in Alberta before her family moved to the coast of British Columbia. She married her highschool sweetheart and they live with their two terrific sons in the Vancouver area.

All through school, Judy could never decide on her future. Since then she's worked at so many jobs she can't remember them all, though they must have involved bookkeeping. At age thirty she threw a 'what-do-you-want-to-be-when-you-grow-up costume party.' Judy, of course, couldn't make up *her* mind so printed 50 different jobs on slips of paper and pinned them to her maternity smock! Now she lives vicariously through her characters' professions.

With hindsight, Judy knows her career began as a child, entertaining her friends with imaginative stories. Telling 'stories' was so much fun, Judy never stopped. Thanks to *Scarlet*, she can continue to entertain people with her stories and get paid for it!

Other *Scarlet* title available this month:

THE TROUBLE WITH TAMSIN – Julie Garratt

JUDY JACKSON

FIND HER, KEEP HER

SCARLET

Enquiries to:
Robinson Publishing Ltd
7 Kensington Church Court
London W8 4SP

First published in the UK by Scarlet, 1998

A copy of the British Library Cataloguing in
Publication data is available from the British Library

1-85487-562-0

Printed and bound in the EC

10 9 8 7 6 5 4 3 2 1

This book is dedicated to my extended family, the Jacksons and the McAnerins. Luckily for me they chose varied and interesting careers and have the kindness to answer all my questions.

To my friends Joyce David and Shirley Mann, who let me pick their brains on what it's like to be a female private detective.

PROLOGUE

'I am sorry, Miss Phillips. I'm afraid we have nothing suitable right now but we'll keep your application on file.'

He didn't mean it. She could tell. She could always tell.

Where now? Searching for a job was hard for any twenty-year-old woman with only a high-school education and no friends or family to give her a helping hand. Someone like her had even fewer choices.

If only she was even slightly pretty. Beautiful women never had trouble finding a good job. Probably because most bosses were men.

As soon as she left today, her application would go straight into the garbage. Jess sat straighter in her chair, shifted her feet to hide the hole in her sneakers, and forced her lips to curve into a smile as she looked the scrawny personnel manager in the eyes.

'I learn fast and I'm a very hard worker. Lambert Investigations advertised a trainee position, Mr Cockell.'

He looked down at her application form on his desk, a form she knew was probably either incomplete or incorrect in almost every section, though she'd done her best. Personnel managers were as bad as every teacher she'd ever been tortured by; they couldn't see past their forms and their rules to *her*, the person.

'Yes, you are correct. However, there appear to be a few problems with your . . . qualifications.'

She swallowed around the lump in her throat and blinked hard. She wouldn't cry. Jess Phillips never cried. 'I'll work for minimum wage. I'm young and strong, I can run errands, answer the phones –'

'I'm sorry, Miss Phillips.' He stood up, waiting for her to leave.

She gathered her woven bag from the floor at her feet, aware of all the clerks in the busy office who'd been watching and listening to her humiliation.

The bag was heavy, but she didn't care. The people at the YWCA hostel seemed nice but she never left her bits and pieces in the room, just in case. She didn't own much, but it was all she had and she'd be damned before she left it lying around for some stranger to steal.

She twisted the bag's handles around her fingers and gripped hard as she stood up. She had to get this job; she'd tried everywhere else.

She didn't want to spend the rest of her life scraping old grease and smelly muck off the floors in crummy diners. She'd been looking for something better for almost two years and was losing hope.

'I'll do two weeks, no wages.' Jess rubbed the bridge of her nose where she'd broken it in her fourth foster home. Or was it the sixth? 'Once you see what I can do, I'm sure you'll hire me.'

'Your time is up, Miss Phillips. I have other people to interview.'

'One week. Just give me one week.' She stepped up to his desk, leaned forward until they were almost nose to nose. 'I'll work damned harder than anyone you've ever hired. Give me a chance to prove myself or you'll regret it.'

'Are you threatening me, young woman?' He reached for the phone and started dialing. 'I can have security here in three minutes.'

'No, no, I didn't mean . . . Shit, don't do that.' Great, now she was going to be tossed out of here by goons in uniforms unless she could make this jerk understand. She reached out and slapped her hand down on the button to disconnect the call.

He glared at her.

'I just need a job, dammit. That's all.'

'Please leave immediately.'

'Why won't big shots like you give people like me a chance, huh? No, instead you crap on us every chance you get!'

'Mr Cockell.' A man's gravelly voice came from directly behind Jess and she twisted around. A stocky, middle-aged man in a plaid jacket stood within arm's reach, but he'd moved so quietly she hadn't heard his approach. 'I need a new assistant.'

'I'm in charge of hiring staff, Harvey.' The personnel manager shook his head slightly, obviously trying to hint the newcomer away.

'Not the people who work for me.' The guy smiled and held out his hand for her application. The personnel manager sighed, then reluctantly handed over the form. It was scanned, then dropped back on the manager's blotter.

Harvey leaned against the desk and tucked his hands in his pockets. 'Obviously you are persistent, but are you smart?'

'Yes.' She clutched her bag tight against her chest.

'Are you quick on your feet?'

'Yes.' Her heart began to pound.

'Do you *listen*? You have to be able to really listen in this job, not just wait until it's your turn to talk.'

'Yes, sir.' Dared she hope? She stood very still while he studied her face.

'Describe our receptionist, without turning around to look at her.'

'Mid-forties. Her blonde hair is a bad dye job; her natural color is brown. Very bad eyesight. Likes to read and uses the public library. Has more than one kid and at least one of them is a boy.'

'This is preposterous!' Cockell exploded. 'How could she know all that?'

'Dark eyebrows and uneven roots,' Jess answered promptly. 'Unusually thick glasses. The bandage on her finger is one of the cartoon type kids like. Beside her typewriter there's a very large stack of well-used

4

books. Most of the books have the library's white and blue stickers on the spine.

'Her purse is sitting open on the floor under her desk and inside I could see one of those soother things adults plug in the mouths of cranky babies. She also has a handful of toy cars and a box of crayons. I guessed a woman like her would only carry toy cars for a son.'

The personnel manager scowled. 'Where did you learn to do that?'

'From Sherlock Holmes.' Jess smirked. 'I also know you have a white dog and use a laundry service.'

Cockell gaped at her.

'Very observant,' Harvey said. 'One more question. If you could have anything you wanted, what would it be?'

'Money.' What's with this guy? Any idiot should know the answer to that one just by looking at her.

'A reasonable answer but not what I was looking for.' She felt as if he was trying to see into her soul. 'Say you had money. What's the first thing you'd buy?'

'What does this have to do with the job?'

He waited in silence. Eventually her gaze dropped and she mumbled something toward her hands still clenched at her chest.

'I'm sorry, I didn't hear you.'

She straightened and glared into his eyes. 'A cat! I'd get a damned cat from the damned pound, okay?'

'Okay.' A very slight smile lifted one corner of his lips and crinkled the corners of his eyes. 'First rule, Ms Phillips. I don't allow cursing. And if you want to work

5

for me, you have to abide by my rules or you'll be out on your ear.'

'No sh– uh, no problem.' She'd expected to have to jump through a few hoops to get this job. Telling him about her dream of having her own pet hadn't been easy but she'd done it. Cutting out a few swear words couldn't be too damned hard.

'My name is Harvey Tate. You start tomorrow at eight. Mr Cockell will take care of the paperwork.' He held out his hand and slowly, not quite believing it was real, she offered hers.

'Thank you, Mr Tate.'

'Call me Harvey.' He shook her hand twice, firmly, and when he released it, there were folded bills in her palm.

'That's twenty bucks.' He chuckled. 'Go buy yourself a pair of sturdy, comfortable shoes that won't trip you up. You're going to be very busy because you've got a lot to learn.'

She stared after him as he walked away. He didn't have a harp or white fluffy wings or a shiny halo but so what?

Jess knew an angel when she saw one.

CHAPTER 1

Jess leaned back in her desk chair and pressed her fingertips against her chest, trying to catch her breath. So, this was how it felt to have your heart broken.

'Nothing's going to change for at least six months, maybe a year. I thought it would be best to tell you now, so you can decide what you want to do.' Harvey stood in the doorway between their offices, his stocky frame dwarfed by the over-height opening.

She forced herself to look clearly at the only man who'd ever shown her any affection, to study the signs her mind had been hiding from for so long. What she saw scared her. She *hated* being scared.

When they'd met eleven years ago he'd already been middle-aged but looked much younger. He hadn't changed much a couple years later when he suggested they form their own firm and she'd named it Finders Keepers. Now his thinning brown hair was more salt than pepper and his shoulders sagged as his seemingly inexhaustible stores of zip and vigor waned.

'What about Sophy? Have you told her?'

'No, but I will before I go out today. I wanted to tell you first. Sophy will be fine. She's just like those cats of yours; always lands on her feet.'

'I don't believe this is happening. You *can't* do it.'

'I'm sorry.' He tucked his hands in his pockets and rocked back on his heels. 'I know you weren't expecting this.'

'Gosh darned straight I didn't expect this. I don't understand.' Her voice cracked on the last word and she cleared her throat, determined not to cry. Jess Phillips *did not* cry.

She scooped Nora into her arms and the cat's purr rumbled as Jess rubbed behind her ears.

'I'm old and tired, sweetheart, and it's time I thought about retiring.'

'Where . . . what will you do?' She burrowed her fingers into Nora's pillowy grey fur, seeking comfort from the cat's simple needs.

She remembered the day five years before when Nick and Nora had come into her life. She'd been hired to find a stolen cat and ended up breaking a pet-napping ring. She'd been able to return all the various pets to their owners except for two of the cats.

Rather than send them to the pound she'd adopted them. Or had they adopted her? She'd named them after Nick and Nora Charles, the comical husband-and-wife detective team in *The Thin Man*, an old movie she'd watched their first night in her home.

'I've been checking out the price of a cottage on a

little piece of the Florida coast,' he said after a long moment of silence.

Her fingers tightened involuntarily and Nora yeowled in protest, then jumped out of her arms. 'You're leaving Vancouver?'

'It's not that I don't care about you. You know I do. I just think it would be best all round for me to move on.'

'Best for who? Not me.' Fight this, she ordered herself. Convince him. 'What about Finders Keepers? I don't have enough money to buy you out.'

'I know, sweetheart, and it's okay. I don't expect you to. I'll find a way to get the money I need to buy the cottage. For the next few years you can send me a percentage of the profits until we're even.'

'I can't do this without you.'

'You're wrong. You've been the driving force in Finders Keepers for the last two years, not me. If you don't want to work alone, you could hire on at another agency or throw in with a new partner.'

'I don't want to work with someone else. I need you.'

'Your instincts put you head and shoulders above most of the other detectives working in British Columbia. No matter how much formal training or how many university degrees those other guys have, they can't duplicate what you have naturally.'

'Oh, yeah?' she grumbled, though she couldn't help feeling flattered. Harvey didn't give compliments often, to anybody. 'And what might that be?'

'You manage to find things other people have given

9

up on. Then there's your intuition about people and the way you sense something isn't right.'

'You and Sophy hate it when I get curious about something.'

'Only when you go shooting off in all directions without doing any planning or talking it over with us first. Then you get yourself, and us, into trouble. Sometimes dangerous trouble.'

'You get hunches.'

'Now and then, maybe. Not like yours. Many times I don't even have a clue what stirred your curiosity in the first place. A lot of people think you're some kind of psychic.' He held up his hand to stop her fiery denial.

'Don't bite my head off. Explain it however you want. Doesn't change the fact you have the best instincts for this business I've ever seen.'

'You've taught me everything I needed to do this job.'

He waved her comment off. 'Maybe a few techniques and some self-discipline. That's all. You've become a darned good investigator, but I've realized that as long as I'm around you won't believe it.'

'Don't talk rot. You're my best friend,' she said, appalled to hear the pleading in her voice.

All her life, starting as a kid being shuffled from one foster home to the next, she'd had to ask, even beg, for what she'd needed. Once she was an adult, she'd sworn never to put herself in that position again. But this was *Harvey*. She'd do anything, say anything, even beg if it would convince him not to leave her.

She stiffened as his hand rested on her shoulder. 'Sophy and I are your only friends and that's wrong. You're young. You should be out having fun with other young people. Dating some of the guys who are always asking you out.'

'I'm not interested in getting involved with any of those men. And even if I was, it's not as though I'd have my pick.'

'Don't kid yourself, sweetheart. Any one of those young men would jump through hoops to have you.'

'You're biased, Harvey. Now, stop being so bull-headed and tell me the real reason you're talking stupid.'

'Don't be cheeky.' He gave her a stern look. 'I know about the offer from Fenleck. I think you should take it.'

'This is my place. I belong here with you and Sophy. Those jerks at Fenleck's won't give me anything good. Heck, they even offered to "ease" me in gently.' She pursed her lips; the nasty taste left by that conversation still lingered.

'They also have better benefits, higher salaries, and a bigger operation with support staff.'

'Who needs it? Besides, what about Nick and Nora? What about Sophy? Fenleck wouldn't let me bring them with me. I asked.'

'You asked about me, too, didn't you?'

She bit her lip.

'They said I was too old, didn't they?' He smiled wryly. 'They're right, Jess.'

11

'You know why I can't take a job there, Harvey.'

He shook his head. 'I think you're wrong. You're not giving yourself a fair shake. You've worked really hard and come a long way. I bet if you took Fenleck's offer, you'd kick the other operatives' lazy butts real good. You'd be their best operative by Christmas and that other stuff wouldn't matter.'

'I'm glad you think so, Harvey. I don't happen to agree with you so we're both going to stay right here.' A familiar tide of affection and gratitude swept through her. God, she loved him. 'End of discussion.'

What would she do without him? It didn't bear thinking about, much less talking. She jumped to her feet. 'Where's the St Clair file?'

'Refusing to talk about my retirement isn't going to make it go away. It's gonna happen, Jess. I'll be leaving as soon as I can afford my place in the sun.'

'Lieutenant Masters' family will be here in twenty minutes. I need to get ready.' She began flipping through the racks of color-coded cassette tapes stacked along one wall of her office, whistling a tune she'd heard on the radio that morning as if she didn't have a care in the world.

'Whistling isn't going to drown me out, Jess. Sitting on the beach for the rest of my life sounds just about perfect.'

'You'd die of boredom alone on the beach and you know it.' When she reached the end of the bottom row of the last rack she spun around and began opening and slamming the drawers of her battered desk. 'You'd go crazy spending all your time staring out of a cottage window at waves and sky.'

'You'll visit me, won't you?'

'Yeah, sure,' she snorted. 'With the amount of spare cash and time I get, I'll see you once a year. Twice if we're real lucky.'

'Jess, you're not listening to me.'

Yes, she was. And she refused to listen to it any more. Time to change the subject. 'You're just cranky because the client's husband got away from you yesterday. You shouldn't have chased him on foot.'

She patted his slight paunch as she walked by to kneel in front of the cardboard box she kept in the corner, half hidden by the sofa. 'Now stop talking nonsense and help me find the St Clair file.'

'When are you going to learn to put things away properly so you can find them?' He sighed audibly, then shook his head. 'Whether you're willing to talk about it or not, the time's comin' when I won't be around to sort things out for you.'

She glanced up, relieved to see the serious expression in his faded blue eyes was gone, replaced by his usual youthful twinkle. The crisis was over. Her heart was safe for now; she'd bought herself some time to convince him not to leave her. 'No such luck. You'll still be bossing me around when I'm an old woman.'

She grinned at him, then shoved the box back behind the sofa, sneezing when a cloud of dust exploded upward. She stood and surveyed her office while refastening the clip holding her long hair at the nape of her neck. 'Now, where the heck is the St Clair file? I want to review the tape.'

'Calm down, Jess. You know the information backwards and forwards and Hurricane Sophy typed up the client's written report before she left.'

He pointed at the filing cabinet beside the other door. A folder and cassette tape were partially hidden underneath her other cat, Nick, who was curled up asleep on top of the cabinet.

'What's happened to you?' he asked. 'You seem unusually flustered about this case.'

'This is the first time the lieutenant has sent us business. If he's pleased, it'll improve our relationship with the police department. Finders Keepers might even get some well-paying business because, if he likes the results, he might point some lawyers our way when they need some help from a private detective.'

'Get real, Jess. Tom Masters hasn't asked us to do anything even remotely earth-shaking. His wife hired us to do background checks on her brother's girlfriends. And, speaking of which, why did we do it? Aren't you the one always preaching ethics to me?'

'With the world the way it is today, every reasonable, responsible person should check out potential mates before making a final commitment. It's not unethical.'

She accidentally nudged Nick while retrieving the file. He opened one eye and batted at her hand. Jess kissed him on the nose and the Siamese's whiskers twitched. The tip of his tail had been broken, bent permanently to one side before Jess found him. Now it switched back and forth in disapproval at having his rest disturbed.

'But the man isn't our client, his nosy sisters are.'

She felt a twinge of guilt but shoved it away, as she'd been doing ever since she'd met with Masters' wife. Business was business and the results spoke for themselves.

'Any sane man would be glad he'd been told the truth regarding those women before it was too late and, from what we learned about Daniel St Clair, he'll be more pleased than most.' Not that she'd met him, of course. But, as usual, she'd checked him and his family out, too. Never again was a lying client going to trick her into doing something wrong.

St Clair was so highly respected in the academic world he probably spent most of his time in the rarefied air at the very top of an ivory tower. She doubted he even spoke the same language as ordinary people like herself. As if that wasn't enough, he was also filthy rich.

He'd started out working for a human resource firm, but his management and organizational skills eventually made him highly desirable as a consultant in the business world. Even the universities vied for his services as a visiting professor.

Nowadays he ran his fancy-dancy business school with high-end clients from corporations and governments all over the world. Judging by the fees his 'students' paid, he could probably afford to lease his office space in downtown Vancouver's Waterfront

15

Tower without putting a crimp in his wallet.

All in all, she'd bet cold, hard cash that if she ever met him, she wouldn't like him.

There were a few things she didn't understand. Even though his associates had talked freely about the academic and the businessman, everyone she'd interviewed had been oddly tight-lipped about the man, even his sisters.

She also didn't understand the whole family thing. What kind of man would let his sisters stick their noses into his personal life this way? They seemed to think it was perfectly normal to hire a detective to investigate his girlfriends.

And speaking of those girlfriends, how did a man like him, supposedly smarter than ninety-nine per cent of the world's population, get mixed up with these ones? Maybe he'd always had particularly bad taste in women? That might explain his sisters' concern.

She shrugged. It didn't matter. She'd been asked to discover the truth about four women he was dating, not the man himself.

When she sat at her desk Harvey grabbed his jacket off the coat tree just inside his office. 'I have an appointment, but I could stick around if you need me. If St Clair comes he'd probably rather get this kind of information from another man.'

'I am perfectly capable of giving a client some bad news –' Jess's hand froze on the tape she was shoving into the cassette player. 'An appointment? What kind of appointment?'

16

'Now, Jess . . .'

'You're going to see the doctor again, aren't you? Jumpin' juniper, Harvey, you said he gave you a clean bill of health.'

'How did you guess . . . ? Never mind, forget I asked. I'm fine, he just wants me to get some tests done.'

'What tests?'

'Gotta go. See ya later.' He swung his jacket over his shoulder and left before she could ask him any more pointed questions.

She was still sitting there, thinking and worrying, when he stuck his head back around the corner and winked at her.

'Besides, who said I'd be alone on that Florida beach? I might be getting old but I'm not in my dotage yet. I can still appreciate a well-filled bikini.'

She had to laugh. 'Get out of here, you lecherous old man. I've got work to do.' He waved and disappeared.

She was still smiling when she pushed the play button and began listening to her own voice. 'Subject, Daniel Gideon St Clair, owner of St Clair Institute for Leadership Excellence; consulting professor, University of British Columbia. Clients, Mary Masters, Ruth St Clair and Hannah St Clair. Request, background checks on Sally de Graf, Kim Stapleton, Amy . . .'

Pink blossoms from the tree behind Daniel's chair drifted lazily on the soft spring breeze until they settled on the white linen tablecloth, a fragrant decoration amongst the coffee cups and crumpled napkins.

At the other end of the narrow cobblestone alleyway cars raced up Water Street and harried business people rubbed elbows with tourists, street vendors, and vagrants. The restaurant's tranquil courtyard seemed a world away from Vancouver's Gastown area.

He glanced around the table at his sisters' animated faces and enjoyed the moment.

Other men might not fully appreciate such a moment, such a place. He did. He'd fought hard for normalcy, for contentment, and long ago had vowed never to take it for granted.

Sometimes, in the dark places in his soul, he remembered another place and another time . . . He squeezed his fingers around the thigh muscle that still ached, wrenched his thoughts away from the past, and concentrated on the present. On his achievements. On *this* family.

Daniel felt the deeper, almost forgotten, pain recede and smiled as his sisters talked. A blossom settled on the sleeve of his black suit and he glanced at his watch as he brushed it away. Almost one o'clock. If he made it back to the office by two, he'd have time to finish the Becker report today.

'Daniel.' Mary's soft voice held reproof as she shook her head, calm and composed as always. Neat and tidy from her short brown hair to her sensible shoes. Then he noticed the jam fingerprint one of his hellion nephews must have left on her sleeve.

18

Though she was only thirty, four years younger than himself, her inborn mothering instincts had been reinforced both by her position as eldest sister and the years spent raising her own two kids.

He slipped the cuff of his jacket back down to cover his watch but it was too late. The enthusiastic debate between their two younger sisters ceased and all three women glared at him.

'He looked at his watch.' There was no question in Ruth's tone. Using that particular tone in court, he thought wryly, was probably why she had one of the best conviction rates of all the crown prosecutors in the province.

Ruth looked happy but tired. Too tired, he thought, and over-worked. With her hair combed straight back from a high forehead, the premature streak of silver in her black hair glinted brighter than ever. Why wouldn't she let him get her a nice, ordinary position at one of the law firms in the city?

'Daniel St Clair!' Hannah, the baby of the family, punched his shoulder. 'You promised if we kept your birthday party to a lunch for just us four, you wouldn't even think about business.'

'I didn't say a word,' he protested.

'Never mind now. Open your last present.' Hannah pushed aside the colorful tissue paper and crumpled ribbon and handed him a small box wrapped in foil. He opened and took out what looked like a keychain ornament.

'Open it.'

19

He twisted the top and a miniature set of screwdrivers popped up. 'It's interesting. Thank you.'

'Someday it will come in handy, you'll see.'

'Hannah,' Ruth said, 'didn't you have something you wanted to discuss with Daniel? Now would be a good time to get his advice.'

He glanced at his youngest sister. For a moment he thought he saw her impish grin but he must have been mistaken because her expression settled into one of mild anxiety.

'Are you in trouble, Hannah?' He watched over all his sisters but he worried most about the awkward, coltish adolescent who'd grown up into such a beauty. Hannah, sweet Hannah, he thought fondly, always a blaze of color. Today, for some reason, she'd worn orange sneakers, a yellow skirt that was far too short, and a purple sweater with a string of milky white pearls.

'No, Daniel, but I would like your advice on something if you have time.'

'Of course I have time. Do you want to tell me about it now or when we're alone?'

'No, it's okay. The Sisters already know about it.' She looked so woebegone he reached over to pat her arm. Ruth made an odd noise but when he looked her way her head was down as she looked for something in her purse.

'Tell me what can I do to help you.'

'I'd rather show you, if it's all right.' Hannah smiled bravely. 'It's only a block and a half from here.'

'If that's what you want. I'll just ask for the bill and we can go.'

'I knew you'd try to pay for lunch, even though we invited you, so I paid the waiter when I went to wash my hands,' Ruth said triumphantly. 'It's your birthday. Lunch was our treat.'

He studied the determined glint in her eyes and decided not to argue. He waited through the usual bedlam as his sisters gathered their belongings until at last they were out on the street where his younger sisters led the way while he and Mary followed behind.

'The sun's unusually warm for April,' Mary said and tilted her face to its rays. 'I saw Mom this morning when I picked up Hannah for the drive into town for lunch. She likes the new home-care nurses you hired.'

'Good. I told the doctor to make sure Anna had the best.' He cleared his throat. 'How's she feeling?'

'Pretty good, all things considered. She was wearing the leopard brooch. I didn't know you'd had it cleaned and repaired. It looks as beautiful as it must have done the day Dad gave it to her.'

'Hannah mentioned Anna was afraid to wear it because she was worried about the clasp. Did the flowers arrive?'

She nodded. 'Absolutely beautiful yellow roses.'

'I would have taken them to her myself, tonight, but I have a client —'

'Don't worry, Daniel. She understands why you don't go to see her very often.' Mary patted his shoulder. 'She knows you love her.'

'Does she?' He felt an uncomfortable thickness in his chest.

'Yes, she does. Now, slow down.' She tugged on his arm. 'We're not in a foot race.'

He forcibly slowed his steps. 'Sorry.'

'I've been thinking about what you told me last week. Are you sure you're going about this the right way?'

'About what?' he asked, grateful for the change in subject. They both sidestepped a bicycle courier who zoomed around a corner.

'Don't be dense, Daniel, it doesn't suit you. Looking for a wife, of course.'

'I'm thirty-four. Time's running out. I don't want to be an old man when my kids are teenagers.'

'It's perfectly normal for you to want a wife and a family. It's just . . . Don't you think your methods are a little . . .' she hesitated, as if searching for the correct term '. . . unusual? Couldn't you choose one in a more conventional way?'

'Seems to me I'm doing it the same as every other man or woman who's decided to settle down. You associate with many different people until you determine what kind of person you like to spend time with, then you date them more seriously until you can decide if they're the best choice. Once I've found a woman I'm sure I can spend the rest of my life with, I'll propose.'

'You sound like you're proposing a business merger, not a marriage. Most people date the serious possibilities one at a time, brother dear, and the process is usually spread out over several years, not eight months. I don't understand why four decent women would put up with this competition you're running.'

'It's not a competition!' He knew he looked shocked. He felt shocked. How could Mary misunderstand him so completely?

He'd spent his life developing the best management practices and hiring methodology. Corporations and governments around the world endorsed the validity of his systems every day when they spent a gratifyingly large amount of money for their executives to study at his Institute. He'd merely applied a proven system to the process of choosing a wife.

'Once I'd made the decision to marry and start a family, why should I waste effort on an antiquated procedure proven unsound by the current divorce rate?'

'Women have been falling all over themselves and each other ever since you were fifteen, trying to get your interest. Why didn't you marry one of them?'

'I don't know. Somehow it never felt *right*. The time wasn't right or they weren't right.' He broke off and rubbed a finger along his eyebrow. 'Maybe I just wasn't ready.'

'And then, wham! You suddenly decide you *are* ready?'

'It wasn't that abrupt.'

'Yes, Daniel, it was.' A window display of hand-knit sweaters had caught their sisters' attention, so Daniel

23

and Mary stopped to wait. She looked up at him with a concerned smile. 'Do you want to talk about it?'

They were both silent for a while before he decided to answer her. 'Do you remember the night we took Anna to the hospital?'

'That was a bad time. We almost lost her.'

'Until then I'd only thought about the future in terms of business, not of home and family. That night forced me to think about what my life would be like without her.' When he noticed Ruth and Hannah were moving again, he began walking.

Mary slipped her hand into the crook of his elbow and leaned against his shoulder. 'We all did. We were scared. That doesn't mean you have to –'

'I've seen both sides and I know what I want. What I *need*. I need to find a woman with warmth and intelligence and strength to be my wife and the mother of my children. A woman of honor. A woman like Anna.'

'We all want you to get married, Daniel, but this isn't the way to go about it. You're supposed to fall in love first. We're worried about you and want you to think this over more carefully.'

'We?' His sisters had always banded together, referring to themselves in the third person as The Sisters. Thankfully he'd seldom been the target of their meddling. 'You felt the need to share our private conversation with those two?'

'The Sisters think you need to figure out why you're looking for a wife this way. Maybe talk to someone who can help you.'

'Are you suggesting I talk to a therapist?' Shock halted him so abruptly she almost stumbled. 'You think my plan is that crazy?'

'No!'

'Good.' Satisfied by her shocked denial, he resumed walking.

'It's just these women you're involved with. We think there's something wrong about them.'

'Oh?'

'Don't get mad, Daniel. We don't understand what's happening with you and we can accept that fact. You're a man and look at the world . . . differently. Some times I don't understand Tom, either. We still love both of you.'

She shook her head in rueful acceptance of the age-old differences between men and women. Daniel had to smile but wisely refrained from commenting.

'What bothers us the most is we don't know why the heck those women are going along with this. Sure, you've got a good job, plenty of money, a great family. And you're sort of good-looking, I guess.'

'Is this what they call "damning with faint praise"?'

She giggled but didn't let herself be sidetracked. 'Okay, okay, for the sake of debate, let's say you're everything a woman could possibly want in a husband. That still doesn't explain why they are allowing you to . . . to audition them for the role of wife.'

'This isn't an audition. All four are intelligent adults who totally support my methods.'

'Do you think I would wait patiently while some

man measured and compared me to a bunch of other women?'

He scowled.

'Absolutely not,' she said. 'It's like you're shopping for grapefruit. You've narrowed the choice down. Now you're checking out their freshness, color, and, I assume, their shape, size, and firmness?'

He felt his cheeks flush at the implied question. 'Mary, I warned you and the others six years ago when the Sisters pulled that trick with the Swanson twins . . . Don't interfere with my private life.'

She pursed her lips in disapproval but dropped the subject of his sex life. 'So, at the moment you're debating which grapefruit is perfect. You've even shown all four to your family to see which one we like the best.'

'Those women are not grapefruit.'

'Exactly. So why are they willing to be treated like fruit?'

His opened his mouth to rebut Mary's comment, then closed it since he couldn't think of an immediate reply to her ridiculous remarks. Thankfully Hannah and Ruth chose that moment to stop in front of one of the old brick warehouses recently renovated into offices.

'We're here,' Hannah announced.

Once inside, he felt as though he'd stepped through a time warp into the '40s or '50s. No wonder this building was often used as a movie set.

Hannah led the way to the elevator and on the third

floor they walked down a short hall lined with warm oak paneling. The top half of each office door held a frosted glass panel with a business name painted in black square lettering. At the end of the hall she stopped in front of a door and he read the name on its glass panel.

'Finders Keepers? What's this?' Suddenly he realized his other sisters had huddled around and behind him, herding him forward as Hannah opened the door into an office that looked like it, too, existed in the 1940s.

As soon as the door opened they were treated to a very talented whistler's performance of a tune from *Phantom of the Opera*.

At the far end of the fairly spacious waiting room squatted an empty desk, squarely facing the door, as if guarding the offices beyond. Two brown vinyl sofas with sagging cushions flanked the desk. A delicate fern hung from the ceiling in one corner, its fronds trailing almost to the floor.

He had to look twice when he saw the box right in the corner beneath the fern. Was that a cat's litter box? In an office?

There were no windows in the room and, other than the desk lamp of green glass and brass, the only light shone through frosted glass panels set into the wall around the three doors beyond the desk. All three doors were ajar. Behind two he thought he could see offices while the third appeared to be used for storage.

The only objects on the squat desk's highly polished

wood surface were a sleek telephone with a display screen surrounded by buttons, a manual typewriter, and a fistful of dandelions someone had thrust into an empty soup can. He knew the typewriter wasn't a decorative museum piece because an unfinished letter with today's date stuck out from the carriage.

He was wondering why someone still used a typewriter in this day and age when he noticed the state-of-the-art computer on the low table beside the desk.

'Please have a seat, Mrs Masters.' A velvety, feminine voice floated out from one of the inner offices. 'I'll be right with you.'

'Mrs Masters? I thought we were here for Hannah.' Daniel's glance roved across each of his sisters' guilty expressions and stopped at Mary. 'I sense a conspiracy. What is this place?'

'Now, Daniel, you know we love you,' she said. 'All we ask is for you to listen to Ms Phillips with an open mind.'

He stiffened. 'I think you owe me an explanation.'

Mary opened her mouth to answer him as one of the inner doors behind him swung open. He spun on his heel and was stunned into silence.

Vibrant was the only word he could think of to adequately describe the tall, slender woman. Electricity pulsed in the air around her and shone in her wide smile, deep dimples, and bright hazel eyes. Even the baggy mannish trousers and Oxford cloth shirt clung to her subtly curved body as if they teemed with static.

'Hello.' She greeted his sisters with a nod, then

stepped forward and extended her hand. 'You must be Mr St Clair. I'm Jess Phillips.'

In what felt like a daze, he reached out to shake her hand. The moment they touched he felt his palm tingle. The firm clasp of her hand reminded him of the time he'd accidentally touched a bare wire sticking out from the fuse box. He slipped his fingers free of hers and quickly smoothed down the hair on the nape of his neck.

'I'm glad you could come today. My services will be so much more effective if we work together. Please, come in.' She stepped back and waved her hand, indicating they should enter her private office.

He took a step forward, then realized his sisters were backing away. Ruth had already opened the hall door.

'Where are you going?' he asked.

'It's best if we leave, Daniel. I know you'd rather do this alone.' Mary patted his cheek, then followed Ruth into the hall. Hannah went on tiptoe to kiss his cheek. 'Happy birthday, big brother,' she whispered.

'Hannah, what have The Sisters done now?' he asked, firmly, menace in his tone.

She didn't answer him, but her impish grin was in full view as she pulled the door shut behind her.

'Mr St Clair?' The woman's voice reminded him she was still waiting for him.

He stepped closer to the private office, then halted abruptly when he remembered Mary's suggestion just before they'd entered the building. Surely The Sisters hadn't . . .

Even if they believed the idiocy about him talking to somebody regarding his search for a suitable wife, they wouldn't arrange for him to see a therapist without even asking him first. Would they?

If they had . . . As much as he liked to indulge their whims for the sake of family harmony, this time they'd gone too far. For a moment Daniel allowed himself to contemplate which methods of revenge would be most effective in teaching The Sisters to stop trying to rearrange his life.

In the meantime, he'd give Ms Phillips exactly five minutes of his time while he explained how his sisters had made a mistake and he had no intention of discussing his personal life with a stranger.

CHAPTER 2

Jess gulped for breath when he turned to look at her. Or rather, look down at her. He must be a good three or four inches taller than her own five foot ten, she thought, and the fancy tailored suit emphasized lean but powerful muscles. His blue-gray eyes were oddly compelling and though some women might say he was a beautiful man, she wouldn't. His chin was too square, his lips too narrow, his gaze too sharp.

Too bad all the softness in his expression had vanished when his sisters left. His jaw was so tense it could have been carved from granite and his eyes . . . She shivered.

She'd never had a boss or teacher who looked so good, not with all that wavy brown hair. Or that body. And when their hands had touched . . . wow! Judging by the look on his face he'd felt it too, the sensation of connection, of affinity. It made her wonder if there was something to all the talk-show nonsense about instant sexual chemistry. Maybe she should touch him again –

Stop right there, she ordered her unruly thoughts.

31

Two groups of professionals had made her adolescence a miserable experience and this man represented both. He was a teacher *and* a business executive, for heaven's sake. The sensation she'd felt when they touched was only a moment of . . . of . . . a moment of craziness, she finally decided.

His eyebrows were curious though. She'd never seen brows slashed upward at the temples in quite that way. She'd bet when he frowned he looked positively diabolic.

She straightened her shoulders and lifted her chin. No man was allowed to intimidate her, not even one as rich and powerful as Daniel St Clair. Nevertheless, she decided to leave her office door open.

'If you would make yourself comfortable, please, we could begin.'

At her gesture he walked past her but came to an abrupt stop two steps inside her office.

'What kind of business are you running here? I can't believe they'd . . . How could they think I would . . . ?'

He sounded angry. And appalled.

'Excuse me?' Jess peered around his shoulder, trying to see what had annoyed him.

She'd only been in the outer office for a few minutes. Even Nick and Nora couldn't cause too much trouble in a short space of time. She scanned the room but everything looked normal. Messy, but normal. Nick still slept on the filing cabinet. Nora washed her paws on the sunny windowsill while keeping an eye on pedestrians on the street below.

Jess studied St Clair's frowning face for clues and discovered she'd been right about his eyebrows . . . he did look rather sinister at the moment. He was staring directly at the big comfy sofa under the windows behind her desk. She slept on it when she was too lazy or too busy to go home at night but today the afghans were folded neatly and the extra cushions she used for pillows were stacked at one end.

'What's the problem, Mr St Clair? Were you expecting a larger agency? I assure you my work is thorough and professional and my prices are very reasonable. I'm very good at my job.'

'I don't care how good you are at . . . what you do. I'm leaving.'

He was past her, through the door, and halfway across the outer office before she realized what was happening. At that moment she literally saw red. She'd worked darned hard on his case and, for some probably snobbish reason, he didn't want to hear her report.

Fine. What the heck. Who cared? Not her.

It didn't mean his family was going to dodge paying her bill, though.

'There's the small matter of my bill, Mr St Clair.'

'Your bill?' He stopped but didn't turn around.

'My time is valuable and your sisters agreed to the hourly rate, plus expenses.'

'Plus expenses!' He swore, then turned and steadily paced closer until he loomed over her. She stood her ground but it wasn't easy. 'How the hell can there be expenses when I've only been here five minutes?'

'I've put in a lot of hours on your case and you *will* pay me.'

His expression altered suddenly. 'My case?'

'Yes.'

'Ms Phillips, what exactly is your job here?'

'I'm a detective, Mr St Clair, and a darned good one.' She crossed her arms on her chest and waited with her chin thrust out, daring him to disagree.

She watched in amazement as his face turned faintly red. If anything, his jaw looked more like chiseled granite than ever. He stared at her without blinking for longer than she'd have thought humanly possible.

Why was he blushing? She glanced back into her office, puzzled, then looked at him again. 'Just what did you think my job was, Mr St Clair?'

'I thought you were a therapist. Or a psychologist. Obviously I was mistaken. I apologize.'

'I can't believe this.' She started to laugh. 'Me, a therapist, helping someone else sort out their psyche. Harvey's going to laugh himself sick.'

'Harvey?'

'My partner. He would have been here, but he had an appointment.' Jess hiccuped as she tried to stop laughing.

'This is wasting time. Why did my sisters hire you, Ms Phillips?'

'Perhaps we should go into in my office and discuss this calmly and professionally? The report is on my desk.' She glanced into her office, noticed Nick was now curled up on the sofa Daniel St Clair must have

34

thought was a therapist's couch. She smiled but sobered immediately when she noticed his face still held a heavy frown.

'Just answer the question. Please.'

'Your sisters hired me to investigate the four women you are considering for the role of your wife, Mr St Clair.'

She watched, fascinated, as his jaw tightened further, wondering if a person could break his own jaw that way. Even granite would eventually shatter if one applied enough pressure.

He rubbed his eyebrow with one hand, an action which shaded his eyes, and she waited in silence for him to say something. Eventually he dropped his hand to his side, the frown magically smoothed from his expression. 'Perhaps we'd better sit down, Ms Phillips.'

Jess sat behind her desk as St Clair settled into one of the two chairs she kept for clients. He leaned back and crossed his legs with an air of resignation, as if he were dealing with a pesky employee or forced to straighten out a wayward student.

Either way, it was darned annoying. This was *her* office, not his.

'I regret my sisters wasted your time, Ms Phillips. In the past they have occasionally over-reacted to a situation which is perfectly ordinary. I see they've done it again but I don't fault them for it because their motives were good. I'm sure you understand.'

She opened her mouth to reply but he pressed on,

staring over her shoulder, not quite meeting her gaze.

'I have no doubt you are fully capable of providing your usual clients with a satisfactory resolution to their difficulties.'

'My *usual* clients?'

'We both know there was no real need for your services in this instance. However, I'm sure we will be able to arrive at a mutually agreeable settlement of my family's financial obligation to your firm and then we can consider the matter settled.'

It was all Jess could do not to stare at him with her mouth hanging open. She hadn't heard such irritating, patronizing twaddle since she was twenty and desperate.

'Are you quite finished?'

Her caustic tone must have startled him because for the first time since they'd touched, he really looked at her directly.

'So tell me if I've got this straight.' She rocked back in her chair and rested her feet on the bottom desk drawer that would never quite close. 'You believe your sisters were dead wrong in their opinion of these four women and my inquiries were a waste of time?'

'Essentially, yes.' A faint expression of impatience appeared in his eyes and those eyebrows were beginning to tilt into another frown.

'But, despite this, you are willing to pay my bill?'

'If it's reasonable, yes. After all, you were hired to do a job and deserve to be paid for your work. No matter how unnecessary.'

'And you don't want to see the reports?'

'No. My friends might be hurt if they knew they'd been investigated even though I, personally, was unaware of your actions.'

'So . . .' She reached for the thick file beside the tape player and opened it to the first closely typed sheet. 'You're telling me these women's pasts won't matter one jot when you ask one of them to marry you?'

'Of course it matters. Choosing a spouse is just as important as hiring someone to manage a business. Many things in a person's past affect their ability to fulfill the expectations of their spouse or employer.'

'Really?' She flipped to the second page of the report. 'Yet you're not interested in the information I gathered.' She lifted out the invoice Sophy had typed that morning, closed the file, and tossed both down on the desk between them.

He eyed the file and the invoice but didn't reach for either. 'I've known these women for some time and we've shared many conversations. I'm reasonably conversant with their history, as they are with mine. They would never dream of investigating my past.'

'Oh, really,' she murmured. Then she smiled, just a little. For a businessman with lots of female employees and students plus three sisters, he knew squat about women.

'What do you mean by that comment?'

'One of these women not only had your past checked out, she had your whole family investigated.' He jerked upright in his chair.

'I didn't try to find out what information she discovered since it wasn't part of my contract with your sisters.'

'Who . . . ?'

'I'm not sure who did it but I do have proof it happened and the researcher was a woman. I expect I could find out her exact identity if I had a little more time but your sister made this appointment before I could do any more work.'

'I've heard it's now a common practice for women to check out the stability and genetic background of any potential father for her children.' He leaned back in his chair again, casually crossed his legs, and smiled in a superior way. 'I don't see why I need to know who instigated the search.'

'Really? Kim Stapleton put herself through college working as an exotic dancer. Personally, I admire her determination to get a degree. Nowadays she only performs when she needs a little extra cash. She's currently performing at a local nightclub called the Peacock Arms. Still not interested?'

'Ahh . . .'

'Amy Jones changed her name to hide a prison record for extortion and fraud, though she claims her then-boyfriend framed her. Thérèse Richard has been married four times and gave birth to two kids. I can't call her their mother since she hasn't seen either since they were babies.'

'Are you finished?' He asked in a stilted voice.

'Sally de Graf was a little harder to pin down,

probably because she's very good at her chosen career as a corporate spy. Her real name is Sarah Graff. I believe she was hired by one of your competitors and is using the relationship as cover for corporate espionage. I don't believe she has any intention of actually marrying you.'

He sat absolutely still and silent, staring directly at her, no expression on his face. Her heart lurched unexpectedly. Poor man.

She could hear the clock in Harvey's office ticking away the seconds and she began to regret the way she'd dumped the bad news on St Clair.

Just because her life had exploded into little bits today was no reason to be careless of other people's feelings.

Harvey was always telling her she should be more sensitive about other people's feelings and failings. This was yet one more example.

She should have considered how the information could, and probably would, bruise his male pride. After all, no matter how much she disliked people like him, St Clair was a wealthy client and a possible source of future business. Harvey would not be pleased by her unprofessional behaviour.

Even though he often accused her of being paranoid about having lots of cash stashed away, safe in the bank, her partner might wonder if she'd sabotaged this chance deliberately. After all, if Finders Keepers didn't make enough profit Harvey wouldn't be able to afford his beachfront property.

'I'm sorry,' she said, meaning it. She was glad the information she'd discovered would keep him from making a bad mistake. Marriage was enough of a crap shoot for ordinary people. Rich people obviously had to be even more careful.

Eventually St Clair stirred, glanced at his watch, then picked up the file and invoice. 'I have a meeting. I'll mail you a cheque.'

She leaped to her feet and hurried around her desk to follow him out into the waiting room. 'My number is on the paperwork. If you have any questions, please call.'

She instantly regretted the offer when a pained expression crossed his face. 'Thank you,' he replied politely.

Geez, Jess, you really blew it this time, she thought. No way are we going to see any business from this guy. The thought of all those possible clients evaporating before her very eyes, along with any possible fees, made her rush into speech.

'I'm sorry if I was too blunt, Mr St Clair, but I felt it was important for you to know what I'd found out.'

'Thank you. I appreciate your concern.' There was absolutely no gratitude in his voice.

'It might be a good idea to find out who, exactly, was checking into your background and your family's history, and why. I could get it done by Monday. No extra charge.'

'That won't be necessary.' He paused with his hand on the doorknob. 'I think you've –'

The knob turned under his hand and swept inward with a hurricane-force Sophy. He hurriedly stepped back out of the way in an effort not to be bowled over and became entangled with a coat tree hidden in the corner behind the door.

'Hi, Jessica. Don't I look great?' The voluptuous woman who kept the agency running smoothly burst into the office. Sophy dropped her purse on to one of the vinyl sofas and carefully removed a silk scarf, revealing a shoulder-length mane of golden ringlets seldom seen on any 55-year-old woman.

Jess blinked at the golden mass, then tried to get her attention so she would know they weren't alone. 'Sophy, this is –'

'I don't care what you think –' Sophy noticed him standing behind her and smiled flirtatiously. 'Oh, my! You're a big handsome hunk of a man, aren't you? Don't just stand there, Jessica. Introduce me.' She held out her hand and batted her false eyelashes in his direction.

'Sophy, this is Daniel St Clair. Mr St Clair, this is our office manager, Sophy Westlake.' Jess noticed Daniel didn't quite smile as he clasped Sophy's hand in what he had obviously intended to be a brief handshake.

'You're Danny St Clair? Oh, you poor man.' She tightened her grip on his hand and tugged him closer so she could reach up and pat him on the shoulder. She extended the touch into an admiring massage of his bicep. 'I was so shocked when I typed up your file yesterday. I can't imagine any woman treating you that way!'

'Thank you. I think.' He tried to ease away from her, toward the door and freedom, but she clung to his hand and moved with him.

'Mr St Clair is a client, Sophy, and his case is confidential. You shouldn't be discussing it, even with him.' Jess's stern reprimand was somewhat spoiled by her struggle to control the overwhelming urge to laugh. It was obvious he didn't know what to make of her secretary.

Sophy ignored her.

'If you want my advice, you should consider marrying a woman slightly older than yourself, who knows and likes your family.' She patted her ringlets with her free hand and wiggled her hips suggestively. 'Your sweet sisters and I really hit it off.'

'If you'll excuse me.' He tried to pull free but it didn't do any good. She didn't release his hand.

'Of course, if you prefer younger women . . .' her tone made it clear that, if true, she questioned his taste '. . . my darling Jessica would be a perfect choice for your wife. She's so smart and so talented!'

'Sophy!' Jess decided it was time to end this little comedy. She put her arm around the older woman's shoulders and coaxed her away from Daniel. 'Mr St Clair was just leaving.'

He sidled sideways, out of reach, until he could open the door. He didn't speak again until he was beyond the dubious safety of the wood and glass barrier.

'Goodbye, Ms Phillips, Ms Westlake. It's been . . . interesting.'

As soon as they were alone Sophy turned on Jess. 'How could you let that happen?'

'What?' Jess asked, bewildered.

'I set up a perfect opportunity for you to finally get yourself a man and you let him walk away. Such a shame when he has such lovely muscles and smells so good.' She sighed.

'Daniel St Clair would *not* be interested in me. He wasn't happy with our meeting.'

'After you saved him from those awful women? He should have kissed your feet.'

'He was angry, Sophy, and probably embarrassed. His sisters hadn't told him what I was doing, plus I didn't handle the interview very well. Harvey was right, I should have let him deal with this one.'

'Pshaw. I saw the way the man looked at you. He was interested.'

'You're imagining things. By the way, I meant what I said. You shouldn't discuss the things you learn in the office.'

'Why, as if I would.' She looked wounded. 'I don't see what's so wrong with mentioning it to him, though. He already knew everything.'

'The client might wonder if you talk about his case to everyone.'

'Oh. I didn't think of it.' She frowned, then brightened. 'Next time he comes to the office, I'll assure him of my discretion, shall I?'

Jess sighed but decided not to argue. They'd already had the same conversation umpteen times because Sophy seldom chose discretion if it went counter to her own agenda. Luckily for Jess and Harvey the older woman was darned good at her job. The agency would not have grown and thrived without her.

Besides, what were the chances Daniel St Clair would ever again set foot in Finders Keepers?

'I've got work to do. If Harvey calls, put him through to me, okay? I'd better tell him what happened.'

'Sure, honey. Maybe Harvey could help you smooth things over with that lovely man.'

'You're a dreamer, Sophy.' Jess shook her head. 'By the way, did Harvey talk to you today?'

'My, you're looking awful serious . . . Oh, you mean his silly plan to move to Florida?'

'You don't seem upset.'

'Of course not.' Sophy winked. 'I'm going with him.'

'You are?' Jess felt doubly betrayed. 'He didn't tell me.'

'He doesn't know, not yet. And you're not to tell him, understand? I'll tell him when the time is right.'

'I didn't think you were serious about Harvey.'

'I should have known you'd notice I had my eye on him. He thinks I haven't seen him looking at me.' She patted her ringlets and looked coy. 'He wants me.'

'He does?'

'You're as blind to the truth as he is. Harvey's a good

man and a hard worker, just a little slow. Good thing for him I'm not.' She made a shooing motion with her hands. 'Now you get back to work and think of some way you can fix yourself up with Mr St Clair.'

Jess chuckled and obeyed the first part of Sophy's instructions.

Inside her office she leaned back against the closed door and rubbed her palm against her hip, thinking about how her hand had tingled with Daniel's touch. She'd felt intense, eager, like when she was close to solving a particularly tricky case. Never before had she associated this particular feeling with a man.

Not that she wanted a man.

Her parents had died when she was six and, like any other product of the foster system, she'd seen a lot of different families and marriages from the inside. As a temporary visitor in their homes, she'd often felt invisible as she watched wives and husbands interacting. Good, sad, or indifferent, she'd never been impressed.

By the time she turned fourteen she'd decided marriage was a trap for women and a waste of time, at least for her. Even then she'd still wanted to believe in love and as she grew up, she'd tried dating.

Over the years she'd spent time with three very nice men but none of them had stirred her blood at all, much less with one touch. As for having a lover, eventually she'd accepted that sex was seriously over-rated and happy-ever-after wasn't going to happen for her.

Touching Daniel St Clair made Jess wonder if she'd been a little hasty with that decision.

How different would this first meeting have gone if he hadn't been a client? If the case hadn't been so personal, so embarrassing for him? If he wasn't part of the two professions she most despised?

Or if he'd shown her the slightest appreciation for saving his gorgeous butt.

Yeah, right. As if she would have a chance to make it to the final round in his wife-selection process. Those four women might be frauds but every one was elegant and gorgeous, with a university degree.

For her, school had been a constant struggle, followed by the hell of finding and losing a series of menial jobs. Most of her life she'd been treated like she was stupid. Eventually she'd begun to wonder if they were right.

One day, when things had been at their worst, she'd wondered if the teachers had arranged for her to graduate just to get rid of her and her problems.

If it hadn't been for Harvey . . . He'd trained her and when he went out on his own he'd invited her to be his junior partner. What would she do if he really moved to Florida and left her here, alone?

Jess dragged in a deep breath and moved briskly away from the door. She picked up the fat envelope of photographs and negatives and sat at her desk. No sense borrowing trouble, she told herself as she began sorting the pictures she'd taken for the woman who thought her daughter was mixed up with a bad crowd.

Concentrate on work, she told herself. Tomorrow could take care of itself.

How did it happen? Living with Anna and her daughters should have been all the training he needed to understand all women inside and out. He'd built a career on his ability to judge people, men or women. He'd spent years and made a lot of money teaching others to hone that instinct. What had distorted his judgment so badly in this, the important process of choosing a wife?

Daniel used both hands to shove open the heavy doors to his offices, resenting the hydraulic hinges that kept them from slamming in a satisfactory manner. He'd done the walk back from the detective's office in Gastown in only four minutes instead of the usual ten or twelve but even the furious pace hadn't given physical relief to his frustration.

He'd wasted almost a year and now he had to start over, beginning with completely reworking the selection process.

As he strode past this week's new receptionist he nodded curtly. None of the kids from Ruth's newest pet project, School-Work, stayed long enough for him to learn their names and each new kid seemed younger than the last. A competent office manager like Chris should be able to find them something to do away from him; the training program's constant changeover was one more irritant he didn't need.

He might not remember this one's name but he did

remember *her*. This morning as he was leaving to meet his sisters, she'd spilled juice on the switchboard, shorting it out. Since she was now using the system, apparently Chris had managed to get it repaired.

'Mr St Clair!' She jumped up with a stack of message slips in her hand.

'Not now.' He didn't pause as he passed her desk.

'But –'

'I said not *now*.' As soon as the words were out of his mouth he regretted them. He could tell his brusque tone had alarmed her so he stopped and turned back.

'I'm sorry. I have to deal with a few things first, then I'll look at my messages. Please ask Chris Houston to come to my office at –' he glanced at his watch '– two-thirty.'

She nodded tentatively and twisted her fingers in the straggly ends of her long hair. 'I don't know where she is, sir.'

He could feel his jaw tensing up again. 'Then you'll have to find her, won't you?'

'Okey-doke. Your mother phoned to say how much she liked the roses.'

Ouch. There it was . . . the guilt, despite what Mary had said. Anna St Clair had always made a big deal of family birthdays and he knew damn well she'd be disappointed if he didn't visit her tonight.

His hand began to ache and he looked down, surprised to discover he was gripping the detective's report so tightly the papers were almost cutting into his palm.

48

'Oh, I almost forgot . . . There was a lady waiting in your office but she left.'

'In my office? Who?'

'Your ladyfriend. She said her name's Sally.'

Sally, alone in his office, perhaps looking through his files? Suddenly he had visions of her using the time to conceal listening devices. Or was she checking on some she'd hidden months before? Daniel resisted the urge to fire the girl. 'I'm sorry, I've forgotten your name.'

'It's Gwen, sir.' Her glasses slipped down her nose and she pushed them back up with one finger.

'Well, Gwen, it's not a good idea to allow strangers into anyone's private office without his or her specific permission,' he said, very gently. 'You might want to remember that in your next job.'

She gulped for air. 'Yes, sir.'

'Did O'Keefe leave for New York as scheduled?' She nodded mournfully. 'Then, when you find Chris, would you please ask her to meet me in O'Keefe's office at two-thirty?'

As he left he heard her frantically pushing buttons on the switchboard, probably disconnecting calls while she tried to find the office manager.

He stopped in his own office long enough to lock the detective's report in the safe and pick up his address book. He had some phone calls to make.

CHAPTER 3

Back in the hall he passed all the other executives' offices until he reached David O'Keefe's, a junior employee who assisted with follow-up on past clients. Even if Sally had managed to bug most of the offices, he judged she wouldn't have had the time or opportunity to bother with this one.

He dropped into a chair, picked up the phone, and punched out a number.

'Is Lieutenant Masters in, please? Daniel St Clair. Thanks, I'll hold.' While he waited he picked up the photograph of O'Keefe's smiling sons and adoring young wife. When his brother-in-law answered he placed the frame face down on the desk so he wouldn't have to look at the happy little family.

'Hi, Tom. I was wondering what you knew about the Sisters' latest scheme.' He listened to Tom's defensive maneuvers for a few minutes before he interrupted.

'I don't blame you for helping them. Hell, I know how hard it is to say "no" to Mary and she's only my sister. You're married to her. I just have a few questions. What do you know about Jessica Phillips? How capable is she?'

Daniel drummed his fingers on the chair's arm while he listened. 'That good, eh? So if I had something important, business-wise, you'd definitely recommend her?'

Tom agreed, then asked a question.

Daniel snorted. 'No, I'm not getting married. But if you want to know what Ms Phillips found out, you'll have to buy me a drink after our racquetball game tomorrow night. Fine, I'll see you then.' He dialed again.

'Rick? This is Daniel. Fine, thanks. You met Sally de Graf at the company Christmas party, didn't you? Yes, the blonde. Yes, she's really something.' He waited for a few minutes until his voluble company lawyer finished congratulating him on her looks and intelligence.

'She's a corporate spy. Her real name is Sarah Graff.' There was dead silence from the other man for several seconds before Rick burst into questions. Eventually he asked one Daniel could answer.

'She's probably working for the new firm in Chicago.'

Rick's next question made Daniel wince.

'How I found out is immaterial. We'll have to discover what, if any, classified information has been compromised. No, she doesn't know her deception has been discovered.' He swung around to face the window. 'We were supposed to go to Whistler for the weekend. I thought I'd better talk to you before canceling. How should this be handled?'

Silence thrummed on the line again. He assumed Rick was absorbing this uncomfortable reminder that Daniel had been intimately involved with the de Graf woman. The man's next comment was tentative.

'Yes, it is a difficult situation.' Daniel angled the chair to catch the afternoon sun and leaned back. The humiliation he'd experienced in Jessica Phillips' office was compounding by the minute but at least the sunlight felt warm and soothing. 'No, I'm calling from O'Keefe's office. I'd already considered the possibility she might have managed to install listening devices.'

He listened in silence as the lawyer debated with himself about possible repercussions. 'Perhaps you should do some checking and get back to me as soon as possible. I'll use this office for now. Thanks.'

Daniel disconnected the call and dialed again.

'Kim? We need to talk. Yes, I've made my choice. I'd like to meet with you tonight, if you have time. I understand your show at the Peacock Arms is over at eleven.' He winced as she slammed down the phone. Two down, two to go. He dialed again.

'Amy? I was wondering if you'd mind coming with me to the police station this afternoon. Yes, I'm finally ready to make my decision. There's just one more step, the security clearance.' He waited impassively while she scolded him sweetly, explaining how trust was an important part of love and marriage.

'I'm sorry, but we really have no choice. Because I have government clients, my wife has to pass the standard police background check, as do all my employees.' After a moment of silence Amy told him what she thought of him and his business in a handful of succinct curses. *Then* she slammed the phone in his ear.

One to go. His lips thinned in disgust as he thought about this last phone call. With Thérèse, more than the other three, he'd shared many conversations comparing their views on raising children. Several times she'd professed a deep longing to hold her very own babies, his babies, in her arms.

Until today he'd thought his decision to marry and have children had been well planned, a logical progression in his life. But somehow she'd sensed and used his own unvoiced, unrecognized urge for children. His damned biological clock had made him such an easy mark, he'd come very close to choosing her for his wife. May she rot in hell!

He dialed. 'Thérèse? This is Daniel. I'm ending our relationship. Why? Because I refuse to be involved with a woman who would bring two babies into this world, only to abandon them.'

Her voice was shrill as she scrambled to explain, to justify, but he ended the call by gently replacing the receiver.

He slouched deeper into his chair, closed his eyes, and toyed with the thought of calling Jess Phillips to tell her he was no longer involved with any of the women she'd investigated. He owed her a 'thank you' and an apology, in any case. Between the Sisters' deception and Jess Phillips' bombshell revelations, he hadn't handled the meeting at all well.

Maybe he should call and make an appointment to see her, perhaps take her out to dinner. The restaurant where he'd had lunch with his sisters was good and nearby. Quiet. Secluded. Two people could have privacy with their dinner conversation.

He was smiling, contemplating an evening with Jess, when a passing cloud blocked the lazy heat of the sun for a few minutes, nudging him back to reality.

Forget it, St Clair. Between his foolish performance in her office today and what she knew about his judgment when it came to companions, the woman hadn't seen much in him to admire. Just because his hand tingled when it touched hers didn't mean she'd thought it anything more than simple static electricity. Best to write a note to thank her, attach it to the check, and put both in the mail.

He heard raised voices outside the door, followed by an abrupt rap on the wood before Rick burst through with Chris on his heels, both talking at the same time.

'Daniel wanted this information immediately. It's urgent.'

'He asked to see me at two-thirty.' The sultry brunette pointed at her watch. 'I must go first, I have people waiting for me.'

'This is serious.' Rick leaned forward to brace his hands on the desk. 'We have to get moving on this. You were right, she's working for the Chicago group. From what I've been able to trace so far, there are at least two clients who have been approached. We should talk to them immediately.'

'Daniel, I've got newspaper reporters in my office, waiting to interview me about our participation in the School-Work Project. I've got to get back there.'

'Okay, okay.' He held up one hand for quiet. 'Chris, you should probably hear this and it will only take a couple minutes. I'm sure you're going to be involved in Rick's inquiries.'

'Inquiries?' She braced one hand on the back of a chair, a startled expression on her face. 'What have you –?' She pinched her lips firmly closed, abruptly cutting off what she'd been about to say.

'You had a question?' Daniel asked.

'No.' She smiled. 'Go ahead.'

'This afternoon I found out a woman has been here under false pretenses.' Daniel thought he heard her utter an odd sound but when she said nothing more, he attributed it to her customary impatience. It was probably driving her crazy to keep those reporters waiting.

'I know you met Sally de Graf at the Christmas party. She's been using our personal connection to scrutinize the company and report back to our competitors in Chicago.'

'Oh!' she said. 'Yes, I remember her.'

'We have to determine how deeply our operation has been compromised.'

55

'Are you sure it has been? I mean, how could she get access –?'

'On top of all the other situations that have arisen since we began participating in the School-Work Project, today the girl on the front desk allowed Sally time alone in my office. It might not be the first time. I want you to have them all work in less sensitive areas from now on.'

'I'll talk to Gwen. She's young –'

'Move her, Chris. Now.'

'Yes, sir.'

Rick had been pacing and fidgeting with the ends of his mustache. 'We're wasting time. We've got to move fast on this. First we have to know if, and where, the office is bugged, so we know how much and what type of information she had access to. We should hire an investigator –'

'No,' Chris protested sharply.

Rick's jaw dropped at her interruption and Daniel looked at her in surprise.

'Why, Chris?'

'Yes, Rick should get the office electronically swept by a professional, but without telling them anything else. We should keep this amongst us three, at least until we know for sure what's involved. If we bring in outsiders, who knows what might happen or whom they'll talk to?'

'No, we'd be throwing away precious time. Time we might need for damage control.'

'What if she bribed someone on staff? What about

the kids in the School-Work Project? They seem like good kids, but have no reason to feel company loyalty. Pressures at home could make them vulnerable to someone like her.'

Daniel leaned back and contemplated the woman standing stiffly before him. Why was she so tense? 'You seem very concerned.'

She was silent for a moment. 'My job is very important to me and this could put the company in a precarious situation. We have to be careful.'

'I'm glad you feel that way, Chris, especially since you've been here less than a year. And I agree we need to be cautious.' He was going to say more but her relief was so obvious, he refrained. She had people waiting and there'd be time enough to deal with her misgivings after he'd made his decision.

'You'd better get back to those reporters. Rick and I will talk things over and fill you in later.'

She hesitated, looking back and forth between the two men before she reluctantly agreed.

'You can't agree with her,' the other man blurted out as soon as the door closed behind her.

'Chris made several good points.'

'Yeah, maybe, but enough to justify not hiring an investigator? A good P.I. could find out if any staff members were involved without giving away information to the wrong person.'

'You're probably right.' Daniel laced his fingers together and rested his chin on his knuckles while he thought.

Jess Phillips was good at her work and already familiar with some aspects of his problem. Logically, he should hire her.

'I'll make some calls and hire an investigator this afternoon.'

'No. I'll take care of it. I think I know just the P.I. for the job.' He noticed Rick looking at him oddly. Daniel decided not to attempt an explanation. The circumstances of his meeting with Jess were not something he would willingly share with an employee.

At the moment she probably thought him a complete buffoon. She'd have to see him differently once they'd worked closely together on the investigation. His decision to hire her had nothing to do with the fact she was unlike any woman he'd ever met.

Of course he'd feel compelled to improve that low opinion, no matter who held it. So why did he feel like he was making excuses to himself, searching for reasons why he should hire Jess?

Rick was still looking at him oddly.

'Don't worry, I'll deal with it. In the meantime, you do a few quiet, random checks on some clients to see if they've been approached by another firm.' They walked out of the office together.

'Don't you think you should talk to the detective today, Daniel?'

'I want to think it over.' Daniel checked his watch. Too late to do anything constructive about this now. If he hurried, he'd be able to get to Anna's in time to share her dinner. He could phone from the car so she'd know he was coming. 'Besides, I've got something more important to do tonight.'

'I ate too much.' Daniel held Anna's arm as she settled into the rocking chair, then draped the blue afghan around her legs. It might be spring but the evenings were still cool. 'The lasagna was almost as good as yours.'

'I'm glad you came.'

'So am I.' He was about to move away when she nudged the nearby stool with her toe.

'Could you sit here, Daniel, like you did when you were young? Sometimes I think about the quiet evenings we used to share when the girls were asleep and Sam was out tending to someone in the parish. You and I would talk about all sorts of things.'

'Yes, I remember.' He pulled the stool closer and sat down within reach, though they didn't touch.

His throat felt tight as he watched her blue-veined hand pluck at the purple flowers crocheted into the blanket. Arthritis had thickened her knuckles. Illness had thinned and mottled her skin. She looked so fragile, so much older than her years.

And he was a damned coward. He knew she wanted him to visit more often but he couldn't. He told her how busy he was at work and she accepted his excuses. But they both knew he stayed away because he couldn't bear to see her like this.

Sitting so close, he could smell her perfume. Lavender. She'd always worn the same scent. As a boy and even a young man there had been nights when the terrors would come, clawing at his mind in the hours before dawn. Somehow she always knew. He'd smell lavender, know she was there with him, and he could go back to sleep.

He looked back at her weary face. He should go home.

As he'd done so often lately, he wondered why he called it that. The apartment wasn't a *home*. This house had been the only place in his life resembling a home and Anna was its heart. If she –

No, dammit. Ruthlessly he made himself face the truth.

Anna was getting weaker. The damned doctors fumbled around, doing test after test, making suggestions and excuses while she faded before their eyes. The occasional rushed trip to the hospital was shocking but not surprising.

One day she wouldn't be able to come home from the hospital, no matter how many nurses he hired. And when she was gone he'd have no home. No warmth. No place.

'Warren Hellmann came to visit me last week,' she said.

'How is he?'

'He said he was fine but he seemed tense. Edgy. So different from when he and Sam were in university together. Warren was always so relaxed, even mellow, about everything.'

'One of the many reasons he was so popular as a

college professor. When he took early retirement during my senior year to start up his own business his students held a demonstration, hoping to persuade him to stay.'

'I remember.' She chuckled. 'He was flattered, but I wasn't surprised when it didn't work. He told me more than once he was tired of teaching. Between you and me, I think what really bugged him was how little teachers are paid compared to what he could make in business.'

'From what I've seen and heard, he's been successful.'

'Warren hasn't visited often since Sam died but the last few years I'm always surprised to see what an old man he's become.' She smiled. 'I sometimes forget that if Sam had lived, he'd be an old man now, too.'

They both looked across at the large chair that had always held position beside the fireplace. She and the girls always called it Sam's chair, as if the man still sat in it every evening. Even now his daughters curled up in it whenever they needed comfort, as if to be held by the soft cushions and wide padded arms was to be held in their father's lap.

Daniel never sat in it. He'd never felt as if he had the right.

'Warren asked after you.'

'I should call him. It's been a few months since we got together.'

'He told me he'd never met anyone as brilliant, as determined, or as focused as you. He's as proud of your success as the girls and I are. As Sam would be.'

'Without Warren's help, things would have been a heck of a lot tougher both in university and when I first started teaching. He used his influence to help me get my business off the ground. His advice and his contacts got me to where I am today.'

She shook her head in disagreement. 'No, Daniel. You earned your success.'

She seemed to be getting too tense so he decided to change the subject.

'The girls looked great at lunch.'

'Mary says Tom might be promoted soon, to captain. I say it's about time he had a desk job. Their boys need a father who's not risking his neck to stop creeps who'd rather steal than work.' She chuckled. 'Did she tell you what those little imps did last week?'

And she was off, chattering about her two beloved grandchildren. He closed his eyes and smiled, enjoying the youthful lilt in her voice. This way he could forget her age, her illness, and how they were losing her by inches.

With his eyes closed it was easier to remember her as she used to be. As she'd been that night so long ago when she'd taken a lost, angry boy into this home and into her arms. As always, when he thought about that time, his hand clenched on his thigh. The ache was phantom, the physical memory of a wound healed so many years ago he bore no visible scar.

'Daniel.' The rhythmic squeak of her rocking chair stopped.

He opened his eyes and saw her smile.

'Where'd you go, son?'

'Nowhere, Anna. Nowhere.' He returned her smile, and shut away the memories.

'The roses are beautiful. Their scent is so lovely I had the nurse put some in my bedroom.' They both looked to where the bouquet gleamed against the river rock fireplace. 'Sam bought me yellow roses for our tenth anniversary. Only it was the wrong month.' She shook her head. 'The man never could remember birthdays or such.'

'I still remember the time he forgot about a wedding until the groom called here to say the church was full of people waiting for the minister. I don't think the bride's mother ever forgave him, did she?'

'Oh, eventually. No one stayed mad at my Sam for long, not even Mrs Worth. And our Hannah has the same magic touch with people.'

She lifted her hand to touch the antique leopard brooch pinned to her dress. 'Thank you for having this repaired, Daniel. I'd missed wearing it.'

'It was my pleasure.'

'Sam gave me this on our wedding day.' Her smile was more fond than sad. 'He's been gone almost twenty years and I still miss him.'

'Everyone does.'

'But we had a lot of happy years together. I want that for you, too. Why don't you find a wife and settle down? Have some kids?'

He almost laughed, considering the day he'd had.

She laid her hand over his where it still gripped his thigh. 'What's bothering you, Daniel?'

'Nothing. Everything's fine.'

'I know you, Daniel. I know when something's bothering –'

'I had lunch with the Sisters today,' he interrupted her. 'Mary told me you like the new nurses.'

She gave him a long look, telling him she knew he was avoiding the subject but she'd allow it. For now.

'Yes, they're both nice women. Thank you for hiring them. Hannah was spending so much time helping me I worried she was neglecting her schoolwork. Ruth says . . .'

While she talked about Ruth's opinions, he stood, shoved the stool out of the way, and stretched out on the carpet at her feet. He lay on his side, propped on one elbow, and watched her as they talked.

This is what I want, he thought, as the shadows lengthened and darkened and the evening passed. This is what a home should be. Peace. Contentment. Sanctuary.

Until last year, he hadn't felt any lack when he returned to his apartment. As long as he had a comfortable bed, a full fridge, and an address for the mail . . . what more did a man need? He spent most of his life either in his office, a classroom, or visiting clients, so he'd been satisfied.

But last year, when Anna had had the bad turn, he'd realized this place, this house, this woman, wouldn't be here forever. He needed his own home, his own sanctuary.

He just had to find the right woman to be his wife and the mother of his children. The sooner, the better. Tomorrow he'd go over his selection process, decide where he'd gone wrong, and work out new search parameters.

Jess stared at Harvey in disbelief. 'You did what?'

He'd dropped the bombshell as soon as he came back from escorting their morning appointment out to the elevator. How could he do this? He knew she didn't want to work for Scratten, the director of the brain trust, or his two smarmy lawyers. He knew she didn't trust any covert group with so much influence in high places.

'I told them we'd do it.'

'But . . . we've always talked things over before we took on a new client. What about the problems we had with the preliminary check? They could be lying or trying to use us for something illegal.'

'I'll do it alone, whether you help or not.' He turned his back on her, avoiding her gaze, staring down at the street through the cracks in the dusty venetian blinds.

'I don't trust them. Something about their organization doesn't smell right.' Jess dropped into his client chair and Nick jumped into her lap. What's with Harvey lately? Once upon a time he'd have refused to deal with sleazeballs like these. 'There's more going on than we've been told.'

'Concept House is a think tank full of Mensa-types

who are paid to sit around thinking up solutions to problems. They have been around for years. Don't you think if they were breaking the law, they'd have been closed down a long time ago?' Harvey grumbled. 'Besides, I already said we'd do it.'

'I don't like Scratten. He and his pet lawyers made my skin crawl.'

'They gave me the retainer this morning.' He reached into the sagging pocket of his cardigan and pulled out a fat envelope. He tossed it toward his desk and she gasped when a wad of hundred-dollar bills scattered across the blotter.

Steady, girl, she warned herself. This is another warning sign. People who offer too much money are usually trying to muzzle a person's common sense. 'Send it back.'

'They're willing to pay big bucks for our services.' He returned to his position in front of the window.

'Too big and it makes me nervous.' When she stopped stroking Nick, the cat butted his head against Jess's hand in complaint but she ignored him. One by one, she checked off her objections on her fingers.

'He wants Finders Keepers to find out who's been sneaking into their buildings but won't tell us what's missing. He won't provide a list of their staff, past or present. He won't tell you the names of the board members, if they even have any. They don't release any financial data or publish an annual report.'

'Nothing odd about that. It's not a publicly traded company.'

'You told me yourself the paperwork filed with the government can only be described as skimpy.'

'It's okay, Jess. My sources tell me Concept House filed the proper paperwork, though they said it would be worth their job to let me see it.' The metal slats crackled when he pulled down on a few, opening a gap just large enough to peer at something or someone in the office directly opposite.

'And that's supposed to make me feel better? What kind of people have enough clout to make lowly *government clerks* keep their mouths shut, for heaven's sake?'

'You're being paranoid.'

'Security at Concept House is as high tech as any I've ever seen and, in my opinion, just this side of deadly. When we tried to trace their financial backing and ownership, we received a visit from a federal agent who told us to back off or we'd lose our business license.'

'Concept House is entitled to their privacy. It won't keep us from getting the job done.'

'I won't help you. I can't.'

'I've worked alone on cases before.'

'I can't think of a single ethical reason why they'd refuse to sign a contract and insist on paying us in cash.' Desperate, she used her trump card. 'We could lose our investigator licenses.'

'You're jumping at shadows, kid.'

'Send the money back, Harvey.'

'No.' The blinds crackled and snapped shut as he let

go to rub a hand over his face as his shoulders sagged.

Why was he acting so weird? Why, for the first time since they'd worked together, was he breaking his own rules? 'What's wrong, Harvey? Does this sudden change in attitude have something to do with your doctor's appointment yesterday?'

'Absolutely not.' He fiddled with the dangling cord, tilting the blinds to let in more sunlight. 'Remember the piece of property in Florida? My share of the fee for this case will provide a large chunk of what I need to close the deal.'

'Oh.' She blinked, her eyes watering in the sudden glare. 'I'd hoped you'd changed your mind about leaving Vancouver.'

'I haven't.' He turned to look at her, his blue eyes regretful but his expression determined. 'I'm going to start working the case, Jess, whether you like it or not. Whether you help me or not.'

'Harvey, I –' She stopped. She'd already said everything she could think of, both about him leaving and about this case, and none of it had changed the stubborn old cuss's mind. She put Nick on the floor and stood.

'Fine! You go right ahead. But don't blame me when we're both flat broke and out on the street because they took away our licenses.'

'Jess –'

'And when it happens, at least then you won't be able to take off for Florida because all your money'll be gone.' She stomped back to her own office and Nick followed her, his nose in the air. She slumped into her own chair and stared at the racks holding hundreds of tapes . . . all the cases they'd worked together.

Who cared if he went to live in Florida? Not her. She'd buy him out. Finders Keepers would be better than ever because she'd finally be able to do things her own way without anyone interfering.

At that moment Sophy's distinctive neighing laugh rattled Jess's ear drums and she shook her head ruefully. She'd forgotten about Sophy, who firmly believed she ruled this particular roost.

Just then she heard Harvey's voice in the outer office, saying goodbye to Sophy, and Jess resisted the urge to run after him to patch up their quarrel. They'd never had a serious disagreement about anything. Now he was making decisions for the partnership without her input and planning to move thousands of miles away. It hurt. It hurt bad and she wasn't ready to let it go.

Maybe by this afternoon they'd both be calmer. Then they could sit down and talk things over. Heck, he'd probably started the argument so she wouldn't have a chance to grill him about his doctor's appointment.

She bent her head over a file and tape, refusing to look up as his footsteps paused outside her door. She waited stubbornly for him to speak, but he kept going, across the office and out the door.

A single tear plopped onto the file and she angrily wiped it away, smudging the ink.

CHAPTER 4

'Do you think he means it, Nick?'

The cat in her arms pointed his nose at the ceiling and purred approvingly as she scratched his neck. She hadn't turned on the lights when she came back from following an architect's errant secretary and now her office filled with shadows as the sun sank beyond the city's skyline.

She was alone in the office with Nick and Nora. Sophy had gone home a while ago and Harvey, the coward, hadn't come back after their argument.

'There must be some way to get him to forget about Florida,' she muttered. 'Maybe I should hire him an assistant. Heaven knows there's more than enough work and he always perks up when he has someone young and keen to train. Nothing he likes better than the image of himself as the wise mentor sharing his hard-won secrets and methods.'

Nick meowed.

'Yes, you're right. I wasn't being nice. Harvey's not like that at all. I should know better than anyone else that he just likes helping the kids, teaching them how to do the job right so they can earn a living.'

She yawned and thought about returning the message Daniel St Clair had left on her voice mail. Nope, she didn't feel like talking to him. Since Sophy liked him so much, she could make the call herself tomorrow morning.

Time to go home. 'Come on, guys. Let's hit the road.' Nora leaped gracefully from the windowsill to the floor and pranced to the outer office. When Jess didn't follow immediately, the cat looked back over her shoulder and meowed emphatically.

'I know, I know. You're hungry. So am I. How about Chinese take-out tonight?'

Nick growled a warning.

'Yes, sir. I won't forget the shrimp this time.' She put him down, then donned her hat and overcoat after making sure her wallet was stowed in the pocket.

She'd found the man's coat at a second-hand store on Fourth Avenue one day when she was on a case and needed a quick disguise. The quality of the fabric was good, plus its ample folds and roomy pockets were very useful, so she'd worn it ever since.

Besides, it made her feel like Sam Spade or Philip Marlowe, especially when she wore her hat. She peeked in Sophy's mirror to make sure the brown fedora was tilted to the correct angle and adjusted the brim with a trembling hand. Harvey had given it to her as a joke when they left the other agency and formed Finders Keepers. She'd worn it ever since for luck.

71

She swallowed hard, then followed Nick and Nora into the hall. While Jess locked the office the elevator pinged its arrival, the doors opened, and Daniel St Clair stepped out.

What was he doing here? She looked down at the keys still dangling in the lock. Don't be foolish, woman. He wants to talk about the work she'd done for him, of course. But did she want to talk to him, alone in the office, tonight?

Her heart thumped hard a time or two, then resumed beating normally, if a little fast. Not that she blamed herself for it. Who would? He was the living, breathing embodiment of every woman's dream lover.

What red-blooded woman wouldn't be attracted to a man with those brown curls rakishly tumbled over his forehead, the faint air of frustration, the blue jeans taut across his hips and thighs, the leather jacket rustling as he moved . . . She inhaled as he stopped next to her. Darn, he even smelled good.

'Ms Phillips?' His voice was a little rough as he rammed his hands into the pockets of his jacket.

She jumped, then glanced up as she slid the keys out of the lock and into her pocket. 'Hello, Mr St Clair.'

'I'm glad I caught you before you left.'

'I'm sorry, you'll have to call Sophy in the morning for an appointment. We were just going home.'

'We?' He looked around the hallway.

'Me and Nick and Nora.'

'Oh.' He looked at the two cats who were waiting for her beside the elevator. 'I'd really like to talk to you tonight. I called earlier but got your voice mail.'

'Oh?' Recalling her decision not to return his call, she blushed. She could tell he wasn't too impressed with a business that didn't return messages.

Nora meowed pitifully, reminding her mistress of the promise to feed them.

'I have to go.' She stepped around St Clair and pushed the call button.

'Look, this really is important. I would have come here to talk to you earlier but I couldn't get away from the office until now.'

When the doors slid open, he followed her and the cats inside. The already small space immediately felt tiny. The elevator shuddered as it slowly dropped one floor.

The doors creaked open and Jess smiled at the woman who joined them. 'Hi, Marie. Nice suit.'

'Thanks.' The elevator shuddered into motion again as she smiled politely at Daniel, then crouched to pet the cats. 'Hi, Nick, hi, Nora.' When she stood up she grinned at Jess. 'I was hoping I'd see you today. Guess what?'

'Roy proposed?'

'Yes!' Her arms shot up in the air and she did a little victory dance. 'Yes, yes!'

Jess saw Daniel blink when Marie squealed. She didn't blame him, the sound hurt her ears, too. Nick's and Nora's complaints were more vocal.

'Congratulations.' Jess knew she had to say it but she sure didn't feel it. She'd realized a long time ago that

73

most women didn't agree with Jess on the subject of marriage.

'I'm so excited.' The elevator groaned and the door creaked open on the ground floor. 'I've got to run, Roy's waiting. I'll give you a call.' She dashed away, high heels clicking on the tile floor.

'You don't appear pleased for your friend.'

'I'm not.' They both followed the cats into the lobby. 'She's throwing away her career and for what? A man who expects her to worship and support him and put his career first while she has his babies and waits on him hand and foot. Bah! Marriage was made for men, not women.'

'I disagree. The institution of marriage has something to offer both men and women, if they choose their partner carefully.'

Jess suddenly realized she was spilling her guts to a man she barely knew, who obviously didn't understand. 'Never mind. You had something you wanted to talk to me about.'

'Your report. I've done some checking.' He held the outside door, looking slightly bewildered when Nick escorted Nora out first. On the sidewalk both cats stayed close to her side, away from the traffic, as they walked to the parking garage next to her building.

'My lawyer has confirmed your information about Sally de Graf. Now we need to pinpoint exactly what information she managed to access and how she did it. To do so will require special skills and equipment.

You're already familiar with the details so I've decided to hire you.'

'You have?'

'Do you think we'd be able to find out?'

'Yes, but . . .' For that she'd need to spend time at his executive school. Maybe the university. Why would she willingly put herself in a place she knew would make her feel stupid?

'You do have the proper equipment to check our offices for listening devices, don't you?'

'Yes, I have access to them. That's not the problem.'

It only took a few minutes to reach her Volkswagen. Ever since some jerk smashed one of its windows and scratched the dark green paint, she'd leased a spot within sight of the cashier's booth and tipped the men a little extra every month to keep an eye on her beloved Beetle.

'There's a problem?'

Yes, she thought, you're entirely too appealing for me to spend any time with, which was very confusing. She didn't even *like* people like him. Or, she never had, till now. On the other hand, if Harvey knew about this potential job for St Clair, he might be willing to give up the Concept House case.

'I'll talk to my partner and give you our answer tomorrow. We always do some preliminary checking and talk things over together before we agree to take on a case.' At least we have till now, she thought sourly.

'Can't we go somewhere, have something to eat or perhaps a drink while we discuss this? I really wanted to get this settled today.' He stepped closer.

Why was she tempted to say 'yes' immediately?

Because of Finders Keepers she had to do work for people like him, but she didn't have to admire them to take their money. Certainly she'd never before considered having a drink with someone who was either a boss or a teacher, much less both. Must be a reaction to the man's physical presence.

She shrugged. This, too, would pass. She unlocked and opened the door, then turned to face him from behind its sturdy frame.

'I'm sorry, that won't be possible.'

The cats jumped into the car where Nora draped herself across the back seat and promptly fell asleep. Nick took his accustomed place as co-pilot in the passenger seat, perched on the extra cushion she kept there for him so he could watch the traffic. The poor baby became ill if he couldn't see out the window.

'I'll call you after I've had a chance to talk to my partner.' She slid into the driver's seat.

'But –' He braced one hand on the open door, the other on the car's roof, and looked down at her.

'Excuse me, I have to get home. Nick and Nora want their dinner.' She looked pointedly at his hand on the door until he removed it. 'Thank you.' She closed the door, then rolled down the window as she turned the key in the ignition. She smiled in his general direction and put the car into gear. 'Goodnight.'

'But –'

Jess glanced in the rear-view mirror as she drove up

the ramp past the cashier. Daniel hadn't moved, reminding her of a western movie she'd seen a few years back. The gunfighter had stared at his opponent, poised for battle, tense, ready, feet spread wide for balance. With his thumbs hooked in the front pockets of his jeans Daniel looked a lot like that gunfighter, whose hands had hovered over the pearl handles of his revolvers.

She dragged her gaze away from him and flicked on her turn signal. As she pulled into traffic she decided not to keep him waiting. She'd better talk to Harvey tonight about Daniel's job offer, right after she fed the cats.

No sense in annoying a man like Daniel St Clair any more than was absolutely necessary.

'What do you think?' Jess crouched beside the pair of cupboards she called a kitchen and rummaged through the tiny refrigerator for two bottles of beer. She'd called Harvey and invited him to join her and the cats for their dinner of Chinese food take-out.

So far, neither had mentioned their argument about the Concept House case. She didn't know whether to be glad or sorry they were both avoiding that topic.

'What I think is, this place is too small. Why do you keep renting a room in this boarding house when you can afford to rent, or even buy, a proper house?' He glanced around the third-floor attic she called home.

At one end of the room the cats were curled up asleep on the double bed she'd tucked under the steeply sloped ceiling. A flowered curtain hid the hooks and wire shelves where she kept her clothes.

Across the middle wall, opposite the door, she'd installed the fridge beside the cupboards that held a miniature sink, a hot plate, a toaster oven, and a microwave. At the other end she'd arranged one aging sofa, a top-of-the-line VCR, and a television with a 36-inch screen. The crates behind the couch held her extensive collection of classic movie videos.

'The price is right, there's a garage for my Beetle, and my landlady watches Nick and Nora if I have to go out of town. Besides, I like it.'

'You don't even have your own bathroom.'

'The women on the second floor work nights and I usually work days. It's perfect.' She picked up the bag of fortune cookies in her free hand and brought it over to the sofa.

'I'll never understand why you break open a whole bag of those but never eat them.'

'Too many calories.'

'Then why buy them?'

'Some people read horoscopes, some visit psychics. I buy fortune cookies.'

'I guess you're allowed. Everyone has one or two weird quirks and yours could be worse.' He poked his fork into one of the greasy cartons and dragged it closer. 'What are you doing tomorrow?'

'Paige Spencer hired us to check out nursing homes for her uncle. Sophy's going to give me a hand by pretending to be my ailing mother. While I tour the facilities, she's going to sit in the lounge and see what she can find out by talking to the residents.'

'So she finally talked you into letting her help with fieldwork, huh? If she likes it, you know this means we'll have to hire someone else to take over her secretarial and bookkeeping work.'

'I don't think so, at least not full-time. She understands going undercover means she has to dress in character but she's not impressed with the outfit I gave her to wear.' Jess grinned. 'That reminds me, did she ask you about hiring a part-timer to help her with the paperwork?'

'I told her it'd have to wait until . . .' His voice trailed off.

'Yeah. Until.' She didn't want to talk about his retirement either, so she nudged him with the toe of her sneaker. 'So, do we check out the Graff woman for St Clair?'

She twisted off the bottle caps, tossed them in the wicker basket beside the sofa, and handed one of the beers to Harvey as she flopped down beside him.

'You know what I think?' Harvey slouched back into the sagging cushions on her old sofa and put his feet up on the wooden plank she'd laid across two cinder blocks for use as a coffee table. 'I think you like him.'

'Yeah, right.' She cracked open a cookie, read the fortune, then tossed it back into the bag with the crumbs. 'He's a teacher, for heaven's sake, and a big-shot businessman. As if I'd be interested in him.'

'Who are you trying to convince? Me or you?' He

lifted his eyebrows. 'Maybe you should give the attraction a try. He might be the man you've been waiting for.'

'I'm not waiting for any man. And besides, he'd never be interested in someone like me.'

'Uh huh.' He forked up another mouthful of chop suey from the cardboard container balanced on his stomach. 'Sophy told me a different story.'

Jess looked at his beloved, rumpled face and wondered when Sophy was going to tell him her plans for his future. She cracked open another cookie and read it aloud. ' "Find love where you least expect it." This one's for you.'

'What are you talking about?'

'You'll find out.' She sipped at the bottle, then broke open a cookie. 'This one's for you, too. "Be careful what you wish for." Obviously warning you away from Florida.' She handed him the slip of paper. 'The St Clair case should bring in a fair bit of money and Sophy told me we have two other new clients tomorrow. Things are picking up.'

'Jess –'

'We can give Concept House back their money.'

'Jess, honey . . .' He studied the bottle's label, then drained it and put it on the makeshift table along with the empty chop suey box. He glanced at his watch and heaved himself to his feet. 'It's late.'

'How 'bout a movie?' She reached over the back of the couch, scooped a video from the nearest crate. 'We haven't seen *The Big Sleep* in months.'

'Not tonight. I have something to follow up before I can get to bed and we've both got a long day tomorrow.' He picked up his windbreaker and baseball cap. 'Look, you decide if we should check into St Clair's problem, it doesn't matter to me.'

'Harvey –' She followed him to the door.

'In the meantime, think about why you're so anxious to take on his case.' He brushed a goodbye kiss across her forehead. 'In my opinion, it hasn't anything to do with money, or me, or the Concept House business.'

'What's that supposed to mean?'

He smiled, faintly. 'Think about it.'

After he was gone she stared at the closed door for a moment, wondering what his last comment meant, then threw up her hands and decided to forget about it. She seldom understood Harvey when he turned profound.

She dropped *The Big Sleep* back into the crate and slid *Casablanca* into the machine, then nestled into the sofa with her bag of fortune cookies.

When Humphrey Bogart spoke those immortal lines as he first caught sight of Ingrid Bergman in his bar, it hit her like a body blow.

Her office was no gin joint but, thanks to Daniel St Clair walking into her life, she knew exactly how Bogie's character felt.

'I hate this,' Jess muttered. Why was this happening? She'd always prided herself on her ability to focus on the job at hand but now, for the first time, something was getting in her way.

Or rather, some*one*. A particular someone.

She was in the middle of another case and she couldn't turn off the stray thoughts about Daniel St Clair, thoughts that had nothing to do with investigating nursing homes or corporate spies.

'Why should *you* hate it?' Sophy craned her head around so she could glare at Jess from her seat in the wheelchair. They'd borrowed it from Terry, who managed the medical supply company in the ground-floor storefront below Finders Keepers. 'I'm the one who looks like the back end of a bus.'

'Shush. Someone might hear you and blow our cover. I wasn't talking about this investigation and you're supposed to be a helpless old lady, remember?' She checked her pockets for spare batteries and tapes, then slipped the voice-activated recorder into the hidden pocket behind the lapel of her coat.

'I still don't think it was necessary for me to wear this get-up.' Sophy lifted the skirt of the prim, flowered polyester dress and shook it disdainfully. 'No make-up. No fingernail polish. A grey wig. Geez, Jess, just because a person decides to live in one of these places doesn't mean she can't look good.'

'You're the one who wanted to go undercover and your role is a nice, ordinary senior of comfortable means and failing health. If you looked your usual glamorous self, they'd never believe you need to live in any of the places we've checked out.'

'I still don't see why I couldn't have worn slacks and a shirt like you.'

Jess tightened her grip on the wheelchair's handles and strained to push it up the sloping path leading from the parking lot to the front entrance of Shaughnessy Manor. The white buildings cast a glare in the afternoon sun and she wished for the dark glasses she'd left in the car. 'Whew, it's hot today.'

'You wouldn't be roasting if you'd left your coat at the office like I suggested.'

'I need the pockets to hold all my stuff.' She ignored Sophy's superior look and spoke into the tape recorder. 'Neatly trimmed lawns. Tulips, daffodils, and some kind of purple flower are blooming in precisely arranged beds. Paige said a nice garden was important to her uncle.'

After an almost sleepless night spent weighing the pros and cons of working for St Clair, she still couldn't make up her mind. In the meantime, she worried her jumbled thoughts might mess up one of her cases. Life got complicated when a person's good sense went to war with her hormones.

'At least you get to see around the place with the manager. I have to sit in the lounge, chatting with a bunch of old people. Not exactly exciting.'

Jess swallowed the urge to laugh at Sophy's disgruntled expression. 'And if you hadn't been sitting and chatting at the last place, would we have known the truth about the awful food? And it was you who noticed the kindness and personal service of the staff at the second home.'

'Humpf.'

'We're almost done. This place was the last on the client's list.' Jess paused for a moment to catch her breath, then sighed and bent over the handles again. Was it her imagination, or was this slope getting steeper?

When they went around a large rhododendron bush the path flattened out and she almost moaned in relief.

'Want me to walk a bit?' Sophy asked. 'You look exhausted.'

Jess was shaking her head when she saw how their path merged with a beautiful driveway which swept toward the buildings. Fifty exhausting yards of fancy brickwork separated them from the formal portico shading the main entrance.

'Thanks, but you can't. Somebody might see us.' She took a deep breath and braced herself, then shoved hard. The chair rattled as they moved onto the bricks.

'This makes a gawdawful noise,' Sophy said and tightened her grip on both the chair and the huge white vinyl handbag in her lap.

'Long, noisy walk from parking lot,' Jess said breathlessly, for the benefit of the tape, 'for a place that's supposed to be wheelchair-accessible.'

She was glad of the shade as they finally moved under the portico. Glass doors swished open as an electric eye sensed their approach, inviting them into a lobby with subdued elegance, soft music, and, more important in her opinion, air conditioning.

'Nice digs.' Sophy relaxed her grip and turned on

the tape recorder in her handbag. 'So what's had your knickers in a twist all morning?'

'Daniel St Clair dropped by the office last night. He wants us to do some work for him. Find out something more about Sarah Graff.' She was about to explain how irritated she felt about her indecision when Sophy spoke up.

'He does? Wonderful. I'm sorry I missed his visit. You know why he came, don't you? He liked you. I told you he'd be back. He wants you.'

'Don't be absurd.'

'There was electricity in the air between you two that day. If *I'd* been the one he looked at that way . . .' Sophy closed her eyes and licked her lips. 'Yummy. All those firm muscles. Did you notice his hands? Big and strong, but so gentle. A man like him would make sure a woman enjoyed herself in his bed.'

'Good for him, but your fantasy's got nothing to do with me. Right now we have to concentrate on nursing homes.'

'I bet you felt the heat, didn't you? Why won't you admit it? Come on, Jess, live a little. Ask him out.'

'Will you *please* stop telling me to get involved with Daniel St Clair,' she said. 'I am not interested.'

'Good afternoon, can I help you?' asked the uniformed nurse behind the reception desk.

'I have an appointment with the manager, Lucas Nillson.'

'If you'd like to wait in the sitting room, he'll be right with you.'

Jess thanked her and wheeled Sophy away.

'If you're not interested in Daniel St Clair, you're either blind or stupid,' Sophy muttered.

'Behave yourself,' Jess hissed through gritted teeth as she faked a smile for the man walking toward her, hand extended to shake hers. 'It's show time.'

'I'm glad that's over with.' Sophy leaned sideways in her seat to help wedge the folded wheelchair into the back of the Beetle. 'Maybe if you turned it.'

'Don't do that.' Jess heard the sharp edge in her voice and winced. 'I'm sorry. It's hot and I'm tired but that's no excuse. I meant to say thanks, but I got the darned thing in and out at all the other places. I'll manage this time because I want us to stay in character.'

'Why? Shaughnessy Manor was the best of all the homes we've seen. The price is comparable to the others but this one beats them hands-down on locale, decor, garden, room size, lots of staff . . . Even the food tasted better. Anybody'd like to live here, including you and me.'

'Not me. They wouldn't allow Nick and Nora.'

'Okay, so no pets. But we both know this place is perfect for the client's uncle. Doesn't that mean you're finished here?'

'Yes. Sort of.' Jess inched the wheelchair in a little farther and let the driver's seat fall back into place. She slipped off her coat and tossed it on top of the chair. Then she climbed behind the wheel and collapsed into a panting heap.

'What more do you need?'

'Shaughnessy Manor is much larger than any of the other nursing homes we saw.' Jess pulled herself together, wound down the window to get some fresh air, and started the car. 'Three times the staff. A separate wing or building for the different levels of care and all of them immaculate and beautifully decorated. I'd say it was *very* expensive to maintain.'

'So?'

'Someone's invested a big chunk of change in that place. It's odd their prices aren't any higher than the other homes we've seen.' When she drove out of the parking lot, instead of turning left to head back to Finders Keepers, she turned right.

'Maybe they're better organized or better managed. What does it matter? Where are we going?'

'I'm curious.'

'Oh, Lord, here she goes again.' Sophy looked up to the sky, as if expecting help from that quarter. 'So tell me what you saw and I missed?'

'Better turn your tape recorder back on.' She waited a moment while Sophy wrestled it out of the handbag. 'None of the other nursing homes had so many security guards. Plus, as we were finishing the tour, did you see the manager's reaction when I got curious about the north wing?'

'Yeah, now you mention it. He was real emphatic about the area being off-limits.'

'They had a guard stationed by the entrance to the wing and he was the only one who wore a jacket.'

'Aren't you the one who's always telling me to stop staring at men? He wasn't even good looking. Maybe he has thin blood.'

'I think he was armed.'

'A gun?' Sophy squealed. 'He can't be, only cops are allowed to carry guns. How on earth would you know if the man had a gun?'

'I'm not sure. Probably the expression in his eyes and the way he moved. He was way more alert than the other guards.' Just beyond a row of cedar trees they left the road and drove the car down a bumpy lane. 'I want to have a look at the backside of their property and the outside of the north wing.'

Sophy braced herself as the lane narrowed and overgrown bushes brushed the sides of the car. 'I don't think cars drive down here very often.' Her voice shook as they jolted across ruts and exposed roots.

'Someone comes this way often enough to make that necessary.' Jess pointed out the side windows. 'The big branches on the bushes and trees have been lopped off to keep the lane passable as long as the driver doesn't care about their paint job. Any vehicle bigger than mine would get badly scratched.'

'Enough to discourage most people.' She shook her head.

Jess grinned. 'Not me.'

They didn't get far though before they were stopped by a brick wall. Jess plucked the recorder out of Sophy's hand and began speaking.

'The nursing home has a brick privacy fence. About eight-feet high with a padlocked gate, both topped by coils of wire. A sign nailed to the gate warns off trespassers.'

Jess handed it back to Sophy, then slid the car into reverse and backed out. As soon as they were back on the main road, Sophy turned in her seat to face Jess. 'Barbed wire. They mean business.'

'No, razor wire. *Real* serious stuff.'

'They sure are paranoid about their privacy.'

'Or they have something to hide.'

'I guess we tell our client to take Shaughnessy Manor off her list, huh?'

Jess had to laugh. 'I think we'd better.'

'I don't like the look in your eye.' Sophy put her hand on Jess's arm. 'You're done with that place, right? Something tells me these people won't take kindly to you snooping around in their business.'

For a moment Jess felt a powerful urge to discover the secrets of Shaughnessy Manor just for the heck of it. The thought made her feel young, like the old days when she dove into any situation that made her curious, just because she wanted answers.

However, she was older now and the urge didn't last long once she thought about the realities of the situation.

'Don't worry, Sophy. Without a client to pay for my time, Shaughnessy Manor is safe enough from my curiosity. I'm having enough problems with Harvey right now.'

Jess slowed for the turn into the parking garage where she kept her car and waved as they passed the attendant who was reading a book in his little glass booth.

'Speaking of men, you mentioned Daniel St Clair came to the office last night to hire us. When will we be seeing him again?'

'We won't.' Jess slid the car into park, turned off the engine, and got out of the car. She reached into the backseat for her coat and put it on so she wouldn't have to carry it. 'Could you help me wrestle this darned thing out of the back seat?'

'Why?'

'Because I told Terry we'd bring it back right away.'

'I wasn't talking about the wheelchair. Honestly, Jess . . .' She shook her head but leaned in on her side to give the wheelchair a shove. 'Sometimes I just don't understand you, girl. I think we should take the man's case just on principle.'

'What principle?'

'Actually two principles. He's easy on the eyes, plus we know he'll be able to pay our bill.' She braced herself and shoved harder. 'I'd better not break a nail doing this.'

At that moment the chair came free and Jess stumbled backwards, her arms full. Off balance, she plopped onto her rear.

'Darnit! I just had this cleaned.' She leaped to her feet, leaned the wheelchair against a nearby pillar, then grabbed the hem of her coat, tugging it around so she could see the disgusting streaks of muck and oil the fabric had collected from the filthy floor. 'Gosh darn it anyway!'

'About Daniel –'

'Drop it, Sophy.' Jess locked the car and picked up the chair.

Sophy, however, apparently had no intention of dropping the subject because she nattered about it as they walked out of the parking garage and down the street to their building. The medical supply store was beside the main entrance and the one-sided debate continued while she returned the wheelchair to Terry. By the time they were leaving, Jess had had enough.

The moment they stepped back out on the sidewalk, she swung around to confront her. But the blistering scold died on her lips when Jess caught sight of a reflection in the window behind Sophy. Her instincts screamed a warning and she froze, grabbing Sophy's hand to keep her still.

'Talk about something, anything,' she whispered, her attention on the distorted image in the mirror-like window. The older woman looked bewildered until understanding and excitement flashed in her eyes and she began chattering.

Jess watched two men leave her office building. They wore black suits, dark glasses hid their eyes, and the menacing way they moved sent shivers down her spine. Everyone on the crowded sidewalk scurried out of their path.

While she pretended to listen to Sophy, she slipped a

palm-sized mirror out of her coat pocket and used it to get a clearer look over her shoulder at the men.

Both looked like thugs. One was wrapping a handkerchief around bloody knuckles, the other brushed dirt from his jacket. They climbed into a dark grey BMW parked illegally at the curb.

She broke into Sophy's prattle. 'Can you read the BMW's license plate?'

'Where? Oh. GJF 424.'

The minute the BMW pushed into traffic, she took off for their building at a dead run, Sophy sputtering right behind her. 'What's up? Who were those men, Jess? Did you recognize them? Jess?'

'I have a bad feeling.' In the lobby she jabbed impatiently at the elevator's call button, but when the doors didn't open immediately she ran for the stairs. She pushed open the fire door but it only moved a couple inches before it was slammed shut in her face.

'Someone's blocking this,' she panted as she thrust her shoulder against the door. 'Help me.' Her feet scrambled for a better grip on the tile floor.

Sophy looked horrified and her hands fluttered. 'Oh, no, Jess. I couldn't . . .'

Just then a muffled voice from the other side of the door ordered them to leave and said the police were on the way.

Jess went still. 'Harvey? Is that you?'

There was silence for a moment. 'Jess?'

Sophy began to giggle.

CHAPTER 5

'You should have seen Jess's face when she realized that was you on the other side of her fight for the door.' Sophy handed Harvey a cup of coffee. She turned on another lamp in his office, then settled into a nearby chair with her own cup. 'It was priceless.'

The moment Jess parked herself in front of Harvey's desk Nick leaped into her arms. 'Today proves I was right. It's time to tell Scratten you're off the case.' She glared at both of them. Nick glared, too, his tail twitching.

Harvey leaned back in his chair, concentrating on brushing a faint smear of dust off his tweed jacket.

'I've been chased before,' he said mildly. 'So have you. It's part of the job.'

'Those two thugs could have hurt you.'

'Then why were they the ones with a cut hand and dirty clothes?' Harvey asked. 'They never got within arm's reach of me but I still managed to beat them at their own game.'

'They'll be back now they know who you are and where we work.'

'Nope. I was following one of those guys when he must've made me and called in the other goon on his cell phone. The second guy swooped down on us in his car and I took off. As far as they know, this just happens to be the building I ducked into to get away from them.'

'So it's all a coincidence? Tell me another one.'

'They're not even sure what I look like 'cause I was wearing these.' He pointed to the scraggly fake beard on his desk then pulled something out of his pocket and tossed it in her direction. She managed to catch the ball cap without dropping Nick and saw it was one to which she'd glued a blonde ponytail.

Jess stared at him, wadded it into a ball, and threw it back. Then she snarled with frustration and swung around to pace. Nick snarled, too.

'Calm down, Jess.' Sophy took a sip of her coffee. 'After ten years working for you guys, even I know he's been through much worse than this without any permanent damage.'

Jess buried her nose in Nick's fur. Why couldn't they see it was different this time?

'Daniel St Clair came to see Jess yesterday,' Sophy said.

'Yeah, she told me.' Harvey linked his fingers behind his head and leaned back. 'Hey, Sophy, why do you suppose she's making a fuss over what should be a very simple decision?'

'A good question.' She contemplated Jess over the rim of her coffee cup. 'It's not as though he can't pay for our services. We know the man's problem is legitimate.' She leaned forward and lowered her voice to a husky whisper, pitched just loud enough to make sure Jess heard every word.

'She told me to have a letter delivered to his office tomorrow morning, turning down the case. But you know what I think?' She winked at Harvey. 'I think she's attracted to him and it scares her to death.'

'I've had enough of this abuse.' She raised her voice. 'We are going home.' Nick leaped out of her arms and headed for Jess's office. Nora didn't move from beneath Sophy's stroking fingers.

Nick stopped in the doorway and hissed. Nora arched and purred under Sophy's hand, ignoring him and Jess, as if to make sure they both knew their place in the scheme of things. Eventually she rose to her feet, and slowly, gracefully followed her mate.

Jess picked up her coat and folded it so the filth from the garage floor was inside where it couldn't come off on her clothes. She rubbed her hand across the silky lining for a minute, thinking.

'I'm scared for you, Harvey.'

His grin faded. 'I'll be fine, Jess.'

'You said my intuition is good about people. Why won't you listen when I say we shouldn't be involved with Scratten? He's bad news.'

'Because you're allowing your emotions to color your judgment. I think you're getting bent out of shape about the Concept House case because it's going to fund my retirement to Florida.'

Could Harvey be right? Even so, that didn't change the fact her instincts were shouting warnings about Scratten. Somehow she *knew* he was bad news. But what could she do now? Harvey had made it very clear nothing she said or did would sway him.

He was determined to work for Concept House. He was determined to quit Finders Keepers and go to Florida.

He was determined to leave her.

She looked from him to Sophy. On the other hand, maybe there was one more way she could try to stir things around to her advantage. She almost felt like smiling.

'Okay, I'll make you guys a deal. You will both stop nagging me about St Clair and his case. In return, I'll concede there's a possibility, a slight possibility, you could be right about why I dislike the idea of you working for Scratten.'

Harvey agreed and then Jess looked at Sophy pointedly until the older woman finally, reluctantly, nodded.

'So that's settled. We all back off. But, before you book your trip to Florida, I'd suggest you have a talk with Sophy.'

Harvey looked puzzled. Sophy, however, was scowling. Watching them, Jess managed a smile.

She thought about hanging around to see what happened next but decided against it. Throwing the cat amongst the pigeons might be fun, and no more than Sophy deserved after trying to interfere in Jess's life, but actually having to watch the carnage wasn't to her taste.

The next morning Jess retraced her steps to the window, cracked the blinds so she could see the street, then looked down at her watch. Ten-thirty.

Where was Harvey?

She'd been in and out herself this morning, to get her coat cleaned and pick up doughnuts for breakfast so she'd hadn't noticed his absence right away.

Sophy told her he hadn't come into the office at his usual time. He wasn't answering his portable phone, though she and Sophy had both been dialing the number off and on for hours.

Neither of these actions were like him. By nature, he couldn't sit there and listen to his phone ring without picking it up to see who was calling.

And in all the years she'd known him he'd only once arrived at work after eight a.m. That day a car accident had blocked Lion's Gate Bridge and thousands of people missed half a day's work. Harvey only missed an hour.

She couldn't stop thinking about those doctor appointments he refused to talk about. Hopefully Sophy would be able to get some answers with a phone call to his doctor's office. What if he'd collapsed somewhere and couldn't get help?

The door to her office slammed open and Sophy

swirled through. 'The receptionist wouldn't tell me anything because we're not "family" so I called all the hospitals in the lower mainland. They don't have his name on their admitting records. I think you should call Lieutenant Masters.'

'You know the cops won't get involved with a missing adult for at least twenty-four hours. They don't have enough time or manpower.'

'We've got to do something.'

'I called Scratten. Supposedly he hasn't heard from Harvey since he left Concept House about noon yesterday.'

'Do you think . . . ?' Sophy's voice trailed off.

'That his absence has something to do with Scratten's case?' Jess dropped into her chair. 'I don't know. Scratten sounded odd when I called. And I'm still worried about those two men who almost cornered Harvey yesterday.'

Jess smacked her hands against the chair's arms and Sophy jumped.

'What was that for?'

'I wish I'd asked Scratten the questions face-to-face. The man's a pretty good liar but he fumbles a bit if you look him in the eye.'

Jess wished she'd resisted trying to mix things up between Harvey and Sophy. If they all hadn't been in a snit last night he might have said something about his plans.

Then she might have had some idea where to start looking for him. 'After I left yesterday, are you *sure*

Harvey didn't tell you anything about where he was going last night or today?'

'Like I've told you a dozen times already, *no*. We talked about . . . other stuff.' She played with one of her ringlets.

'I'm sorry, Sophy.'

'Will you please stop apologizing? Like I told you first thing this morning, I understood. You probably hoped if he knew my feelings, he'd change his mind about retiring.' She shook her finger at Jess. 'Doesn't mean I'll let you get away with it again, understand?'

'Yes, ma'am.'

'Now, let's stick to our present problem. What can we do about Harvey?'

'I don't know, but I'd bet this has something to do with Concept House. I wish I knew what angle Harvey was pursuing.'

'What about the list we found in his top drawer?'

'The company directors? Hmm, you might have a point.' She frowned. 'When you read me the list I realized I recognized almost every name on it. They're all big shots in business or society or both. I wonder . . .'

Sitting on her rear wasn't going to make Harvey appear, she thought. Time to do something useful. The chair crashed against the wall when she stood.

'When you were reading the paper this morning, didn't you mention some private club is hosting a society event tonight? Seems to me you said a whole bunch of VIP types were sponsoring it.'

99

'Yeah, but I don't see what that's got to do with Harvey.'

'Call St Clair. Tell him I'll take the job and I can come to his office right now.'

'But, Jess . . . I thought you didn't want anything to do with him. What about the letter you had me print up this morning? He'd have it now if we hadn't become so worried about Harvey, I forgot to call the courier.'

'That was then. Things are different now.'

'What's different?' Sophy looked bewildered even as she picked up the phone to dial.

'This morning I didn't need to ask the man a favour,' Jess muttered while Sophy talked to someone at St Clair's office.

'He can see you in twenty minutes.'

Jess nodded once, then picked up Nora who was snoozing on top of her coat. She cuddled the cat, then handed her to Sophy. 'Feed them for me, okay? I might be a while.'

'Sure.' Sophy trailed her out to the reception area. 'You didn't finish telling me what's different now.'

'St Clair's problems are simple enough. He needs to know if Graff put listening devices in his office. I'll do an electronic sweep of his office and with any luck he'll agree to give me what I need.'

'What you need?'

'Scratten was too busy to see me today and when I asked him about tonight, he said something about an important party he couldn't miss. *This* party.' Jess shrugged into her coat, then slipped the recorder into one inside pocket and her wallet into the other. Automatically she checked for spare tapes and batteries.

'So?'

'If Harvey's disappearance has something to do with the men and women who run Concept House, I've got to find a way to get into their world without making them suspicious.' She plucked her fedora off the rack.

'I only know one person who moves in the same circles as those people.' She turned the hat in her hands for a few minutes before she put it on. When the brim was angled just right, she looked at Sophy. 'St Clair.'

'Oh, Lord.'

'I bet he has tickets to the society thing. And thanks to the excellent services of Finders Keepers, he won't need the second ticket.' She smiled grimly.

'This isn't smart, Jess.'

'If I can get myself in the door, I'll be able to corner Scratten long enough to get some answers. I might even make a few useful contacts.'

'What are you going to tell St Clair when he finds out you're using him to investigate his friends?'

'Nothing.' She went into the storeroom to get the case of electronic gadgets and hooked its carry-strap over her shoulder. 'He won't notice a thing. And if he does, I'll figure out some believable excuse to account for my actions.'

'Ha! You're taking a big risk. He can't be as blind as you think, not a man that successful. I also doubt he's the type to smile and shrug when he finds out you've been stringing him along.'

'It doesn't matter.' Jess looked back at Sophy who had Nora cuddled under her chin. 'This is for Harvey.'

Jess hovered in the empty hallway on the eighteenth floor of Waterfront Tower while she sucked in gulps of air and fought to stay calm.

According to Harvey's report from the earlier investigation, St Clair's offices were on this floor and the entrance had large brass letters on a wood surface.

Why the heck hadn't he told her that on this particular floor there were two businesses with brass letters?

The entire hall was paneled in a dark reddish wood that shouted money. The wall on her left boasted curly brass letters about a foot high. To the right, a string of raised brass letters glinted beside enormous doors.

Which was St Clair's? She glanced frantically from left to right. Someone was going to come out, see her standing there and ask what she wanted. Then they'd guess she couldn't read the darned signs.

With her luck, it would be Daniel, himself. What a way for him to discover her secret. Men like him always thought people like her were stupid. Then he'd change his mind about hiring her and there would go her only chance to get her hands on the ticket.

Okay, calm down. Take a breath. First step was to get herself through the correct door and for that she had to be able to think clearly.

Jess closed her eyes and ran through one of the calming routines Sophy had taught her years before.

If the exercises could get her through all the medical testing which diagnosed her dyslexia when she was twenty-four, surely they could get her through this.

As she breathed, slowly and deeply, she could feel the heavy pounding of her heart ease into a more natural rhythm.

Her eyes blinked open and she focused on the first letters of the two signs. What was the name of his firm? Oh, yeah. St Clair Institute for Executive Learning.

She snorted. It still sounded self-important.

Jess focused straight ahead and visualized the first word as she'd seen it on Sophy's typed report. 'S'. Followed by a 't'.

Then she raised her hand and used one finger to draw the 's' shape in the air. Once she had it clearly in her mind she studied both sets of letters. Bingo. The longer string of words began with an 's'.

She stiffened her spine, tugged the equipment bag's strap higher on her shoulder, and shoved open one of the enormous doors. After she stepped through it began to swing shut with a ghostly sigh.

She jumped out of the way, then looked sharply to the left when she heard a giggle. Behind an equally massive desk made out of the same expensive-looking wood as the doors, a young woman with scraggly hair and heavy black eyeglass frames wore an apologetic smirk.

Not at all the type of person she'd expected to see working for Daniel St Clair, Jess thought. Behind and above the receptionist's head, on a wall painted a deep burgundy, she saw more of the squarish brass lettering. On the opposite wall she saw several framed photographs featuring St Clair and what appeared to be a series of important men and women shaking his hand and smiling for the camera. Many were autographed.

The photographs confirmed it. She'd finally found the man's school.

Though she doubted 'school' was an accurate description. Not by any stretch of her imagination could she see any resemblance between this place and one of the many schools where she'd wasted her time. As she crossed to the desk, at each step her shoes sank into the sea of ivory carpet.

'My name is Jess Phillips. I'm here to see Daniel St Clair.'

'Sure thing, Ms Phillips.' She toyed with her hair. 'I'm sorry about what happened before, laughing when you came in. Those doors have got hydraulic hinges and it's kinda funny how most people jump when they come through the first time.'

'I understand. What's your name?'

'Gwen. Sit down and I'll let them know you're here. Please.' The last was added after a distinct pause and a nervous glance to her left, toward an arched doorway. She appeared relieved when she saw the hall was empty.

Jess glanced around and saw a seating nook she hadn't noticed when she came in. She lingered near one of the leather sofas, half-afraid to sit down, until she realized what was happening to her.

Great. Already intimidated and she was barely inside the man's office. That was the moment she decided she never wanted to work for him. And if it weren't for the darned ticket, she'd have been out of there so fast the receptionist wouldn't have seen her for dust.

Jess laced her fingers around the case's strap and hung on tightly. Who said she had to take on the entire investigation? When he talked to her in the parking garage, St Clair had only mentioned checking his office for bugs. So, that's what she'd offer in exchange for the ticket. No more.

If he wanted something else checked, he could hire another firm.

Feeling better now she could see the end to her involvement with him, Jess relaxed. A couple minutes later a slender, dark-haired woman wearing a severe navy blue suit and a chilly expression appeared beneath the arch.

'Good afternoon, Ms Phillips. My name is Chris Houston. I'm the Institute's office manager.' She didn't smile or extend her hand in greeting. 'Did Gwen offer you something to drink?'

Jess was about to say no, when she noticed the flash of panic on the receptionist's face. 'Yes, she did, but I wasn't thirsty.'

'If you'll come with me?'

As Jess followed her, they passed quite a few closed doors before the other woman paused and wordlessly indicated Jess should enter an empty office.

A much smaller space than she'd expected for a man who owned this business, Jess thought. She glanced around at the plain desk and credenza, the over-flowing filing cabinets. Crowded and messy, too, which also surprised her.

'Mr St Clair will be here shortly.' She stood stiff and sour-faced just beside the desk, not quite meeting Jess's gaze.

Well, Jess thought as she dropped her heavy case beside a chair, that's odd. The office manager's attitude and expression seemed almost antagonistic. Interesting.

But Jess's twinge of curiosity was overwhelmed, then forgotten, when Daniel St Clair walked through the door.

Daniel escorted the Japanese trade commissioner to the door and exchanged bows as the man and his staff left in the elevator. The lucrative contract between their government and his firm had been formally approved. The paperwork was signed.

He allowed himself a moment to enjoy an experience he would have considered routine, up until two days ago.

Ever since his sisters introduced him to Jess Phillips, everything in his life had gone haywire. Finally something had transpired as planned. Now it was time to deal with what Rick had labeled 'the Sally situation'.

Past time.

Inside the lobby, he tried not to scowl at the inept

106

girl behind the reception desk who smiled nervously as he walked past her toward O'Keefe's office. Why had he allowed Chris to persuade him to give her another chance at the position?

He hadn't gone far when he realized the odd sound he heard was his own feet. Stomping.

He immediately stopped, braced his hands on his hips, and drew a few calming breaths, struggling for control. His feet hadn't been loud on the thick carpeting but that wasn't the point.

The distractions caused by Jess Phillips, the mess caused by Sarah Graff, and the recent problems with the Institute staff were beginning to get to him and that couldn't be allowed, no matter how tired and irritated he felt.

It didn't matter that he had good cause for annoyance. After all, it had been over thirty-six hours since Jess Phillips had driven off with her cats and left him standing in her exhaust.

He wanted his own office back.

He was tired of working out of someone else's office. He'd even had to set up a temporary space suitable for consulting with clients like the ones who'd just left. Irked by her casual dismissal in the parking garage and annoyed he hadn't heard back from her right away, part of him regretted offering the job to Jess Phillips.

If he hadn't been so busy all morning he'd have considered hiring a different detective.

Which brought up another subject irritating the hell out of him . . . Rick and Chris were still at loggerheads over Daniel's decision to hire a detective and it was beginning to affect office dynamics.

He adjusted the fit of his jacket and continued down the hall. From this point forward, things had better go smoothly and cooperatively.

Jess Phillips would do whatever was needed to resolve this situation and she'd do it immediately or he'd hire someone else to do the investigation. Even Rick and Chris might be out looking for new jobs if they didn't stop squabbling.

No more fooling around. He wouldn't allow it.

Inside his temporary quarters Chris was standing at attention, not bothering to hide her disapproval.

Then he saw Jess. The breath shuddered in his lungs even though he'd thought himself prepared for this meeting.

The impact of her presence was just as powerful, just as vibrant as before. As he made himself breathe normally again he smelled something unfamiliar in his office. Green apples. He inhaled again. And spring.

It had to be Jess. Chris used some kind of flowery scent and Rick always used Old Spice. Neither of them ever smelled like green apples and spring.

He barely restrained the urge to touch Jess, then pulled himself together when he realized Chris was staring at them both with a speculative look in her eyes.

'Ms Phillips.' He nodded to Jess as he walked around to stand behind the desk. 'So good of you to come.' He didn't actually say 'at last', but judging by the way her lips tightened he knew she'd heard it in his voice. Good.

'Where's Rick?' he asked Chris.

'He said to tell you he'd be along in a few minutes. Now you're here, I'll get back to work.' She slipped out of the office.

'Rick Gorley is the company lawyer,' he told Jess. 'I wanted you to meet him and Chris since you will likely need their assistance in your investigation.'

She hesitated, looked as if she would disagree, then shrugged. 'Fine by me.'

His jaw clenched at her casual tone and attitude but he didn't respond.

'About my fee –' She was interrupted when Rick rushed in, already talking at full speed.

'Sorry, Daniel, got here as quick as I could. Becker called. I know the Sally situation is urgent but he needed soothing. I told him I'd call right back after this meeting –' When he saw Jess his rapid spiel dried up and his jaw dropped.

'Jess, this is Rick Gorley.' They shook hands; Rick looked dazed. Good, Daniel thought. At least I'm not the only idiot who reacts to her so strongly and foolishly.

Daniel frowned when he noticed the vivid, friendly smile she gave Rick. She hadn't smiled at him that way since the day they met.

'They'll help you at any time I'm unavailable,' he said. 'The rest of my staff don't know you're a detective or why I hired you.'

Rick leaned against the desk near Jess. 'Daniel will be glad to get back into his own office. As a matter of fact, if you're ready to get started, I could show you where everything is right now.' He eyed the case at her feet. 'I was wondering . . .'

'Yes?'

'I'm curious about how you're going to check the office for bugs. Any chance I can watch?'

Before she could answer, Daniel spoke, 'You owe Becker a call, remember?'

'Oh, yeah.' He shook her hand. 'Nice meeting you, Ms Phillips.'

Once they were alone, Daniel shoved back from the desk and stretched out his legs. 'Is that all the equipment you'll need to do the sweep?' He indicated the case with his chin.

'Yes.'

'I believe the less people who know what you're doing, the better. So after you do my work area and the conference rooms, I'd like you to complete the check on the other executive offices tonight, after everyone else has left for the day. I also . . .'

'No!' The moment the word blurted out of her mouth she looked as though she wanted to call it back. 'I already have something I need to do tonight.'

He braced his elbows on the chair arms and looked at her over his steepled fingers. 'Ms Phillips, I have never before had so much trouble hiring a consultant. Have you ever heard of the old business adage, the client is always right?'

'I could do your private office now, but it would be more practical for me to come in tomorrow morning to finish the rest.'

'It would have to be early. Though it's Saturday, we're running a management seminar tomorrow afternoon.'

'Fine. Could Mr Gorley or Ms Houston be here to let me in?'

He nodded, reluctantly. 'It could be arranged *if* you're sure the delay is necessary. I would prefer to have this completely taken care of today.' He waited for her to apologize and agree to his timetable.

She didn't.

Jess realized she was annoying him but couldn't help it. She needed him to hand over the ticket as quickly as possible so she could get back out there and spend the next few hours looking for Harvey. Plus, if she had to confront Ralph Scratten tonight, she needed time to do some research of her own.

'I can't waste my afternoon hanging around your offices, waiting for people to go home.'

'I expected you to move on this yesterday.'

Jess almost replied she hadn't intended to move on it at all but managed to bite her tongue. Better not to antagonize the man just before she asked him for a favor.

'I had to consult with my partner and finish up another case. We're sorry for the delay.' She decided to dive right in with a straightforward question. 'About my fee. I was wondering . . . Do you have tickets to the charity thing at the Hotel Galleria tonight?'

He looked baffled.

She didn't blame him. After all, what did this have to do with checking his offices for listening devices?

'I just thought . . . under the circumstances . . .' That's when it occurred to her it might be awkward to refer to the other women he'd been dating. How to ask him if she could use his spare ticket, without mentioning the reason she knew he might have one?

'I need a ticket.' Jess stuck her hands in her pockets. 'I thought we could do a swap. I'll sweep your offices for half the usual rate, in exchange for your extra ticket.'

'I have an invitation, not tickets. No one can use it except me and my companion or guest.'

Just for a moment, a very brief moment, Jess had a dazzling vision of herself on an elegant date with Daniel. It didn't last long. She'd never fancied herself as Cinderella and so far she hadn't noticed any tendency in him to play Prince Charming.

As if glass shoes, a pretty dress, and one dance could magically create a love strong enough to erase all the fundamental differences between a prince and a housemaid. Bah! Instant love would never wipe away inequalities between two people, allowing them to live happily ever after.

Even as a kid she hadn't bought into that fantasy.

'Invitation?' she asked, hoping she'd heard wrong.

'Issued in my name. It can't be used by anyone else, not even my "guest", unless I attend.'

'There has to be a way around this.'

'There isn't.'

'Can't you talk to someone, get me a ticket?'

'Sorry. The event is sold out.'

She tensed when she realized she'd have to ask for exactly the circumstances she didn't want . . . more time alone with Daniel. 'How about if we went together?'

'I wasn't going to attend. Too busy. However, maybe we could work out a deal . . .' He rubbed a finger along one eyebrow as he considered. 'I need to know if any of my employees were helping Graff.'

'Good idea.' Get on with it, she groaned. Either refuse or agree, just stop wasting time she couldn't spare.

'What action would you recommend?' he asked.

'Someone could work in your office undercover as an office temp for a few days, getting to know the staff. It wouldn't take them long to get an idea of who, if anyone, might be involved. If you suspect anybody in particular, a background check could expose a motive.'

'Motive?'

'People usually have a reason for taking money to betray their employer. They could be broke or greedy or a gambler. Or they might have wanted revenge against you personally.'

His brows lowered into one of his sinister-looking frowns. Obviously he didn't like that idea. Too bad.

'I have a counter-offer,' he said. 'I'll escort you

tonight if you'll agree to sweep the office plus check out my employees.'

Now it was Jess's turn to consider. Not that she had much choice when he knew he held the upper hand. 'You'll pay my usual rate plus expenses for the background checks and undercover work.'

'Done. How soon can I expect answers?'

'Someone from my agency will be available to start work here day after tomorrow. I can't guarantee how long it will take us to check out all your employees.'

She bounced to her feet, unable to sit in the small room with him another instant. 'I'll be here at five tomorrow morning with my equipment to do the entire office.'

'Jess.' His voice stopped her halfway out the door. 'I'll need your home address.'

'Why?'

'I'll pick you up there tonight at seven-thirty.'

'No!' She definitely didn't want him in her home. But she also didn't want him to know how her gut churned at the thought. Time to assert herself, even if only in a small way.

'I've got work to do. Pick me up at the office. At eight.' She took off out of there like a scalded cat.

She nodded briefly to the young woman behind the reception desk and actually had her hand on the outer door when she heard him call her again.

'Jess?'

She pulled the door open as she turned toward him, determined to escape as quickly as possible.

114

She could swear the smug jerk was hiding a grin. Winning obviously didn't become him.

'Yeah?' she asked, her voice perilously close to a growl.

'I have to pick you up by seven-thirty so we're not late for dinner.'

For the first time since the first year after she'd met Harvey, controlling the urge to curse was a real struggle.

'Also,' he said, 'just thought I should mention . . . it's black tie.'

Black tie. Oh, my God. And she didn't own even one formal outfit.

'I'm looking forward to tonight,' he said.

She tossed her head and swept out, intending to slam the door. Nothing happened. It eased shut with the same ghostly sigh as when she'd arrived.

Even the man's darned door was against her.

It seemed to her he'd got his own way today from the moment she'd arrived. Well, tonight would be different. As soon as he walked her into the ballroom, he was on his own.

No way would she confront Scratten with St Clair at her side.

CHAPTER 6

As Daniel stopped the Jaguar in front of Jess's building, half a block away the steam clock blew its one-note warning. Seven-fifteen.

He was early. Time enough to do some thinking, he decided as he leaned back in the leather seat and loosened his tie. He grimaced when the compact disk on the passenger seat caught his eye.

Some of Hannah's friends had been inspired to perform their own interpretations of the music of Mozart, Chopin, and Tchaikovsky. This CD was the result and he'd promised to listen to it. She had some vague idea that he could help these guys to a career.

She'd asked sweetly, he agreed reluctantly. That's the way it always was with Hannah, he reflected.

Might as well get it over with. This evening couldn't get any more painful. He slid the CD into the machine and hit play.

Maybe it *could* get worse, he thought as the music assaulted his eardrums. But since he'd promised

Hannah to listen to the entire CD, he turned down the volume rather than turning it off.

He rested one wrist on the steering wheel and watched the street through his car's rain-streaked windshield. Gastown's old-fashioned street lamps cast a warm yellow glow on the wet cobblestones. Bold neon signs in every hue of the rainbow flashed in store windows. They both glimmered and refracted in the oily puddles along the gutter.

Well-dressed restaurant patrons and business people scurried along beneath their umbrellas, ignoring the beggars and their illiterate cardboard signs claiming hunger and thirst.

Vancouver, bordered by mountains, farmland, and ocean. City of contrasts. A living, struggling dichotomy.

As were his feelings about Jess Phillips.

She wasn't anything like his mother or sisters. He couldn't imagine her as a woman content in the dual roles of wife and mother. Yet . . . he liked her.

She'd made it clear she didn't want to work for him. Then, when she had asked for the ticket, he saw her vulnerability and without a moment's hesitation he'd forced the issue. Why?

Any competent investigator could help him deal with Sarah Graff. How had it come about that he wanted this particular detective and no other? Now she'd be working for him, spending time in his life, and he wished he'd never met her.

Yet he hadn't told either Rick or Chris about the five

o'clock appointment tomorrow morning, intending to be there himself.

Why? His future was all planned. Sure he'd hit a snag, thanks to the Sisters' interference, but he didn't have to abandon his strategy altogether. He just needed time to analyse where it had gone wrong and rework the system.

His plan hadn't been, couldn't be, affected by the sheer fact of her existence, not in any way. Unless he hired her to do a background check on all his potential wives?

No. A good idea, but not if it involved Jess.

He leaned forward and turned off his car. To hell with this tangled thinking. Time to take charge.

Daniel pulled his cell phone out of his coat pocket and punched out a number. 'Chris? Ms Phillips is going to be at the office at five tomorrow morning to perform the sweep. I need you to be there. Thanks.'

As he disconnected the call, the steam clock blew again, indicating the half-hour. Time to go. He straightened his tie and picked up his umbrella from the back seat. Then he locked the doors and crossed the dimly lit lobby toward the elevator.

The rising elevator car rattled and shook as it passed the other floors. As he watched the numbers change on the floor indicator, he realized it wouldn't be prudent to spend the entire evening with her. Once dinner was over, the guests would be mingling. No one would notice her or the fact she was alone, much less question her right to be there. He could leave.

She'd made it clear she didn't want his company tonight. She had her own reasons for being there, reasons which had nothing to do with him.

For a moment Daniel allowed himself to speculate on what those might be, but realized he didn't know enough about her to do so. He shook his head as the elevator's raucous ping announced his arrival.

Her reasons didn't matter.

As soon as he saw her, he'd explain he was leaving immediately after dinner and if she wanted to stay, she was on her own.

'*Nada*. Nothing. Zilch.' Jess smoothed on a pair of pantyhose and yanked her only dress, a sleeveless black sheath, over her head. 'Nobody seems to know where Harvey is. And I couldn't track down Ralph Scratten, either. Get the zipper for me, would you?'

'Here, use this.' Sophy handed her the brush, then slid the long zipper closed.

Jess ruthlessly dragged the brush through her tangled hair. She'd crisscrossed the city like a mad woman. Tracked down everybody who knew, or knew of, Harvey. Visited almost every hospital and clinic in the city. Tried coercing his doctor's secretary into spilling her guts.

She'd discovered nothing.

It was like he'd disappeared into thin air. She glanced over at Sophy. 'Why are you so calm?'

'Because if something terrible had happened to Harvey, I know you would have sensed it.' Her expression serene, she patted Jess's hand.

'Yes, I would.' Jess wrapped her arm around Sophy's shoulders and squeezed. 'That doesn't mean he doesn't need our help. He could be hurt.'

'The only thing I don't understand is why you can't find him. It's your talent.'

'I need a clue, Sophy. Otherwise I'm in the dark, same as everybody else.'

'Are you sure cornering Scratten tonight is a good idea?' She got Jess's one pair of high heels from the bottom drawer of her desk and dropped them on the floor near her feet.

'Good or not, it's the only idea I have left. I just wish I didn't have to spend even part of my evening with Mr Big Shot. I intend to lose him as soon as possible.'

'You were hoping you'd find some clues this afternoon so you wouldn't have to go tonight, weren't you? Why don't you ease up? You might enjoy yourself.'

'I might have to go to this thing but I'm *not* going to have a good time.' She winced when the brush hit a knot.

'Here, let me do it.' Sophy snatched the brush from Jess. 'You're making it an even worse mess.'

Sophy separated out a handful and began trying to untangle it.

'Ouch!' Jess flinched. 'Take it easy, will you?'

'Big baby.' She picked up another handful of hair. 'Gertrude came to see me today. She still wants us to find her cousins.'

'Absolutely not, we still haven't been paid for

finding her dog. I don't care if she's a friend of yours. She's a flake.'

'Like I've told you, she's not exactly a friend, she's my hairdresser.'

'She charges for doing your hair, doesn't she? So why does she expect us to work for free?'

She tapped her foot, waiting. Sophy didn't answer.

'You're afraid, aren't you?' Jess tried to twist around to see Sophy's face and got the brush rapped on her shoulder.

'Stop fidgeting.'

'I can't believe you're so intimidated by your hairdresser. Why don't you change to a new one?'

'Only someone like you who trims their own hair would say that. Do you know how bad the odds are against me being able to find another hairdresser who does my hair exactly right? I don't want to risk it.'

'Fine. Then you do the work for her, on your own time.'

'Maybe I will.'

'Great, that's settled,' Jess said. 'She'll have to wait, though. You'll be busy for the rest of the week, maybe longer.'

'Doing what?'

'Pretending to be the temporary receptionist at St Clair's office, starting day after tomorrow. He wants us to check out his employees to find out if any of them have been providing Graff with inside information. If you turn up any likely candidates, we'll do a background check.'

'Why can't you work there?'

'Yeah, right. And how am I supposed to write down phone messages and file paperwork? I'd be tripping over my own lies from the moment I walked in the door. Nobody would believe for more than a minute that I'm an experienced office temp.'

'But Gertrude –'

Worry, fear, tension . . . Suddenly her emotions and her control were swept away. She slapped her hand down on the desk. 'Please, Sophy! You have to do it, we don't have any choice. It's part of the deal St Clair made with me so I could go to this party tonight. Get it?'

'Yes, I get it,' Sophy said placidly.

Instantly Jess felt terrible. Yelling wouldn't make this whole mess go away and Sophy deserved better. 'I am really sorry.'

'I understand, dear.' Sophy patted her on the shoulder, then resumed brushing. When the tangles were finally gone, Sophy began stroking the brush through Jess's long hair, from top to bottom, over and over. She closed her eyes. Oh, that felt good.

'Don't you think it's time you retired this dress and bought a new one?'

'Why? It's perfectly good for the few times a year I need one.'

'It's at least five years old, maybe more.' Sophy dropped the brush on to the desk.

'That's exactly why I paid a lot of money for a classic style in good fabric. So it would last and never go out of style.' Jess stepped into her shoes, grimaced, then began searching through her desk. 'I only need it for funerals or weddings. Or maybe the rare time on a case when I have to wear a dress to blend in.'

'You're not going to go to a fancy affair at the Hotel Galleria with your hair bundled back with an elastic, are you?'

'He's going to be here any minute. I don't have time to fuss with it, even if I wanted to.'

'Follow me.' Sophy led the way to the file cabinet in the outer office and opened the bottom drawer. She rummaged through the jumble of accessories she kept in the office for fashion emergencies. 'Sit down.'

As soon as Jess obeyed, Sophy grabbed handfuls of her hair and twisted them around each other, fastening the mass on top of Jess's head with a jeweled clip. Then she tugged a few wispy strands loose at Jess's temples and the nape of her neck.

She stood back to study her work, then leaned forward to make a few adjustments before she grabbed a non-aerosol spray bottle from the drawer.

'Don't use that stuff, Sophy. You know I don't like the flowery smell —'

'I suggest you shut your mouth or you'll find out how awful it tastes.' She covered Jess's eyes with one hand and sprayed the makeshift hair-style into submission. 'Looks good. There's just one more thing.'

'What?' Jess felt exasperated and didn't care if it showed. Why was Sophy doing this? Now the darned man would think she'd fussed to look good for him.

123

'The dress is too long. If I had your legs, I'd show them off.' She shifted things around in the drawer, eventually pulling out a large square scarf, one with lots of bright jewel-tone colors and metallic gold embroidery.

She tied it around Jess's hips at an angle, leaving the corners to dangle from a knot at one hip. Then she grabbed handfuls of the dress above the scarf and tugged until the fabric bloused loosely at Jess's waist and the hem rode up an inch or two.

'Ooops, I almost forgot.' She shut the file drawer and reached under her desk for a purple patent leather purse. 'You'll need this. I got it ready while you were in the bathroom washing up.'

'You really have a thing for shiny vinyl, don't you?' The purse's shoulder strap, a heavy gold-coloured chain, jingled and jangled as Sophy tossed it into Jess's unwillingly hands. 'You know I hate using these. They always get in my way.'

'I imagine you want to take your tape recorder and stuff with you, right? You'd look a little odd wearing your coat all night, so this will have to do. Sorry about the color, it's all I had on hand. Unless you'd prefer the white monstrosity you made me use with my disguise two days ago?'

'No, thanks. This will do fi–'

At that moment she heard one solid rap on the outer door. Jess could see a man's silhouette through the opaque glass. The purse's chain jingled again as her arms dropped to her sides. 'He's here.'

'Of course he is. Didn't you hear the steam clock blow the half-hour? He strikes me as the type of man who likes to be exactly on time. Aren't you going to let him in?'

'Maybe this whole thing was a bad idea.' When Jess didn't move Sophy tsk-tsked and opened the door herself.

'Hello, Danny, my boy. Come right in. She's almost ready.'

'Good evening, Ms Westlake. I prefer "Daniel" if you don't mind.'

Jess filed that little fact away in her mind. So, he preferred Daniel, did he? As she recalled, even his sisters called him Daniel. Perhaps, if he got a little too bossy tonight, she'd use the nickname to let some hot air out of his balloon.

'My dear boy, of course not.' Sophy shook his hand, then stepped back and allowed Daniel and Jess to get their first glimpse of each other.

They stared. In silence.

Jess felt dizzy.

No. Stunned.

No. Stunned *and* dizzy. The man looked positively lethal in a dinner jacket.

Eventually Sophy cleared her throat. 'You two kids had better be on your way or you'll miss the dinner.

'I'll . . . I'll get my coat. It's in the other . . .' Her voice trailed off as she dashed for her office. Breathing space. She needed breathing space.

She was gulping a glass of cold water from the dispenser when Sophy slipped in, pulling the door closed behind her.

'Did you see that?' she whispered. 'He seemed absolutely poleaxed when he saw you. He didn't say a word and, truth be told, I'd swear he couldn't think one, either. Not that you were exactly eloquent.'

'I'm taking the cell phone. Call me if you hear from Harvey and I'll leave immediately.' Jess heard the hoarseness in her voice and held down the lever to refill her glass.

'Of course I will. Why are you hiding in your office, talking to me? He's waiting.'

Jess downed the second glass of water, then reached for her coat.

'You can't wear that old thing. Use this.' She brought her hand out from behind her back, with an air of a magician producing a rabbit, and shook out a cloud of lacy black wool. Jess realized it was a delicate knitted shawl.

'It'll keep you warm.'

She shifted restlessly while Sophy draped the shawl around her shoulders. Thanks to Sophy's fooling around, Jess hadn't felt or looked so feminine in years.

'If he gets the wrong idea from all this primping, Sophy, I'm going to punish you.'

'Ooh, what a threat. I'm so scared. Now get out there or you'll have to start clucking like all the other chickens.'

'Okay.' Jess drew a deep breath. 'I'm ready.' Sophy

126

followed her into the outer office where Jess greeted him with a curt nod and a terse hello. His response was equally brief. Sophy smiled and said nothing.

Jess tried not to be too aware of Daniel as they waited for the elevator, rode down to the lobby in silence, and settled into his car. But it was hard when he looked and smelled so darned good.

Before he started the car, he inhaled, then smiled. 'It *was* you.'

'Pardon me?'

'Your perfume. This morning, when you were in my office, I thought I could smell green apples.'

'It's my shampoo.'

'Oh.'

They were halfway through the ten-minute drive when he spoke. 'Before we arrive, I have something I want to say to you.'

'Yes?'

'Hmm.' He seemed to be working himself up to saying something unpleasant. 'I want to thank you for not mentioning the full circumstances in front of my staff.'

'The full circumstances?'

'About my sisters hiring you. No one outside your agency and my family knows how I found out about Sally's . . . Sarah Graff's real purpose. Or the truth about the other women.'

'Hey, no problem. I understand how it might be a little –' She stopped, deciding the less said on *that* subject, the better.

127

His fingers tapped restlessly on the steering wheel. 'You look beautiful.'

'Thanks. You clean up pretty good yourself.'

He'd been looking pretty grim, but after her comment his shoulders seemed to relax.

'Nice car,' she said.

'Thanks. It cleans up pretty good, too.'

Conversation dried up again and they rode the rest of the way in silence. Well, almost silence, Jess thought.

Some kind of music filled with brassy trills, cymbal clashes, and the plucking of stringed instruments vibrated from hidden stereo speakers. She didn't ask about it, though, because he'd probably start talking about 'classical' music.

It figured his tastes would be so opposite to her own. In her opinion, the true classics were performances of people like the Beatles or Elvis Presley or Buddy Holly. Anything by them was a thousand times better than this . . . this noise.

They joined a line of cars inching their way toward the hotel. Once they reached the entrance, two valet-parking attendants scurried to open the Jaguar's doors.

The boy on the driver's side straightened his burgundy jacket on thin shoulders and stood at attention as Daniel stepped out. 'Hi, Mr St Clair. How's it hangin'?'

She didn't hear Daniel's reply because another young man was opening her door and offering a greeting but the first attendant grinned as he caught the keys tossed his way.

Daniel took her elbow as they merged with the crowd flowing into the hotel. Merely a polite gesture, she knew, but it emphasized how much bigger and taller he was than herself.

'Do you know the parking guy?'

'Ruth likes to get me involved in her special projects. Michael was part of a group of kids she convinced me to sponsor a couple years ago.' He shrugged. 'He's a good kid. Always takes care of the Jag for me, if he's on duty.'

Jess sensed there was a lot more to the story. While she debated asking a few more questions, she was distracted by a nearby scuffle. She looked over, noticed a couple men and women with cameras and microphones. 'What the heck . . . ?'

She jerked her hands up to guard her eyes but it was too late. A bright flash blinded her. 'Jumpin' juniper!'

'Sorry, I should have known they'd be here and warned you not to look directly at them. Are you okay?'

'Yeah, I think so,' she muttered. She blinked several times until her eyes could focus again. The first thing she saw was his concerned face. 'Why are they taking our picture?'

He shrugged. She fumed. He seemed to do that a lot when he didn't want to answer a question. She didn't push the issue, though, because they were at the entrance to the ballroom.

Two uniformed staff guarded the door, checking invitations and comparing them to a list on their clipboard. Some of the guests were greeted by name, as he was. Others were asked to show identification.

She'd been skeptical about his claim that she couldn't get into this event by herself, even with the invitation. Evidently he'd been telling her the simple truth.

She'd even wondered if this whole thing hadn't been a ploy of some kind. Though why he'd go that far to force her to work for him and spend time with him tonight, she hadn't been able to imagine.

It's not as though a man like him would be hurting for a date, even at the last minute.

That thought was emphasized for her the moment they entered the beautiful but crowded ballroom. The round tables were covered in floor length ivory damask tablecloths and held a centerpiece of creamy white roses, ivory candles, and purple crocuses. Every chair looked like a throne, slip-covered in the same ivory fabric and bound by purple cords.

She only had a few minutes to admire the crystal chandeliers, reflecting endlessly into the mirrored walls and ceiling, before several gorgeous women rushed over to dote on Daniel.

He kept a firm grip on her elbow when she tried to dodge the perfumed mob, forcing her to stand there and listen to the adoration.

Impatient to get out of there as soon as possible, she began looking around the room for Scratten. She noticed more than one bald head but couldn't see him. However, she did see the Premier of British

Columbia chatting with the wife of the American Vice President and a minor British royal.

Nearby a millionaire athlete and an aging movie star held court. Beyond them, she could see two local mayors fawning over the biggest star in computer technology's firmament. She'd heard he was considering expanding into British Columbia, which explained why the two male mayors were looking at him with the same lustful gaze as the women clustered around Daniel.

And these were only a few of the people she recognized out of the hundreds of lavishly dressed people milling around, sipping champagne.

'What the heck *is* this event, anyway?' She didn't realize she'd asked the question loud enough to be heard until Daniel spoke quietly near her ear.

'Feeling a little awestruck?'

'Of course I am. There's some famous people here tonight.' Awestruck was probably the right word, she thought, because until he spoke, she hadn't noticed Daniel's admirers were gone. 'I had no idea.'

'Really?' The look in his eyes told her he didn't believe her.

Oh, my. He probably thought she'd wangled her way into attending this party with him because she wanted to hang around famous people.

'Yes, really. I knew there was a function here tonight. I needed to talk to one of the guests and I hoped you might have a ticket, considering the published list of sponsors.'

'Was my name on the list?'

'No, but they seemed to be your kind of people. I thought, because of my report on those women, you might not have a date for tonight. Which is why I made the offer of a swap. And that was *all* I knew.'

'Really?'

'It's true. Oh, I'd heard there might be a few big shots here but I expected people like you, not them.' She pointed to where a gold-medal figure skater shook hands with a man who'd won more trophies and held more records than any other professional hockey player.

'Oh, you mean truly important people who have accomplished big things?' He smiled wryly. 'Not just businessmen and women.'

'Yes . . .' Jess was all prepared to continue her heated arguments when she realized what she'd just said. Ooops. 'I didn't mean . . .'

Amazingly, he laughed. 'No, no, don't bother making excuses. No doubt it's good for me to be told what other people think of me. Humility is good for the soul, or so I've heard.'

'So, tell me, what's going on here tonight? This is quite a turn-out.'

'You see before you a gathering of notables, celebrities, politicians, and business leaders who are here to lend support to charity and to be seen doing so, hence the reporters who blinded you outside,' he murmured as they began strolling around the edge of the immense room.

'Then there are the ambitious up-and-comers who plan to connect with someone they believe will help their career. The rest are fairly ordinary, if wealthy, people who paid a thousand dollars a plate for the opportunity to meet and mingle with the aforementioned notables.'

Jess stumbled over her own feet, barely noticing when he gripped her arm in support. She heard the cynical amusement in his voice but only one thing he said really stood out in her shocked mind.

A thousand dollars a plate?

She couldn't quite believe what he'd said.

'A thousand dollars a plate? You mean it's going to cost you a grand for me to be here?'

'Five grand, actually,' he replied casually.

Jess went stock-still, unable to speak. She couldn't believe she'd offered to swap a couple of hours of her professional services for a ticket worth five thousand dollars.

But to her the really big question was, why did he accept? And how could he be so offhand about so much money?

She massaged her temple where she could feel the beginnings of a headache. Did this obligate her to help him complete the investigation into Sarah Graff's actions? Oh, no! Jess almost stamped her foot.

What was she going to do? It didn't matter that the man hadn't *intended* to take her. The truth was, she'd asked him for something that cost him five thousand dollars. How could she dump him the moment she found Scratten?

Especially when she'd practically forced Daniel to bring her? How dare he put her in this position? He should have told her how far this would put her in his debt.

'Jess, we're creating a bit of a traffic jam.' When he tugged on her arm, she resumed moving.

'Why on earth am I here, with you? You could have brought almost anyone as your date, and probably should have, at that price.'

'To me the money was a donation to charity. I had no intention of showing up until you asked about it and I wouldn't be here now, if I could have just given you the invitation.'

'That's a lot of money for any banquet dinner, no matter how many famous people you get to meet.'

'The organizers set one thousand as the minimum. Attendees were invited to donate more, if they so chose, and my sister can be very persuasive. She convinced me to give ten thousand to the cause.'

'Your sister?'

'I assumed you knew . . .' Daniel raised one hand to acknowledge someone waving at a table near the front of the room. He grasped her elbow again to steer her in the right direction. 'Ruth is one of the people running this little shindig.'

'Your sister knows all these people?'

'We're often surprised by exactly who and what she knows.'

Right at the front of the room a stringed quartet performed background music at one end of a small stage. At the other end, small potted palms flanked a podium and microphone. Flowers and greenery were banked high behind and around the musicians and the empty stage.

At a round table directly in front of the stage, Ruth smiled at them, her eyes bright, from behind one of three empty chairs.

'Hi, big brother. I thought you'd never get here.' She leaned over to kiss Daniel's cheek, then shook Jess's hand. 'Hello, so nice to see you again. Daniel didn't tell me you'd be his guest tonight. Let me introduce everybody.'

The three men at the table all stood politely. Ruth put her hand on the sleeve of the man to her left. 'This is my friend, Ian Blake.' He patted her hand, then held it possessively.

'How do you do?' The red-head's smile showed way too many of his big, shiny white teeth as he put his free arm around Ruth's shoulders but Jess couldn't see any real sincerity or warmth in his expression. 'Ruth sure knows how to throw a real humdinger of a party.' He smacked a kiss on her cheek, 'Don't you, baby?'

Ruth smiled but turned to the woman to his left. 'Liz Harper, my indispensable right hand for these events, and her husband, Craig.'

The petite brunette nodded shyly. A woman of restrained elegance, Jess concluded, especially compared to the woman sitting on her husband's left.

Craig Harper, a burly giant in an ill-fitting suit with an unexpectedly sweet smile, leaned across the table to shake their hands. 'Nice to meet you at last,' he said to Daniel. 'Liz talks about you all the time.' His wife blushed.

'Nice to meet you, Liz and Craig. Ruth raves about Liz all the time.'

'Eve Spender, one of the most generous contributors to this event.' Jess wondered at the sudden chill in Ruth's tone until she saw the predatory way the Spender woman looked at Craig. She wanted him and didn't care who knew it.

Eve Spender's attention turned to Daniel when he extended his hand to shake hers. She ran the tips of her fingers across his wrist and palm. 'My *good* friends call me . . . anytime,' she breathed. Then she giggled, a sharp-edged trill that climbed through two octaves. The sound grated on Jess's nerves.

'Eve.' Daniel greeted her as if he hadn't noticed her suggestive actions or words.

'And her brother, James Campbell.'

Campbell acknowledged the introduction with a slight inclination of his head, then noticed the politician at the next table was momentarily alone. 'If you'll excuse me?' He left the table.

He's a cold man, if she'd ever seen one, Jess thought. Evidently, whatever else this evening brought, dinner wouldn't be fun or cozy.

★　★　★

By the time the first two hours had passed, Jess could feel the pain in her temples begin to throb in earnest. The clip in her hair was digging into her scalp. The stupid chain on the purse made too much noise. And she sincerely disliked Eve Spender.

Why hadn't someone conked that woman on the head a long time ago? It would have been a service to the human race and put the rest of the world out of it's misery.

After watching her domineer Ruth, bully Liz, ogle Craig, and flirt with Daniel, Jess was very close to telling the woman to shut up. Though Craig had too much class to give her any encouragement, Jess couldn't say the same for Daniel.

Besides, her stupid giggle was beginning to cut through Jess's skull like a buzz saw.

After another hour, Jess wondered if she could arrange to have Ian and Eve dumped down a bottomless pit together. They deserved each other.

Throughout the dinner and after several interesting speakers, quite a few people came over to congratulate Ruth on the success of the event. If they were a celebrity Ian cut into the conversation, even occasionally excluding Ruth. Otherwise he ignored everyone at the table while he gawked at the crowd.

Jess no longer cared if this dinner was costing Daniel a truck load of money. He should have to pay *twice* as much for inflicting these people on her.

Worst of all, she'd pretended to visit the ladies'

room three times, touring through different parts of the ballroom each time, all without seeing Ralph Scratten. What if he didn't show up? What if she'd wasted all these hours, endured these people, and put herself in debt to St Clair – for nothing?

Don't think about it, she told herself.

Scratten had definitely told her he'd be here to-night. He'd had no reason to lie. No doubt he knew, under normal circumstances, she wouldn't have been able to get near the ballroom tonight, much less inside.

Lucky for her, normal circumstances seemed to have gone out the window after she met Daniel St Clair. Or perhaps meeting him was merely one more calamity in a very unlucky week?

Jess played with her water goblet and tried to look as if she were listening to Campbell's silly political opinions. It was getting very late and if Scratten wasn't going to show, she'd have to think of another place to find information about Harvey.

But first, she'd better take one more walk around the ballroom, just to make sure Scratten hadn't come in since her last tour.

Either way, she wasn't coming back to this table. She was fed up. Since he seemed amply entertained by Eve, Daniel probably wouldn't even notice Jess was gone. She could leave a message for him with the guys guarding the door or with the young kid who'd parked the Jag.

Jess gathered up the shawl and the purple purse, smiled politely and got to her feet, intending to slip away. At the exact same moment St Clair stood up, startling them both.

CHAPTER 7

Daniel decided he'd discovered an entirely new form of torture. Even thumbscrews might be more enjoyable than spending hours beside Jess while she chatted amiably with every man but him.

Look at her now, engrossed in Campbell's absurd theories.

It was an odd feeling to have irrefutable proof of one's own idiocy, a new and uncomfortable sensation he'd never experienced until Jess barged into his life.

Earlier tonight he'd thought things over carefully and made a logical decision. Then he saw Jess, delectably gorgeous, looking as uncertain as he felt, and he no longer wanted to leave her to her own devices at the party.

As they'd approached the hotel he'd struggled with the nearly overwhelming urge to drive on past and never stop, just so he could keep her all to himself.

As a result, he'd spent too much time sitting here listening to Eve Spender's blandishments and wishing she was Jess, thinking about Jess. He glanced at his watch, surprised to see it was only just after ten. It felt like midnight.

He nodded idly in response to a comment or question from Eve, he wasn't sure which, and her voice swelled in volume followed by another annoying laugh.

She'd been talking at him all evening, needing only the slightest response from him to keep her entertained. A small sacrifice on his part if it kept her away from Craig Harper which, judging by her grateful smile, pleased his sister.

As of now, Craig and Liz Harper would have to fight off the dragon by themselves because he'd had enough of wallowing in emotion and uncertainty. He didn't give a damn if Jess spent the rest of the evening hanging on Campbell's words. He was going home.

He stood abruptly, as did Jess.

'It's getting late –'

'Goodnight.'

They stopped to look at each other in confusion, quickly masked. Jess managed a quicker recovery.

'I'm sorry but I have to go. I have an appointment early tomorrow morning,' she said, her expression regretful.

Eve pouted elegantly while Campbell looked shocked anyone would interrupt his lecture.

'Are you sure you have to go?' Ruth asked. 'We're going to hear a lovely soprano later.'

'Yes, we're sure. 'Night, sis.' Daniel bent to kiss Ruth's cheek. 'I promised to have Jess home before eleven.'

'Don't worry about me, Daniel. You stay and enjoy the party, I'll take a cab.'

'You know what they say, Jess.' She looked annoyed so he smiled. 'You leave with the guy who brung ya.'

'Fine. It was, umm . . . nice meeting all of you. Lovely party, Ruth.'

'Have fun, you two.' She winked.

Daniel almost groaned when he realized Ruth thought they were leaving early so they could be alone together. Now she'd tell the Sisters he was involved with Jess.

He glanced at Jess to see if she'd noticed Ruth's innuendo but, judging by her expression, she was still thinking about his insistence on taking her home.

He could tell she wasn't pleased. He wondered why. It was as if . . . Daniel had to stifle a laugh when he realized Jess must have hoped leaving early would get rid of unwanted company. Him. How ironic. If she only knew.

'You lied to your sister,' Jess whispered as she led the way across the ballroom.

'So did you.'

'She's not my sister.'

'Doesn't really matter. She knew we were lying.'

Jess appeared startled. 'She couldn't.'

'Ruth always knows when people are lying. A useful talent for a prosecutor.' He stopped watching the sway of her hips long enough to notice she was leading him away from the exit. 'You're going the wrong way.'

'I have to freshen up. Why don't you go collect the

car? I'll meet you out front in a few minutes.' She sidestepped a cluster of women and he sidestepped right after her.

So, she still wanted to get rid of him, hmm? If he did as she suggested, would he be sitting in the car, waiting for her long after she'd left through another door?

Or perhaps this had to do with her reason for wanting to attend the party in the first place. All night he'd sensed her urgency and anxiety, even when she was sitting still. Though she'd participated in discussions all evening, her gaze had kept darting here and there, watching people.

He recalled her mentioning she was here because she needed to talk to one of the other guests. That might explain her frequent and lengthy absences from their table and why she'd returned from a different direction each time.

He was tempted to play along. Why not? She was more than capable of getting a cab to take her home. She obviously didn't want to spend any time with him and, in fact, considered him an obstacle to her plans.

What about his decision to escape early, leaving her to pursue her own aims? This was the second time she'd given him the opportunity to do so, virtually ordering him to leave without her. So . . . why wasn't he already gone?

He could almost hear the Sisters laughing at that one. Of course he wasn't gone. He didn't take orders well. He gave them.

'Tell me who you're looking for,' he said.

'How did you . . ?'

'You mentioned it earlier, when we arrived.'

'Why do you want to know?'

'So I can help you, since it's clear you're not willing to leave until this is done.'

'I said you could go without me.' She lowered her voice because Ruth was at the microphone, introducing the soprano.

'I was raised to be a gentleman,' he said softly. 'I have to escort you safely to your door or I'll hear about it from Anna.'

She spun around, fists propped on her hips, her words no less fierce for her quiet tone. 'How on earth will your mother know what we do tonight?'

He chuckled, drawing the attention of those around them. 'Oh, Ruth will make sure Anna and the Sisters know everything that happened tonight, whether it happened in fact or in her imagination.'

Jess wondered what he meant by that comment but she didn't bother asking. She'd already wasted enough time on this conversation. 'We'd better hurry, the performer's going to start as soon as Ruth stops talking. I'm looking for Ralph Scratten.'

'Never heard of him. Do you know who he came with?'

'No, but he's completely bald, about five foot ten, and a snappy dresser.' She started walking, feeling as though Daniel was dogging her steps as she quartered the room, scanning the crowded tables for Scratten.

Time after time either she or Daniel caught a glimpse of a bald pate. She'd move closer, only to be disappointed. Who knew there could be so many bald men in one room?

Just as the lights began to dim for the soprano's opening number, she recognized her quarry among a few men leaving the ballroom for the lobby.

'There he is.' She broke into a run, bobbing and weaving through tables, chairs, and people. The purse's heavy chain clanked as she ran.

'Wait,' Daniel called.

'No!'

First he cursed, then he laughed and dashed after her, pausing only to scoop up the shawl she'd dropped. Jess had the lead as they burst out into the lobby but he was only seconds behind when she caught up with her quarry.

Only one man was still standing near him by the time she caught up.

'Mr Scratten,' she panted. 'I need to talk to you.'

'Ms Phillips.' He quickly smoothed the annoyance from his expression. 'I didn't expect to see you to-night.'

'I know.' She heard Daniel arrive at her side, breathing heavily, but she didn't let him distract her from Scratten.

'You could be in serious trouble with security for gatecrashing the party.'

'I had a ticket.'

'I seriously doubt it.' He raised one hand to call over

145

the guards who were watching suspiciously, not pleased by their behaviour, but he slowly lowered it when Daniel spoke up.

'She's with me.' Daniel put out his hand to greet the tall, stooped man with Scratten. 'Good to see you, Warren.'

'Hello, my boy.' He clasped Daniel's hand warmly. 'How are you?'

'A little winded at the moment. I'd like to introduce you to Jess Phillips. Jess, this is Warren Hellmann, an old friend of my family.'

'Hi, how are you.' Intent on her prey, Jess barely noticed the introduction. 'If you'll excuse us, I'd like to have a private word with Ralph.'

'Maybe later. I was just . . .' Scratten half-smiled and pointed at the swinging door beside them. It bore a sign indicating the men's washroom. 'You understand, I'm sure,' he said.

'No.' Jess straightened her spine and thought about why she was here. Harvey wouldn't waffle if she was the one in trouble. 'The only reason I'm here tonight is to get some answers from you. Don't think you can avoid me again by going in there. Because if I have to follow you in, I will.'

Hellmann looked shocked and Daniel laughed out loud.

'You wouldn't dare,' Scratten spluttered his outrage.

'Never underestimate a woman on a mission,' Daniel said. 'I suggest you give the lady five minutes of your time before, uh . . .' He pointed his thumb at the swinging door and grinned.

A cell phone rang.

At first they all looked at each other blankly, then the men reached into their jacket pockets while Jess opened the purple purse.

Jess flipped open her phone and put it to her ear. 'Hello?'

When she heard the voice on the other end, her knees sagged with relief. 'Harvey.'

Daniel put his arm around her for support and she allowed herself to lean into his strength.

'Yes, Harvey. Everything's okay? Are you sure? He's right here. No, I haven't, not yet.' She eyed Scratten, who was shifting his weight from foot to foot. 'Okay. I'll be there soon.'

She closed the phone and pressed her forehead against Daniel's shoulder.

'You okay?' he asked.

She smiled weakly, pulled away from him and slipped the phone back inside the purse. 'Yes. I am now.'

'You sure?'

'Yeah. I have to get back to the office. Is that mine? I didn't know I'd dropped it.' She reached for the shawl he still held.

'Yes, in our mad race through the ballroom.' He shook it out and draped it around her shoulders. 'Jess . . . ?'

'What?'

147

He bent down so his lips were next to her ear. When he spoke, she felt his breath caress her skin. 'Are you going to talk to Scratten?'

She frowned. Harvey wanted her to apologize, then walk away and forget the whole thing. She couldn't do that. Not when she *knew* the man was up to no good. She grabbed the ends of the shawl, tightening it around her shoulders as she wrapped her arms around her chest.

Maybe she could manage to be a little more polite, since Harvey was okay.

'I'm sorry, Mr Scratten, if I was rude. My only excuse is I was worried about someone I love. If you want to, uh . . .' She bit her lip. 'I'll wait out here in the lobby and talk to you when you're, uh . . . later.'

Hellmann slapped Scratten on the back. 'Give the lady five minutes, Ralph. Heck, I wish a woman loved me that much. Makes me envious.'

'Yes, sir.'

Daniel waited beside Warren as the other two moved away a few feet for privacy. He felt envious, too. His sisters loved him but he couldn't see them acting the way Jess had tonight, just because they were worried about him.

What a magnificent wife and mother she'd be, willing to do whatever was necessary to protect someone she loved. When he'd thought tonight was about just another case, another client, her behaviour had seemed a little off the wall. Not any more.

'She's quite a woman,' Warren said as he watched Jess.

'Yes, she is,' Daniel agreed. Too bad she wasn't the kind of woman he was looking for to be his wife.

'I bet your mother likes her.'

'They haven't met.' Watching Jess and Scratten was like watching a pantomime.

She asked him a couple questions. Evidently she didn't like his answers. He shook his head, then backed up a step when she put her fists on her hips and leaned forward.

'You'd better get the two of them together in one room at least once before you find yourself married,' Warren said. 'If you don't, you'll really annoy Anna.'

'We're not a couple. Jess needed to be here tonight and I didn't have a guest. Simple enough.'

'If you say so.' He pulled a big fat cigar out of his pocket and stuck it in his mouth, unlit. 'In all the confusion I didn't get a chance to introduce you to Ralph Scratten, did I? He's been my chief financial officer for about a year, a real find.'

'How are things at Concept House?' Daniel asked, most of his attention still focused on Jess and Scratten.

She asked him another question, arms crossed, foot tapping. He held his hands out to the sides and shook his head, the very picture of blameless innocence. Obviously she didn't buy his act because she began pacing back and forth in front of him, talking fast.

'Business looks pretty rosy,' Warren said. 'Profits are up for the last two quarters and the government's off my back about those defense contracts. Ralph brought in some new blood and they're generating business hand over fist.'

'Great.'

'Thanks again for bailing me out last year. We should be able to generate some dividends soon.'

'Don't worry about it, Warren. It was the least I could do.'

'Why don't you take your seat on the Board? With the size of your investment, you deserve some say in how things are run.'

'No, thanks, I'll leave Concept House in your very capable hands. Between teaching at the university and running my own businesses, I already have enough to do.'

It looked like the confrontation was winding down. Judging by their body language, Scratten no longer feared he was going to get punched in the nose and Jess looked calmer, if not pleased.

'Looks like they're done,' Daniel said. 'Goodnight, Warren.' He started walking toward her.

Jess gazed at Ralph with loathing. She'd been right. He was a slick liar who claimed to know nothing about what happened to Harvey but she could see the lies in his eyes.

By the time Daniel touched her arm she was more than ready to leave. Ralph wasn't going to admit to anything tonight. She had to be satisfied with knowing who to confront if anything else happened to Harvey while he worked for Concept House.

She wasn't sorry for cornering him tonight. It

couldn't hurt for the man to know *she* was suspicious of him. To know she watched out for Harvey.

Jess was aware of Daniel's thoughtful gaze as they crossed the lobby to the hotel entrance but he didn't say anything until after he'd asked the valet to bring around the Jag.

'I was wondering,' he said, 'whether to ask if the talk with Scratten was helpful.'

'Don't ask.'

'Hey, no problem. Consider it unasked.' He chuckled and lifted his hands, palms out, as if fending off danger. 'I've seen you in action.'

His foolishness made her smile. 'Be afraid. Be very afraid.'

'Yes, ma'am. Looks like we weren't the only ones who decided to leave early.' He pointed to where Craig helped Liz tenderly into a car.

'I'm not surprised.' The Jaguar pulled up to the curb as the Harpers drove away. 'When I met her in the Ladies' room earlier tonight, she told me she's pregnant. Craig's been so over-protective he's driving her nuts.'

'No wonder my sister wanted me to keep the dragon away.' Daniel smiled as he tipped the valet who'd brought the car.

'What dragon?' She'd had enough of the jeweled clip digging into her scalp so she reached up and pulled it out of her hair. Oh, the relief! She sighed, then combed the mass back from her face with her fingers.

When he didn't answer she looked over, to see him

151

watching her every move. 'Sorry, I couldn't stand it another minute.'

'No.' He cleared his throat. 'No, that's okay.'

'You mentioned a dragon?'

'Ruth asked me to divert the Spender woman's attention because her behavior was making Liz unhappy.' He started the car and drove away from the hotel. 'At least the evening was sacrificed in a good cause.'

Darn. Jess slouched lower in the seat as she realized she'd misjudged him. Far from enjoying Eve's flattery, he'd merely tolerated it. She sure hoped she wasn't going to have to start admiring him.

The city streets were almost empty at that time of night so the drive back to her office went quickly. When Daniel stopped the car in front of her building, she didn't let him turn off the ignition.

'No. Don't come in.' She released her seatbelt. 'Harvey and Sophy are waiting for me.' She opened the door but paused. She couldn't leave like this. She put her hand on his arm, the fabric of his jacket sleeve felt cool and smooth beneath her fingertips.

'Thanks.'

When he smiled, his teeth shone white in the shadows. 'You're welcome. All in all, an interesting evening and I'm glad I went with you. I haven't laughed so much in years. I hope you got what you needed.'

Impulsively she leaned forward and kissed his cheek. Her sensible side cried out a warning but she jerked back too late, her lips already tingling from contact with his skin, rough with late-night stubble.

He captured her hand on his sleeve. 'Jess.'

'Yes?'

She knew he was watching her, though she couldn't see his eyes. His fingers tightened over hers, then let go. 'Nothing.'

She swung her legs out the open door, then stooped to look back at him. 'I'll meet you at your office at five tomorrow morning.'

'I won't be there.' She could see his profile, so he must have been looking straight ahead through the windshield, not at her. 'Chris will let you in.'

'Oh. Well, that's that, then.' She fiddled with the purse's chain, listening as it clanked in her hands. 'Goodbye.'

He nodded sharply and she closed the car door. She used her key to open the building's street entrance, locked at nine every night, then walked briskly across the lobby to call the elevator. He was still there as she stepped inside but as the doors closed she saw his car surge into traffic. He was gone. Determined to put Daniel out of her mind, she concentrated on Harvey. Upstairs she flung open the door to Finders Keepers. 'Harvey?'

'In here, sweetheart.'

She tossed the purse and shawl on to Sophy's desk and ran into her own office. He half-lay on her sofa-bed; Sophy sat beside him, his hand clasped tightly in both of hers. Both cats were sitting on the back of the sofa by his head.

'Harvey!' She dropped to her knees at his side and flung her arms around him in an extravagant hug. 'I'm so glad you're okay!'

He winced. 'Careful.'

She pulled back. 'You're hurt? You told me you were fine.'

'Just stiff. Bruised at bit around the edges, like my ego, but it's my own darned fault.'

'Old fool,' Sophy said, with affection.

'What happened?' Jess demanded.

'I'm not exactly sure. Last night I was keeping watch across the street from Concept House, tracking who came and went and at what time, trying to spot any secretive visitors.' Whiskey sloshed in his glass as he lifted it for a sip. 'Just before dawn they got the drop on me. I didn't see or hear them coming.'

'Who?' When Jess sat down cross-legged on the floor Nora jumped down and curled up in her lap.

'I don't know. One guy pulled a pillowcase over my head. Then he and another fellow tied me up and tossed me into a car trunk. They drove for miles but, heck, we could've been going in circles for all I know. Eventually they stopped. One of them opened the trunk and stuck a rag with chloroform over my face. When I woke up it was early this afternoon.'

'Where were you?'

'It looked like a small hospital room, very antiseptic. The only windows were narrow and barred, up along the ceiling.'

'Could you hear anything? Traffic? Sirens? Church bells? Other people?'

'Absolutely nothing. Either I was all alone in the building or they have incredible sound-proofing. I spent the whole day watching sunbeams move across the ceiling. Not very interesting except as a way to keep track of time because my watch got smashed when they threw me in the trunk.'

'How did you get away?'

'I know it was after eight because I'd watched the sun go down. At a guess, I'd say they filled the room with some kind of knock-out gas because one minute I was laying on the bed, feeling sorry for myself, and the next I woke up, the darned pillowcase over my head, tied up again, and back in the trunk of the car.' He emptied the glass in one swallow.

'They drove around for a long while but finally stopped the car, tossed me on the ground and cut the ropes. By the time I got untangled and the pillowcase off my head, they were gone. I'd been dumped into a farmer's muddy field out in Abbotsford. Not to mention I had a doozy of a headache.'

'Did you call the police?'

'No, and you're not allowed to either. I've got no proof, no suspects, no leads. I'll look like a darned fool.'

'You *are* a darned fool, in my opinion,' Sophy said. 'Only an idiot would sit out all night in the cold at your age. Humpf.'

'You never saw their faces?' Jess asked. 'Could it

have been the same two thugs? Where's the pillowcase and the ropes?'

'Nope. Maybe. In a plastic garbage bag in my office.' He fell back against the pillows. 'Common nylon rope available at any builder's supply. Industrial issue pillowcase, Nielson's laundry mark.'

'No help there. Nielson's does the laundry for most of the hospitals and clinics in the lower mainland.'

'I know.'

Jess rubbed Nora's tummy. 'I'm worried about you.'

'You don't need to be, they won't catch me by surprise again.'

'Harvey –'

'Enough.' Sophy took the empty glass out of his hand. 'He's going home to bed. You two can rehash this to your heart's content, tomorrow.'

'I've got an appointment at five a.m., but I'll come over as soon as I'm done.'

'No, you won't,' Sophy announced. 'If you arrive on his doorstep before dinnertime, I won't let you in.'

'*You* won't?' Harvey asked.

'Yes, *I* won't.' Sophy stuck out her chin. 'I'm taking you home now and I'm staying to make sure you take it easy. You got anything to say?'

'Nope,' Harvey denied. 'Just clarifyin'.' He winked at Jess.

'Okay, then.' Sophy looked as if she didn't know what to say next. Jess had to smile.

Sophy had probably prepared herself for a long debate and the easy victory left her at a loss, not

156

knowing what to say next. Harvey was good at doing that to a person, Jess reflected.

'So. I guess I'll go shut down the computers for the night.' Sophy hovered for a moment. 'Jess, would you please give me a hand?'

Jess was surprised but put Nora down and followed Sophy out to her desk.

'There's something else I want to say,' Sophy whispered, then took a deep breath. 'I can't convince Harvey to see the doctor but he did promise to take it easy for two or three days.'

'That's great.' Jess's nervousness had her whispering, too.

'Here.' Sophy shoved two audio tape cassettes into her hand.

'What's this?'

'A transcript of Harvey's case notes on Concept House.'

Jess almost dropped the cassettes. 'Harvey's going to hit the roof. You know how picky he is about anyone seeing his rough notes.'

'Tonight while I was waiting to hear from you or Harvey, I decided I couldn't just sit here and do nothing. So I got out his notes and read them into the tape for you. I thought they might help if you couldn't track down Scratten at the party.'

'But I did find Scratten, though a fat lot of good he was, and Harvey's home safe.'

'For now. I've tried to talk to him about dropping Concept House, too. He won't listen. But what if you did a little digging over the next day or two while he's incommunicado? Could you get it all taken care of before he's mobile again?'

'I don't know, Sophy.' Jess turned the cassettes over and over in her hand. 'Depends what's involved.'

'So find out!'

'If I do this, he's going to be real pissed off with us. It's one thing for him to complain about getting old, quite another for me to step in and try to protect him.'

'They've already kidnapped him. Who knows how far they'll go next time he gets in their way, unless you stop them first? Isn't that worth the risk of making him mad at us?'

'Yes, it is.' Jess slipped the cassettes into her pocket. 'What's the worst he could do? Break off the partnership? He's already planning that one.'

'There's one more thing. For this to work, I'm going to have to be right beside him, making sure he does take it easy or you'll be blundering into each other. That means you'll have to do the work at St Clair's office yourself.'

'I can't pretend to be an office temp, you *know* that.'

'Maybe not, but I'm sure you'll think of a different cover that will work just as good, as soon as you set your mind to it. Besides, you're better than me at reading people. You usually know right away if someone's trying to pull a quick one.'

'You don't understand!'

'I understand, Jess. You're afraid of what you feel when you're with Daniel.'

'I am not!'

'No? Then why is this the very first time, in all these years, you've asked me to work undercover alone? Oh, I've helped you with simple stuff like the other day at the nursing homes, but I've never done anything for a client outside the office by myself.'

Jess opened her mouth to argue but closed it again when she realized Sophy was right. And it wasn't acceptable.

'Okay, you've made your point.'

'Good. And while I'm making sure Harvey behaves himself, I can help by starting the paperwork for the background checks. Now, why don't you go talk to Harvey while I take care of a few things.'

Jess wandered back into her office and began fussing with the papers on her desk. 'We were worried about you,' she said to him.

'I gathered that. Sophy told me where you were and why. What possessed you to track down Scratten?'

'I had to do something. I tried everything else we could think of.'

'He wouldn't tell you anything, especially if you were right about his involvement.'

'I know, but I thought it was worth a shot. At the very least, when we're face-to-face I can tell if he's lying or not. It could help me narrow down the possibilities.'

'I was a detective long before you were born, a darned good one. Smart, too.' Harvey swung his feet onto the floor, groaning a little as he stood up. She didn't offer to help, knowing he'd feel insulted.

'I had a lot of time to think while I was shut up in that room today.'

'Yeah?'

'The fact they could take me so easily should prove, even to you, it's time for me to retire.'

'I'll make you a deal,' she said.

'What?' he asked suspiciously.

'You give Scratten back his money first thing tomorrow morning and I'll accept your decision to give up field work.'

'Jess –'

'No, think about it! This could be a good thing! We hire some more people, a clerk, a couple more agents. You run the office, business booms, and we all get rich. Then you can take a holiday on the beach in Florida every year. Twice a year, if you want.'

'I can't give it back. The money's gone. I put a deposit on the cottage and it's non-refundable.'

She felt as though she'd been flattened, just like when he first told her his plans.

'Can we please drop this for now?' he asked, looking weary.

That was fine with her. If the money was already gone, she was just wasting her breath. They had no choice but to complete the case. That meant she had to follow Sophy's suggestion, no matter how angry Harvey would be later.

Hopefully he'd remember this was his own stubborn fault when he found out what they'd done.

160

She'd also better start looking for an agent-trainee. If she convinced Harvey he was the only one who could train the new employee properly, at least he'd always have back-up while he worked for Concept House.

Back in her own rooms, Jess fed the cats, then stuck a frozen dinner in the microwave for herself. While it heated she changed into her pajamas and poured a glass of milk.

While she ate the lasagna she listened to both tapes. Harvey had gotten a lot further in his investigation than she'd realized. He must have paid attention to her warnings because he'd looked into Scratten's rather checkered background.

Harvey's notes to himself on what to do next were both interesting and helpful, though one name he mentioned only in passing really caught her attention.

After listening to the tapes a second time, she set the alarm for four a.m. and went to bed. It was some time before she slept, though. Maybe it was just as well Daniel wasn't going to be there in the morning, she thought. Otherwise she'd have had to find a way to ask him some questions about his family's good friend, Warren Hellmann, the man who owned Concept House. The delay would give her time to figure out how to handle this information.

Jess didn't like coincidences, never had. Nine times out of ten a person found out later, often too late, the coincidence had been arranged.

And Daniel's sisters had seemed like such nice women. She decided to give the St Clair family the benefit of the doubt because Tom Masters was one of the few straight-arrow cops she knew.

CHAPTER 8

When Daniel went to bed the night before, he'd felt satisfied he'd made the right decision. Spending time alone with Jess would be a mistake. She'd made her opinions of marriage and motherhood very clear.

He'd enjoyed the evening but he had long-term plans that couldn't include her. Sure, he felt attracted to her, what man wouldn't? She was exciting and beautiful. But since the attraction couldn't be acted upon, a smart man would avoid her.

As the restless hours passed, he'd begun to second-guess himself. Sure, Chris was capable of assisting Jess, but she'd made it clear she didn't support his decision to hire a detective. Was Chris the best person to handle the arrangements for something so vital?

As dawn approached he wondered why he should stay away. His company, his livelihood, was at stake. He was a rational man, in control of his actions and emotions. A man with a goal he believed in.

Granted, he needed a new plan to achieve that goal, but first he had to take care of business, making sure

163

Sarah Graff's trickery had done no lasting damage to the Institute.

In the meantime, surely he could be in the same room as Jess without losing his head?

As he drank a cup of tea and ate his bran cereal a little earlier than usual for a normal work day, he realized he'd been wrong. Of course he should be there to watch out for his interests.

As he left his apartment, he understood exactly why and where he was going and what was going to happen once he got there.

And there would be absolutely no problem avoiding any personal involvement with Jess Phillips.

Jess looked around Daniel's office as she packed away the last of her equipment.

Impressive. Granted, she hadn't seen inside the offices of many wealthy or powerful people, but she thought Daniel's must be unique.

The huge corner office's two glass walls framed the breathtaking panorama of Burrard Inlet and Stanley Park. The view's natural colours were reflected in the slate-blue carpet, the soft greys of the upholstered furniture, and the natural oak in the wood pieces. Even the gauzy blinds echoed the early morning haze she could see on the north shore mountains.

Most surprising of all, he didn't have one of those massive status-symbol desks most executives hid behind. He didn't have a desk at all. Low shelving and filing cabinets lined the only two solid walls of his office. Comfortable sofas and upholstered chairs formed a conversation area near the windows.

She figured he worked at the sturdy conference table, because the cabinet nearest the head of the table held a framed photo of his family, a computer, and a telephone.

The artwork – animal sculptures carved in soapstone and jade and two large watercolours of forest scenes – reminded her of her one and only camping trip with her fifth foster family. Or was it the third?

No matter, she'd never forgotten how it felt to stay beside a mountain lake at the back of beyond, surrounded by trees and rocks; lying in a tent wide awake all night, listening to the sounds of wild animals roaming nearby.

She shuddered. Creepy crawlies, awful food, never warm. Never again. She'd rather appreciate the world's natural beauties from a safe distance, thank you very much.

Jess zipped the equipment case closed. Time to stop admiring the man's office and start dealing with his problem, as promised. She put the last of the miniature electronic devices she'd found into a plastic evidence bag, then labeled and sealed it.

She'd been surprised at how basic all the gadgets were. Nothing real high-tech or expensive. Obviously Graff had been working for a budget-conscious client. She recorded that bit of information; Daniel might find it useful.

She leaned against the table, tapping the recorder

165

against her lips as she considered her next move. First, make arrangements to work here for a few days. She still had no idea what kind of work experience she should fake for a day or two but hopefully she'd think of something.

Second, get a list of employees and photocopies of their employment applications so she could arrange for the background checks. And since Chris was the person who could provide both those things, she guessed she'd have go track the woman down in her office.

She sighed.

Chris Houston hadn't seemed exactly pleased or pleasant when she'd arrived this morning; more like an android than a real human. Basic information had been exchanged and that was all. No offers to share coffee. No chit-chat about the weather. She hadn't even stuck around to watch Jess work. Of course, Chris might not be a morning person.

Perhaps she didn't like private investigators, in general, or Jess specifically.

Or she might have something to hide, Jess thought. Pretty funny if they went through the whole under-cover and investigation process, only to find out later the disloyal employee was in on the secret from the beginning.

She clicked on the recorder. 'Get Sophy to do Chris Houston's background check first.'

She pocketed the recorder, picked up her equipment case and the plastic bags of gadgets, and went looking for Chris. She wasn't worried about being seen; it was still early and Chris had said the staff wouldn't start arriving until eight.

So she was surprised to hear voices as she neared the reception area. Jess, mindful Daniel didn't want his staff to know what she was doing, hesitated in the hallway.

'Yesterday afternoon, when I told the staff they weren't to come in today until eight a.m., wasn't it clear I meant *all* staff, including you?' Chris asked.

'I only came in early so I could do the filing,' a female voice wailed. 'I didn't want Mr St Clair to get mad at me because it wasn't finished.'

'Didn't I mention the directive came directly from Mr St Clair?'

'Yes, ma'am,' the voice said meekly, 'but –'

'Haven't you already been involved in several disruptive incidents this week?'

'I always told Mr St Clair I was sorry. And I never did any of those things twice, did I? Our teacher says it's important to show an employer we can learn from our mistakes.'

Jess had to smile at the young woman's naïve zeal, especially coupled with such faith in her employer's tolerance. Obviously someone without much experience in the real world.

She peeked around the corner in time to see Chris's head sink into her hands. From where Jess stood, it looked like the office manager was hiding a reluctant smile from the employee. Maybe Chris was human after all.

Then she leaned a little further, trying to see who Chris was talking to and recognized the young receptionist.

She pulled back. Now what? This looked like it was going to be a long, drawn-out discussion and she couldn't hide in the hallway forever while Chris scolded Gwen.

'When I talked to you after the orange-juice incident, you begged for one more chance, assuring me there would be no more trouble.'

'Please don't fire me.'

Jess had heard enough. Besides, she didn't mind delaying poor Gwen's fate, temporarily at least. Maybe by the time Chris cooled down a little, the poor girl wouldn't lose her job, especially if Jess was able to show there'd been no harm done.

She stuffed the evidence bags into her case and pulled out a few props. Over-sized sunglasses with plastic diamonds imbedded in the frame, a blonde wig to hide her own hair, and a long flimsy scarf tied around her waist in a big floppy bow all did wonders to change how people perceived her.

Even though Gwen had met her, she wouldn't recognize Jess under this get-up.

She made sure the equipment case, along with her distinctive hat and coat, were out of sight in the hall. She unbuttoned the top three buttons on her shirt to show some cleavage, took a deep breath, and swept into the room, already talking full speed and two octaves higher than her normal voice.

'Oh, darlings, I'm so glad Danny arranged for me to be alone this morning. My muse could never create with all those people around.' She clutched her hands to her heaving bosom and fluttered her eyelashes and her voice. She played it to the hilt, more southern belle than even Scarlet O'Hara at her best.

'It's going to be so much fun. Can't you'all just picture him surrounded by pale greens and blues? Danny is going to be so pleased with me, he really is.'

Both women were looking at her, mouths hanging open in shock.

'He expects so much from me. But then he always has, naughty boy!' She managed a high-pitched titter. 'But, darlings, don't worry. Ella Mae will take care of everything.'

'Ella Mae?' Chris asked, having found her voice at last.

'Yes, Christine? I can call you Christine, can't I? I don't want to offend you, dear, but to me the name Chris has always seemed so manly. Not that I don't like manly things,' she tittered again, 'as Danny would tell you if he were here.

'Now, where was I? Oh, yes . . . Danny's new office. Won't he look handsome surrounded by pale green and blue? He can imagine himself at the bottom of the sea.'

'I thought the bottom of the sea is mostly dark because sunlight won't reach that deep,' Gwen said.

'Is it?' 'Ella Mae' waved a careless hand. 'No matter. I'm an artiste and I can't be concerned with reality. What I desperately need is a cappuccino. Would you be a dear and make me one with just a teensy-weensy extra cream?'

'Gwen can pour you some coffee.'

'That won't do. That absolutely won't do. I *told* Danny I couldn't work without my cappuccino. Will you be a sweet girl, Gwen, and run down the street to the dear little coffee bar to get me one?'

'Sure.' She glanced at Chris uncertainly. 'I guess so.' She picked up her purse and sweater. 'Um, that place is expensive, though.'

'Not to worry. Christine will give you the money, won't you, dear?'

Chris looked grim as she handed Gwen a five-dollar bill.

'Now, don't forget, dear, a large cappuccino with double cream.' Jess watched to make sure Gwen actually got into the elevator. As she stepped back into the office, she loosened the scarf from around her waist and cast it over her shoulder.

'Thank heavens that's over,' Jess said in her normal voice. 'I'd hate to keep that role going for any length of time. My throat already hurts.'

'You're an accomplished actress.'

'Thanks. It's a useful talent in my business. So are you; you followed my lead very well.'

'Was the farce really necessary?'

'You tell me. I got rid of her without answering a lot of questions, didn't I? Now you won't have to fire her.'

'I imagine you have no intention of actually redecorating Daniel's office so Gwen's going to wonder why she never sees Ella Mae again.'

'No, right now she's probably wondering how on earth Ella Mae wangled her way into St Clair's life. She'd find it more surprising if Ella Mae actually did redo his office.'

'What if she tells the other employees about Ella Mae?'

'I think St Clair's reputation can withstand a little gossip linking him to an airhead decorator, don't you? Now, you and I have some arrangements to make, so let's get on with it. I'd better be gone before Gwen comes back.'

'What about the coffee?'

'What the heck, you drink it. It's your five bucks.'

She was about to take off the sunglasses when the door swung open. Jess and Chris both froze, fearing Gwen had returned.

'Chris?' Daniel thought the two women standing beside the reception desk looked unnaturally rigid. 'Is there a problem?'

'No.' Chris's expression was odd as she looked back and forth between him and the other woman. 'But perhaps I should introduce you to Ella Mae.'

As if in slow motion the stranger pivoted to face him. Huge black sunglasses covered half her face beneath curly blonde hair. The creamy curves partially revealed by her gaping shirt captured his attention.

'Hello, Daniel.' She slid the dark glasses down her

nose and he recognized Jess. How many different women *was* she? he wondered, as he tried but failed to avert his eyes as she buttoned the shirt.

'Why the disguise?' he asked.

'Because you didn't want anyone to know why I was here.'

'Ella Mae was planning to redecorate your office in blue and green,' Chris said. 'You'd be able to imagine you were working at the bottom of the sea.'

'Redecorate my office?'

'As good a cover story as any.' When Jess pulled off the wig, her own thick hair tumbled loose around her shoulders and, even with Chris standing right there watching, Daniel had to resist the urge to bury his fingers in it.

Jess used an elastic from her pocket to confine the mass at her nape. 'You'll be dumping Ella Mae, though, so your undersea adventure won't happen.'

'Thank you. I think.' He watched as she transformed herself back into the Jess he first met.

Yet, how could he forget that beneath the business-like exterior existed the sexy goddess of last night and the temptress of a few minutes ago? He felt a powerful hunger to discover what other women existed as part of the multi-faceted Jess Phillips.

'You're very welcome.' She reached around the corner into the hall for her belongings. 'I'd better get out of here before someone else on your staff shows up for work –'

172

'Or Gwen comes back with the cappuccino,' Chris said drily.

'Yeah.' Jess grinned. 'Anyway, there are a couple things we need to get settled before I go.'

She put her props back into the case and showed Daniel the bags of gadgets she'd removed from the senior executives' offices.

'I found these this morning. You can go back to working in your own office now. I'll send you a written report late this afternoon, detailing their purpose and range and where they were found. That should help you pinpoint where you'll need to do damage control.'

Daniel tried to concentrate, to ignore the hunger so he could make sense of her words.

'Thanks.' He picked up the coat and held it for her to put on. She looked surprised, as if she wasn't used to the courtesy. The collar snagged her pony tail and when he lifted it out, her natural electricity caused the silken strands to cling to his fingers.

He took a deep breath. 'What about your other recommendations?'

'I'll need a list of your employees, copies of their employment applications, along with their addresses, including those who quit or were let go in the last year or two.'

'Chris can get you the copies and computer print-outs this morning. What else?'

'I'll need a cover story to explain why I'm here for a couple of days and to give me an excuse to wander at will around the office, talking to all your employees.'

'Yesterday you suggested some kind of office temp, like a receptionist or bookkeeper.'

'Absolutely not. A bad idea.'

Her vehemence finally jarred Daniel out of the sensual fog. Why the abrupt reversal from what she'd recommended just the day before? 'How come?'

'Too slow. You said you wanted this resolved right away. To do that I need to be free to come and go all day, talking to everybody. I thought maybe we could pretend I was some kind of consultant.'

'Should you stick with Ella Mae?' Chris asked.

Jess's expression of dismay was so comical, Chris and Daniel both laughed.

'Not funny. Ella Mae is gone forever. Besides, your offices are so beautiful, no one would believe you'd hired a decorator, especially one like her.'

'How about you pretend to be a trainee from a mature-student program?' Chris asked.

'Won't work. I'd have to sit in one place to learn a particular job. I'd only be able to question the people training me.'

'Too bad, you'd blend right in,' Daniel muttered. 'Thanks to Ruth we've already got too many student trainees in this place.'

'A computer consultant?' 'Time and motion studies?' 'An observer from another management school?'

They took turns tossing out ideas but none seemed right, with Jess vetoing some he thought would probably have worked.

'Could you be an authority on ergonomics and

healthy offices?' Chris finally asked. 'You could talk to every employee when you visit their work area to measure for things like white noise, light strength, and chair positioning. Some of the staff have even asked me about it recently, so they won't be surprised when you show up.'

'I don't know anything about that stuff,' Jess said doubtfully.

'Since I'd already planned to talk to Daniel about it, I've done some preliminary research into the subject. You could take my paperwork home with you now and look through it before you come in tomorrow.'

Daniel wondered why Chris's suggestion seemed to bother Jess.

'I wouldn't want to claim to be an expert,' she said. 'If someone took one of my comments seriously, they could be in big trouble.'

'How about a decorator who specializes in healthy offices?' he asked. 'That covers all your criteria.'

Jess was silent for a moment, thinking. 'It could work. Especially if I played the role nosy and mixed in a little of Ella Mae's personality.'

A picture of Jess with her blouse undone almost to her navel flashed into his mind. Could he be around her all day for two or three days, with her dressed like that, and still maintain his sanity and a safe distance?

'When I was here the first time, was anyone told what I do for a living?'

'No. Only Rick and Chris know more than your name.'

'Since Gwen's seen me twice now, once as myself and once as Ella Mae, I'd better stick with my own name and appearance. Less chance of her realizing I'm not what I seem.'

Daniel wondered if he felt glad or sorry he'd never see Ella Mae again. 'Have we covered everything?'

'What about the business people who are your students? Do they have access to the private offices? Have any of them been in and out with unusual frequency the last few months?'

'No. Classes are conducted in our meeting rooms on the nineteenth floor unless there's a very large group, in which case we hire space in the convention center across the street. Many are long-distance students who take the courses via e-mail and fax. I don't see how any of them can be involved.' Daniel glanced at his watch. 'Almost eight.'

'I'll get my research papers for you now,' Chris said. 'Do you want to wait for the print-outs or should I send them over to your office?'

'Send them to my home address, just in case one of your clerks notices the address on the package.' Jess took out a business card and handed it to Chris.

'I'll be right back,' she said, and hurried down the hall toward her office.

Daniel watched Jess and tried to remember why staying away from her was so critical.

A few minutes later Chris returned with a fat file folder. 'Here you go.'

'Thanks,' Jess said. 'I'd better leave.'

'I'll walk you out,' Daniel said. He held the door for her; as she walked past him, she smelled of green apples again. This time he was careful not to let her see him sniffing her hair. The same scent still lingered in his car from last night.

Neither spoke while they waited for the elevator but he noticed she jumped when it pinged to signal its arrival.

After she stepped in, he saluted her with two fingers to his temple, and backed away. He felt as surprised as she looked when, on impulse, at the last minute he blocked the doors as they were closing.

She reached out and pressed the button to hold them open. 'Was there something else?' she asked.

'Yes.' Damn, he thought. Now what? 'Have dinner with me tonight.'

Double damn. Why did I say that? he wondered, and hoped she would refuse.

She watched him, her gaze steady and unsmiling.

The elevator buzzed angrily, indicating they'd held it on this floor too long. She took her finger off the button and as the doors began to close, she spoke. 'Yes.'

He was left staring at his reflection in the shiny metal. Staring at the man who'd told himself less than an hour ago there would be absolutely no problem avoiding any personal involvement with Jess Phillips.

What a fool.

Jess pulled the Beetle into Harvey's driveway, still not sure if she'd made a dumb decision.

This would be business, not a Cinderella fantasy. Dinner would be the perfect place and opportunity to slip in a few questions about Warren Hellmann and Concept House. But even if eating dinner alone with Daniel might be useful, that didn't make it smart.

As she walked up the front steps, she tried not to drop the box of scones or spill the tray of paper coffee cups.

She also debated telling Harvey what she'd discovered. If she told him about this new development, he'd find out what she and Sophy were doing. But what were the odds there was no connection between Daniel's sisters hiring her only a few weeks before Warren Hellmann's employee hired Harvey?

Slim, very slim.

She balanced the box on the railing and tapped out her signature rat-a-tat with the lion's head door knocker. By the time Sophy appeared, Jess had decided to keep this latest development to herself, for now. Until Harvey was up and around again, what he didn't know wouldn't hurt her and Sophy.

'Why are you here –' Sophy held the robe's lapels high around her neck and squinted sleepy-eyed at Jess '– at nine-fifteen in the morning? I could swear I told you dinner time.'

'Good morning, Sophy. I brought breakfast instead. Here, take these.'

She pushed the food and drinks into Sophy's hands and dashed back to the car. She opened the passenger door, grabbed Chris's papers and scooped up the tape recorder and its trailing wires. She pushed the lock

178

button with her elbow and pushed the door shut with her hip.

'I asked why you're here.'

'This is why.' Jess held up the fat file folder and walked past Sophy into the house. 'Is Harvey awake?'

'How would I know?' she answered indignantly, but with a blush.

Jess looked at her, all innocence. 'Maybe because you'd talked to him this morning?'

'Oh. Well, I haven't. Hopefully he slept through your racket.'

'Good, because I have to talk to you.' She sat down at the kitchen nook, pushed aside Harvey's stack of crossword magazines, and set out the file folder and the tape recorder. 'I went by the office and forwarded the phone so it will ring here. You can stay here and take care of the stubborn old coot.'

'Thanks.'

'Chris Houston is Daniel St Clair's office manager. This is her research into the science of healthy offices and I have to learn some of it before tomorrow morning.'

Sophy sighed, made room for the scones and coffee on the table, then plopped down onto the bench beside her. 'And you want me to read it into a microphone right now.'

'Please. That's why I stopped by the office to get the tape recorder.'

'Don't tell me. Tomorrow you're going to pretend to be an expert in healthy offices.'

'Not quite. A nosy, slightly ditsy decorator who advises about healthy offices.'

'Think you can pull it off?'

'Yes. My only real concern is, because his offices are so nice, it's not likely anybody will believe he's hired a new decorator already. It should be okay, though, because Chris says quite a few of the staff have approached her about getting this checked. They'll think I'm there in response to their own requests.'

Sophy flipped through the papers. 'There's a lot of technical stuff here.'

'Just tape enough of the theory and the jargon so I'll sound authentic instead of foolish. I can listen to it this afternoon at Bailey's.'

'I forgot today's your last day washing floors at the restaurant. Figured out what's happening?'

'Yeah. I think take-out orders are prepared, delivered, and paid for but only half are entered in the computer system. Then the cook and the delivery guy split the difference. I have to double-check one thing, but I'm giving Mr Bailey my verbal report today.'

Jess laughed. 'I remember when I first went to work for Harvey. I swore I'd never wash another floor and now look at me.'

'Speaking of Harvey, what did you want to talk about that he can't hear, Jess?'

'I've been thinking.' Jess fiddled with the sharpened pencils he kept in an old mug. 'If we hire a trainee and convince Harvey he's the only one who can teach them properly, he won't be alone while he's working a case.'

'Might be kind of risky for a rookie if those thugs showed up again.'

'I doubt it. We both know Harvey would make sure the trainee was safe. I'd feel better if he wasn't out there alone and there's no way he'll let either of us stay with him.'

'Do you have someone in mind?'

'Maybe. Chris Houston is sending their employee records to my place this afternoon so you can start the background checks first thing tomorrow morning. There are two in particular I want you to complete as soon as possible.'

'You're going to steal one of his employees?'

'St Clair's Institute is involved in one of those programs to give students actual work experience. Gwen's not suited for corporate life, but I liked her.'

'Who's the other priority?'

'Chris Houston.'

'Daniel's office manager?

Jess nodded. 'She's hiding something.'

'But she already knows –'

'All about the investigation. I know.' Jess shrugged. 'Either she thinks she's smarter than me or whatever she's hiding has nothing to do with Sarah Graff. We'll have to find out which.'

'Are you going to eat one of these scones you brought?'

'I'm not hungry. I ate while I was at the coffee house across the street from Shaughnessy Manor.'

'Don't tell me. You couldn't leave it alone, could you?'

'I thought maybe since it was so close, some of the staff might come over there for coffee or a meal, just to get away from their own cafeteria food. I sat at the counter and groused about my boss, the doctor. One of the women agreed with me and we compared notes.'

'So did you satisfy your curiosity about the mysterious north wing?'

'The rest of the place really is a seniors home, but the north wing is used as a private hospital for rich people who need some place safe and secluded to put family members. They sometimes also do plastic surgery there for celebrities.'

'What about the guard you thought was armed?'

Jess chuckled. 'No gun. Turns out he's an ex-cop, who started working there after he got fired from the force. She said he has an attitude problem. I gather he doesn't approve when the other guards don't wear their jackets. Considers it out of uniform.'

They jumped guiltily when a clatter at the other end of the house was followed by a bellow of pain. Harvey's progress through the house to the kitchen was punctuated by groans and complaints.

'I told him he'd feel stiff today,' Sophy said. 'Maybe now he'll believe me and use some painkillers.'

'Look, I'm going to take off. I have time to do some work on you-know-what before I go to Bailey's. Call me on the cell phone when the tape's done, and I'll swing by to pick it up, okay?'

182

'Aren't you going to stay and have breakfast with us?'

'Nope, he's all yours, Sophy. Got a busy day in front of me. Not to mention a stress-filled evening.' Harvey appeared in the kitchen, rumpled and grumpy, holding his back and groaning.

'Hi, Harvey.' She kissed his stubbled cheek as she breezed past. 'Bye, Harvey.'

CHAPTER 9

'Is that guy trying to get your attention?' Mr Bailey pointed across the packed restaurant. Jess looked up and her heart skipped a beat.

Daniel looked wonderful but seriously out of place in Bailey's. Somehow his Armani suit and shiny black wing-tips didn't quite suit a decor of orange-and-red plastic booths and blue linoleum.

'Probably. He's a . . . friend of mine. Are we done now, Mr Bailey?'

'Yes. I'm really glad you caught them, Jess. They could have put me out of business. And thanks for sticking around – I've never had to deal with anything like this before.'

'You're welcome.' She shook his hand.

'Why don't you and your friend stay for a late lunch and watch the show? On the house.'

She smiled, tempted by the thought of watching Daniel eat a sloppy hamburger and fries, surrounded by noisy families. 'No, but thank you.'

Jess made her way over to Daniel. 'Hi. Watch out!'

She shoved him out of the way as a little boy careened down a nearby slide, milkshake in hand. The milkshake went flying and the splatters just missed Daniel's wing-tips.

Her orange polyester uniform wasn't so lucky. Jess tugged off her red apron and used it to wipe chocolate off her arm. 'You have to stay alert in a place like this.'

'So I see,' he said. 'Thanks. I came by to give you the –'

Daniel's voice was drowned out as a chorus of squeals rose from the throats of all the children in the restaurant. Berty, the most popular clown in the city, was about to start his performance.

Knowing that, for the next half-hour, no adult would be able to make their voices heard, Jess crooked her finger at Daniel, indicating he should follow her. She led the way to the nearest exit, which just happened to be through the kitchens.

As soon as the doors swung shut behind them, the noise faded to a tolerable roar. 'Wow,' he said. 'What was that?'

'A big star, at least to those kids.' Jess opened the door to the alley. 'How'd you find me? And why?'

'The photocopies and print-outs were ready so I told Chris I'd drop them off on my way to a meeting. Here.' He handed her two large well-stuffed envelopes. Their fingers brushed, lingered. 'Ms Westlake told me where to find you.'

Jess pulled her hand away and started breathing again. 'She did?'

Time to have another word with Sophy, Jess thought as she pulled off the earphones that hung around her neck. She held the portable tape player in one hand while rummaging in her coat pockets for her keys.

'About tonight . . . I made reservations at La Minuet for eight o'clock.'

He seemed strangely uncertain. Had he hoped she'd cancel? 'I've heard they serve terrific food.'

'They do. Possibly the best in the city.'

Together they rounded the corner on to the street where Jess had parked her Beetle. She saw Bailey's former delivery man scratching a key through its beautiful green paint and cried out. 'Get away from my car!'

The guy barely acknowledged her, other than to call her a bitch, and used two hands to pick up a piece of broken cement the size of a small boulder from the gutter. When he aimed it at the car, she jumped on his back, whacking him over the head with the envelopes, yanking on his arm to keep him from smashing in the windows.

'Jess!' Daniel pulled her away and stepped between them to knock the cement out of the man's hands. Then he twisted his fist tightly in the fabric of the man's shirt between the shoulder blades to hold him in place. 'What the hell's going on?'

She ran her fingers over the deep gashes in the green paint. 'Look what he did.'

'Yeah? Well, you deserved it, bitch. You got me fired!' He'd been hanging in Daniel's grip, content to mutter threats, but he exploded into furious struggles, broke free, and lunged for Jess.

She screamed and flung herself sideways.

Daniel cursed, his body seemed to flow, and next thing she knew the guy was flat on his back, struggling to breathe.

'Jess?' Daniel's hands were gentle as he urged her to her feet but when she looked into his eyes she could see his ice-cold fury. 'Are you okay?'

'Yes. Thanks.' When she stood up, she noticed a crowd had gathered.

He handed her his cell phone. 'Call the police.' He crouched and moved his hands over the chest and throat of the man on the ground. She couldn't see what he was doing but the man began to breathe easier.

'What was this about?' Daniel asked when she finished talking to the dispatcher.

'This jerk did deliveries here until he was fired this afternoon. I proved he was in cahoots with the cook to rob Mr Bailey.'

'How did he find out you were involved?'

'Mr Bailey wasn't quite sure . . . He didn't want to handle it alone.' Daniel's eyebrows were tilting more ominously with every word she spoke. 'He's never had to fire anyone for employee theft until now.'

'So you volunteered to help him? Are you crazy?'

'If there had been any sign he'd react this way, I would have told Mr Bailey to hire a security guard for a day or two.' She knew she was being curt, but how dare he question her ability to do her job properly?

'What if I hadn't been here? He could have hurt you.'

'I've been doing my job for years without your help, Daniel. I would have handled it.'

They heard sirens and the man on the ground stirred. Daniel looked down at him and said one word. 'Don't.'

The man lay still.

Twenty-five minutes later Jess stood on the street alone, bewilderment quickly turning to outrage.

Daniel and the man who'd attacked her had both been handcuffed and taken away in the back of separate police cars. She'd told the police how Daniel had defended her but it seems most of the witnesses claimed they'd seen Daniel attack and almost kill the man on the ground with some kind of martial arts.

So the police had decided to take them both to the station to get things straightened out. As they'd shut the door on him, Daniel told her to go home and he'd pick her up at seven-thirty for dinner, as arranged. Then he told her not to worry.

Why were men such stupid macho idiots? Of course she was worried. He'd been wrongfully arrested for protecting her. She had to go down there and get him out.

Jess found her car keys, then tossed the envelopes and the tape player into the passenger seat. She started the car with shaking hands, then had to think a minute to remember the location of the police station. Why? She'd been there hundreds of times.

She'd parked the car and was running toward the station when she saw Daniel and Tom Masters stroll out. Daniel shook his brother-in-law's hand. Lieutenant Masters laughed, slapped him on the back, then turned and went back inside.

Jess stumbled to a halt. What an idiot *she'd* been. So overwrought she'd forgotten the dratted man was related to a senior officer. She turned around and left, glad he hadn't seen her there.

Keep it simple, he told himself. Keep it light and fun, bring her home, then walk away.

Daniel shifted the bouquet of roses to his other hand and knocked on the screen door of the restored Victorian. Though he didn't think the original owners would have chosen fluorescent purple and pink trim for their two-tone grey house.

The inner door stood wide open and wonderful smells like tomato sauce and garlic were wafting toward him from a distant kitchen. He could hear what sounded like two dozen people arguing, laughing, and singing . . . all at the same time and as loud as humanly possible.

He rapped again, harder, but had little hope someone would hear him. He searched again for a doorbell or buzzer of some kind to announce his presence but there was nothing.

Well, it seemed he had two choices, walk in or leave. He might wish he'd never asked her out but since he had, leaving was not an option. Daniel pulled open the screen door and walked in. 'Hello?' he called.

Three struggling bodies spilled into the entryway from the kitchen. Daniel narrowly avoided a flailing arm.

'That's enough fighting, boys. You almost knocked that man over.' A grandmotherly woman wiping her hands on a tea towel joined them in the entry hall and shooed the boys away. 'What lovely roses.'

'Hello, Daniel.' Jess's voice, all cool velvet promise, floated down to him.

He looked up, saw her descending the stairs, and felt his mouth go dry. Tonight she wore another slim black dress but this time it hung straight from her shoulders, clinging to every curve and molding to her lithe thighs with every step. Her coat was over her arm.

'Your young man brought you pink roses, Jess.'

'So I see.' Her heels clicked as she stepped down onto the worn parquet floor. 'They're lovely.'

'Not as lovely as you,' he said and presented them to her.

'Thank you.' She touched the petals, running one fingertip across the edges of a barely opened bud, then held them out. 'Would you put them in water for me, Mrs Martelli? We have reservations and I don't want to make us late.'

'Of course. I'll even lend you one of my vases.' She took the roses and beamed at them both. 'Run along and have a good time.'

'I fed Nick and Nora so you don't need to check on them.'

190

Daniel was sitting in the car beside Jess before he realized what was bothering him. She'd said everything proper and polite but she hadn't seemed to *care* much about the roses. 'The roses –'

'Mrs Martelli will put them in my room. She's the best landlady I've ever had.'

'I thought she was a relative.'

'She takes in boarders. I rent the attic. It's wonderful and usually very quiet but once a month she has all her nieces and nephews over for a big family dinner. It can get rowdy, but they always have a lot of fun.'

Daniel couldn't stop wondering why she hadn't reacted to the roses in any of the ways all the other women in his life usually did, whether it was his mother, sisters, or past lovers.

'You don't like roses?'

'The flowers were very nice.'

Nice?

'Are you allergic? Or are you annoyed with me for some reason?'

She looked surprised. 'No, I don't have any allergies. And how could I be annoyed with you after what you did for me this afternoon? Speaking of which, I want to thank you.'

'I'm glad I was there.' Every time he thought about what could have happened to her, it made him furious. If he thought she would listen, he'd try again to make her see the stupid chance she'd taken.

'Where did you learn how to do that . . . what you did to him at the end?'

'At ten I was a skinny little runt who always managed to find trouble. So Sam chose a martial art with a philosophy he liked, then enrolled me, hoping it would help me build some self-esteem and muscles. It's good exercise, mentally and physically, so I've kept it up.'

'Philosophy?'

'Besides learning to defend themselves, students of martial arts are often expected to learn self-discipline, courtesy, and ethics.'

'Sounds . . . consuming.'

'It can be.'

'Did you miss your meeting because the police took you down to the station?'

'No. Tom Masters was on duty so he had a word with the arresting officers. They charged the other guy and let me go.' Daniel felt compelled to get an explanation for the undercurrents he sensed flowing between and around them. He stopped for a red light. 'I don't understand –'

'The light's turned green.'

Daniel realized he was holding up traffic and stomped on the gas. For the next few minutes he concentrated on getting them to La Minuet on Granville Island and parking the car. When she would have opened her door to get out, he put his hand on her arm. 'Wait.'

'Is there a problem?' she asked.

'You tell me. I need to know what was wrong with the roses.'

'What is it with you and the roses? They're very nice and I thanked you. End of story.' He could tell she was becoming exasperated. 'Now let's go before they give away our reservation.' She got out of the car.

Inside the restaurant she was charmed by the white twinkle lights in the potted trees at the corners of the room and in the garden outside. She adored the medieval-style tapestries on the walls. She admired the crystal candle holders on every table, the wine he chose, and the soup served for their first course.

Every man in the place watched her and envied him. All in all, the perfect dinner guest.

Daniel couldn't stop thinking about the roses. So he asked her again.

'Are you sure you want to have this conversation?' Jess asked after the waiter topped up their wine glasses and left.

'Yes.'

'I don't know if I can put it into words.'

'Try.' He played with his wine glass, spinning it slowly and watching the ruby liquid gleam in the candlelight.

'You've probably given roses to dozens of women. Family, employees, dates, friends.'

'I don't keep track but, yes, I imagine I have.'

'I enjoy flowers. I enjoy receiving gifts, maybe because I never got many after my parents died when I was six and I grew up in foster homes. If I happened to be with a family at Christmas time, they made sure there was something under the tree for me to open.'

'Must have been tough.'

She half-smiled. 'Nothing particularly bad or good ever happened to me, so they'll never make a "Movie of the Week" about my life. Just constant moves and nobody who really cared about what was going on in my head. So, to me the true significance of any gift is what it means to the *giver*.'

'I don't understand.'

'I bet you always give flowers to a woman the first time you take her out.'

'And that's wrong?'

She held up her hand. 'You started this. Now hear me out.'

He hesitated, then nodded. 'Okay.' Sensing he might not like what he was about to hear, he fortified himself with a sip of wine.

'It's a polite habit that greases the wheels of your relationships with women. We're not dating, we're not even potentially dating, yet you brought flowers. You've given flowers to so many women it's become virtually meaningless to you. A pretty gesture.'

Daniel put down the wine glass and moved his hand away from its delicate stem, afraid it would snap in his fingers.

'The roses were not personal to *me*,' she said. 'They weren't chosen because of what you've learned about my character, my interests, or what's important to me.'

'You think they're nice but insignificant,' he said. This conversation wasn't light, wasn't fun, and it wasn't simple, he thought. Were his encounters with

Jess ever going to go the way he'd planned?

'Yes. So, like I said before . . . thank you for the roses. I'll enjoy their beauty and their scent, but don't expect me to get emotional about them.'

Jess toyed with the silverware and waited for him to say something. Anything. His jaw was back to resembling granite, like the first time she'd met him, and his eyebrows twitched into a thoughtful frown.

What was it about this man? He could push her into saying things, exposing herself emotionally in ways she never had with any other person, even Harvey.

A smart woman would limit the time she spent with him. After tonight all contact should be kept short and sweet, she decided, strictly business.

If he was angry at her explanation, their dinner might be over with the soup course. She hadn't even had a chance to slip in a few questions about Hellmann, her reason for accepting Daniel's dinner invitation.

'Would you like more wine?' he asked as he summoned the waiter. Glasses were filled and the entree served. When the waiter left, Daniel began chatting about sports and his nephews.

Typical male, she thought. Gets uncomfortable with an intimate conversation, so he pretends it didn't happen. Fine with her. If she managed it properly, talking about his nephews could lead very naturally to the topic of his old family friend, Warren Hellmann.

The edge to her smile was almost as sharp as the knife she used to cut into the grilled lamb chops.

* * *

Jess set her elbows on the table and propped her chin in her hands to watch the harpist seated on the small dais in the center of the restaurant. While the waiter served their after-dinner coffee, a woman wearing a long blue velvet gown had seated herself behind the harp.

From the first moment she'd laid her fingers on the strings, Jess had been enthralled. Every move the woman made, every stroke of the strings was graceful. Every magical note rang true, producing butterflies in Jess's stomach and yearning in her heart.

She sat shoulder to shoulder with Daniel because he'd turned his chair sideways to watch in comfort, resting his arm on the tablecloth. Sitting so close, she felt the yearnings spread from her heart to more dangerous places in her body.

Listening to Daniel talk about his family had made her feel peculiar, as if she were listening to another fairy tale, but this one was real. A mother and a father, a big brother like Daniel and sisters like Mary, Ruth and Hannah. A fairy tale life so many people took for granted. But not her.

Daniel didn't seem to take it for granted either, which was unusual. But then, he seemed to be an unusual man in many ways.

'Superb, isn't it?' Daniel murmured next to her ear, his voice husky with emotion, which surprised her until she turned her head to answer and found herself hypnotized by his hot blue gaze. He was looking at her, not the harpist.

'Yes,' she breathed. He leaned closer, so close she

could see the gray flecks in his blue eyes, so close she felt his breath on her lips.

Oh, my . . . he was going to kiss her.

Her breathing faltered as her heart began to beat faster. Her lips parted and she tilted her head, just a little, waiting. His mouth brushed hers once. Twice.

The woman seated behind Daniel slid her chair back and bumped into him, whispering an apology as she stood up.

The spell was broken. He looked away, shoulders tensed, his fingers pressed against the tablecloth.

'Daniel?'

He relaxed and smiled at her, bland, friendly, as if it had never happened, then faced the harpist again.

Jess swallowed hard. Could he really turn it off so easily? Then she caught a glimpse of his other hand beneath the table, clenched in a fist on his thigh, and realized it was all an act.

She fought the urge to slide her hand beneath his where it lay on the table, afraid, yet wanting to see passion in his eyes again.

This was for the best. She should be glad the moment was gone. No matter how her body reacted to his, she knew it couldn't be right, they were too different. And yet . . .

No. With a twinge of regret, Jess tuned out Daniel and the seductive music, concentrating on what she'd learned about Hellmann.

He was an old college roommate of Daniel's father. He'd been a highly respected university professor until the entrepreneur bug bit him and he created Concept House. When Daniel was a young man, Hellmann had been his mentor, using his influence to promote Daniel's career. Indeed, Daniel's first job after graduation had been at Concept House.

His ties to Warren Hellmann were strong, built on affection and gratitude. She'd have to be careful because if he found out she was investigating his old family friend, she had no doubt he'd protect Hellmann even if he had to ride roughshod over her to do it.

The harpist's fingers drew a final rippling cascade of sound from the strings, then pushed the instrument upright. She curtsied to enthusiastic applause and left the dais.

Daniel tasted his coffee and grimaced. Jess tried her own and realized the coffee had gone cold unnoticed.

'Did you enjoy it?' he asked.

'Yes.'

'A far cry from the so-called music Hannah's friends create. She has some misguided idea I can introduce them to a music producer.' He asked the waiter for the bill. 'Which is why we were subjected to a racket on the way to the hotel the other night. I'd promised to listen to their CD.'

So. He hadn't been listening to that noise because he enjoyed it. She hadn't realized how comforting her little misconceptions were until they were shot down.

As they stepped out onto the sidewalk, she looked up at the starry sky and drew in a deep breath of the cool spring night air.

'Feels good, doesn't it?' Daniel helped her into her coat. 'Want to take a walk?'

'Why not?' she said, trying not to think about the almost-kiss, ignoring the tiny voice in her mind warning her this wasn't a good idea. They followed a path down to the boardwalk and joined the other couples strolling along the water's edge. 'It's a nice evening.'

The guard rail had lamps, low to the ground, to light the way and every forty yards or so they passed beneath a street light. City traffic raced by high overhead on Granville Bridge, but it was faint and seemed far away.

Much closer she could hear water slapping against the pilings beneath them. Sailboats, yachts, and powerboats creaked as they rode the low swells in the nearby marina.

Jess watched enviously as the couple in front of them cuddled and kissed as they walked arm in arm. She overlapped the fronts of her coat and hugged it to her body.

'Jess, I've been doing some thinking about Sarah Graff and I have a suggestion. Please consider it carefully before you answer.'

'I'm listening.'

'I'd like to be part of your investigation.'

'What do you mean, part of it? I'll give you regular reports and consult with you or your staff whenever I need input.'

'I prefer to be more hands-on. As much as possible, given my own heavy schedule, I'd like to work *with* you to fix this. It's my business at risk. I know Sally – I mean, Sarah Graff. I know my competitors better than you could.'

'One of the first things Harvey taught me about this business is that it's a very bad idea to involve the client in the work. It's a rule that's stood me in good stead.'

There was an even more important rule she had no intention of mentioning to Daniel: don't let yourself become sexually attracted to a client because it usually clouds your judgment.

Since she couldn't seem to stop thinking about sex whenever she was with Daniel, despite his teaching degree and business position, no way was she going to complicate things by breaking both rules.

'I talked to Tom and he says you're very good at your job.'

Jess felt a glow of pride. 'That's nice.'

'But I'm going to insist on full participation.'

'You're going to insist?' Jess opened her mouth to tell him where he could shove the whole darned case when she experienced one of those random thoughts that so often turn a person's life around. At least she hoped it would turn one in particular around . . . Harvey's.

So, Daniel wanted to help, did he? Then she'd put him to good use. Time to negotiate. She stopped under one of the street lights so she could read his expression.

'I'm working on another case that's proving difficult. Maybe we could do a deal.'

'What kind of a deal?' Daniel looked distinctly wary.

A breeze started to blow in over the water and Jess huddled deeper in her coat.

'I'm not sure yet. I might need introductions to people you're acquainted with or invites to a few social functions. You get me in the door if and where necessary and we'll work together on your case.'

Daniel appeared to be considering her offer. He flipped up his collar against the strengthening breeze. 'It's getting chilly. Let's head back, shall we?'

He offered his arm. Jess tucked her hand inside his elbow and they matched steps.

'Let me see if I've got this straight,' he said. 'You'll allow me to give input on my own case *if* I risk my reputation for you.'

'Risk! What risk?'

'Hey, it's my name that's going to get you in those doors, lady. If, or I should say *when*, you do something crazy, they'll blame me because I arranged for you to be there. And if you think that kind of gossip won't spread like wild fire, you're naïve.'

'You're exaggerating.'

'Remember, I've seen you in action. If you're on the scent, you focus on your goal and ignore everything in your way.' His lips twitched like he was trying not to smile. 'In the Galleria's ballroom the other night, you didn't care what anybody thought in your single-minded pursuit of Scratten.'

'The circumstances were unique. It wouldn't happen again.'

'Really? Here's my counter-offer. I participate fully

in my own case and I go with you to any of these functions, to protect my own interests and reputation.'

Jess didn't answer right away. If she agreed to this, she might have to spend more time with Daniel than she'd hoped. On the other hand, this would give her inside access to places and people who would otherwise be difficult or even impossible for her or Harvey to approach.

'Okay.' Jess stuck out her hand and they shook on it. His palm was warm against hers, the grip of his fingers firm. It felt good.

Daniel resumed walking and she fell into step beside him. After a minute, he reached for her hand and tucked it into the crook of his elbow again. It felt very good. Down, girl, she told herself.

Think about something else, like what part of the arrangements with Daniel, if any, she should tell Harvey. Would he welcome her help on his case or would he be angry? By the time they reached the Jag, she'd made a decision.

Take as long as possible to tell Harvey as little as possible.

When they pulled up in front of Mrs Martelli's, the boarding house was dark except for the lights beside the front door and her own windows up under the eaves.

During the drive home the silence had grown thicker, tenser. Jess could tell he was thinking about the kiss, as she was, and she wondered if he would kiss her again, now. She searched for something to say, anything to change the mood.

'What are you going to tell your staff when I get there tomorrow?'

He half-smiled, as if he knew what she was doing and why.

'I asked Chris to talk to them before they went home this afternoon,' he finally answered, 'to explain you were coming for a few days and would be talking to all of them about their work stations. When I spoke to her afterward, she said they had a lot of questions.'

'That's normal. You don't need to worry.'

'So you're ready for tomorrow?' he asked.

'Of course,' she said. Never let the client see you sweat, as Harvey would say.

CHAPTER 10

Jess slipped into Daniel's office, shut the door, and braced herself against it, tempted to turn the lock. How could she, or anybody else, have been ready for this hoopla?

Why hadn't Chris warned her Daniel's staff took such an avid interest in his love life? Though the woman looked so haggard lately, she probably had more important things on her mind than Jess's comfort.

Only halfway through the second day and she'd had all she could take. The really unfair part of this whole thing was, from what she could see, Daniel wasn't suffering nearly as much as her.

After all, what employee would ask the boss to his face if he was sleeping with, or engaged to, or just toying with, his ditsy decorator? As a matter of fact, he seemed to be enjoying the speculation. Maybe a little too much.

How many times today had she been faced with an employee delicately digging for gossip, only to look up and see him grinning from ear to ear? Under those circumstances, how could he blame her for having a little fun of her own? After all, using the nickname fit the role she'd chosen to play.

Maybe that's where she'd made her mistake. Instead of choosing to play an open, friendly character who liked to talk to everybody, she should have come in here tougher than Attila the Hun and wearing the polyester dress she'd made Sophy put on for visiting the nursing homes.

As it was, she'd spent more time deflecting their questions about her supposed affair with Daniel than delving into their lives.

From what Jess could piece together, the present situation had been inevitable from the moment Gwen told her two best friends about Ella Mae's underwater plans for Daniel's office.

From there the story spread through the rest of the staff. Debate on whether or not Daniel would actually enjoy working in an office resembling the set of a Disney movie had only primed the pump, as it were. Having a different female decorator show up two days later had started a flood of conjecture.

At first the staff had tried to pry information out of Chris, but she'd frustrated them with her usual stone-wall tactics. Then they'd turned to Rick who, along with Chris, was known to have been in on the original meeting between Jess and Daniel.

Rick, oddly enough, was not a good liar. His evasive maneuverings had only served to convince the staff Jess and Daniel were an 'item'.

It didn't help that Daniel's demand to be involved in the investigation required the two of them to have several private conversations during the day, usually in his office.

The staff had added two and two, came up with five, and decided Daniel had hired her because they were having a torrid affair.

Which wouldn't have been a huge issue, by itself. The real problems came from the scorching thoughts in her own head. She was becoming more confused every minute she spent with him. She was even beginning to wonder if she'd be able to say no if he suggested an affair, yet wishing he would.

She knew darned well he would never consider her as a potential wife. Not that it mattered because she didn't want a husband or family, anyway. The white picket fence and attendant responsibilities weren't for her.

Jess ignored a twinge of regret, peeled herself off the door and wandered over to sit down in front of the window.

Daniel shoved open the door, then slammed it shut behind himself. 'Don't walk away when I'm talking to you, and don't call me Danny.'

'Sorry. It slipped out.'

'Tell me how it can "slip" out four times in one day?'

'It's going to continue to slip out every time you think it's funny when one of your employees asks me, ever so coyly –' she changed her voice to a cutsey tone ' "How long have you two, tee hee, *known* each other?" '

'You'd laugh too if you could have seen your face.'

'Consider this a warning, Danny boy.' She pursed her lips, pretended to blow him a kiss and began to whistle 'Oh, Danny Boy'.

'You wouldn't.'

'Yes, I would. In the hallway, in the coffee room, in the elevator. One more grin, and you'll be hearing it in your sleep.'

Daniel scowled at her and for the first time in two days she felt like smiling. Oh, she'd smiled all day until her cheeks ached, but not because she felt amused.

'In your rush to get away from me, you forgot your notepad.'

Jess froze. She'd been carrying it around, pretending to take notes as part of her role. Her real observations on the employees were in the recorder she'd hidden in her pocket.

'Thanks,' she said casually and held out her hand. He tossed it, she missed, and it fell to the floor, open to a page full of meaningless scribbles.

'Sorry.' He stooped to pick it up for her before she could get there. 'Some kind of personal shorthand?'

'No.' She had to control the urge to snatch it out of his hand.

'Thanks.' She shoved it in her pocket. 'Not that the silly thing matters. It's a prop, for heaven's sake, full of chicken scratches. Heck, why write down all this healthy office stuff when it's just a ruse?'

'I thought you were making notes for the case.'

'Sure, but not in that. If one of your employees saw it

207

by accident, like you just did, and recognized stuff about themselves, we'd be in a fine mess.'

She breathed a sigh of relief when he seemed to accept her explanation.

'Have you found anybody yet who might be in league with Sarah Graff?'

'No, but the day's not over.'

Daniel spent the rest of the afternoon watching Jess move. Not by choice, but because he couldn't help himself. Not a productive way to spend a work day but an interesting one.

Away from the office or alone with him, she was herself, her body fluid, each movement flowing into the next. Her aura was electric, almost visible as it clung to her. Even her eyes seemed to change color constantly, from emerald green to golden brown to every shade in between. The velvet in her voice rubbed against his skin.

Outside his private office, in her role of decorator from hell, she bounced like she was made of springs, reminding him of Tigger from the *Winnie the Pooh* novel he had read to Hannah when she was little. Even Jess's voice bounced, with her tone shooting up and down with every sentence she spoke. She brought new meaning to the term perky. So different from her own self, and yet somehow just as real.

How could one woman become another so convincingly between one breath and the next? She'd be a star if she ever went on the stage, he thought.

208

He couldn't stop thinking about kissing her and wanting to get her alone so he could do it again. Thinking that if he did, it might have been as good as he was afraid it would be. None of this made sense.

She was driving him nuts.

Every time he walked through the office, he looked for her to see what she would do next. He manufactured excuses to do so. Like now, when he stood beside the photocopier, duplicating a document he could have printed from his computer.

Across the busy room, Jess bustled around the desk of the junior accounting clerk. Measuring, talking, moving, talking. The clerk watched her, fascinated, as he answered the questions she slipped into the conversation.

Daniel knew she was aware of his presence because she'd had to work hard avoiding his gaze.

The clerk asked a question. Jess's brows lowered in a quick frown. Daniel only caught a couple words but, putting it together with the look on her face, he could tell the young man wanted to know if she was really involved with the boss.

She looked at Daniel, a threat in her eyes.

He couldn't help it. He grinned.

She stood up, put her hands on her hips, looked him straight in the eye, and began to whistle. The entire office slowly went quiet as, one by one, all his employees realized what was happening.

He frowned.

Jess's mouth went dry when his eyebrows tilted

ominously. Her whistle faltered but she wet her lips and kept going. She'd warned him. Now he had to be taught Jess Phillips meant what she said.

After the first verse a few voices began to hum along. Nobody moved, so it was hard to tell which hardy souls had braved their boss's displeasure to join in.

Word of unusual doings must have swept through the private offices because as she whistled another verse, the doorways filled up with people who wanted to watch. More voices swelled the humming, adding harmony.

She swept through a third verse and finished with a rousing rendition of the chorus. The scattered applause died away as people saw Daniel's expression of icy disapproval.

Gradually the chill in his eyes dissipated and his lips tilted into a smile. Then an unwilling chuckle escaped and a moment later Daniel laughed out loud, reminding Jess of the time she watched a frozen river break free in spring.

He continued to laugh and soon the whole room was filled with happy sounds as everyone joined in.

That's when she saw Hannah and Mary standing just inside the room. They must have seen the whole thing. It wasn't until she saw the disbelief in their faces that she wondered if she'd gone too far to make her point. Now they'd dislike her for embarrassing their beloved brother, even if she thought he was all the better for some loosening up.

* * *

'I like her, Daniel,' Mary said as she sat down in his office.

So did he. Too much. Yet he had no idea of how she felt except for one fact. She didn't want the life he needed.

Daniel stood in the middle of the room, too tense to sit down, trying to figure out how he'd ended up enjoying himself while Jess teased him in front of his employees. Office discipline had gone right out the window and he was having a hard time making himself believe it was a bad thing.

What was happening to him?

'I like her, too.' Hannah hugged him, then kicked off her sneakers and sprawled on a couch. 'She makes you laugh.'

'What's so odd about that?'

'Come on, Daniel, get real. Before you met Jess, when was the last time you laughed from the gut and out loud?'

He didn't give her an answer because he couldn't think of one.

'Thought so. Report has it you had a good time at the party the other night, too.'

'You talked to Ruth,' he said.

'Yup. She said you chased Jess through the ballroom just when the soprano was going to sing and neither of you came back. Not that I blame you, but you have to admit that's weird behaviour for you.'

'There were extenuating circumstances,' he muttered.

'And that's not all I know.' Hannah smirked. 'One of my friends saw you and a pretty brown-haired lady at La Minuet last night. Betcha she was Jess, right?'

'Are you two dating?' Mary asked.

'No,' he said. Then he grinned. 'But most of my staff have been asking her that question since yesterday morning and it's driving her crazy. She's doing some work for me, but all the speculation is getting in her way.'

'She's working for you? As a detective?' Hannah sat up quickly. 'How exciting. What's she looking for? An embezzler? A corporate spy?'

'That's confidential.' He dropped into the chair beside Mary. 'Why are you guys here?'

'Mom's feeling better and she wants to have us all over for a barbecue on Sunday.'

'A barbecue? In April?'

'Hey, I'm not going to argue with her. I'm too happy she's still here to order us around.'

'Don't sweat it, Danny.' Hannah giggled when he glared at her. 'Daniel. The deck's enclosed and heated.'

'Hannah and I were coming downtown anyway to do some shopping so we said we'd swing by to tell you and then pick up supplies on the way home.'

'Are you sure she's up to it?'

'I don't know,' Mary said. She leaned into the cushions and sighed. 'But if it makes her happy, who are we to say no? She already told the nurses we'd be there and gave them the day off. I figure if we do all the work and take turns keeping an eye on her, it'll be okay. If she gets over-tired, we'll all go home.'

Jess hovered outside Daniel's office, unable to bring herself to knock. *Come on, girl, anyone seeing you here will think you're a coward.* So what if his sisters witnessed the scene she'd just caused?

Finders Keepers' operatives always reported to the client before leaving. This day and these people were no exception. *Bite the bullet and get it over with before someone walks down this hallway and sees you trembling outside this door like a school kid outside the principal's office.*

She drew a deep breath, released it slowly, then rapped at the closed door.

'Come in,' Daniel called.

Jess opened it a few inches and stuck her head in. All three of them looked at her and, just for an instant, she was struck dumb.

'Yes?' he asked impatiently.

She leaped into speech. 'Sorry to interrupt, but I wanted to tell you I'm leaving now. My preliminary report should be ready by Wednesday morning.'

'Thanks. Will you need to come back?'

'As your healthy-office authority, you mean? No, she can make a graceful exit, thank heavens.'

'Hey there, Jess.' Hannah stuck her hand up and waved. 'Didn't get much chance to say hello before. Daniel hustled us away too fast. You're a heck of a whistler.'

213

'Thanks, Hannah.' Jess wondered if Daniel agreed with her and forced a smile. 'Hello, Mrs Masters.'

'Please, call me Mary,' she said. 'Could you come in for a minute?'

Jess felt slightly ill but she nodded and stepped inside. 'Sure. What's up?'

'First, the Sisters want to thank you for the work you did. Daniel wouldn't tell us the results –'

'He said we're too nosy.' Hannah pouted.

'– but he did mention you were competent and thorough,' Mary continued as if their younger sister hadn't spoken.

'Thank you.' Jess felt herself blush and immediately wondered why. She'd received many compliments from satisfied clients. Why did praise from Daniel feel special, even when it was only passed on this way?

'I'm glad you're here,' Mary said, 'because it saves me calling you tonight. I have a message from our mother. She'd like you to join the family for dinner on Sunday.'

Daniel's brows lowered. Jess could tell he'd been caught by surprise and didn't much like the idea as he said, 'Uh, I thought we were going to keep it small and simple. Just family.'

Jess could tell when she wasn't welcome, even if he was too polite to say so directly, right in front of her. Not that she *wanted* to meet the rest of his family.

'I don't think –' Jess didn't get a chance to finish her refusal before Mary spoke.

'Well, it's mostly family but Mom really wants to

214

meet Jess. Besides, she's also invited a couple of her old friends and Warren.'

'Warren Hellmann?' Jess asked.

'Yes. Do you know him?'

'Daniel introduced us the other night.' Jess was torn. Here was her chance to talk to Hellmann, to help Harvey. All she had to do was get more involved in Daniel's personal life. Something that obviously didn't please him any more than it did her.

'So you'll come?' Mary asked.

'Yes. I'd like that.'

'Good. We'll have lots of fun,' Hannah said.

When she got back to Finders Keepers, Jess poked her head into Harvey's office. 'Got a minute?'

He looked up from a stack of papers. 'Sure, sweetheart.'

Jess flopped down in a chair and heaved a sigh.

'Bad day?'

'No, not really. Tiring. Daniel's employees almost drove me crazy trying to find out if we were a "hot item". He thought it was amusing, which annoyed me. I did manage to talk to everyone on his staff though, except those who are out of town.'

'Any possibles?'

'Nope. Not on the surface. Have to wait and see what Sophy's search turns up, but I don't think we'll find anything. Sarah Graff strikes me as the type who works alone. What about you? Did you find out anything about your mysterious abduction?'

'I still don't know where they took me, but I think I found out why. I got a peek at Scratten's appointment calendar this afternoon. During the period in question he was expecting visitors, very hush-hush; his secretary didn't know their names. He also knew I was watching the building. He couldn't ask me to absent myself, because it would look suspicious. He couldn't let me see his shy visitors and record their description. Ergo, he is responsible for my little adventure.'

'You could be right. Why else would they kidnap you, hold you for a time, then let you go, all for no visible reason?'

'Maybe they thought I needed a rest?'

She laughed, then lay back and pretended to close her eyes, while watching him from under her lashes.

'Did I tell you about all the interesting people I met at the charity thing the other night? There were lots of celebrities and Ruth St Clair seemed to know them all, though none of them sat at our table. Oh, did I tell you I met an old friend of Daniel's family when I talked to Scratten? Warren Hellmann.'

Bingo, she thought. A definite reaction to the name. She pretended to yawn, then got up.

'I'm glad you had fun.'

'I did. I'd better get going, lots to do. It's housework tonight.' Just before she left the office she hesitated. 'St Clair's sisters invited me to Sunday dinner at their family home.'

'Don't get involved with a client, Jess.'

'I won't. It's just that I've never been to a family

Sunday dinner and I'm curious. Plus Tom Masters is supposed to be there and I thought I'd schmooze a little, see if he can send us any more business. Hannah St Clair assured me it's going to be fun.'

'Yeah, right.' He snorted. 'You're going to feel like a fish out of water.'

Jess shifted restlessly, trying to get comfortable in the wooden deck chair. She'd been uncomfortable ever since she sat down in it three hours ago, but she doubted it was the chair's fault.

She didn't belong here.

She didn't belong in the suburbs at all.

It wasn't her clothes because her lavender sweatshirt and black jeans blended right in. Everyone under sixty was wearing jeans. For the first time ever she'd left her room in a mess, discarded clothes strewn anyhow. She'd never had so much trouble deciding what to wear.

The house was exactly what she'd expected, a family home. Comfortable, full of mementos and knick-knacks. Clean but lived-in, unashamed of the hard wear that showed years of family living. Big comfy furniture a person wouldn't be afraid to sit on. Anybody could tell this house had seen lots of happy kids through its rooms.

Like today, when there were lots of people running around. Too many. The St Clair family seemed to enjoy the atmosphere of barely controlled mayhem. She didn't.

217

The only time everyone sat down quietly together was when the Sisters told them about Jess's whistling and, somehow, persuaded her to put on a performance that was met with a round of energetic and ego-boosting applause.

For the rest of the afternoon, Daniel's mother, Anna, sat across from Jess, enthroned on a padded lounge, a blanket across her legs, the calm at the eye of the hurricane. Two elderly ladies and Warren Hellmann clustered around her, and all four talked non-stop while they watched the younger generations, making suggestions that were sometimes heeded.

Daniel and Tom Masters had fought cheerfully over who flipped the best burgers and mixed the best drinks. The three women had swirled around, setting the buffet table, bringing casseroles from the kitchen, debating what to do and how to do it.

Before and after dinner, the Masters' two sons dashed back and forth between the wide expanse of lawn outside and the enclosed deck, getting in everyone's way as they snatched raw vegetables or snack food from the table their mother and aunts were trying to organize.

Early on she'd offered to help and been immensely grateful when they refused. Family dinner was obviously a complicated routine they'd perfected over the years and she knew she'd be distinctly out of step if they'd accepted her offer. Much like if she tried to join in a performance by an established dance troupe; she'd probably trip them up and make a fool of herself.

Through it all she'd listened as they maintained a running commentary on the weather, the latest political scandals, the school system, each other's jobs, and how best to fix the world. One sibling would start a sentence, then another would complete it, though none of them shared exactly the same attitude toward anything.

Which made for some lively conversations in which they'd all tried to include her. Asking her opinion, explaining the inside jokes while they giggled help-lessly, endlessly at things that made no sense to her.

Once everyone sat down to eat, the constant move-ment had stopped, but not the talk. She hadn't felt so alone in a long time.

In the middle of things, yet not part of them. Why should it bother her this time? She was used to it, expected nothing else. After all those years visiting in foster homes, she knew she wasn't comfortable with 'family' stuff.

Daniel had been perfectly polite all evening, but distant. It took most of the evening for her to admit to herself she'd hoped for more.

At least coming here hadn't been a total waste of time. She'd learned quite a bit about Hellmann by listening to conversations. He was Anna's friend, her kids' honorary uncle and they all trusted him.

They teased about his academic successes and the switch to business. In a quiet moment, she'd overheard him apologizing and explaining to Anna why Concept House hadn't been able to pay out any dividends this year.

She'd even had several chances to chat with him herself. He hadn't blinked when she'd mentioned Harvey's name or her job. So maybe he was Ralph's dupe; just another academic who couldn't cope in the real world.

Either that, or he was a cold-blooded man who'd cheat friends, a man who could look her straight in the eye with a fatherly smile and lie through his teeth.

For the first time Jess wondered if she could trust her instincts. Nothing was clear. Was she afraid of what Daniel would do if . . . no, when he found out she was investigating Hellmann's business? She felt uncomfortable deceiving the St Clairs about why she was here today.

How would they feel about her if she exposed corruption at Concept House? A scandal like that would rock, maybe destroy Warren Hellmann. What if Anna's investment was lost?

Would Harvey forgive her for interfering?

And yet she had to do what was right. Not just for Harvey's sake, but for everyone who trusted Hellmann and Ralph.

Jess rolled her shoulders, trying to ease the growing tension in her neck and back. The answers weren't going to be discovered in the St Clair home. So why was she still sitting here?

'Thirsty?'

Jess glanced up and saw Tom offering her a glass of cola, condensation already forming on its sides.

'Yes. Thanks.' She was having a hard time adjusting to seeing the lieutenant this way, enjoying himself with his family, playing with his sons. Before today she'd only seen him as the no-nonsense policeman with no tolerance for fools.

He groaned as he lowered himself into the chair beside her. 'Lord, I'm getting too old, my boys are going to be the death of me.'

She laughed.

He sipped his own drink. 'The St Clairs are quite a group, aren't they? I still remember the first time I ate dinner here. Takes getting used to.'

'Yes, I bet it does.'

'And this is only a small event. Before she got ill, Anna loved to throw parties and she's darned good at it, too. I think that's why Ruth is so good at those charity bashes she runs; she inherited the hostess gene from her mother.'

'I couldn't do it.'

'Once every summer Anna has her kids invite all their friends and they have a big party, out on the lawns. She told me once she and Sam started the tradition when the girls were little so they'd know what was happening in their kids' lives. Lots of fun but it's a circus. The boys and their friends go wild.'

'Are you insulting our sons again?' Mary bent over to kiss her husband's cheek and he swept her on to his lap.

'No. Telling Jess about your mother's summer party.'

Mary laughed. 'I have to admit it gets a little wild. But so much fun, Jess, you'll see.'

There was a burst of laughter, Hannah called for Mary to come support her in an argument with Daniel. The boys started wrestling among the table legs and Tom rushed to separate them.

She bit her lip. It almost sounded like Mary expected Jess to still be part of their lives come summer. But how could that be? Like always, she was just passing through.

Tom and Daniel began organizing a volleyball tournament, to be fought to the death in the backyard. As they chose up sides, Jess saw Ruth clearing the table and jumped to her feet, determined to do something useful tonight. Maybe she'd have been in the way preparing the meal but she was a champion cleaner and dishwasher, thanks to the years before she met Harvey.

'Can I help?'

Ruth looked up from where she was scraping the plates. 'Don't you want to play volleyball?'

'I'm not very good at sports.'

Ruth laughed. 'None of us are what you'd call athletes, except maybe Daniel. We just have fun playing together.'

'I'll take care of these if you want to go play.'

'Thanks, but . . .' Ruth glanced out to the deck and lowered her voice '. . . we decided to take turns watching over Mom today, to make sure she doesn't overdo it. It's my turn so I volunteered for kitchen

222

duty. But if you're sure you want to help, I'd like the company.'

Jess and Ruth were finishing up the kitchen as the sun began to sink behind the trees. Anna's two friends had to leave and Hellmann offered to drive them home so, while Jess dried the last wine glasses, Ruth went to say goodbye and walk them out to the car.

For the first time since she'd arrived Jess was in a room where, despite the shouts echoing from the backyard, everything was relatively quiet. She put away the last wine glass, folded the tea towels and hung them on the oven handle.

She looked around the kitchen. It was a big room, where one could feed a large family with ease.

Ruth had been working in the walk-in pantry on the other side of the kitchen, putting away the pots and pan, and storing the boxes and cans that hadn't been used for dinner. Jess wasn't ready to rejoin the others so she decided to finish the job.

She found places for the last few clean pots, put away a box of pasta and a canister of flour. When she turned to leave she noticed vertical rows of pencil marks on the inside of the door. On top of each row was a name and beside each mark was a date. Someone had been keeping track of each child's height as he or she grew.

She assumed the two shortest belonged to Mary's sons. The tallest row had to be Daniel's. Her heart beat faster and her hand trembled as she reached out to run her finger down the marks beneath his name. She could imagine Anna teasing but proud as he grew. She'd probably needed to stand on a ladder or a chair when he grew so tall she couldn't reach the top of his head.

Daniel and his sisters were very lucky people.

On the bottom half of the door, the marks were fainter or smudged, perhaps by people accidentally brushing against them as they went in and out of the pantry. She slid her finger down, imagining the years passing, visualizing Daniel as a young man, then as a teenager.

The marks ended abruptly. Jess stooped to look closer, puzzled. His sisters' dates were there, beside his, but there were none for Daniel below about four foot two. She looked at the date on the lowest one, taking her time to figure out what the numbers meant.

Daniel would have been ten.

She could imagine many different, simple reasons to explain how and why Daniel wasn't represented on the family growth chart before he was ten. But her intuition told her nothing to do with Daniel was as simple as it seemed.

His life was probably full of stories she'd never hear.

'Jess? Are you in here?' At the sound of Anna's voice, she jerked to her feet, feeling guilty, as if she'd been caught snooping.

'Yes, Mrs St Clair?' When she stepped out of the pantry, Anna was leaning heavily against the kitchen table, looking much frailer than she had earlier. Jess rushed over to take her elbow. 'Here, let me help you.'

'Didn't I tell you to call me Anna, my dear?' She allowed Jess to guide her a few feet to a straight chair where she sat down quickly.

'Yes, Anna.' Jess felt a twinge of discomfort at the informality. 'Can I get you something? A glass of cold water?'

'That would be nice.'

Jess filled a glass from the filtered jug in the fridge, then sat beside Anna as she sipped.

'Mom!' someone called from the deck, then Ruth rushed into the kitchen. Jess could see the relief on her face when she saw her mother. 'Oh, there you are.'

'Thank you for seeing my friends to their car, Ruth,' Anna said. 'Are they gone?'

'Yes, Mom.'

'How's it going in here?' Daniel stood in the doorway, sweat-dampened hair in wild disorder and grass stains on his shirt. 'Mary and I are losing the battle to Tom, Hannah, and the boys so I came to recruit another player. How about it, Jess?'

'I'd rather not. I've never played sports.'

'You'll be fine. We always go easy on beginners.'

'Leave the girl alone, Daniel. Ruth will play. I'm going to sit in the living-room and Jess can keep me company.'

'I can play next time, Mom.'

Jess was glad to see she wasn't the only one who got that particular non-answer from him.

'Nonsense, Ruth. You get out there and show them what a real competitor can do.'

Ruth looked at Daniel, a question in her eyes. He shrugged.

Anna struggled to her feet and Daniel rushed to help her. Ruth and Jess trailed after them as he supported her into the living-room.

'If Mom has a problem,' Ruth whispered, 'the nurse is upstairs in her sitting room and we're right outside. Just call.'

She nodded and followed Ruth into the living-room, which at first glance appeared to be over-full of mismatched but comfortable furniture. One wall was mostly window, one was fireplace, and the third was totally covered in framed photographs. Daniel held Anna's arm as she lowered herself into a rocking chair.

'How about a small fire, son? I know it's not really chilly enough, but I feel like looking at the flames tonight.'

Daniel knelt to build a fire while Ruth spread an afghan over Anna's legs.

Jess wandered across the room to look at the photographs. Formal shots, candid shots, even awkward shots were there. A montage of family life spanning several generations, judging by the coloring of the shots and the clothing the subjects wore.

How did it feel to know what your ancestors looked like? Not that she ever thought about it much, except perhaps when she was faced with a display like this one.

Daniel came over to stand beside her.

'This is Sam.' He pointed to one of the formal shots, this one of a smiling man in black robes and a white collar.

'He was a minister?'

'Yes.' He pointed to another of the same smiling man, this time with Anna seated by his side and the three oldest kids grouped around them. The little one on his lap must have been Hannah. 'These were taken about a month before he died. I was seventeen.'

'He looks like a good man.'

'He was. The best.' She could hear the old sorrow in his voice but when she looked up at him, he was smiling. 'He preached a mean sermon. Anna used to say all but the most determined of sinners paid attention when Sam spoke.'

'Come on, Daniel. Let's go show Tom and those boys exactly what losing feels like.' Ruth put the glass of water she'd refilled down on the small table at Anna's elbow.

'It's nice of you to sit with her,' Daniel said, his voice pitched low. 'She enjoys meeting new people.' His hand rested on Jess's shoulder, then slid down to the small of her back.

'I like your Mom.' Jess heard the tremor in her voice and hoped he didn't sense how weak his touch made her feel. His hand tightened on her waist, then he released her and left with Ruth.

Accompanied by the rhythmic squeak of the rocking chair, Jess drifted along the wall, watching the St Clair family grow up in the photos. She smiled when Tom began appearing at Mary's side, tall and gangly but in his shiny-new patrolman's uniform.

'You should have known him back then,' Anna said. 'He was so idealistic! He believed he could save the world.'

'Tom?' Jess looked at her in surprise. 'But he's –' She managed to stop what she was about to say.

'Yes, I know. Ruth tells me he's got quite a reputation at work for being a cynical you-know-what.'

'Yes, he does.'

'He's a marshmallow with Mary and the boys, though, and nothing else matters to me. I wasn't happy when he wanted to marry her because he was five years older than her and a cop. But it's worked out.'

'He's certainly a different man at your house today than the one I've met at the police station.'

'I understand it was Tom who suggested my girls come see you about the mess Daniel had got himself into.'

'Yes.'

'I don't think my son would have actually married one of those women but his sisters weren't so sure. If he had, he would have been a very unhappy man, which is one of the reasons I invited you here today. I wanted to thank you, personally.'

'You're welcome,' Jess said, flustered. 'It was just another case.'

'Not to us.' Anna looked at her, a shrewd look in her eyes. 'And, I suspect, not to you.'

CHAPTER 11

Jess didn't know what to say to Anna so she pointed to a nearby picture. 'He looks like he's got the world by the tail.'

A young Daniel wore a baggy white jacket and pants with a black sash tied around his waist. His face was twisted into what he'd probably thought of as the fierce expression of a warrior. A huge trophy stood beside his bare feet. Sam stood at his shoulder, a proud grin on his face.

'Daniel won the Canadian championship that day. He was supposed to go to Japan a few months later to compete for the world title. He'd trained hard and was the favourite to win.'

'What happened?'

'Just before he left, we found out Sam was ill. Daniel refused to leave me and the girls alone to cope.'

Jess traced his boyish features with one finger, an unfamiliar lump of emotion in her throat. He must have been fifteen or sixteen, already a foot taller than his father, but in the boy's face she could see the man he had become.

'Come and sit down, my dear.'

'Sure.' Jess looked around the assortment of seats but in the end chose the plump stool between Anna's rocking chair and the fire.

'That was always Daniel's favorite seat.' Anna picked up her glass and studied Jess over the rim as she drank. 'Tell me about your family.'

'I have none.'

'None?'

'My parents died when I was young and neither of them had family so I ended up in the foster care system.'

'Life's difficult for children on their own. Many of them don't become successful, productive adults. You seem to have beaten the odds.'

Her tone was matter of fact, which surprised Jess. Most people offered unwanted sympathy when they found out about her past.

'I was one of the lucky ones, I guess.' Jess felt warmed by Anna's interest. 'Never hurt or abused, never really unhappy. They moved me to a different foster family every year or two, mostly because of bad luck when I was little. But when I was older, it happened because of my own bad attitude.'

'Stubborn, were you?' Anna's eyes twinkled.

'I had a few problems.

'You learned to deal with them.'

'Mostly thanks to my partner, Harvey, and Sophy, who works for us. They've been wonderful.'

'Sounds like you love them.'

'Yes, I do,' Jess said, fiercely.

'So you do have a family,' Anna said. 'One you chose.'

'Yes, I guess I did.' Jess hadn't thought about it quite that way before. She did now, looked at it from all sides, and liked what she saw. She, Harvey, and Sophy were family.

In the fireplace a log crackled and sparks flew, several landing out on the hearth. Jess grabbed the little broom from on top of the log basket, kneeling to sweep the glowing embers back where they belonged.

She stayed there, staring into the dancing flames.

She had a family. And no matter how far away Harvey and Sophy lived, they'd still be bound, all three, by ties as strong as shared blood and genes.

That amazing thought ran round and round in her brain, leaving her more content than she'd been in a long time, thanks to Anna.

The rocking chair's squeak slowed, then stopped, but she didn't think anything of it until she heard a gasp, then a whimper. Jess spun around, saw Daniel's mother tilted sideways in her chair.

'Anna? Anna!'

At Jess's frantic cry, Anna's eyes flickered but didn't open. She scrambled across the carpet on her hands and knees and pressed two trembling fingers to Anna's throat, praying hard until she felt a ragged pulse.

'Hold on, Anna. Hold on!' Jess leaped to her feet and ran through the house faster than she'd ever run in her life. In the kitchen she grabbed the phone and dialed emergency services.

While it rang she slammed open the window between her and the back yard and screamed, 'Daniel!'

Daniel stepped out of the intensive care unit into the hospital's main corridor, scrubbing his face with both hands in an effort to wake himself up.

Anna was going to make it, thank God. Another reprieve.

He tried to straighten his shoulders but gave it up, exhausted right to his bones. Three nights with virtually no sleep followed by a night like this one had left him drained of energy. Intensive care at three in the morning was a very desolate experience, one he'd had far too often this last year as her condition worsened.

Hospitals were very different places at night when the lights were dimmed. The underlying stench of pain and despair seemed stronger. The long, echoing corridors were full of shadows and silence except the nurses' stations, each one an oasis of light and subdued bustle.

He managed a nod for the nurse who was beginning her rounds, then spotted the pay phones on the wall in the waiting area and remembered his promise to Mary. Shortly after the emergency room doctors stabilized Anna's condition she'd had to leave to take care of her boys because Tom had been called into work. She'd asked Daniel to phone, no matter how late, once the doctors made a decision and told the family the prognosis.

He picked up the receiver and leaned against the wall, grateful for the support, while he fished in his pocket for change to feed into the phone. Mary picked up on the first ring. He bent his knees and slid down to sit on the floor as he talked.

'Hi. It's me. She's going to be okay but they're keeping her in the I.C.U. till morning, then in the hospital for a day or two for observation.' Mary's response was a string of broken sentences and swallowed sobs, and he realized she felt guilty for leaving the hospital. 'Anna understood her grandsons couldn't be left alone. Besides, Ruth, Hannah, and I were all here. Are the boys finally asleep?'

Daniel straightened his legs and rested his head against the wall while he listened. 'No, don't worry about my car. I'll take a taxi home and get the Jag from you tomorrow or the next day. Ruth is prosecuting today but she's going to stay until seven. No, no. You come down after the boys go to school in the morning. Hannah will stay with Anna until you get here.

'The nurse brought in a cot so they can take turns sleeping. I was going to stay, too, but the Sisters kicked me out. Said I was in the way.'

He pinched the bridge of his nose and closed his burning eyes. 'Did Tom take care of everything at the house before he left? Did he remember to put out the fire? Great. Jess? No, I imagine she's home in bed. Last time I saw her she was standing in the driveway with

233

Tom and the boys as we followed the ambulance.'

He endured several jaw-cracking yawns while Mary answered, so at first he didn't quite catch everything she was saying. Once the general gist sank in, the information jerked him awake, if not quite alert. 'You saw her where?'

He dragged himself to his feet and scanned the shadowed waiting area with it rows of hard vinyl chairs and sofas and a few tables. When he came in to use the phone, he'd noticed what seemed to be a heap of rumpled blankets on a sofa at the far side, but other than that, the place still looked empty.

'You're sure? You saw her here when you left? Thanks. You get some sleep and I'll talk to you in the morning.' Daniel hung up the phone. Why would Jess come down to the hospital and spend most of the night waiting for news of a woman she barely knew?

Then he noticed a hat on the table nearest the blankets. The hat looked a lot like the one Jess always wore. He walked over to pick it up, thinking she'd left it behind, when the mound of fabric shifted and one arm flopped out. He looked closer and recognized Jess, sound asleep, wrapped in her coat and a hospital blanket. She'd folded another blanket to use as a pillow.

Daniel considered leaving. He really did.

He reminded himself they were wrong for each other. Reminded himself of the possible, indeed probable, consequences of getting involved with her. Thought about how dangerous it would be to spend time alone with her when, due to stress and lack of sleep, his control and good sense were close to non-existent.

Told himself a smart man would leave. Especially a man who'd been kept awake by thoughts of her for three nights straight.

But he couldn't.

Because he also kept thinking about the things they did have in common. Of the times he'd seen evidence of her well-protected but caring heart. Of her intelligence and how she made him laugh. How she stirred his senses in ways no woman ever had.

Daniel tucked her arm back under the blankets at her side, then made himself as comfortable as possible in the chair opposite where she lay. He stretched out his legs, linked his hands on his belly, and contemplated her face.

Sleep muted the vibrancy of her personality, dimmed the electricity she generated, but it didn't lessen her appeal. Jess was the only woman Anna and the Sisters truly liked. Hell, even Tom liked her and respected her professionally.

Was it possible he'd found the right woman to be his wife and the mother of his children, but had been so focused on the goal he hadn't seen her there, right under his nose?

He needed to do some serious thinking because it was clear he had two big problems. First, her own stated aversion to marriage. He'd have to be careful she didn't find out his changing intentions too soon or

235

she'd cut him out of her life. He needed time to change her mind.

Second, he had to figure out if these thoughts were driven by his libido taking control, rather than his reason.

He knew damned well he was too tired to think clearly tonight. So he decided to put off thinking until tomorrow.

He considered waking her, he really did. And he would. Soon. At the moment he wanted to watch her sleep, just a little longer.

Jess swam upward through the layers of consciousness, gradually becoming aware of a stiff back, an unusually hard bed, and a rough pillow.

She was obviously getting too old to spend nights on the sofa in her office, she thought. She groaned and flopped over on her stomach, reluctant to wake up. That lasted until she buried her face in her makeshift pillow and got a good whiff of the unique aroma achieved by combining medicine and disinfectant. Then she remembered where she was and why.

Anna.

Guilt crashed down on her again. She should have noticed sooner that Anna was in trouble instead of wallowing in her own problems.

But she hadn't. And that's why she was in a hospital waiting room in the middle of the night to check on Anna's condition. She'd been here a couple of hours when she met Mary beside the nurses' station. That had been distressing; running into Daniel would probably have been worse.

Once she got over her initial surprise at seeing Jess, Mary had tried to convince her there was nothing more she could have done. Jess knew better, though she appreciated the impulsive hug from Mary before she left.

The nurses had wasted considerable energy trying to convince Jess to go home and phone in for information, but eventually they'd realized she really would stay until Anna was out of danger. As night deepened, Jess had huddled into her coat until one of the younger nurses took pity on her and slipped her a couple of blankets for warmth.

She stretched, loosening the kinks in her spine. Time to check on Anna and, if all was well, she'd head home. She didn't want to risk running into Daniel.

She rolled over on to her back, slowly opened her eyes. Daniel's weary face was the first thing she saw. The heat in his sleepy gaze was the second. Alarm bells rang in her head but he blinked and it was gone, leaving her to wonder if she'd imagined the desire in his eyes.

'Hello, Jess,' he said. 'Mary told me you were here.'

'Oh, no,' she moaned and flipped the blanket over her head, hoping he'd go away. When she realized he wasn't going anywhere, she pushed it away from her face and sat up and untangled her legs from the blanket, feeling a little silly.

'Gee, what time is it?' Knowing she probably looked like she'd been through a hurricane, she released her

237

ponytail, smoothed her hair back with her hands, then wrapped the elastic around it again. 'I stopped by to find out how your mother was doing and must have fallen asleep.'

'Anna's going to be okay.'

'I'm glad.' She stood, scooped up her coat, and plopped the hat on her head. 'Must be going.'

Daniel stood up, too, then swayed, as if he'd moved too fast. Jess grabbed for his arm and held on until he steadied.

'Thanks,' he said. 'I feel punchy, like I've had a few too many drinks.' He tried to follow her through the furniture and swayed again, knocking against a table lamp.

Jess grabbed on to his arm and this time didn't let go as she led him toward the lobby.

'Guess I'm more tired than I thought,' he said.

Judging by the dark rings under his eyes and the grey hue of his skin, Jess felt she'd have to agree with him. Even his voice was slurring.

'Maybe you shouldn't drive.'

'I can't. Mary took my car home.' He spotted the taxi company's direct phone on the wall near the doors and veered in that direction. 'I'm supposed to take a cab.' He reached into his back pocket, then looked at his hand blankly when it came out empty. After a moment, he began searching them all.

'Guess not. Seem to have misplaced my wallet. I'll call Tom to come . . . no, that's why Mary had to take my car. He had to go solve a murder.'

'I'll drop you off at your apartment.'

'You sure?

'No,' she muttered.

'Huh?'

'I mean, yes, I'm sure. Let's go.' Jess wrapped her hand around his upper arm and led him toward the parking garage. Once he'd folded his long legs into the front of the Beetle, he put on the seatbelt and promptly fell asleep.

Jess started the car, then drove out of the parking garage. Thank heavens she knew where he lived because he wasn't going to be any help as a navigator. She was halfway across town to his apartment when she was struck by a thought. Mary had his car. Had he thought to keep the keys to his apartment? Somehow she doubted it.

'Daniel?' She shook his shoulder. 'Daniel!'

'Uhuh? Whatzhappenin'?' His bleary eyes blinked open.

'Where are your keys?'

He slapped at his pockets a few times, but his hand fell into his lap as he fell into sleep again.

'Daniel?' She poked him this time. 'Where's the keys to your apartment?'

'Mary's got 'em.'

So, no keys. Which meant he couldn't get into his apartment.

With his wallet missing, along with his cash, credit cards, and identification, dropping him at a hotel was out of the question. They'd think he was a drunk and no hotel would give him a room in that condition without at least a credit card and her credit cards were all maxed out.

She was faced with two choices. She could drive an hour and a half to his mother's locked house and help him break and enter which, the way her luck was running, would probably get some unpleasant attention from the police.

Or she could take him to her place.

Jess swung the car around at the next intersection and headed back to her boarding house. As she passed through the part of town where Harvey lived, she considered dropping Daniel off there but decided it wasn't a good idea.

Come morning, the two men would sit together over coffee and probably start talking about the only thing they had in common – her. Not a good idea if there was the slightest chance they'd put together enough information for Harvey to realize she'd been meddling.

No, having an overnight guest was preferable to that scenario. Her only remaining problem was figuring out how to get her guest, who was taller than her and outweighed her, up the steep flights of stairs to her attic aerie.

Jess twisted the key, shoved her door open, flicked on the top light, then turned to face the man propped against the jamb.

She ignored Nick's questioning meow, sucked in a deep breath, then grasped Daniel's dangling hand, ducked under his arm and braced her shoulder under his armpit as support. She tried to keep his arm across both her shoulders as they lurched toward the bed together, like some absurd parody of a three-legged race.

As soon as her knees touched the mattress, Jess used the last of her strength to heave Daniel's dead weight upward and forward and he fell face down across the bed. Both cats leaped out of the way just in time, complaining loudly. For the sake of her linens, she removed his shoes before she tossed a quilt over his unconscious form.

Jess pivoted and staggered over to lean on the sink while she downed a large glass of cold water. She poured a second glass but this time felt strong enough to walk over to collapse on the sofa where she could sip it in comfort. Nora stalked to the corner where Jess kept a soft pad for the days they didn't choose to sleep on her bed, twitched her tail in disdain, and lay down with her back to Jess.

Nick jumped into Jess's lap and prodded her chin with his nose.

'Hi,' she whispered and absently began rubbing his ears. Eventually he gave up trying for her undivided attention, jumped down and curled up with Nora.

Jess sat there, unable to think about anything other than the fact Daniel was asleep in her bed. Nick was the only male who'd ever slept in that bed.

Eventually she shook herself out of the fantasy world where Daniel was there because he loved her.

Tomorrow was a work day and it was long past time she got some sleep herself.

While she put out food and water for the cats, she thought about Daniel, asleep in her bed. She got out the extra pillows, sheets, and a quilt to make herself comfortable on the sofa, and thought about him. She went about her usual bedtime routine of gathering her pajamas, a towel, and her toiletries and thought about him. She made the trip down to the second floor, where she had a shower and brushed her teeth and thought about him.

Jess climbed back up the stairs to her room but paused with her hand on the doorknob. She had to stop thinking about him as a man, especially an attractive man, or she'd get herself into trouble. Bad trouble. Heart trouble.

He was a client she was helping out of a jam, no more. Shouldn't be too hard to keep her distance when he's passed out cold, she told herself.

Certain she'd made the right decision and could face this situation with indifference, she tucked the bag under her arm, stiffened her spine, and opened her door . . .

. . . to see Daniel, dressed only in a pair of plaid boxers as he swayed unsteadily in the middle of the floor, legs planted wide apart for balance, looking around her home in confusion.

'Daniel, what are you doing?'

'Jess?' he asked, bewildered.

She averted her eyes but it didn't do any good. She'd

seen his nearly naked body now and couldn't, wouldn't forget it.

'Where am I?'

'My place.' Jess looked for his clothes and saw them piled neatly on the floor beside the bed. He must have taken them off before he woke up enough to realize he wasn't in his own home. 'What are you doing? You're supposed to be asleep.'

She looked at him again, being careful to keep her gaze centered on his face, where she was relieved to see some of his normal alertness returning.

'It's disconcerting to wake up and have no idea where you are.' He shoved his fingers through his hair. 'Can I use your washroom?'

'Oh. Down one flight, first door on the left.' He moved to the door. 'Uh, Daniel? Maybe you should wear your jeans. Just in case you run into one of the other tenants or Mrs Martelli.'

He looked down at himself, and she could tell that's when he realized he was clad only in his underwear. A rueful grin twisted his lips. 'Good idea.'

She looked the other way as he bent to pick up the jeans and stepped into them. It was the sound of the zipper that set her to opening and closing her cupboards.

'Here's a towel and some soap if you want to get cleaned up.' She laid them down on the counter while she put her own things away.

'Thanks. Any chance you have an extra toothbrush and some toothpaste?'

She handed them over, careful not to touch his fingers.

'When I get back, perhaps you'll explain why and how I got here.' It was more of an order than a question, a sure sign he was almost himself again.

Part of Jess felt sorry to see the last of the helpless man who'd totally depended on her. Not that she preferred Daniel in that state, but it had been kind of fun while it lasted.

He opened the door, then paused, giving her an excellent view of his broad shoulders. 'Cute PJs.'

No matter how innocent the words, his look and tone were thick with sensual overtones.

Now it was her turn to look down at herself. What man could think her old cotton pajamas looked sexy? Heck, it had been at least a year, maybe more, since she bought them in the menswear department at the mall. They'd been washed so often they'd lost what little shape they ever had and even the multi-coloured stripes had faded.

Still, better safe than sorry.

Jess dashed behind the curtain and began a hurried search for Harvey's Christmas gift from a few years ago, a long thick robe she'd never worn. Finally she noticed a corner of green terrycloth at the back of a shelf and tugged until it came down, bringing a stack of sweaters with it. She pulled the robe on, kicked the sweaters back into the corner, and yanked the curtain shut to hide the mess.

After tying the sash tightly around her waist, she

went to wait on the sofa. If the man wanted to talk, they'd talk.

She sat there for a minute, then realized her pillow and blankets were still spread out on the sofa. She couldn't sit with him on what was essentially a bed! She scooped up the bedding and tossed it behind the curtain on top of the sweaters.

Then she went back to sitting and waiting. When her fingers began to drum on the sofa's arm, she twisted both hands together and held them in her lap. When her knees began jittering up and down, she held on to her thighs.

Why should she feel nervous? This was her home, her territory, not his. It took her a minute to realize what was bothering her. There was something so intimate about sharing conversation alone at night, when the rest of the city was in bed, doing whatever people do in bed.

Talking in the dark, not seeing the face of the other person clearly, somehow released inhibitions and people said more than they should. She didn't think it was a good idea to sit together with Daniel like this.

She shivered. Maybe it was a really bad idea.

Morning would be much better. Smarter.

She scurried to where she'd tossed the bedding, swept it into her arms and dumped it back on the sofa. Then she ran over to the double bed and flicked on the little light clipped to the headboard. She dashed back to the door and, as she flicked off the switches for the top lights, heard a faint noise on the other side of the door. Daniel was on the stairs!

She leaped over the back of the sofa, hauled the blankets over her body, and huddled down, concentrating real hard on being asleep.

Daniel shifted the damp towel on to his bare shoulder and pushed open her door, not sure what kind of reception he'd find inside.

The last thing he remembered was her offering him a ride home from the hospital. How had he ended up at her place?

The room was in total darkness except for a circle of light cast on the bed where he'd woken up. Since it was the only bed in the place, he imagined it was hers. And since it was still empty, Jess must be curled up on the sofa.

There was just enough light for him to avoid any obstacles as he made his way to the counter to put down the items she'd lent him, then hung his wet towel on a drying rack beside hers.

Guess this meant he'd have to wait till morning to find out what happened, he thought, and switched off the lamp.

Daniel reached for the snap on his jeans, then thought better of taking them off. He tossed the quilt to one side, stretched out on the bed, crossed his arms behind his head, and thought about Jess.

Moonbeams shone through the room's only window over the kitchen sink, creating a square of pale light near the sofa. He could just see her pillow and the top of her head.

She lay still. Unnaturally still.

She wasn't asleep. She was hiding.

Daniel knew what he wanted . . . to get to know Jess, to find out if she was the woman for him. Whatever the Sisters might say about his earlier search for a wife, because of it he'd learned the importance of knowing a woman's secrets, her dreams, and her motives. Either that or risk marrying a woman like Thérèse or Amy or Kim.

Jess responded to the truth, to vulnerability. To use that, he'd have to be willing to open up about the tough subjects himself, first.

'I always have a hard time going back to sleep once I take the edge off with a nap,' he said, thoughtfully. 'What about you?'

There was a long silence before she answered.

'Yes,' she whispered.

'Sometimes I can get back to sleep if I read.'

'For me it's movies. Takes me out of my own problems, especially the old classics and mysteries.'

'So that's it! The *Thin Man* movies. I thought your cats' names rang a bell.'

She sat up to look at him over the back of the sofa. 'You've seen the movies?'

Daniel felt a certain amount of grim satisfaction to know he'd been right. He had her hooked. Now he'd got her talking, it would be simple to slide the conversation into more personal areas.

'When I was a student at the university the student union often organized theme film festivals that could

247

last as long as a week. Once I sat through all the Nick and Nora movies in one night.'

'Sounds like fun.'

'Probably. My memory's a little foggy due to our martini consumption. Every time Nick drank one, so did the guys. The girls drank with Nora. We were all stupid drunk and sick as dogs by the end of the night.' He shook his head in disgust. 'Idiotic kids.'

She laughed. 'I bet you've never had another martini.'

'Can't bear the taste. Why do you like the old movies best, Jess?'

'I'm not sure. Sometimes I think it's the element of mystery or fantasy. Nowadays we're told almost every detail about an actor's life, even to what kind of underwear they prefer or who they're in bed with. Sometimes their real life gets in the way of the role they're portraying and ruins the film.'

'Surely a competent actor can make you forget the real person?'

'The other day I went to see a romantic comedy. It would have been a really good movie, except I couldn't quite believe they were falling in love when I already knew the two actors fought from the start of filming and got divorced before it was over.'

'Those kind of things happened to the actors back then, too.'

'Maybe.' She leaned her arms along the back of the sofa and rested her chin on her laced fingers. 'But I don't know about it.'

'Do you have a favorite actor?' he asked. 'Or movie?'

'That's a hard one. I think it depends on my mood. Sometimes I need cheering up, sometimes I want to be challenged by the story. Sometimes I just want to escape.'

'Nobody did tough guys like Humphrey Bogart,' he said.

'You think so? To me his characters always seemed lonely.'

The odd note in her voice made him wonder if she was ready to broach a more sensitive subject. 'You knew all about lonely when you were young, didn't you?'

'Yes.'

'We have that in common.'

'Yeah, sure.' She snorted. 'With your sisters? I don't think so.'

He hesitated. Could he do this? Daniel's fingers dug deep into his aching thigh as he thought about exposing old pain. But if he wanted Jess, did he have any choice?

'The St Clairs adopted me when I was ten.'

Jess sat up to stare in his direction but couldn't see more than a shadowy outline against the white sheets. This explained so many things, like the marks on the cupboard door and why he called his mother Anna.

'Adopted?' How could she and Harvey have missed that fact in their initial investigation? 'You were one of the lucky ones, then, weren't you? Nobody ever wanted to adopt me.'

249

'Lucky?' He moved and she thought he was rubbing his thigh again, like she'd seen him do so many times.

'The interesting thing about luck,' he said, 'is some people believe you make your own with hard work and tenacity. Others believe it has to fall into your life, like a gift.'

'And you, Daniel? What do you believe?'

'I think it's a very bad idea to wait for luck to make your life better. Hard work is much more reliable. On the other hand, I've always thought the day I met Sam was the luckiest of my life.'

Her throat felt thick. 'Yeah?' she asked softly.

'Until now.' The room seemed to grow very still, his voice very quiet. 'Meeting you was a gift, Jess.'

'Oh.' The intensity she felt radiating from him made Jess feel threatened, as if he were demanding a response from her. 'I don't know what to say.'

'You don't have to say anything.'

'What happened to your family, Daniel? Did your parents die, too?

'I have no idea what happened to them but, if there's any justice in this world, they are dead.'

She was shocked by the depth of his bitterness.

'I met Sam in an emergency room. He was there comforting one of his ill parishioners. I was in the next bed because my stepfather had knocked me off our apartment's balcony. My thigh broke when I landed on top of a cement wall. The social worker declared it was an accident and said I'd have to go back there when I left the hospital.'

250

'Oh, Daniel.' Jess impulsively stood up and rushed over to sit on the bed. She touched his hand where it lay on the sheets. He gripped her fingers.

'The doctor kept me in the hospital because it wasn't healing well. My parents –' he spat the word '– didn't give a damn about anything except drinking, but Sam and Anna came every day. They asked to adopt me and my parents signed me over fast enough.'

To hate his birth parents this way must hurt him, deep inside. 'Maybe they did it because they knew it would be best for you.'

'They did it for the money.'

'I don't understand.'

'Did you notice the brooch Anna was wearing at dinner yesterday?'

'The leopard? It's beautiful.'

'It's also valuable. It's a family heirloom passed down through five generations in Sam's family. He gave it to her on their wedding day.' He turned on his side and drew her closer until she was sitting in the curve of his body, his hand warm on her hip.

'My parents agreed to sign the adoption papers if Sam forked out over a thousand dollars. Sam and Anna didn't have that kind of money. Hell, he was a minister with two little girls. But they knew I'd probably end up dead if I was sent back, so they pawned the brooch.'

'They pawned it!'

'It took Sam many years to pay it off, even with my help. So you see, I'm in the unusual position of knowing exactly how much I'm worth.'

'That's got nothing to do with it!' She grabbed him by the shoulders, as if the physical contact would make him listen better. 'A person's worth can't be measured in money. It's measured by things like the happiness they give to others.'

Jess had more to say but it went out of her mind when she looked at her hands where they gripped his flesh, his muscles moving smoothly under lightly tanned skin.

He didn't touch her, he didn't move at all, but she suddenly felt enveloped, as if the intensity that was so much a part of his aura had expanded, wrapping around her.

Daniel's empty stomach chose that moment to rumble.

'You're hungry!' She jumped up.

'No. I can wait until morning.'

'Nonsense. I'll get you something small, just to fill up the empty spaces until morning.' She bustled over to the kitchen area. 'I've got some fortune cookies here, somewhere.'

Daniel reached up over his head and clicked on the headboard lamp.

'I'm not hungry for food, Jess.' His voice was deep and rough, dragging over her senses.

CHAPTER 12

Jess stood still, one hand on the cupboard, half afraid to look at him.

'Jess?'

Slowly her hand dropped and she pivoted to face him. With the one light in the dark room focused on him where he lay on the bed, he looked like a bronze sculpture she once saw in a museum, a nude of a Roman warrior resting after battle. At the time she'd been fascinated by the warrior, even slid her hand over his shoulder and torso.

He'd looked warm yet felt so cold.

Daniel propped himself up on one elbow, the rest of his body stretched out, his jean-clad legs crossed at the ankle. The light glinted off his hair, gilding his brown curls gold, like a tousled crown, leaving his face in shadows, making it hard for her to read his expression.

Because of the angle of the light, every ripple of every muscle on his chest and shoulders and abdomen was clearly defined, as if sculpted. Her palm tingled as

253

she thought about sliding her hand across his skin. Daniel wouldn't feel cold.

He held out his hand. 'Come here, Jess. We'll fill up the empty spaces together.'

'We shouldn't do this.' She took one reluctant step toward him and then another. She felt her old prejudices crumbling, the old fears fading. Why couldn't she make love with Daniel? He wasn't like all those teachers and bosses who'd rejected her all her life. He was different.

'It'll change everything. We won't be able to go back to what we were before,' she said.

'I know. I don't want to go back.'

This wasn't permanent or knowing each other's secrets, she assured herself. This wasn't forever inside a picket fence. This was about a man and a woman wanting each other. While it lasted, it would be beautiful. She already knew he intended to find a wife and she'd told him she would never get married.

What could be wrong about them sharing some happiness now?

'I need you, Jess.'

'Oh, Daniel!' She sped across the room and flung herself on to his chest.

He caught her in his arms but not quite quick enough. He fell onto his back and air whooshed from his lungs with the force of her landing. Their feet tangled and he held her on top of him while he chuckled. 'I'll have to remember that once you've made a decision, you move fast.'

He held her gaze as his chuckle died away and his expression grew serious. 'I want to remember everything about you.' He reached up and removed the elastic in her hair so it fell around both of them like a veil.

'You're sure about this?'

'Very sure,' he said as he undid the sash, slipped the robe off her shoulders, and tossed it on the floor.

He slid his fingers into her hair, cupped her head, and drew her down for a kiss. The kiss turned hungry as soon as their lips touched. His mouth moved on hers, nibbling, exploring. When his tongue swept across her lips, she opened her mouth and let him in.

When he ended the kiss she moaned a soft protest. He turned them both until she lay on the mattress looking up at him, one of his legs across hers, holding her down, his erection heavy against her hip. She ran her hands over his shoulders, tracing the bones and the muscles, the bumps in his spine.

His lips moved on her neck as his hand moved down the buttons of her pajama top until he parted the fabric. Cool night air touched her breasts and he lowered his head to take one nipple in his mouth, covering her other breast with his hand.

Jess arched her back and gave herself up to sensation, to the wet heat of his mouth. She felt her body growing heavier, the heat and dampness between her legs. They both had too many clothes on.

She slid her hand down his side and around the front of his hips until she cupped his hardness in her hand.

Slowly she tightened and rubbed her fingers over the denim and he shuddered.

'You feel so good,' he groaned, and she felt his breath against her nipple, damp from his mouth.

'I could feel even better.' She tugged suggestively at the waistband of his jeans.

He dropped his head on her shoulder and chuckled. 'How do you do it?'

'If you ever get out of these jeans, you might find out.'

'You know I meant make me laugh in the middle of making love, you little devil.' He closed his teeth on her skin, and growled, pretending to bite her. Then he kissed the spot and rolled to his feet. He swept the pajama bottoms down and off her legs, then took a condom out of his pocket before discarding his jeans.

'Sex doesn't have to be serious, does it?' She watched as he rolled on the condom, wishing she'd thought to do it herself.

'No –' he lowered himself over her, 'I guess it doesn't.'

She wrapped her arms around him and parted her legs, welcoming the feel of him probing for entrance to her body. Their breathing grew ragged and he groaned as he thrust deep inside her.

Jess muffled her scream against his shoulder and went still, drowning in new sensations. She'd never felt this explosion of feeling before, as if all her nerve endings were exposed.

'Are you okay? Jess?' He started to pull out and she

wrapped her legs around his hips, holding him close, keeping him inside.

'No. I'm not okay,' she gasped. 'I'll never be okay again. And if you stop, I'll have to hurt you.'

He laughed as he started moving inside her again. But he didn't laugh for long, as his harsh breathing and her soft moans blended with the sound of their bodies coming together.

She felt the pressure inside her building, her body demanding release as the tension coiled tighter. 'Daniel!' she begged.

He lifted himself off her, and she whimpered, grasping at his shoulders to hold him closer, afraid he was leaving her. He braced himself above her with one hand on the mattress and, hips still moving, slid a finger between them, rubbing her, finding the heart of her.

Jess screamed again as the tension exploded. She arched her hips and held her breath, trying to hold on to the glorious sensation.

He moved his hand away from her, bracing himself with both hands on the mattress as his hips moved faster and faster, until finally he flung his head up, groaning, as his body pulsed in release. He collapsed against her and sighed.

'Can I stop now?' he whispered. She laughed.

He withdrew gently, leaned over the side of the bed and dropped the used condom into the trash can. Then he lay down and nuzzled his nose up to her ear, pressed his lips against her neck. When she shifted, just a little,

257

he put his leg across her thighs and wrapped his arm across her chest, cupping her breast, as if to make sure she didn't leave him.

She was glad he wasn't the type of man who turned away from a woman as soon as he was done. He was obviously a sensitive and caring lover, who wanted to share with her the gradual easing of the passion they'd shared.

The delicious aftershocks quivering through her body were somehow better with him still holding her close.

'That was wonderful.' She trailed her fingertips down his spine and waited for him to answer. 'Daniel?'

She twisted her head to an awkward angle so she could see his face.

Daniel had fallen asleep.

He gradually became aware of a series of soft thuds and rustlings. Even with his face buried in the pillow, he knew right away he wasn't in his own bed. He slid a hand out to his side, searching for Jess, but the bed was empty.

He turned his head on the pillow and opened his eyes.

She was tiptoeing toward the door, dressed, hat and coat in hand, the cats at her heels.

'What time is it?' he asked as he rolled over, then sat up. He put his bare feet on the floor and flinched. 'Ow, that's cold!'

She froze mid-step, then cautiously looked at him over her shoulder. 'You're awake.'

'Almost.' He flipped back the sheet and stood up to stretch some of the kinks from his spine. Lord, he felt stiff. Daniel grinned as he remembered what they'd done in the night.

Jess had averted her eyes and he realized she was shy about his nudity. Little prude, he thought tenderly. She'd get used to seeing him like this eventually, but it was rather sweet. And arousing, he thought, as he felt himself responding to her, to memories of making love with her.

He walked up behind her and slid his arms around her waist. 'Good morning, honey.' He slid his hands up to cup her breasts, his fingertips massaged her hardening nipples, and bent his head to kiss the side of her neck. She trembled. 'Come back to bed.'

'I . . .' She blushed and cleared her throat. 'I've got to go to work.'

'How can I convince you?' He slid one hand down across her stomach to stroke back and forth between her legs. She had to be aware of his erection pressing against her bottom.

'I'm sorry I fell asleep last night. What a waste of a night when we could have been . . .' He whispered all the erotic thoughts he'd been having about her since they'd met, thoroughly arousing them both.

Her arms went loose at her sides and she dropped the coat and hat. He could hear her breathing grow as uneven as his own and her heart was beating fast under his hand.

Daniel swept her up into his arms and carried her back to bed.

'Good mornin', sleepyhead,' Sophy sang out when Jess finally arrived at the office.

'Morning.' She hurried by Sophy's desk without looking up, hoping to avoid any conversation about why she was late. She was so confused and embarrassed, the last thing she wanted right now was for Sophy to find out she'd been with Daniel all night.

Where and how had she lost her common sense?

'You were supposed to call me last night and tell me what you found out at dinner.'

'Shh, Harvey's going to hear you. He's not supposed to know I'm doing this, remember?'

'He's not here. He's feeling better, so he went down to the public library to do some research.' Sophy followed Jess into her office and waited, arms crossed, while Jess hung up her hat and coat. 'He doesn't have a clue what we're doing. Yet. You know we can't hide it from him for long.'

'I know.' She yanked on the cord to raise the blinds. She needed some fresh air.

'I called your place this morning but you'd already left, according to the nice man who answered your phone.'

Jess's hand stilled in the act of opening the window. She groaned and closed her eyes, resting her forehead on the cool glass.

'Invited Daniel for breakfast, did we? And then left

him there to lock up? What happened, did you get first dibs on the shower?'

'I'm not going to talk about it, Sophy.'

'Are you going to tell Harvey you broke one of his rules and got involved with a client?'

'No, I am not!' Jess realized she was shouting and dropped into her chair. 'I'm sorry. I'm tired. Besides, I won't have to tell Harvey, he'll probably know it the minute he sees me.'

Sophy put her hand on Jess's shoulder. 'I know I teased you about Daniel, sweetheart, but you'll be careful, won't you? I don't want to see you hurt.'

'I'm going to get his case finished and that'll be the end of it. I already know he's wants a wife and children and the station wagon in the suburbs. He knows I don't. So we'll enjoy each other and when it's over, it's over.'

'It's never that easy, Jess.'

'I didn't say it would be easy. But that's the way it's going to be, an enjoyable interlude for both of us. In the meantime, let's get to work. How are the background checks going? I told Daniel we'd have a report for him on Wednesday morning.'

'Nothing so far. I just have two more to do.'

'Great. While you finish, I'll see what I can find out about Sarah Graff, aka Sally de Graf. Daniel's counting on me.'

Daniel tried to look like he was paying attention to the speaker, but it was tough going. Now Anna was home

261

from the hospital and feeling better, he'd intended to spend the evening helping Jess track down some information and then all night making love to her.

But Ruth had called, upset. Ian Blake had dumped her for a political aide and she needed an escort to a dinner honoring the retirement of the Deputy Attorney-General.

So here he was, sitting with two hundred and fifty people, listening as the man's friends and enemies praised his years of service. Some were earnest, some were dull, some were both. One or two were witty enough to give the evening a spark. He leaned over and whispered in Ruth's ear, 'What time was this supposed to be over?'

'Shush.' She frowned.

The chair creaked when Daniel leaned back, trying to get comfortable. He hoped they would run into Ian Blake on the way out of this place, just so his fist could run into the man's face. Partly because he'd hurt Ruth but, since he figured she was better off without him, mostly for his own satisfaction.

After all, it was Blake's fault he was sitting here in an overly warm room instead of where he wanted to be, playing assistant detective and making love with Jess.

If he could, he'd have slipped out for a breath of fresh air. As it was, Ruth's position and reputation ensured they were seated center front and he would have had to walk out with the entire room as an audience.

He looked around, idly wondering how many of the

guests he knew, when he caught sight of a long-legged woman dressed in a sexy French maid's costume, her short black dress complete with white frilly apron and ruffled slip. Her hair was bundled into a messy top knot crowned by a little white cap. She was flitting along the side of the room, pausing behind each pillar to eye the crowd before she moved on.

He wasn't the only one who'd noticed her. The occupants of the tables she passed stared after her, whispering among themselves. He had to smile. Who would have the audacity to come to a formal affair like this dressed in a tiny little burlesque costume?

He was admiring the woman's world-class legs when it suddenly struck him. He recognized those legs.

She wouldn't . . .

Who was he kidding? Jess would do anything, given what she considered to be sufficient reason.

He watched while Jess worked her way closer to the front of the room, wondering what she was up to. Eventually she darted behind the nearest pillar and peered around it. She saw he was looking at her and gestured urgently for him to join her.

'I think you'd better go before the whole room is watching her instead of the speaker,' Ruth whispered wryly. 'Don't bother coming back, big brother. I'll be fine now, I just didn't want to walk in alone while Ian was supposed to be here with his new girlfriend.'

'Are you sure you're okay?' She nodded and he leaned over to kiss her cheek. 'Thanks, sis. I'll call you tomorrow.'

Daniel walked quickly to where Jess waited impatiently. She started to speak but he shook his head and hustled her out of a side door. They burst through a service entrance into the kitchens where he wrapped his arms around her waist and kissed her.

'First, I have to thank you for rescuing me. Then you can explain why you're here and why you're dressed in this.'

'No time for that now,' she said. 'Where's your car?'

'I had the valet service park it when we arrived so I imagine it's in the garage.'

A white-jacketed employee of the hotel tapped Daniel's shoulder. 'Excuse me. You're not supposed to be in here.'

Jess grabbed the guy's sleeve. 'Do you know a really fast way to the lobby?'

'Well, sure, but it's for employees only.'

Jess beamed at the man while she tugged Daniel down so she could whisper in his ear. 'Bribe him. We've got to get out of here.'

He obediently slipped the man a ten-dollar bill. The employee made it disappear so fast Daniel couldn't tell which pocket he'd put it in. 'This way,' he said, and pointed to their left.

Jess grabbed Daniel's hand and urged their guide to go faster several times until they were running through the hotel, slowing when they reached occupied sections, then speeding up again.

He was glad they didn't pass any other employees, Daniel thought as he pounded after her. She'd probably have told him to bribe all of them and in a hotel this size, he'd soon run out of money. Finally the guy shoved open a soundproof door to the lobby.

Jess hurried Daniel over to the valet stand, requested his car, and made him bribe the valet so they'd get top-speed service.

Once they were finally seated in the Jaguar, Daniel turned the engine on but looked at her instead of driving away. 'What's going on, Jess?'

'I arranged to be a waitress at a party Sarah Graff attended tonight.'

'Which explains the outfit.'

'The male owner of the catering company insists all his female staff dress like this. Macho idiot.'

Daniel smiled at the disdain in her voice. 'And Graff was there?'

'I overheard her making arrangements to meet a man at one a.m. at her townhouse. She was giving him the address and directions.'

'You hustled me out of the hotel to tell me about her sex life?' Daniel felt totally baffled.

'Of course not. He asked her if she had the promised items and they started arguing about her fee. I got the impression he hasn't paid her what he promised and she'd refused to hand over most of her information until he did. I think it means she's still got your stuff and if we get there first, we can get it from her.'

'I'm curious. How much did they agree to pay her?'

'A couple of hundred thousand. Now, either get the

car moving or I'll drive. I've already wasted too much time looking for you. If I hadn't promised you'd be in on this, I would have gone alone. She's still at the same address as when you were dating her. Do you remember how to get there?'

Daniel shifted gears and drove. 'You said you think we can get it all back? How?'

'With smoke and mirrors and Harvey's help. He's going to meet us there but for this to work, you have to stay out of sight.' She tugged the lace cap off her hair and tossed it into the back seat. The apron followed. 'Your job is to keep watch and warn us when the real guy shows up.'

'Just a sec.' Daniel shifted gears, smoothly working the clutch and the brakes, weaving his way through a traffic jam at Howe and Georgia. Once they were clear, he stomped his foot down on the accelerator again. 'Okay, go on.'

'When we get there, Harvey and I are going to pretend we were sent by the guy because he couldn't come himself. I'm the messenger, Harvey is the boss's enforcer.'

She released her seatbelt, then reached up under her skirt, grabbed the ruffled half-slip and began wiggling it down over her hips. By the time she was able to pull the slip off over her feet, the hem of the dress was around her waist.

'Will Graff believe it?' He shifted gears again, trying to concentrate on threading his way through the mass of pedestrians jaywalking across Robson Street, rather

266

than watching her. He glanced at his watch. Twenty minutes to go.

'Yeah, I think so.' Jess smoothed the skirt of the black dress back down over her thighs and refastened her seatbelt. 'She let him know she didn't like his habit of sending underlings to conduct his business with her. She can be quite snooty, can't she?'

'I guess so. I never really noticed.'

'You wouldn't. She was playing a role when she was with you and acting like a snob would have spoiled the image. Got a comb?'

'In the glove compartment.'

Jess released the catch and rustled through his registration papers until she came up with a small make-up bag. Inside she found a brush, a comb, two lipsticks, and a purse-sized perfume spray.

'These yours?' She looked in his direction, her eyes sparkling with amusement.

'The Sisters keep it in my car for emergencies. Not me.'

'What a relief.' She removed the elastic supporting her topknot and ruthlessly dragged the comb through her hair until it was hanging in a smooth curtain. She held up one of the lipsticks. 'Think they'd mind if I used this?'

'Go for it.'

'When you get to Graff's, park across the street and down a couple just in case she's watching out the window.' When she flipped down the visor the little light imbedded in the mirror frame came on.

Daniel's body responded as he watched her outline her mouth in blood-red. This was the most dangerous driving he'd done in his life.

She zipped the case and stored it away, then reached up, opened the cover for the ceiling light, and loosened the bulb. 'Don't want anyone to be able to identify us when we open the car doors.'

'We're here.' Daniel maneuvered the car into a narrow space and turned it off. When he looked at her he was amazed at how much she'd changed her appearance with so little. The woman was a bloody chameleon. 'What now?'

'Let's go find Harvey.'

When Daniel walked around the car to meet Jess she smiled up at him and winked.

'Pssst!' The sibilant hail came from the bushes beside a townhouse almost directly across the street from Graff's. 'Over here.'

Daniel followed Jess around to the side yard. Teeth gleamed in the darkness as a man smiled and moved out of the shadows. He was dressed completely in black, even his shirt and tie. A black slouch hat, pulled low over one eye, effectively hid half of his face.

'I thought you weren't going to make it in time,' he whispered. 'You must be Daniel.' They shook hands.

'Could you get the stuff we need?' Jess asked.

Harvey showed Jess a metal briefcase. 'Everything's inside.'

'Good.' Jess kept her voice low. 'What have you got

for Daniel in case Graff's real client shows up before we're done?'

'Cats.' He handed Daniel a small tube. 'Stay here in the bushes. The people who own this place are vacationing so you don't need to worry about being seen as long as you're careful. If you have to warn us, blow in there –' he pointed to one end of the tube '– and it'll make an awful noise, like a couple of cats in heat.'

'Give the branches a shake at the same time, just in case he's suspicious about the sound. He'll think he saw an animal moving in the bush,' Jess said.

Daniel turned the gadget over in his hand, then closed his fist around it. 'Let me get this straight. You two are going to go in there and somehow convince her to cooperate. I get to stand out here and pretend to be a cat in heat?'

'That's about it,' Harvey said. He grinned.

'If she sees you, Daniel, this won't work,' Jess said. 'The key is to make her believe we are who we say we are. We have to get it done before her client shows up.'

'What are you going to do about the money they owe her?'

Harvey hefted the briefcase. 'All taken care of. Two hundred thousand in Sophy's play money.'

'Play money? Won't Graff know it's fake?'

'Not the stuff Sophy makes,' Jess said. 'Most people can't tell, which is why we only use thousand-dollar bills. This way Graff can't pass it off on some innocent shopkeeper.'

'Sophy's look real except they only have three or

four different serial numbers because it's copied. Only a very careful mark or a bank teller would notice,' Harvey said. 'Plus the gold square looks real enough as long as you don't look at in the sunlight.'

'What if she does notice? She might be armed.'

'We're safe enough since the deal's happening at night. It only has to satisfy her long enough to get us out the door. And there's always the enforcer here –' she pointed her thumb at Harvey, who grinned '– to protect me.'

Daniel opened his mouth to protest, but Jess pressed her fingers against his lips.

'Stop fussing. We don't have any more time to talk about it now, but I promise everything is going to be okay.' She kissed him, then turned to Harvey. 'It's show time.'

Jess crossed the grass to the sidewalk. She stood still, breathing deeply for a moment or two, changing before his eyes into what even he would say looked like a cold, determined businesswoman.

'Isn't she magnificent?' Harvey murmured. 'Lots of professional actors would pay big bucks for her talent.'

'How does she do that?'

'Posture, mostly. How a person stands and moves gives subconscious messages to the people who see them. Jess has the knack of projecting a personality without saying a word. She also has an exceptional memory.'

He suddenly ceased talking and Daniel look down to see Harvey studying him.

'You don't look like a stupid or cruel man,' he said, 'despite those eyebrows.'

Daniel was startled. 'I hope not.'

'Jess is a very special woman.'

'Yes, she is.' He felt as if Harvey was warning him. But why? 'Are you trying to tell me some –?'

'Tate!' she called.

'Gotta go.' Harvey moved into position slightly behind Jess, walking to her right. He put one hand inside his jacket, as if he carried a gun under his left arm.

They crossed the street and strode quickly down the sidewalk and up Graff's driveway. The door opened after they rang the doorbell, spilling light out on to the porch. Daniel instinctively stepped back and he was glad he had when, after Jess and Harvey moved inside, Graff moved out on to the porch and peered down the road in both directions.

The door shut, leaving him standing in the bushes with an absurd noisemaker in his hand. When he told Jess he wanted to be part of the investigation, somehow he'd imagined a more active and interesting role for himself than this. Not to mention he hated to see Jess taking chances while he was sitting outside.

If something went wrong, by the time he knew about it he'd be too late to help her.

Daniel moved closer to the porch and propped himself against the railing. The address number on the townhouse caught his eye. Twenty-nine. As he recalled, Graff's address was twenty-six.

He was reminded of a show he'd seen on television recently and he began to wonder.

What if he loosened one screw on the nine and it fell down so it looked like a six? And what if he did the same at Graff's so the six looked like a nine?

Jess had heard Graff give her client the address, so chances were he'd never been here. When he showed up, he'd go to the wrong house. When no one answered, he'd eventually leave. He might even think Graff had doublecrossed him. The only potential problem Daniel could see was if the guy could tell the number had been recently moved. Best to start on this set of numbers, just in case it didn't work.

Daniel took out his keys and flipped them around to the small screwdriver. He'd have to tell Hannah she was right, it had come in handy.

Jess stepped out of Sarah Graff's townhouse, shook the woman's hand, and gave Harvey the full briefcase to carry to the car. She didn't allow herself to smile until they were away from the house.

'You sure she gave us everything?' she whispered to Harvey.

'Are you kidding? Once you got started on her, she was too scared to hold anything back. Maybe next time I should be the messenger and you be the enforcer.'

'She dragged it out so long, I expected her real client to show up. I wonder what happened to him?'

Jess's heels clicked on the pavement as they turned on to the sidewalk. As they passed the neighbor's laurel hedge, she relaxed, knowing they weren't in view from Graff's windows until they crossed the street to get the car.

'I know what happened.' The low-voiced, amused comment came from behind the hedge.

Jess and Harvey stumbled to a halt. 'What?'

Daniel stepped out into the moonlight, casually swinging his key chain. 'I said, I know what happened to her client.'

Jess had used up her store of patience dealing with Graff. When Daniel didn't say anything else, she quietly exploded. 'Well, are you going to explain yourself, mister? You were supposed to be in the bushes across the street.'

'Sure, if you'll bear with me for a moment.' He peeked back around the hedge at Graff's house.

Jess came and looked too. 'What are you watching?'

'The lights. Ah, ha!' he exclaimed when the last upstairs light was doused and the townhouse was dark.

Daniel walked quickly across the grass and up the porch stairs. He did something to the front of her porch with his key chain and it took Jess a minute to figure out what she was seeing.

'He changed her address,' Harvey breathed in her ear. 'Clever. Very clever.'

'You think so?' Jess snapped.

Daniel rejoined them behind the hedge. 'Just a couple more minutes. I'll meet you at the car.'

Jess and Harvey waited for him by the front fender

of the Jaguar while he sprinted up to the porch of Graff's vacationing neighbors. This time she could see his movements more clearly as he pushed the nine back up to it's correct position and replaced the screw.

When he joined them, Harvey shook his hand and grinned. 'Like I told Jess, that was clever. If you ever want to change jobs, give me a call.'

'Don't you think we should leave before someone sees us?' she asked pointedly.

'Yeah, you'd better go.' He handed Daniel the briefcase. 'It's all here. Just give the case to Jess when you're done with it.'

'Need a ride, Harvey?' he asked, as he locked it in the trunk.

'Nope, I can walk. My car's stashed in the next block. I gotta get back to work on my own case.'

'Thanks for your help,' Daniel said.

Harvey waved and trotted away.

After they were inside the Jaguar Jess fixed the ceiling light, then watched the traffic out of her side window as they drove off. Neither said anything until finally she couldn't stand the silence any longer.

'That was really stupid. Why didn't you stay with the plan?'

'I couldn't just sit outside and wait while you took chances for me. You should be glad I did it.'

'Yeah, sure.'

'Her client arrived less than ten minutes behind you with two of his own enforcers. You would have been exposed as impostors, and all for nothing because they would have completed their deal. Who knows what would have happened to you and Harvey?'

'We're professionals, you are not. Remember that in future, okay?'

'Okay.' He stopped at a light and leaned over to brush a kiss across her mouth. 'But it was fun. Thanks, Jess.'

Jess cupped her hands around his jaw and held him still for a real kiss. A car horn blared to let them know they were blocking traffic and they leaped apart, laughing. Daniel shifted gears and stepped on the gas.

'Harvey says it's all there,' she said. 'Computer disks, audio tapes, files.'

'What's to prevent her talking about this business?'

'As soon as she tries to deposit the phony money at a bank, at the very least it will be confiscated. They might arrest her for passing counterfeit. She can't implicate us because she doesn't know who we are. She can't talk much or the police will know she's also into corporate espionage.'

'Would she have kept copies?'

'I doubt it because, ironic as it may seem, a client would see it as a breach of confidentiality. That would be bad for business because her profession relies on word of mouth from satisfied clients. Besides, your little trick with the address will annoy her client so much, he'll probably refuse to have anything more to do with her.'

'So . . .' Daniel's voice faded as he stopped the Jaguar in front of Mrs Martelli's.

'I guess that's that. Your Institute is secure and our business is done.' Jess undid her seatbelt and reached into the back seat for the frilly apron, slip, and cap. 'Sophy will send the bill to your office tomorrow.'

'Jess –'

She clipped the little white cap on top of her head and looked up at him from beneath fluttering eyelashes. 'Can I interest Monsieur in zee leetle bon bon?'

Daniel started to grin. 'Yes. Please.'

CHAPTER 13

'Hey, Jess, look at this.'

She looked up from the cheese grater to where Daniel was looking at something he'd taken from the briefcase. Last night Harvey had shoved the stuff in quickly and Daniel had decided to sort through it while she made them her specialty for breakfast, a single omelet the size of a frying pan, stuffed with every goody she could find in her fridge.

Sadly enough, there were no shrimp because Nick and Nora had insisted on eating them all as soon as she took them out of the fridge.

She'd been grating the cheese and whipping the eggs, enjoying the early morning laziness and a sense of general well-being after a great night of sex. It all vanished in a flash flood of panic. Daniel was holding a piece of paper covered in writing.

And he expected her to read it.

'I can't leave this.' She quickly poured the eggs into the frying pan. 'Tell me about it later.'

She knew he kept talking as he sorted but she

277

couldn't hear the words because his voice was drowned out by the fear roaring through her body. Her hands began to shake when she realized how close she'd come to disaster.

She braced herself against the counter because reality hit with a blinding flash, as it so often did. When it happened, she thought, it would be an ordinary moment just like this one, with no warning.

She couldn't bear for him to look at her like she was stupid. She'd been fooling herself about what would happen when he found out. As hard as it had been to endure that reaction in the past, Daniel's disappointment and rejection would devastate her.

But would it be better to tell him herself, to have it end at a moment she chose? Or should she let it ride, like any gambler addicted to the game? Because she couldn't fool herself any longer. Maybe she'd managed to keep herself from loving him, but she was addicted to him.

Jess's nose twitched and she suddenly awoke to the fact the eggs were about to burn. After a couple minutes of flurried activity involving cheese, ham, and onions, she managed to salvage breakfast.

She cut the giant omelet in two and flipped each half on to a plate.

She carried the plates over to the sofa where he was working. 'Breakfast.'

'Thanks. Mmm, smells great.' He closed the briefcase and balanced the plate on top.

'Daniel? Have you ever played roulette?' She sat down

beside him, nestled in the corner of the sofa with her legs curled beneath her. She balanced her plate on the arm.

'Roulette? Sure, once or twice. Why?' He forked up a mouthful of omelet. 'Tastes great, too.'

'You know how sometimes people get on a winning streak and they let it ride, risking everything, every time? Hoping they'll end up a really big winner, knowing they're more likely to lose it all?'

'Yeah. Always seemed pretty stupid to me. Why?'

'Just wondering.'

Jess ran into Finders Keepers, coat tails flying behind her. For the last week she'd been flying and she didn't see an end in sight.

'Any calls for me?' she asked as she ran past Sophy's desk.

'Three and I've got some information on –'

'Not right now, okay? I've got tons to do before the new client arrives in thirty minutes. If you put it on a tape, I'll listen to it in the car later.'

Jess tossed her coat and hat on the sofa, plopped down at her desk, and pushed the play button on her message machine. She didn't realize Sophy had followed her in until she reached out and stopped the machine.

'You're going to talk to me now.' Sophy sat on the edge of the desk, her expression solemn. 'This can't go on, Jess. You've taken on too much. Even I'm having trouble keeping everything straight. I never know where you are or which case you're working on.'

'If this is about getting you an assistant –'

'No, it's not. It's about you, burning the candle at both ends. For the last week you've been seeing Daniel every night, yet taking on more clients than ever. Harvey's no help, what with spending all his time on Concept House.'

'We need the money, Sophy. You know that.'

'Not this bad. Harvey can darned well stay here or get a cheaper cottage.'

Jess realized he hadn't told Sophy the whole truth. It was at times like this Jess really wished she could let go with a really big, bad curse to relieve her feelings. Well, she sure as heck wasn't going to risk Sophy's wrath by covering up for him.

'He's already put the entire retainer from Concept House down as a non-refundable deposit on the cottage. If he can't come up with the rest of the money by June, he'll lose his deposit. He can't drop the case because he can't pay them back the retainer.'

Sophy looked stricken for a minute, then her lips firmed. 'Men! I've wasted enough time trying to be subtle if he's going to go around doing stupid things like that. If this whole thing turns out to be a mid-life crisis, he's going to have another type of crisis on his hands!'

'You're going to talk to him?'

'I'm going to do more than *talk* to him.' She frowned. 'Don't imagine this gets you off the hook, young lady. You're trying to keep too many balls in the air.'

'At the moment I don't have any choice.' Jess tapped her finger against the desk. 'How about we hire some help? No, not Gwen. A professional.'

'That would be expensive.'

'I've got some money saved up. I might as well spend it keeping Harvey's skin whole long enough for him to come to his senses.'

'Whoever we hire can't follow Harvey around to keep an eye on him. When he spots the tail, he'll hit the roof.'

'Then we'll get him to follow Hellmann and I can keep an eye on Harvey while I take care of the other cases.'

'It might work,' Sophy said slowly. 'From what you told me last night, Hellmann hasn't noticed you.'

'I've decided we should know what Scratten is up to, too. After all, he's the one who started this by hiring Harvey.'

'Scratten?'

'I don't think Harvey checked into him thoroughly enough before he took the case.'

'Who should we hire?'

'Why don't you give Fenleck Associates a call? Harvey thinks they'd be the place for me to work after he leaves. It'd be a chance for me to see what they can do.'

'I'll get on it right away.'

'Give them my cell-phone number and make it clear the operatives are to phone right away if there's any developments,' Jess said. 'Was there something else you wanted to talk to me about?'

'Yes. I've finished the background checks for Daniel's employees.'

'And . . . ?'

'All clear except for one.'

Sophy's ominous expression got Jess worried.

'Darn, it's not Gwen, is it? Because I think you'd really like her.'

'No, Gwen's okay. As a matter of fact, I met her for lunch today. I got the impression she doesn't like working at the Institute. She's thrilled by the idea of working for a real detective. And, no, I didn't tell her she'd already met one of the detectives.'

'She doesn't fit in at the Institute.'

'She'll be fine here. Which is why I hired her to help me with the paperwork. I know you wanted her to work with Harvey but I don't think it's a good idea right at first.'

'You did what?' Jess fell back in her chair.

'I hired her. She's starting as soon as she works out her two weeks' notice at the Institute.'

'Okay. That's settled, then.' Jess wondered how Harvey was going to feel about having no say in this but decided to leave any explaining to Sophy. Harvey had done enough surprising things himself lately so he couldn't really complain. 'So, which employee has the problem?'

'Chris Houston.'

'Jumpin' juniper! I knew there was something wrong about that woman. What did you find out?'

'Her personal references were phony so I went back to the records at the university where she got her degree. It's like she didn't exist before she enrolled. There is no family history.'

'She's using an alias?' Whatever Jess had been expecting, this wasn't it.

'Or she deliberately hid her past to become a different person. Another odd thing. After she got her Bachelor of Science degree, her entire career was spent in hospital administration. Then she switched to working for Daniel, which is a completely different field.'

'Unusual but not unheard of.'

'According to one of her former co-workers, Ms Houston left very suddenly last June with no explanation.'

'June?' Another coincidence. As she recalled, June was the month an unknown woman investigated Daniel. 'Keep looking for info on her, Sophy.'

'Are you going to tell Daniel?'

'Tell him what? She didn't lie about her qualifications to get the job. We didn't find evidence she's in cahoots with Sarah Graff.'

'I don't think that's a good idea, Jess. You're already hiding your suspicions about Warren Hellmann. Daniel seems to be the kind of man who –'

The outside door banged open. 'Yoo hoo! Sophy? Are you here? Did you find my cousins yet?'

Jess and Sophy both rolled their eyes.

'Just a minute, Gertrude,' Sophy called. 'As for you, young lady, you'd better think carefully before you add one more ball to your juggling act.'

* * *

'What a beautiful day.' Anna's eyes were bright as Daniel helped her out of the car, her gaze darting from person to place to plant. 'The campus is always lovely but on a bright spring morning, it's truly special.'

He finished making arrangements to meet Anna's nurse in an hour, thanked her for driving her to the university, and shut the car door. 'Why the summons, Anna?'

'Is that what you think of my lunch invitation, I summoned you?' She put on a hurt look but it melted into a smile when he shook his head. 'I thought of it more as a command performance, myself.'

'Are you sure you're well enough for this?' He held out his elbow and she wrapped both hands around his arm as they began to stroll along West Mall.

'I was in town for my specialist's appointment anyway. I remembered it was your day to lecture at U.B.C. and thought it would be nice to have lunch together. That's all. Oh, look . . .'

She pointed to a cluster of kids lounging on the steps of the Student Union Building, enjoying the warm sun and sharing boxes of pizza. Several were reading textbooks, a few were scattering bread crumbs for the birds. 'That looks like fun.'

'We're not eating lunch on the steps of Sub, Anna. *I'm* too old for that.'

'I'm not really hungry, Daniel. Is there someplace we could sit outside and just enjoy the day?'

He worried about Anna getting chilled if they sat

outside but he didn't want to disappoint her. 'I'm scheduled to give a two-hour lecture to three hundred commerce students this afternoon. I can't imagine doing it on an empty stomach.

'I suggest a compromise. There's a café not far from here where the chef makes an excellent tortilla salad. We're early enough to get a seat next to the big windows looking out on a beautiful garden.'

'Sounds wonderful, dear.'

'Great.' He took out his cell-phone. 'I'll phone ahead to tell them we're coming.'

While they walked, the university operator forwarded his call to the café so he could make the reservation. Anna exclaimed over the scolding squirrels and the raucous ravens and the pretty green of the new growth on the evergreens. She even found amusement in watching the seagulls scavenge their lunch in the trash cans.

'Look at that, Daniel! Have you ever seen a rhododendron so large? And the azaleas are beautiful this year.'

It was only a short distance but Daniel could feel her gradually leaning harder on his arm until by the time they arrived at the café, he was supporting most of her weight.

Why was she gadding about this way? She should be at home, not exhausting herself walking around the campus and worrying him sick.

In the café she complimented the waitress on the early pansies in the round concrete planters on the patio outside their entryway. Daniel was glad when he finally got her settled at a table with a menu.

After they placed their orders, she smiled at him. 'This place is lovely.'

'I'm glad you like it. The food's good, too.'

'I know how you met Jess. No –' she held up her hand, '– don't worry, I'm not going to lecture you about those other women. From what I understand, the Sisters have done enough of that already.'

'You have no idea,' he said fervently.

'I wanted to tell you how much I liked Jess. She's special.'

'I agree. We've been spending quite a bit of time together and she has a lot of qualities I admire.' Not to mention she's sexy as hell, he thought.

'But . . . ?'

'No buts.'

Anna reached out to cover his hand where it lay on the table. When he felt the slight tremor in her fingers, he had to fight the urge to pull away.

'Something is troubling you. If you talk about it, perhaps you'll see it more clearly.'

Daniel decided to talk it over with Anna. She always gave him good advice.

'Lately I've wondered if Jess could be hiding something from me. I don't know what or why, it's just a feeling. It's probably all in my imagination.'

'You need to talk to her, son. I know you really care about her and doubts always need to be nipped in the bud before they grow into obstacles.'

'I'm not sure –'

'Thought I recognized you two. Saw you through the window. Mind if I join you?' Warren didn't wait for an invitation before he pulled a chair out from the table. He sat down and used a table napkin to wipe sweat from his face. 'This is going to drive me crazy.'

'What's going on, Warren?' Daniel asked.

Warren leaned close to Daniel to whisper in his ear. Daniel didn't know why he bothered. The man's whisper was always loud enough to be heard two tables away.

'See the guy over by the door? He's wearing a black raincoat.'

Anna and Daniel started to twist around in their seats so they could look.

'Careful! Don't let him know I'm on to him.'

'On to him?' Daniel managed to catch a glimpse of a mousy guy in a black raincoat hovering behind the hanging plants that formed a barrier between the tables and the entryway. 'What's going on, Warren?'

'That guy's been following me for two days at least, maybe more. I can't even use a public washroom without seeing him.'

Daniel had to smile. 'You're imagining things.'

'No, I bloody well am not!' Warren was still perspiring freely and wiped the napkin across his face again.

'Try to calm down, Warren,' Anna said. 'You don't look well. Please remember your high blood pressure.'

'How would anyone look if they were being stalked?'

'Daniel, maybe you should go talk to that man, set Warren's mind at ease.'

'Tell him to leave me alone or I'll call the cops,' Warren said.

Daniel looked at the concern on Anna's face and sighed. Embarrassing or not, if she wanted him to approach a complete stranger to ask the man why he was stalking Warren, he would.

Daniel slowly pushed away from the table. He looked down at Warren. 'Are you sure you want me to do this?' he asked.

'Damned right!'

He shrugged. During the much too short walk through the tables, he tried to think of a tactful way to bring up the subject but resigned himself to enduring an embarrassing moment. As he approached, the man in the black raincoat appeared intent on what looked like a perfectly ordinary fern.

'Excuse me. My friend would like you to stop following him. He intends to call the police if you don't leave him alone.'

The guy appeared astonished. 'Following him? I don't understand. Please assure him,' he looked at Warren. 'I'm just examining this wonderful fern while I wait for my lunch date.' He glanced at his watch. 'It appears I've been stood up again. Women!' He shook his head ruefully. 'I'd better get back to work.'

He pulled open the door and left quickly.

The guy didn't notice the belt from his raincoat had

caught in the closing door and he walked away without it. Daniel scooped it up and looked over at Anna and Warren. 'It was all a misunderstanding. I'll be right back to explain.'

Daniel pulled open the door, expecting to see the guy. The patio and the lawn beyond was empty in all directions. Where could he have gotten to? He walked to the edge of the patio and looked up and down the road both ways, but saw no one in a black raincoat.

He shrugged. Simple enough to leave it with the café's hostess. The guy would probably come back for it once he'd missed it.

Daniel had his hand on the door when he heard the guy's voice and saw him standing behind a cement pagoda at the edge of the patio, talking on a cell phone.

Daniel walked over, intending to get his attention and hand over the belt, but backed away when he heard what the guy was saying.

'Hellmann made me. I'm sorry, Jess. I fed them a story and left. Do you want me to call in another operative? Within the hour. Fine, I'll hang around until he gets here. Hey, I heard you're going to come work with us when Harvey retires. No? Too bad.'

Daniel clamped a lid on the rage simmering deep inside his gut. He wanted answers; results came from a cool brain, not hot emotions.

So, he'd been right to be uneasy about Jess.

Had someone written 'easy mark' on a big sign over his head that could only be seen by women? Kind of ironic if Jess discovered the truth about those other women, then proceeded to use him for her own ends.

He remembered the day the Sisters had invited her to dinner at Anna's. In hindsight he could see she'd been about to refuse the invitation when Mary mentioned Warren was coming. He had no idea why she was interested in his old mentor, but he would soon.

He unobtrusively dropped the belt back where he'd picked it up instead of at the hostess desk inside the café because he didn't want to draw attention to himself. He didn't want Jess's *friend* to wonder if he'd been overheard.

'Anna?' He stood behind the chair he'd sat in earlier. Sitting at his place was the crab salad he'd ordered an eon ago, or so it felt. His stomach churned; his appetite had vanished.

Anna looked up and smiled. 'Did you say it was a misunderstanding?'

'Yes. A big one. Something about a woman who let him down.'

'So Warren doesn't need to worry?'

'No.' He couldn't wait hours to confront Jess. He had to talk to her now. 'Look, something's come up at the office. Warren, would you like to eat lunch with Anna today? My treat.'

'Of course, my boy. I happen to love crab salad.'

'Are you okay, Daniel?' Anna asked.

'Yeah, sure. I'll call the nurse and ask her to pick you up here in forty-five minutes.'

'Yes, dear. I hope, whatever the problem, it turns out okay.' She held up her cheek for his kiss.

'So do I, Anna. You take it easy and I'll talk to you tomorrow.'

'Daniel!' she called after him. 'What about your lecture? Who's going to talk to those three hundred commerce students?'

Daniel forced a smile. 'Thanks for reminding me. I'll take care of it.'

He would have to give the lecture. He'd made the commitment, he wouldn't let them down. Daniel roamed the campus, thinking, while he waited.

Dealing with Jess would have to wait.

He thought about the time they'd spent in the jacuzzi tub in his apartment last night. They'd made love until the water was chilly and the floor awash. Afterward, cuddling together in his bed, she'd chattered about her day. He'd felt so sorry for her, damn him, for what she put herself through for the sake of the job.

He'd enjoyed the honesty they shared, congratulating himself that this time he'd chosen well.

Damn it all to hell. If she thought he would let her walk away now, she was in for a shock.

She'd been careful not to tell him exactly who she was investigating, but he knew exactly where to find her. He'd deal with her later, he promised himself. Later.

Jess shifted from foot to foot, trying to ease the burning in her soles. How did people do this all day, every day?

Reed-Howard, one of the highest of the city's high-end clothing stores, had a small problem. Ladies' lingerie, size extra large, was being stolen at an alarming rate and their own security staff didn't seem capable of stemming the flow.

Highly unacceptable to a new store manager who was still on probation with the owners. The manager, Carol, hired Jess to identify the thief and then arranged for her to get a job in gift wrapping, which was directly across from ladies' lingerie.

From there she'd discovered the culprit was Craig Lynch, head of security. She showed Carol how Lynch had been able to avoid detection because he knew all the hidden camera locations, then explained how to catch him red-handed by either having new cameras added or changing the angles of existing cameras, and presented her invoice for payment. That was yesterday.

Today Carol had decided Jess was the only one who could catch the crook in the act and make it stick for the police. She'd offered Jess double her normal rate if she'd follow through on the case, and triple if he was put in jail.

Which is why Jess had spent four hours yesterday and six today trying to wrap presents for the first time in her life, and wearing the uniform of the store's female staff, which included black pumps with three-inch heels. Her feet were killing her.

When she turned in her final bill for this case she was including a recommendation that store management and directors, men and women, have to stand one full shift in these cruel shoes before they made another employee do so.

With any luck her target would make his move soon so she could go home to soak her feet. Or maybe Daniel would massage her aching feet again, like last night. The thought almost made the pain seem worthwhile.

'Miss? Is my parcel done yet?'

Jess stuck one more piece of adhesive tape on the stubbornly wayward piece of ribbon.

'Sorry for the delay, ma'am,' she said and put the package down on the counter.

The elderly customer's doubtful gaze traveled from Jess, to the parcel, then back to Jess. 'That's not quite what I was expecting it to look like.'

Jess looked at her handiwork and flushed. It might not be a work of art but it was the best she could do and she had the paper cuts to prove it.

'Do you want me to try again, ma'am?'

'No, I think three times is enough.'

'Thanks for shopping at Reed-Howard,' Jess said, her attention already back on the lingerie racks as she slipped the parcel into a store bag and handed it to the customer.

She didn't see Daniel until he spoke. 'Jess.'

She looked up, her smile of welcome fading when she saw the bitter chill in his expression. 'Daniel. Is something wrong? Is it Anna?' She reached for his hand, where it gripped the counter edge, but he pulled away before she could touch him.

He didn't appear to hear her. 'Why did you deceive

293

me, Jess? Because I believed those other women, did you think it would be easy?' He closed his eyes, as if it pained him to look at her, and rubbed his eyebrow.

'I've been a fool, even thinking of marriage. I guess I shouldn't feel too bad, I've seen ample evidence of your talent for deception.'

So, the end had come, just as she'd feared. He didn't want her, she was too stupid for him. How had she betrayed herself? Or had someone told him she couldn't read? Who?

She linked her hands behind her back, determined not to let him see her pain. She wouldn't beg. She looked him straight in the eye.

'I'm sorry to find you're as shallow as all the others,' she said. 'I've been telling myself you were different, that you'd understand, that you cared enough it wouldn't matter.'

'I understand you used me.' His voice rose, drawing the attention of some nearby shoppers.

'You'd better leave, you're going to blow my case. I'll talk to you tonight.'

'I don't give a damn about your case,' he said, though he lowered his voice. 'Do you understand? I want to know why you're doing this and I want it to stop.'

'Fine. Consider it stopped. You don't have to see me again.'

He pointed to the store phone at her elbow. 'Call them now and cancel the surveillance.'

'The surveillance?' The sudden change in subject made her feel dizzy.

'It's useless to deny it. I was there when your *friend* called you at lunch time to report he'd been seen by Warren.'

'Warren? This is about Warren Hellmann?' Now she felt giddy with relief. He didn't know. Her secret was safe.

'You know it is.'

'Don't you think you're over-reacting?'

He planted his hands on the counter and leaned in close. 'I don't know what reason you have for hounding an old man with high blood pressure. I do know it's going to stop now.'

'You can't intimidate me, Daniel.' Jess stuck out her chin and glared back, refusing to retreat an inch. 'If you want to talk about it, I'll see you tonight. In the meantime, go away. I'm working.'

'Seems to me the cops might be interested in a detective who hassles innocent people.'

Hangers on the lingerie racks clattered to the floor and a cardboard display toppled. She looked up and saw Lynch running for the escalator. He must have been loitering among the racks and heard Daniel call her a detective.

'He heard you.' She jumped up on to the counter and shoved at Daniel's shoulder. 'Get out of my way.'

She slid down the other side of the glass case and took off after Lynch. She almost twisted her ankle at the top of the escalator so she kicked off the blasted shoes and sprinted down the moving stairs, her feet bare except for her pantyhose.

Vaguely she heard Daniel call her name. Tough. She didn't have time for him right now. 'Lynch! We already have you on camera. Stop!'

The big guy looked over his shoulder and pushed his way through the customers in front of him.

'Lynch! This is a waste of time!'

A few feet from the bottom he vaulted over the handrail and disappeared from sight. Jess grabbed on to the moving rail and leaned as far over the side as she could, catching a glimpse of him heading toward the back of the store.

The loading dock. He always parked his car beside the first bay in the darned loading dock.

As soon as she was close enough to the ground, she leaped over the side, too, and followed him. He was easy to track because his path through the crowded store was marked by the screams and outraged shouts of the people he knocked out of his way.

Jess could tell she was gaining on him. He might be bigger but she was faster. She gave up yelling for him to stop, saving her breath for running.

He disappeared through the swinging doors in the back wall. She followed him through only minutes later but he was already halfway across the echoing receiving area. He was shouting for someone to open the big door in the first bay. That proved she was right; he was going for his car.

'No!' she screamed but of course they scurried to

follow his orders. As far as they knew, he was head of security dealing with an emergency and she was a nobody. The motor engaged and slowly, majestically, the door moved upward.

Jess dug deep, found some more energy, and picked up speed. He looked back at her, ducked under the rising door, and headed toward the far side of the cement apron where he kept his car.

She thought of the triple fee she was about to lose, thanks to Daniel, because now she might not be able to catch him red-handed. She put her head down and threw herself into a flying tackle, grabbing him around the knees and bringing him down.

He shoved and kicked his way back to his feet but she sank her fingers into the fabric of his suit jacket and hung on. His jacket tore away from the lining, ripping open a hidden pouch between the two layers of fabric, and several pieces of expensive lingerie tumbled out.

'You stupid bitch, look what you've done.' Lynch pulled his meaty fist back to slug her, aiming for her face.

She scrambled sideways on all fours so the punch glanced off her shoulder and chest. Lynch swore and tried again but this time Daniel caught the punch with his own hand, wrapping his fingers around Lynch's fist.

When Lynch cursed and tried to kick Jess, Daniel squeezed. A minute later Lynch was cowering on the ground, begging him to release his hand.

Daniel ignored him. 'Are you okay?' he asked her.

She stood up cautiously, wincing as she became aware of bruises and sore muscles. The scrapes on her hands and knees were raw but not bleeding. Her pantyhose and store uniform were torn but her skin was relatively whole.

'No major damage,' she said. 'Thanks to you.'

He reached inside his pocket and pulled out a cell-phone, coolly ignoring the man sniveling at his feet. He held it out to her.

'Make the call or I'll let him go.'

CHAPTER 14

'Ha! Don't try to bluff me, Daniel,' Jess said. 'I know you too well. Besides, what makes you so sure Hellmann is innocent?'

'I've known him most of my life. He'd never do anything underhanded or illegal.'

'Plee-aase!' Lynch struggled to rise, then moaned and sank back to his knees.

'Quiet!' she hissed at him, then looked back at Daniel. 'How often do we hear the families and friends of criminals say what nice people they always seemed to be? People lie, or things happen and people change.'

'Not Warren.'

Another voice intruded on their conversation. 'Let Mr Lynch go and step away. Now.'

For the first time Daniel and Jess noticed they had collected an audience. Two young and very nervous security guards were standing just out of Daniel's reach but poised to attack. Beyond them a loose circle of employees and customers had gathered to watch the action.

'I can't. He'll run.'

'Let Mr Lynch go!'

'He can't, not until the police arrive.' Jess could tell they were wary of a man who could subdue their boss so easily but were also bravely determined to do what they thought was right.

'I'm a detective hired by your store manager to investigate a series of thefts. Call her, she'll vouch for me, for us.'

They either didn't listen or didn't believe her. One of the security guards stepped closer to Daniel but stopped when, sirens blaring, three police cars raced into the alley. They screeched to a halt, blocking the loading dock. The cops got out of their cars but remained behind the open doors.

Several drew their weapons while one gruff-voiced officer ordered Daniel to put down the object in his hand and back off.

'It's only a phone,' Daniel said and held it up by two fingers so they could see it clearly. 'Look, I'm going to hand it to her, okay? I don't want it to get wrecked if there's a scuffle when I let this bastard go.'

The officer agreed, warning him not to make any sudden moves.

Daniel extended his hand and gingerly dropped it into her palm. Once she had it and moved back, the police holstered their guns and some of the tension eased. Jess began to breathe easier.

'If they arrest me, you'd better call Tom. Looks like

I might need his help again,' he observed wryly. 'That never happened before I met you.'

'See? I told you things and people change.'

He scowled.

'Let go of his hand and back away,' the officer ordered.

'He's a thief and he'll run,' Daniel said. 'Maybe some of your officers should come up here first.'

The cop looked annoyed but followed his suggestion. Sure enough, as soon as Lynch's hand was released he tried to get away. After a short scuffle with police, he was once again pinned to the cement.

Two other officers held Daniel's arms.

'What's going on here? Let me pass.' Carol pushed her way through the crowd. 'Jess? What's going on?'

'Lynch found out I'm a detective and made a run for it. These officers need you to confirm Lynch is a thief and you'll be pressing charges. Then maybe they'll let Daniel go.'

'She's correct. I hired Jess to get evidence so we could have Lynch arrested,' Carol said.

Jess scooped up the garments that had fallen out when Lynch's jacket tore open and handed them to the police officer. 'There's the evidence. Daniel was helping me, so please let him go.'

'I can't do that, ma'am, until we have all the facts.'

'Then here is another fact you should consider. His brother-in-law is Lieutenant Tom Masters of the Vancouver Police. Now let him go.'

★ ★ ★

301

'Do you usually get that belligerent with cops?' Daniel held the door as Jess lowered herself into the front seat of the Jaguar. Tom had gone by Reed-Howard to pick it up on his way to the police station.

'Seems counter-productive,' he said, 'especially for a private detective. Don't you need to keep on their good side?'

'They had no reason to bring us down here. They were just being contrary.' She reached for the seatbelt, moaned and abandoned the attempt to fasten it around herself. 'I'm glad I didn't bring the Beetle today. Driving home would have been painful.'

'This time it was harder for Tom to smooth things over with the officers who brought us in for questioning.' He leaned in and fastened it for her.

She didn't comment but he saw how stiffly she moved. After the tumble she took tackling Lynch, she must be hurting bad. Sitting on a wooden, straight-backed chair in a police station for so long had to have made her body feel even worse.

'Don't go looking for any more trouble tonight, okay, guys?' Tom walked over to stand beside Daniel on the curb, trying not to grin. 'Mary and I have a date for dinner and a movie, without our boys. Another call from the station to rescue you would put a crimp in our evening.'

Jess gave Tom a look that said exactly what she thought of his attempt at humor.

Daniel thanked Tom before he walked around to climb into the driver's seat. As he turned the key in the ignition, Jess closed her eyes and relaxed back into the cushioned seat with a heartfelt sigh.

He moved out into the traffic, wondering. Where did his outrage go? He'd spent most of the last three hours furious with her. How could a few words from her make him question his own judgment?

Traffic slowed enough for him to look over and see if she was okay. She held the seatbelt away from her shoulder and chest with both hands, flinching at every bump in the road.

He figured it would give him nightmares for weeks to come whenever he remembered the way she'd flung herself at the knees of a mean bastard twice her size. She'd brought him down but it had cost her.

Daniel realized he couldn't worry about Warren right now. All he cared about was seeing Jess taken care of.

What she needed was a long hot soak to help those sore muscles. The boarding house only had a shared shower with limited hot water.

She could stretch out full length in the tub at his place and stay as long as she needed to, allowing the water jets to massage away some, if not all, of her aches and pains.

He tried not to think about the previous night when they'd shared the tub.

They were almost at his apartment before Jess opened her eyes and realized he wasn't taking her to her own home.

'I don't want to go to your place. I'm still mad at you.'

Daniel's hands tightened on the steering wheel. He didn't want to think or talk about Warren right now, he wanted to concentrate on Jess. He needed time to take another look at everything that happened today and figure out how he felt about it.

She could have been badly hurt today and it would have been his fault for letting Lynch know she was a detective.

'I suggest we table the subject until tomorrow, when you feel better.'

'You can drop me off at Sophy's or Harvey's.'

'You're going to my place. I'm taking care of you,' he said, flatly.

'Do you remember asking me if I thought it would be easy to deceive you because those other women had?' she asked in a dreamy tone.

'I don't want to talk about it now.'

'It's your arrogance that made you easy to fool. Most men would have wondered why those women were willing to be treated that way, and smelled a rat. You're so darned sure all women think you're wonderful, you couldn't even see they were too good to be true.'

'Damn it, Jess. You're way off base.'

'Remind me to phone Mrs Martelli and ask her to feed Nick and Nora,' was all she said, then closed her eyes again.

She didn't stir when he pulled into the parking lot beneath his apartment building. He opened her door, released the seatbelt, and ran a finger down her cheek.

'Jess? We're home.'

She opened her eyes. When she tried to swing her legs out of the car, she cried out in pain.

'What's the matter?'

'My hip. I must have banged it when I tackled Lynch.'

When he scooped her into his arms she tried to tell him she was too heavy but he gave that all the consideration it deserved.

Her head slid down to rest against his shoulder and she linked her arms around his neck.

'Tired?' he asked.

'Are you kidding? I hurt too much to be sleepy. Boy, am I out of shape.'

'I think your shape is perfect,' he said, longing to run his hands over the warm curves pressed against his chest.

Jess let herself feel warm and safe in his arms as they rode up in the elevator. If it was all going to end tomorrow, so be it. She'd enjoy today.

On his floor he let her legs slide to the floor, still supporting her around the waist while he unlocked the door.

She limped inside under her own power. He locked the door, swung her up in his arms again, and carried her straight into the bathroom.

She was struck anew by the luxury of this room compared to how practical the rest of the apartment looked, even the guest bathroom near the front door. The first time she came to his home, he told her he bought it furnished from the previous tenants who

305

were divorcing. His only contribution had been a king-sized bed.

The apartment's furnishings and decorating could have been copied straight out of a catalogue photo. The master bathroom, however, looked and felt sensual, almost exotic.

One entire wall was made of glass bricks. The huge tub was white marble, set one step up from the green tile floor. Behind the tub a jungle of plants thrived in the moist air.

When she was standing on her own two feet she saw her reflection, ruthlessly illuminated by the fat light bulbs all around the mirror. And if one mirror wouldn't have been bad enough there were three, set at different angles.

'Oh, my heavens. I'm a mess!' One of her sleeves hung loose at the shoulder. The blouse had lost a couple of buttons, luckily none of them vital for modesty. Her skirt was twisted so the zipper was in front of one hip instead of center back. Her pantyhose were shredded around her feet and knees.

The uniform was filthy and so were her arms, legs, and face. Her hair . . . Jess turned her back on the mirrors.

'You get undressed, I'll fill the tub.' He turned the gold-plated taps on full and water gushed from the mouth of a gold dolphin. She watched him remove his jacket and shoes, and roll up his sleeves. He tossed his keys, watch, and wallet onto the green-tiled counter.

'Get naked? With you in the room? You dumped me this afternoon, remember?'

'Nobody's dumped anybody,' he said fiercely. 'And we agreed the subject could wait until tomorrow.'

He left the dolphin gushing hot water and reached for her, pulling her closer to stand on the soft white carpeting of the step leading to the tub. His fingers touched her chin, tilting her head so he could see her eyes.

'I'm taking care of you,' he said, daring her to argue. Jess smiled. 'Okay.'

His fingers were unusually clumsy as he removed her skirt and tossed it into the corner of the room. He made swifter work of the blouse and her bra, though he swore when he saw the bruise already darkening on her shoulder and breast.

Daniel bent his head and brushed his mouth across the mark, his touch lighter than a breath. Jess shivered.

He knelt at her feet and gently slid the pantyhose and panties down her legs at the same time, careful of her scrapes and bruises. Those joined the heap of discarded clothing in the corner.

Then he turned off the taps and helped her to step into the tub, easing her down until she was lying full length, the water just deep enough to lap at her breasts. Jess winced, the breath hissing from her as warm water touched the raw places where her bare skin had connected with the cement. He turned on the water jets to make the water swirl around her.

'It'll only hurt for a little while, honey, but we have

307

to get those scrapes cleaned. The jets will be good for your sore muscles. You lay still, I'll take care of everything.'

And he did. He knelt beside the tub and used the hand-held spray to wash her hair, massaging her scalp with his big hands until she wondered if she'd melt into a little puddle right there. Then he used a terry facecloth and some soap to wash her body, carefully and thoroughly making sure every inch of her was clean.

Her heart began to beat a slow, drugged rhythm as he slowly drew the cloth up her leg to her abdomen. She ran her tongue across her bottom lip and her hips rocked. He'd been watching his hand move on her skin, but when she moved he looked at her, his eyes stormy with need.

'Daniel, please,' she moaned. 'You're driving me crazy.'

'We can't, honey, you're hurt.'

'I don't care.'

'I do.' He slid the cloth up between her thighs, drawing the slightly rough fabric across her, back and forth, back and forth. The gentle friction across her swollen flesh was almost more than she could bear.

'Daniel!'

'I'll take care of you, honey.' He dropped the cloth into the water and cupped her with his hand.

She parted her legs and he slid a finger deep inside, moving his thumb on her. He eased his finger out, then back again. And again.

'Jess, you're so beautiful,' he breathed before he sealed her lips with his mouth, his tongue plunging, mimicking the movement of his hand, faster and faster, harder and harder, until her body clenched, arching out of the water as he gave her release.

She lay in the support of his arm, feeling utterly boneless, her body floating gently with the motion of the water.

After one last caress, he slid his hand from between her legs and rested it on her abdomen. Still leaning over her, he rested against the tub edge, head hanging as if he'd just run a marathon. The room was silent except for the jets pushing the water and his ragged breathing.

She lifted one hand out of the water and ran her fingers down his shoulder. She felt better but the man was hurting. Bad.

She raised her shoulders, high enough to slip her arm under his and around his torso, pressing her wet breasts to his chest. At the touch of her hardening nipples, he shuddered.

'Daniel,' she whispered. 'Come here.' And she pulled him forward. Caught off guard he flopped down into the water on top of her.

'Jess!' He lifted up, braced on his arms to take some of his weight, and looked down at her. 'We can't do this.'

'Yes, we can, if only you'd hurry up and take off your clothes.' She arched her hips and rubbed against his erection. He gasped.

His eyes began to gleam. 'Are you ever going to listen to good advice from me or anybody else?'

'Nope.' Jess wrapped her arms around his neck, closed his mouth with her own, and pulled him under the water.

Later, once they were dry and curled together in his bed, she snuggled her hips back against his groin and placed her hand on his where he cupped her breast. 'Daniel?'

'Yeah?' he said, sleepily.

'About Warren. I –'

'Go to sleep, Jess.'

'Ouch!' Daniel jerked his hand away from the hot frying pan.

Jess stood just outside the kitchen, watching him. What he was cooking smelled good but he looked almost as tasty in his jeans and T-shirt as he'd looked last night wearing nothing at all. She wondered what he would say if she nibbled on him instead of breakfast.

'Damn.'

'Burn yourself?' She tightened the belt of the robe she'd borrowed from his closet.

He didn't look at her. 'I'm fine. Sit down.' He pointed at the table.

Jess smiled when she saw the single rose in the bud vase. A silver rack held toast. Little crystal bowls with strawberry jam and marmalade. Champagne flutes and linen napkins. He'd really put a lot of effort into breakfast.

Now she knew he could do this, she'd have to make sure it happened more often. Pampering was a good thing, one she meant to get used to if she got the chance. It all depended on how their talk about Warren went this morning.

What would happen if she told him everything?

Best case scenario, he accepted the necessity of the investigation and offered to help her. Worst case, he broke off their relationship and warned Warren and Scratten of what she was doing.

There was a lot at risk if she trusted him with the truth and she ended up having to deal with the latter.

'It looks wonderful,' she said.

'The eggs will be ready in a minute.'

'Can I do anything to help?'

'Yeah. Sit down.'

He left the pan for a moment to fill the champagne flutes with orange juice. As soon as he was close enough she grabbed his shirt and pulled him down for a kiss. 'Mornin'.'

'Good morning.' He handed her the glass and went back to the stove.

She sipped. Mmm, champagne and fresh-squeezed orange juice.

He scooped the scrambled eggs out on to two plates and carried them to the table. 'I called Sophy this morning and told her you'd be late for work.'

'I know. She told me when I called her.'

After he sat down across from her, she saluted him

with her glass. 'Quite a spread. I didn't know you were so talented.'

He looked self-conscious. 'Toast and scrambled eggs are simple enough.'

'It's beautiful and I appreciate the effort.'

'Well, then . . . you're welcome. Eat up, before it gets cold.'

They ate silently and she thought he seemed as nervous as she felt, which was good. If he was tense it meant he, too, had a lot riding on the outcome. It meant their relationship was important to him.

They finished together.

'That was delicious,' she said as she pushed back from the table. She picked up both plates and carried them over to the sink.

'I'll clean up.'

'No, you cooked, I'll clean.'

'Would you like some tea?'

'That would be nice. Thanks.' The stilted conversation was amusing, wasn't it? So why wasn't she laughing? Two people with important stuff to discuss, wasting time on silly chatter because they were both afraid.

They worked silently until the kitchen was clean, the tea was made and poured, and they had no more excuses for delay. She followed him into the living-room where she curled up in a big easy chair, tucking the folds of the robe around her bare legs, and sipped from the mug, enjoying the fragrance.

Daniel stood by the empty fireplace and put his mug on the mantel.

'I think it would be best to start with an explanation of why you have someone following Warren.'

She took her time answering. 'I suppose you want the truth.'

'Why else would I ask?'

'Not everybody likes to hear the truth. Not really. Oh, they think so. Seems to me people are always demanding the truth. Sometimes they even pay people like me and Harvey to find it. Then they don't know what to do when it makes them uncomfortable or ruins their illusions.'

'I don't have any illusions about Warren.'

'Yes, you do. Just like you have a mental picture of Anna or Sam or your sisters. Just like I have my own picture of Harvey and Sophy. And if the picture turns out to be a mirage, it hurts.'

'I want to know why you're following Warren and I want to know who hired you.'

'Ever since I went to work for Harvey, people have been asking me questions like that one. And until now, I've never had a problem refusing to answer, unless it was a cop asking the questions.'

'Do you answer the police?'

'Depends.'

'Depends on what?'

'The cop. What's at stake.' She leaned forward to set the mug on the table. 'It's usually better to redirect them before they start asking questions.'

'You mean lie,' he said grimly. 'To the police?'

She smiled. His outrage was really quite amusing. 'I

imagine even you lie now and then, for the sake of business. I wouldn't be good at my business if I wasn't a darn good liar. Harvey once told me it's a useful talent.'

'Are you going to lie to me, Jess?'

'I should. But I won't. I've decided to let it all ride.'

'What do you mean by that?'

'You wouldn't understand, Daniel. You'd never understand.'

After she'd explained exactly how important this case was to her and to Harvey, and shared her suspicions and any hard data about Concept House, Daniel began cross-examining her like a lawyer in court.

'You've done enough dancing around the subject. Just tell me what Warren is doing at Concept House.'

'Money laundering.'

He stared at her dumbfounded, like he'd never heard the term before.

'That's where someone takes another person's illegal income and runs it through their own business so –'

'I know what the hell it is. I worked there after college, dammit. If something like that was happening, I'd have known.'

'How? You were young. Naïve. You trusted your father's old friend. Besides, the think-tank could have been totally legit up till a couple of years ago when he started having financial troubles.'

For the first time since their discussion began, he sat down. He leaned forward, elbows on knees, hands dangling, and stared at her. 'I can't believe this.'

'According to the bank records we . . . found, one of the Concept House accounts has been fluctuating wildly.'

'Warren might not have anything to do with it. Scratten could be working on his own.'

'It started before Scratten went to work at Concept House.'

'How on earth would Warren know how to connect with someone who needed money laundering?'

'In the last week since I've had him tailed, Scratten has met with a suspected leader of a local illegal drug operation and a woman with connections to a terrorist group in Europe.'

'But that doesn't mean –'

'Harvey always says, if you consort with the devil, you'll end up dancing to his tune. That's why I had Sophy peek into Harvey's files on the case. It seems Scratten hired him because he thinks Warren's about to bail out and leave him holding the bag. So Harvey's been spending his time trying to get the goods on Hellmann.'

'And this whole thing started because you didn't like Ralph Scratten?' He flung up his hands and resumed pacing. 'That's hard to believe.'

'Okay, let's try this another way.' She stretched out her legs, flexing and rubbing her left calf. She'd been sitting still for so long the muscle had cramped. 'If a man wanted you to go to his country and set up a training program for his senior civil service, would you go?'

'Yes.'

'And if that same man spent all his time with goons who wore guns, refused to tell you exactly how many people you'd be training, and told you it must be kept hush-hush, would you still go?'

He hesitated. 'Probably.'

'And what if, when your partner seemed uneasy about the arrangements, the man waved a big wad of cash in your face and promised more when the deal was done. By the end of the training, you'll end up with lots of money, five times as much money as it's worth. Then the man refused to give you any time to think it over. Would you still go?'

'No.'

'I rest my case.' She stood up. 'I've told you everything I know, now I'm going to have a shower.' She tugged the lapels closed and tightened the belt. 'When I come back you can tell me what you've decided.'

She wanted, quite desperately, to kiss him. But she didn't want him to think she would try to use sex to convince him.

'You'll need something to wear, I had to throw away the stuff from yesterday. My sisters keep some stuff in the guest room. Pick out whatever you want.'

'Thanks.'

Daniel watched her go, still not sure how she'd persuaded him to doubt the integrity of a man he'd known and trusted for years.

If Jess was right, Concept House was in big trouble. How would it affect the money he and Anna invested in it last year? The St Clair Institute was thriving so they'd both be okay, but Anna had insisted on giving Warren most of her retirement funds. She'd be wiped out.

If Warren's business and career exploded with a big, very public criminal case everyone associated with Concept House, including the directors, would appear tainted.

Oh, my God. Daniel felt sick to his stomach.

Warren had insisted on making him a director.

He shoved open the balcony door and stepped out, dragging in several deep, cleansing breaths of fresh air, trying to think this through.

He'd seen cases where the directors of a company were held accountable for the wrongdoing of the management, even if they were ignorant of the criminal activities.

There'd been a case just a few years back where one of the richest and most influential investors in America got caught up in a similar mess.

Daniel fell on to a chair and dropped his head into his hands. If this ruined his reputation, it could severely damage or even destroy the St Clair Institute. He couldn't take care of Anna and the Sisters if he lost his own business.

Ruth and Tom were both expecting promotions. Their careers could be sent off track by a scandal like this.

Daniel rubbed his temples, trying to ease the pain blooming behind his eyes. He could force Warren to resign and take over himself. Once he was in control of Concept House, it would be a simple matter to fire Scratten and anyone else involved in this mess.

He'd hire the best criminal lawyer in the country to deal with any legal fall-out, before it occurred. The police would be satisfied if he let the company be used to trap one or two of the criminals who delivered their dirty money to Concept House, until word got out it was no longer business as usual. Tom would help arrange things from that end.

He'd make a very public donation to charity of any profits Concept House had earned since Scratten was hired. Ruth could handle that one.

A risky plan, though he didn't doubt his ability to pull it off.

And yet . . . . He knew if he used her information to mitigate the damage to Concept House, Jess would see it as a betrayal and he'd lose her

She didn't trust easily but she'd trusted him today, an incredible gift. Time after time she'd proven herself to be everything he'd thought he wanted in a wife. A woman with warmth, intelligence, and strength. A woman of honour.

She was also a complicated bundle of opinions and attitudes who never hesitated to challenge him, or anyone else, if she thought they were wrong. Never a dull moment around Jess. Despite his headache, he found himself smiling. When would she realize she loved him?

She had to love him. There was no other explanation

for what she'd done. What a woman, he thought with awe. She'd believed in him, believed he'd do what was right, without demanding guarantees.

She had no idea what her trust meant to a man like him. Or maybe she did. What had she said? That the true significance of the gift was what it meant to the giver?

If he couldn't convince her that exposing Warren and Scratten weren't the only way to stop them, he'd have to choose between her and his family, a terrible choice.

Harvey was the key. He'd known the truth about Concept House and still decided to help Scratten. If Harvey and Daniel could work out a plan, Jess would probably go along.

He'd discover some way to make this work. He had to.

He'd finally found her. He was damned well going to keep her.

CHAPTER 15

'No, we will not.' Jess was emphatic and stared out the windshield of the Jaguar.

'Yes, we will.' Daniel was implacable. He turned on to Water Street and began looking for a parking place on one of the side streets near her office. 'I called Sophy while you were in the shower and she agreed with me. She said she'd find Harvey and get him to meet us at Finders Keepers in . . .' he glanced at his watch '. . . twenty minutes.'

'You don't understand. Harvey doesn't know I've been –'

'Meddling? Interfering?'

'Helping. I'd planned on telling him when the time was right.'

'The time's never going to be right, Jess, not as long as you're worried he's going to leave you.' He parked the car and came around to help her out of the car.

'He's not going to like having you tell him what to do.' Jess made sure she was out of the car before he got there. She'd had enough of his help.

When she got out of the shower earlier she'd hoped for the best but steeled herself for the worst. What she got was a shock; Daniel seemed to think someone had put him in charge of her life.

'He doesn't have to like it. Your firm built an excellent reputation because the three of you were a cohesive working unit. That was your strength and things began to fall apart when you lost it. It's time to get it back. We'll pool our information and resources to build a plan that will work for everyone.'

'Ooohh.' She pretended to shiver. 'Listen to Mr Big Business Consultant.'

Jess looked at him out the corner of her eye to see if she'd finally managed to annoy him. Darn. He was still smiling.

'If you and Sophy insist on going through with this, I guess I can't stop you, but I'm going to do the talking.'

'Sure.' He shrugged and held the building's door for her.

She *wished* he wouldn't do that, almost as if he thought she was bluffing. Ha! She'd show him who was in charge.

Jess sailed through the open door with her nose in the air. She punched the elevator call button and decided not to waste any more breath arguing with him. Might as well wait for Harvey to tell Daniel off and save herself the trouble.

In the office Sophy was sitting at her desk, listening to someone on the phone. Her eyes were bright with laughter when she waved them in.

'Yes, I'll tell her.' She hung up the phone.

'That was Carol, at Reed-Howard. She thought you might be interested to know Lynch wanted the lingerie for himself.' She giggled. 'It seems men's underwear and nightshirts aren't soft enough for his delicate skin. He was stealing it because he didn't want anybody to see him buying it.'

Jess and Daniel looked at each other and burst into laughter at the same time. The man had been full of macho bluster and bravado. It was hard to imagine him wearing the silk and lace that fell out of his jacket when she tackled him.

Their laughter died away.

'Did you find Harvey?' Daniel asked as he made himself comfortable on one of the vinyl sofas.

'He'll be here soon.'

'I want it to go on record that I think this is a very bad idea.' Jess plopped herself down on the other sofa and scowled at Sophy, who shrugged but didn't look very apologetic.

The door knob rattled and they all looked up expectantly but it wasn't Harvey. Gertrude swept into the room.

'I am very disappointed,' she announced.

Jess never could understand why she didn't use the royal 'we' since she'd obviously taken Elizabeth the First as her role model. She did royal disdain better than anyone else Jess had ever met, though she thought the tight red curls in Gertrude's hair and lace ruff on all her blouses were going too far.

'I asked you to find my cousins through the Wellesley connection. The white trash who showed up on my doorstep this morning can't possibly be related to *me*. I repudiate their claim.'

'I warned you, Gertrude,' Sophy said in a meek voice. 'I told you. People who search for long-lost relatives are often disappointed.'

'You made an error. I demand you correct it immediately and locate my legitimate relatives.'

'I'm sorry, Gertrude,' Sophy said, even more meekly, 'but those people are the only descendants from the Wellesley branch of your family.'

Jess sighed and rolled her eyes at Sophy's attitude. She hated how this woman treated Sophy but Jess had given up trying to make her stand up to her hairdresser a long time ago.

Jess looked at Daniel to see how he was enjoying his privileged position as front-row observer to Gertrude's performance. He'd propped his elbow on the arm of the sofa and was supporting his chin in such a way that his hand hid his mouth, hiding his expression.

'They are seriously dysfunctional. They arrived this morning with no notice, expecting me to put them up. As if my home is a hotel. I won't have anything more to do with them.'

'Gertrude, I was very careful –'

'Any respectable business is satisfaction guaranteed.' She dropped a piece of paper onto Sophy's desk. 'Since I am not at all satisfied with the quality of the cousins you found, I refuse to pay this invoice. The search was obviously incompetent.'

Jess couldn't keep her mouth shut any longer. 'You'd better pay this bill and the money you still owe us from when I found your dog last year. If your check isn't in this office by the end of next week, I'll send them for collection.'

'Well, I never!'

'As for this search, Sophy did it herself and she's very good at it. Nobody could have done a better job.'

'I've never met such an insolent girl. You've never shown proper respect when you speak to your betters. You will apologize to me at once or I will speak to Mr Tate about how you treat clients –'

'That's enough!' Sophy's quiet tone stopped Gertrude's tirade mid-flight. She stood up behind her desk. 'You will not speak to Ms Phillips that way.'

'Indeed? Need I remind you how difficult it is to get appointments in my salon?'

'Then I'm sure you won't have any trouble filling my regular space. I won't be needing it again.' Sophy looked pale but determined. 'As Ms Phillips said, we expect your account to be paid in full by the end of next week. Goodbye.'

'Well!' When Gertrude tossed her head not one of the red curls moved, as if they were glued down. The glass pane rattled when she slammed the door on her way out.

Sophy dropped into her chair, looking dazed. 'That wasn't so bad.'

'You should have done it a long time ago,' Jess said. 'Now you can find an even better hairdresser.'

'I guess.'

'See?' Jess said to Daniel. 'This is exactly what I was trying to explain to you. Granted, Gertrude isn't a good example –'

'I hope not.'

'People don't deal well when faced with a reality which forces them to give up their illusions. Gertrude's real cousins didn't fit with her image of her family.'

The door opened again and for a moment she thought Gertrude had come back. All three gave a big sigh of relief when they saw it was only Harvey.

'Hi,' Jess said brightly. 'Daniel wants to talk to you.'

After Daniel had them sit down together on the vinyl sofas, he explained everything she'd accomplished so far. Harvey sat beside Daniel on the sofa. He wasn't happy and he didn't say much, but at least he was listening.

Sophy sat opposite Harvey; Jess slouched down beside her and brooded.

Daniel was right. Harvey would leave or he would stay. She couldn't pretend to be a different person or treat him any differently, hoping it would change his mind.

There were lots of questions she would have asked, actions she would have taken, if she'd been thinking clearly rather than reacting emotionally. Worse, she'd been so focused on herself and Harvey, she hadn't looked at this mess from Daniel's point of view. She hadn't been fair to him.

At that moment she heard Daniel say something and she hoped she'd heard wrong. 'You're what?'

'I'm one of the directors for Concept House.'

'You were part of this, one of them, all along?' Jess felt as if her blood had turned to ice.

'Why didn't you tell me while I was spilling my guts this morning? Aren't you the one who got so mad yesterday when you thought I was using you? Which, by the way, wasn't true. After we . . . you know . . . became involved, I didn't ask you for any information or introductions.'

She looked at Harvey. 'I'm sorry. I promise you I didn't know.'

'I did,' he said.

Jess was glad she was sitting down.

'You knew? Why didn't you tell me?'

'Because he's a director on paper only. As far as I could find out, he's never become involved with company and he's had very little contact with Hellmann since bailing him out last year.' He looked at Daniel. 'Right?'

Daniel nodded. 'Last year Warren told me he had some short-term shortages and needed a loan. I agreed because I could afford it and I felt I owed him because he'd helped when I was starting out. He did offer me a place on the Board for my investment, but I was too busy with my own company and I didn't think a successful man like him needed my input.'

'A mistake,' Harvey said quietly.

'Yes, sir, a very big mistake.' The anger in his eyes turned inward. 'It was months before I found out he'd listed me as a director, anyway. Neither the Sisters nor I knew he'd also approached Anna for an investment until she got sick.'

The muscle in his jaw flexed. 'She'll lose everything if Concept House goes bankrupt. Which is one of the reasons why I wanted to have this meeting. I have a proposal I'd like you to consider, but first –'

'You might as well save your breath, son,' Harvey said. 'I'm going to finish this investigation.'

'I'm prepared to help you, if you'll agree to work together.'

'Daniel told me Finders Keepers was so successful because we stuck together. What did he call it?' Jess tapped her chin with one finger. 'Oh, yeah. We're a cohesive working unit, at least until recently. He wants us to pool our information and resources.'

Daniel smiled briefly. 'I didn't think you were listening.'

'I was listening.'

'Don't you think it's time you told us the real reason you're working for Scratten, Harvey?'

'I'm not going to tell you anything. I'm doing this alone and I've wasted enough time on this discussion.' He began to stand up.

'Sit down!' Sophy barked the order and he dropped like he'd been shot. She looked over at Daniel. 'What do you mean, the real reason?'

'Jess talks about Harvey a lot. Quotes his rules and his sayings endlessly.' Daniel smiled at Jess, then turned to look at Harvey. 'Your decision to move to Florida hurt her deeply. She and Sophy have both been so emotionally involved they didn't wonder *why*, with this case, you're not following any of your own rules.'

'Yes, we did,' Jess said indignantly.

'You both wondered why he was hurting you this way, you worried something was wrong with him. You thought about it with your emotions. Try to look at it from a business perspective. Why would a man who'd built a very successful business suddenly throw away all the principles which solved your cases and made him successful?

'Why would a man who preached the benefits of working together, suddenly insist on working alone? You three are a family. Why would he suddenly tell you he was leaving you for good?'

Jess felt as if she'd been sitting in the dark and hadn't noticed until Daniel turned on the lights. She couldn't say a thing.

Sophy could. 'He cut us out deliberately because he didn't want us involved in the Scratten investigation. And that's why you told me you didn't want to get involved with me, isn't it, Harvey?'

'He's protecting us,' Jess said. 'Aren't you?'

He looked over at Daniel, angry but resigned. 'You just had to do it, didn't you?'

'Yes.'

Sophy leaned forward and put her hand on Harvey's knee. 'Please explain, Harvey.'

'When I was a very young man, I fell in love with a wonderful girl. Louise.' Harvey pulled out his wallet and handed Sophy an old photograph. 'Two days before our wedding, she was killed by a drunk driver.'

'She was very pretty,' she said and passed it to Jess.

It was a black and white photo of a smiling girl with dark hair, sitting on a blanket in the sun. A girl with the whole world in front of her and a boy who loved her with his whole heart.

Jess showed the picture to Daniel, then handed it back to Harvey. He looked at the picture, then slid it into his wallet and put them both away.

'The driver wasn't much older than me, the only son of a very rich housing developer and the biggest employer in town. By the time the case got to court all the evidence had gone missing. The only witness moved his family into a brand new house in one of their developments and developed amnesia.

'I was in court when the judge dismissed the criminal charges. He'd killed Louise and still got off free and clear because of his family. The bastard turned around, looked right at me, and laughed. That day I vowed to make him pay, even if took my entire lifetime. He's why I became a detective. I've watched him for thirty years, waiting for him to make a mistake.'

'Is that what this is about, Harvey?' Sophy asked. 'He's finally made a mistake?'

'It can't be Scratten. He's too young,' Jess said.

'It's Warren, isn't it?' Daniel asked. 'He killed Louise.'

'He's given me lots of opportunities over the years, but exposing those would only have embarrassed him, not destroyed him. I'd been hearing some nasty rumors over the last couple years, but couldn't get any proof. Then, one day a couple months ago, I was having a beer with another detective, swapping war stories. He told me about this guy who tried to hire him, but my buddy had too much respect for his license and his skin to take the job. I asked him to give the guy my name.'

'That was Scratten,' Jess said.

'Yes, and with his unwitting help I'm finally going to put Hellmann in jail where he belongs.'

'Why did Scratten hire you?' Daniel asked.

'He thought Warren was double-crossing him. Either that or the cops were on to them. He wanted to find out if it was time to disappear, leaving Hellmann holding the bag.'

'That's why you deliberately cut Sophy and me out of the investigation. Because as soon as Scratten told you what he wanted, and what kind of criminals were involved, you knew it might get dangerous.'

'You're underestimating Jess and Sophy,' Daniel said. 'They are strong, resourceful women.'

'Thank you, Daniel,' Jess said, pleased at his compliment.

'My family has a lot at stake in this mess, but if the four of us work together, I think we can clean it up.'

'No. I'm sorry about your family but it's gonna happen, St Clair. He's going to jail.'

'If we do it your way, my family won't be the only one hurt. Concept House has over a hundred employees who need their jobs. You say you want to punish Warren, but what if I showed you a way you could do it without hurting anyone else?'

'He's going to jail,' Harvey repeated. 'Once it hits the fan, Scratten will testify in return for immunity.'

Daniel leaned forward and rested his elbows on his knees, intent on convincing Harvey.

'I'm sure you know Warren very well after watching him all these years. You know what it would do to him if I took over Concept House, fired him, and his peers knew the cause was incompetence.'

'It would drive him crazy.'

'Would you consider Louise avenged?'

Harvey shook his head.

'Tell me something, St Clair. How would you feel if Jess phoned to tell you she was pregnant and was coming to your office so you could celebrate together? What if on the way a drunk driver swerved into her lane, slammed her car into a gas truck, and she burned to death? What if it was your grief he mocked in the courtroom? Would you be satisfied with getting him fired?'

Daniel's face was wiped clear of all expression and he went deathly still.

'God in heaven. Oh, that poor girl.' Sophy wiped at the tears sliding down her cheeks.

Jess knelt beside him and pressed her cheek to his hand. 'I'm so sorry, Harvey.' He rested his other hand on her head.

'Daniel?' he asked.

Jess turned so she could see Daniel. His hands were fisted so tightly the knuckles were white.

'I'd kill him,' he said in a low voice, as if the words were dragged from his soul. He looked at Harvey. 'Please forgive me. I didn't understand.'

'Of course. It was a long time ago and now, with revenge almost within my grasp, I realize my life was very lonely until the last few years.' He ran his hand across Jess's hair, a regretful smile on his lips.

Life seeped back into Daniel's eyes, along with a deadly purpose. 'We've got a lot of work to do if we're going to make damned sure Warren goes to jail.'

'First rule, St Clair. I don't allow cursing. If you want to work with me, you have to abide by my rules.'

An hour later Jess left Harvey and Daniel huddled over their plans in Harvey's office and went to see what Sophy was up to.

She was sitting at her desk.

'You should see it in there, Daniel's already trying to take over and Harvey doesn't like it a bit. I decided to leave before it got messy.'

Sophy jumped when she heard Jess's voice, then she turned her head away and wiped her eyes.

'You shouldn't be so upset, Sophy. As Harvey said, it happened a long time ago.'

'That's only part of it. He's never going to love me, is he? He still loves Louise.'

'I don't think love has been driving him all these years. I believe he loved her once but it faded and all he had left was revenge. You heard him, living for revenge makes for a cold and lonely life.'

'Enough of this.' Sophy briskly wiped her eyes and blew her nose. 'We've got work to do. While you were in there with the men, I had a phone call. Remember you asked me to see what else I could find out about Chris Houston?'

'Yeah. And . . . ?'

'I can't find anything from the years before she went to university, except a birth certificate . . . and a death certificate.'

'So she's not the real Chris Houston.' Jess rolled her eyes. 'Great. As if there wasn't already enough going on. I guess it's time to tell Daniel about her.'

'Now?'

'Yeah. While I go rescue Daniel from Harvey, would you please give his office a call and see if she's still there? Knowing Daniel, he's going to want to deal with this immediately.'

'Will do.' Sophy picked up the phone.

'I shouldn't be here.' Jess dropped her coat on the conference table in Daniel's office and fiddled with a stack of business magazines. 'This is none of my business.'

'You stayed at the restaurant when Mr Bailey asked

you to.' Daniel made himself comfortable on the sofa.

'He wanted me to help him explain things to those men and he was scared.'

'I need you to help me explain things to Chris.'

'Not likely.'

'I'm scared.'

She snorted inelegantly. 'That'd be the day.'

Daniel chuckled, then responded to a rap on the door.

'Come in.'

'You wanted to see me?' Chris's smile twisted when she noticed Jess. He hadn't understood Chris's opposition to the investigation, but he now realized she'd both feared and expected to be found out.

'Yes, please sit down. Both of you.' He waited until Chris chose a chair opposite him. Jess stayed by the table, but she did sit down.

'We know Chris Houston isn't your real name. I'd like to know why you're living under a false name and what, if anything, it has to do with me.'

All color drained from her face and he watched, horrified, as she seemed to crumple where she sat. She buried her face in her hands as sobs racked her body.

He looked helplessly at Jess, then leaned over to put his hand on Chris's shoulder. She flinched away from his touch; her body huddled into the upholstery as her shoulders convulsed.

She was in such terrible pain, Daniel felt stunned. Jess brought over the box of tissues Daniel kept beside his computer, yanked out several and pressed them into her hand. 'Here, Chris, take these.'

Chris tried to say something, but the words were so torn by her tears, he couldn't understand them.

'It's okay, take your time.' Jess knelt and put her arm around Chris, not allowing her to pull away. A moment later she turned into Jess for comfort.

Jess held her tightly and looked at him, questions in her eyes. He had no answers. All they could do was wait until Chris had calmed down enough to talk.

Gradually her sobs quieted to deep, gasping breaths and irregular shudders that shook both her and Jess.

'Chris?' Jess handed her more tissue.

'It's been so . . . hard. Wondering. Waiting. Hating.'

Despite the breaks in her voice, he could understand her words, if not the meaning.

'I don't understand.' Daniel reached out a hand to touch her, but stopped when he remembered how she'd flinched from his touch.

She pulled away from Jess and sat back in the chair, looking down at the wad of wet tissue in her hands. Jess took them away, tossed them in the garbage and handed her the tissue box, then sat beside Daniel.

'I needed you so, but you never came.' She almost broke down again, but controlled it. 'You never came. I hated you for most of my life and it tore at my soul. I had to know the truth!'

'You hated me?' he asked, astounded.

'When I saw your ad for an office manager, it was

335

perfect. I'd be close but safe. If it didn't work I could walk away. You'd never know. If I liked you, I was going to tell you. When the time was right.'

Daniel felt just as helpless and bewildered now as he had when she was crying.

'But once I started the lie, there was no way out.'

'Chris, I don't understand any of this. You'll have to calm down and explain.'

She dragged in another deep breath, then tidied her jacket and sat straight. 'My name was Megan Porter. My parents were Vince and Meredith Porter.'

'That can't be.' Daniel felt as if his world had taken a quarter turn, leaving him reeling. He felt Jess lay a calming hand on his arm and things settled down again.

'I'm your half-sister. My . . . our mother was pregnant when you left. I was born six months later. They fought about you until the day she died. I used to dream you'd come back and rescue me, take me away with you. Vince –' She closed her eyes and pressed her fist to her mouth.

He stood, lifted her to her feet, and wrapped his arms around her, holding tight.

She didn't need to say more. He knew what Vince was capable of. He couldn't bear to think of her, a defenseless little girl, at that madman's mercy.

She'd needed her big brother and he hadn't even known she existed.

'I didn't know, I didn't know. I'm sorry I wasn't there to protect you.' He felt her arms steal around him, tentatively, as if she was afraid he'd push her away. He rested his cheek on her head and held her tighter. 'I'm here now.'

She began to cry again, peaceful, healing tears that dampened his jacket. He rubbed one hand up and down her back, just like he did for his other sisters when the world got them down.

He looked up at the ceiling and blinked back tears. It was almost too much to take in, to have someone who truly belonged to him. As much as he loved Anna and the Sisters, some part of him had always known he was separate. Apart.

Jess watched him and knew she loved him. Why hadn't she seen it sooner? She'd thought she could enjoy the affair, their time together, then walk away. Regretful but whole.

It wasn't going to happen. She didn't doubt she'd still have to walk away when he found his perfect wife for his perfect life. But now she knew she wouldn't be whole again because he'd taken her heart.

Jess pressed her hand against her chest, to feel her heart beating. Daniel looked up at her and smiled.

Sure he was a teacher, a boss, and a general pain in the neck, but he was a son, a brother, and a lover, too. A man. The only man for her.

'I've got to go,' Jess reminded him. 'Harvey's waiting.'

'She's right.' Daniel brushed Chris's hair back from her damp face. 'We've got someone waiting for us. It's important.'

'No, it's okay, Daniel.' Jess picked up her coat from the table and slipped it on. 'You stay here with your sister. Harvey and I can do this alone.'

'No, you can't. I said I'd be there, and I will.'

Chris wiped her sleeve across her face and gave a shaky laugh. 'Hey, I'm grown-up. I can take care of myself.'

'You've done too much of that,' he said. 'I've got a better idea. Get your purse and coat.'

He took her to Anna.

CHAPTER 16

Jealousy was a very ugly emotion, one Jess had not allowed herself to feel in a very long time. Tonight, it seemed she had no choice and little control. Anna had been pleasantly surprised to see them at her door, inviting them in for a visit. She'd surprised Jess with a brief hug.

Then Daniel had explained about Chris, and Anna had welcomed his half-sister to the St Clair family with tears of joy and love. She'd shooed them off on their errand, promising to take good care of Chris. As they left she'd been busy phoning the Sisters to invite them all over to meet the newest member of the family.

The whole time they were at the house, Jess's guts had churned with a jealousy so sharp she was surprised the others hadn't noticed a green cast to her skin.

She didn't begrudge Chris her welcome. What overwhelmed Jess was the intense yearning for them to invite her in, too. All these years she'd been so sure the whole family thing wasn't for her. Anna had helped

339

her to see that Harvey and Sophy were her family, bu
now Jess wanted more.

She pushed the button for her floor and glanced u
at Daniel. The ride from Anna's home to Finder
Keepers had been very quiet. From the few com
ments he made, she imagined he was thinking abou
Chris.

The last time she'd felt this way, she'd been eight
That year's foster parents gave their son a Boxer pupp
for his birthday. He'd let her play with his puppy an
she'd been so happy for a while.

The following month had been her birthday an
she'd spent the intervening days quietly, desperatel
wishing they'd give her a puppy of her own. They gav
her a very pretty sweater.

She'd gone wild with envy and anger and disap
pointment, crying and hitting out. Before the day wa
over she'd been moved to another family. The socia
worker had explained that a child like her, who move
around a lot, couldn't expect to have what othe
children, normal children, had.

The doors opened and Daniel followed her into th
dimly lit hall. They hadn't gone more than a step o
two toward her office when Jess heard a faint meow
She grabbed Daniel's arm, touched her finger to hi
lips so he wouldn't speak, and looked down the hall i
the opposite direction.

She listened intently and heard it again. Nora! Sh
touched Daniel's arm, pointed to his feet, and ben
down to take off her own shoes. He looked puzzled bu

did as she asked. Then she gestured for him to follow her away from Finders Keepers.

She found her cat nearby, cowering in front of an office door. She handed Daniel her shoes and scooped Nora into her arms. She held the cat in one arm while she fished a thin wire out of her coat sleeve and used it to pick the lock.

A minute later they were inside and she shut the door carefully behind her. She put the wire away then held Nora against her chest, gliding her hands through the cat's fur to let her know she was safe.

'What's the matter?' he said in a low voice. 'Why did we come in here?'

'Nora never leaves by herself. If she's out in the hall, there's something badly wrong in the office.' She bit her lip while she thought.

Jess looked down at herself. Luckily she was wearing dark slacks but the white blouse had to go. Daniel was wearing a thin black sweater under his jacket. 'Take off your sweater.'

She put Nora on the desk and started unbuttoning her blouse. 'Hurry.'

He tossed his jacket on the desk, then pulled the sweater over his head. 'What are you going to do?'

'Reconnoiter.' She tossed her blouse beside his jacket and pulled his sweater on. It was huge on her but it would do. 'Wait here. I'll be right back.'

'Jess, you can't go out there alone.'

'Better me than you. Hold on to Nora for me, okay?'

She cracked the door open, watched quietly for a

couple of heartbeats, then floated down the hall like
ghost. As she neared Finders Keepers she could se
lights through the glass panel in the door. Intending t
listen at the door, she stepped forward. Paper crackle
under her toes and she froze.

She held her breath while she waited but there wa
no response from inside. They hadn't heard the noise

Carefully she moved her foot and stepped aroun
the paper. She pressed her ear to the crack betwee
door and frame and realized why they hadn't heard he
step on the paper. Sophy was scolding someone.

'. . . and you should be ashamed of yourself.'

A man screamed at Sophy, 'Sit down and shut up
you stupid old hag, or I'll shut you up!'

His voice felt familiar but he was so edgy sh
couldn't place it. Another man spoke but so low sh
couldn't hear what he was saying and then the voice
moved away, into one of the inner offices. She waited
but heard nothing more.

Jess picked up the paper and whisked back down th
hall as quietly as she'd come. Daniel was waiting fo
her.

'What did you find out?'

'There's at least two men in there and Sophy i
driving them nuts with her scolding. Whoever it is,
think they're either in Harvey's office or mine.' Sh
held up the paper. 'And this was on the floor, as if i
had been shoved out beneath the door.'

'What is it?'

'I don't know. Let's have a look.' She picked up th

esk lamp and put it down on the floor behind the desk. Hopefully the bulk of the desk will keep the glow from howing through the door into the hall.'

She flicked on the lamp and stared at the paper in lespair. It was handwriting. She didn't have a hope of iguring out what it said.

Jess leaned back against the desk drawers and closed .er eyes. She no longer had a choice. She had to tell .im.

'Jess? What does it say?'

'I don't know. I can't read it.'

'Why?' She sensed him coming around the desk to it on the floor beside her, his arm and leg pressing gainst hers.

'Because I can't read.'

'Jess –'

'I was moved so frequently as a child my problem vasn't diagnosed. Everybody, myself included, hought I was just plain stupid with a rotten atti-ude. I was angry at the world and my own brain ntil Harvey made me go see a doctor and get some help.

'People who can't read have to be really good liars nd actors to protect themselves, so the other kids and he teachers and the bosses don't find out how stupid hey are. Guess I shouldn't complain, it was great raining for my career.'

She didn't open her eyes, waiting for him to say omething, anything. In the ensuing silence she lis-ened to her heart beat, slow and steady.

343

His arm came around her shoulders and he whis
pered her name as his mouth settled over hers.

Jess gasped and Daniel took advantage, slipping hi
tongue inside, teasing until her senses came alive an
she began kissing him back. She dropped the pape
between them and turned into his naked chest, twinin
her arms around his neck and kissing him hungrily, a
if her life depended on being close to him.

And she truly feared it did.

Eventually she realized there was more comfort that
passion in his kiss and she eased away.

'Dyslexia?'

She nodded and held out the paper. 'You'd bette
read it. It might be important.'

He took the paper but didn't look at it. She knew h
was watching her, silently compelling her to look a
him. Eventually she couldn't stand it any longer an
met his gaze.

'I love you, Jess.'

She put up her hand to stop him. 'I don't want to tal
about it.'

'Tough. We're going to settle this right now.'

'The only thing we have to settle is what's happenin
in my office. I'm not going to sit here chatting with you
while Sophy and Harvey are in trouble. Now, read th
paper.'

His lips tightened but he withdrew his arm and ben
over the paper. Jess tried not to feel bereft of hi
warmth. This was for the best. He'd have time t
think, to face the reality of her problem.

Nora meowed and settled into her lap.

'It's from Sophy. She says she's slipping this under the door when they're not looking. She thinks if we see it when we come back, we won't be caught, too.' He read further, then suddenly his fist clenched, crumpling it in his hand.

'Warren and Scratten are both in there. Scratten has a gun and they're waiting for us. Harvey's tied up in your office but they've told Sophy to answer the phones. If we call, she's to tell us to come immediately.'

'Scratten. It was him I heard screaming at Sophy.'

'Seems likely. He's the one with the gun.'

'Do you have your cell-phone with you?' she asked. 'We could phone, pretending to be a client. When Sophy answers, we could find some way to let her know we got her message.'

'Do your phones have call display? If Warren is watching, he might recognize my number.'

'Darn. I think so.' Since she couldn't read the digital display, she'd never paid much attention to it. She looked around the unfamiliar office, hoping for inspiration.

'If we used one of these phones, would they know where we are?'

'It depends on the size of the display screen and if they'd recognize the name of this company.'

'Sophy would. Then she'd know we were close. I say we chance it.' She stood up and set Nora down on the desk. 'Why don't you look for an extension so you can listen, too?'

Daniel prowled around the two other desks. 'Found one.'

'I'll do the talking.' Jess started dialing. When she heard the phone ringing, she signaled for him to pick up.

'Good evening, Finders Keepers.'

She recognized Sophy's voice but changed hers, just in case someone else was listening. 'Hi, this is Gertrude. May I speak to Ms Phillips?'

'I'm sorry, she's not in. May I take a message?'

'Tell her I got the note and I'll be glad to postpone her appointment.'

'That's wonderful! Um, ah, I'll see she gets your –' The connection was cut off.

'I'm scared for them, Daniel.' She set down the phone but didn't take her hand off the receiver. 'At least she knows help is on the way.'

'We'd better notify the police. I'll call Tom.' He disconnected, then dialed again. She heard him say hello to his brother-in-law, then she stopped listening.

Jess remembered the edge on Scratten's voice and tried to deny her growing conviction the police would be too late, but she couldn't. Nora came to weave around her ankles, as if sensing her unease.

Daniel put the phone back into his pocket.

'We can't wait for the police.' She picked up Nora and cuddled her. 'We have to help them now.'

'We can't, Jess. Scratten has a gun.'

'Since we can't go in, we'll have to trick them into coming out.' She scratched under Nora's chin and the

346

cat began to purr. 'What would make them *want* to leave?'

'This is crazy.'

'Fire. If they believed the building was on fire, they'd want to escape. Do you think they'd take Harvey and Sophy with them?'

'How should I know? Jess, listen to yourself.'

'Since they want something from us, they'll take them for hostages. Even if Harvey and Sophy's hands were tied, their legs would be freed to walk out.' She put Nora down and began rummaging in her coat pockets for matches. She knew they were there somewhere.

'And what if they decide it would be easier to just shoot them?' He grabbed her arm so she'd look at him. 'Have you thought of that?'

'Yes, I have. They didn't kill Harvey last time he got in the way, so I don't think they will this time, either.' She looked up him. 'Now let go of me. I'm doing this, either alone or with your help.'

'What if we can't stop them? If we do this before the police arrive, they could get away.'

'Then we'll have to stop them, won't we? We'll need smoke. The fire alarm alone won't be enough.'

She collected the trash cans from beneath the desks and stuffed all the rubbish into one. Then she dribbled a few drops of someone's cold coffee over the papers, just so they were damp enough to smoke.

'Phone Tom back and tell him what we're doing. Maybe you should get him to warn your family, too. If

347

you're right and they get away, then Warren and Scratten are going to need some new hostages.'

He swore and grabbed his phone.

'Open a window,' she ordered when he was done. 'We need a breeze.'

She set the trash can in the hall and set it on fire. After a few minutes it was smoking heavily. She came back into the room where she made a nest for Nora on the floor from the coat and jacket. She hugged Nora and told her to stay. It was risky leaving Nora here, in case something went wrong and the fire spread, but not as risky as taking her out into the hallway where an idiot would be waving a gun around.

She looked at Daniel. She smiled faintly and held out her hand. 'Ready for another adventure?'

He cursed, then grinned and took her hand. 'Why not?'

'Thanks, Daniel.' She kissed him, then began giving orders. 'Just beyond Finders Keepers there's a niche for the fire extinguisher. If you flatten yourself against it, hopefully they won't see you.'

'Where are you going to be?'

'The fire alarm is right by the elevator.' She coughed and began waving a file folder at the smoke, encouraging it in the right direction. She filled another trash can with water and put it near her bonfire, ready to douse the flames, then watched in satisfaction as smoke began to fill the hall.

'I'll pull the alarm, then when they come out, I'll distract them so you can use some of your martial arts magic to jump Scratten and get the gun away. Harvey and Sophy, even with their hands tied, can handle Warren for the few seconds until I get there.'

She tore the sleeves off her blouse, soaked all three pieces in the office's sink, then handed one sleeve to Daniel. 'Tie this over your mouth and nose to protect you from the smoke.' She draped the largest piece of her wet shirt over Nora's nest, hoping it would keep out the worst of the smoke.

She tied the other sleeve over her face while she Daniel tiptoed into position, then she pulled the alarm. The door opened and Warren came out, followed by Sophy and Harvey.

Just as Scratten came through the door, Harvey pretended to stumble and tried to get the gun. Scratten knocked him to the ground, then aimed the gun at his chest.

When Jess realized he really was going to shoot Harvey, she screamed and ran toward them. Scratten looked up, cursed, and pointed the gun at her.

Daniel moved, Scratten screamed and went down.

Sophy shoved Warren and he stumbled forward where he tripped over Jess's foot. She wrestled him on to his front and pinned him, then Sophy sat on his back.

Jess was feeling very pleased with her scheme until she heard a gun shot.

'It went like clockwork,' she said. She sat down cross-legged on top of Sophy's desk. As soon as she was settled, Nick and Nora scrambled up Daniel's body, across the paper he was trying to write on, and into her lap.

He wondered if it was luck that kept their claws from piercing his skin.

'Do you really think so?' Daniel smiled wryly at her obvious satisfaction, then re-read what he'd written. He was no lawyer but, unless Warren chose to dispute it, the wording should hold up in court. Under the circumstances, the old bastard would probably be able to claim he'd signed it under duress.

'Oh, it's just a graze,' Jess said. 'Stop being such a big baby.'

Daniel winced as Sophy tightened the gauze around his arm, then looked over to where Warren lay on the floor beside Scratten. Both were tied up with the ropes they'd used on Harvey and Sophy. Harvey stood over them with Scratten's gun in his hand, daring them to move.

Daniel realized he would have to explain to Warren until he understood how things would get worse, not better, if he tried to dispute the sale of his Concept House shares.

'You think he's over-reacting?' Sophy said. 'So who ran screaming down the hall when she thought Scratten had shot Daniel?' She handed him one of Harvey's extra shirts since Jess was still wearing the sweater.

'That was before I knew it was only a graze.'

'Thanks for the first aid, Sophy,' Daniel said as he

buttoned the shirt. Then he went to stand over Warren. He had some questions that needed answers.

'Why?'

'You know I was having problems, Daniel. After you and Anna gave me money it got worse, not better. I had to do something, I was desperate. Lucas Nillson got me into a deal and it all snowballed on me.'

'Shut up, asshole,' Scratten yelled.

Daniel noticed Jess had stopped playing with the cats and was listening.

'Wouldn't it have been better to let the business fail than get involved with criminals?'

'You don't know what it's like! Once they get their hooks into you, you're screwed. Nillson made me hire Scratten and next thing I knew their buddies were funneling their dirty money through the company. I couldn't stop them.'

'You could have gone to the police.'

'They would have killed me,' Warren whimpered.

'Damn right,' Scratten threatened.

Harvey jammed the gun barrel against Ralph's knee. 'I suggest you be quiet. I wouldn't mind giving you a permanent limp.'

'You've got to help me, Daniel. I can't go to jail. I wouldn't have hurt them, you know that. It was all Scratten's idea.'

'I met Lucas Nillson,' Jess said quietly, 'when Sophy and I were checking out nursing homes for a client. He's the manager of Shaughnessy Manor. The Manor's north wing is kept locked and guarded and I

351

'would bet that's where they kept Harvey the night he was kidnapped.'

'You'd better give that information to Tom as soon as he gets here,' Daniel said. 'He'll want to send several officers to deal with Nillson before this arrest hits the news. But there's one more thing before Tom gets here.'

Daniel had just finished his short, but not sweet, conversation with Warren when the door burst open and Tom led several police officers into the room.

Jess was glad to see the last of the police. They'd asked questions, gathered evidence, and asked everyone to come down to the station in the morning to sign their statements. Several burly officers had escorted a despairing Warren and a defiant Scratten out to the police cars.

Sophy was on the phone, fielding calls from reporters who'd heard the news on their scanners.

Jess had decided she needed to sit down and have a little quiet time with Harvey.

'It's finally over. How do you feel?' Jess walked into her partner's dark office. She could barely see him sitting behind his desk, silhouetted against the tiny bands of light caused by the street lights shining through the venetian blinds.

The connecting door to the her office was closed and she shut the door to the outer office behind her. She wanted one more shot at convincing him to stay in Vancouver. She might not get another chance.

'Where's Daniel?' he asked.

'In my office. He wanted to phone his family and tell them it's over so they wouldn't worry.'

'I feel odd.'

'Huh? Oh.' Jess realized he was answering her question. 'Good odd or bad odd?'

'Just odd. Until now, I never really believed this day would come. It's odd, knowing that tomorrow I'll have to find a new purpose for my life.'

'What about the cottage in Florida? Doesn't that count? Ouch!' She stubbed her toe as she groped her way to a chair.

'Oh, so now you want me to go, do you? Doesn't matter, Sophy canceled the deal. I don't get to have my beach cottage in the sun.'

Jess felt like cheering and dancing a jig.

So she did.

After she'd crashed against his desk a couple times, Harvey lost patience. 'For heaven's sake, just sit down before you break something!'

She did as she was told. Once she'd caught her breath and found the chair again, she worried about his money. 'I thought you said it wasn't refundable.'

'She phoned the agent, told them I was under a doctor's care and not fit mentally to be signing contracts. She persuaded them to send the money back. I believe she did some delicate hinting about her friend, Ruth St Clair, the Crown Prosecutor.'

'Sophy's quite a woman, isn't she?'

He didn't answer.

'I'm glad you're not leaving. I was serious when I said you should stay with the firm. You could run the company and be in charge of training the new operatives we hire. Really go big time. If those guys at Fenleck are anything to go by, we won't have any serious competition.'

'Speaking of which, I'll pay half of their bill, Jess, since this was my case. I can afford it now I'm getting Scratten's retainer back.'

Jess slouched down in the chair and put her feet up on Harvey's desk. 'What now?'

'Revenge must take up quite a bit of space because I feel sort've hollow.'

'Sophy would fill up that space, Harvey. She loves you.'

'Yeah. She told me she did, while those two had us tied up. She also proposed.'

Jess's feet thudded to the floor as she jerked upright. 'She what?'

'Said she'd wasted enough time and I should fish or cut bait. I asked her what that meant and she didn't know, not exactly, so then she told me I should either get off the pot or pee.'

'Colorful sayings. How did you answer her?'

'I told her I'd think about it and get back to her.'

'Is that why you're sitting here in the dark? You haven't made up your mind? Geez. She's afraid you'll always love Louise.'

'She told me that, too. I said I'd analyse the situation and get back to her.'

'Harvey, you are beginning to seriously annoy me.'

His desk light clicked on and she blinked in the sudden glare. 'What about the spaces in *your* life? Are you going to spend the rest of your life hiding up there in your safe little attic, watching films about Sam Spade, Adam Dalgliesh, or Sherlock Holmes?'

'I'm not hiding!'

'Tell Daniel you love him.'

'Later. Maybe tomorrow.'

'You shouldn't postpone something that important, Tess. What if things had gone wrong tonight and that bullet did more than graze him? You would never have had a chance to tell him. When Louise phoned that day I didn't tell her I was happy about the baby. I thought it could wait until I saw her.'

'That was a low blow, Harvey.'

'Hey, it could happen to you.'

'He'll probably ask me to marry him.'

'So marry him.'

'If we have kids, they'll be ashamed of a mom who can't read. I won't even be able to help them with their homework.'

'If they are ashamed, it'll be because of your attitude. And as for homework, you're marrying a teacher, sweetheart. Make him do it.'

'I'm probably getting all worked up about nothing. I doubt he'll consider me wife material now he knows I'm dyslexic.'

'You should be proud of what you've accomplished,'

he said, 'not worrying about what you don't have.
You've got to give Daniel a chance.'

'Tell you what.' Jess leaned forward and crossed her
arms on his desk. 'You have your talk with Sophy now
and I promise to have a talk with Daniel tonight.'

'Deal.' He stuck out his hand, she shook it. 'I think
Daniel is going to surprise you, Jess.'

'I hope so.'

'Does Sophy always get so . . . carried away when she's
happy?' Daniel asked as he watched Jess lock up the
office.

Sophy and Harvey had left twenty minutes ago but
Jess kept telling Daniel there was just one more thing
she *had* to do.

He suspected she'd been hoping he'd get tired of
waiting and leave without her. It wasn't going to
happen. It had been a long, traumatic day for both
of them and she looked as exhausted as he felt, but they
were going to have a talk before this day was over.

'Well, not usually. I'm glad the engagement is now
official,' she said as she dropped the key in her pocket.

They started down the hall. Nick and Nora were
already waiting at the elevator.

'I've never seen Harvey quite that embarrassed
before. It was amusing watching him try to convince
Sophy they should be decorous and businesslike in the
office. Geez, I can't even imagine Sophy trying to be
decorous.'

After they left the building he put his arm around

her waist and steered her toward where he'd left the Jaguar. Jess was too tired to notice, but Nick looked doubtful before nudging Nora in the new direction.

She did notice she wasn't at the Beetle when he opened the car door for her. 'I'll drive my car.'

'You can't. You're too tired.'

'Nick has to ride in the front seat or he'll throw up.'

'Then he can sit with you.' He settled her into the seat, fastened the seatbelt for her, then waited for the cats to jump in. Nora draped herself across the back seat as usual while Nick sat bolt upright on Jess's lap.

'We have to drop by Anna's before I can take you home. She made me promise to come over, no matter how late. She wants to see both of us with her own eyes, to make sure we're okay.'

She nodded, as if it wasn't important, but he noticed a small smile appear on her lips.

When they pulled into the driveway, bedlam erupted as his sisters and nephews came boiling out the door. He felt damn good when he saw Chris was part of the group, though she hung back a little. She looked happy but cautious, as if she wasn't quite sure what they would do next.

Everyone talked as the car doors were opened and Jess, Daniel, and the cats were extracted. Ruth hugged him, Chris clung to his hand, Mary hugged Jess, and Hannah cooed and cuddled Nora.

The boys were going to pick up Nick but backed off respectfully after one contemptuous look from the

Siamese. They waited for him to jump out, then shut all the doors.

'Daniel!' He looked up and saw Anna standing in the doorway, her hand out to him. His sisters let him go and he ran up the stairs to catch her in a hug.

'See? We're in one piece,' he said.

'Tom told Mary that awful man shot you.'

'It was just a scratch, honest.'

Everyone else had crowded onto the porch by that time and Anna turned to Jess.

'Thank God you're both safe.' She hugged Jess and kissed her cheek. 'Is he telling me the truth? You're both okay?'

'Yes.'

'The Sisters made you two some dinner.' She linked arms with Jess and led the way inside.

While Daniel and Jess consumed chicken noodle soup, homemade bread and milk, the family badgered them for the full story about what happened. Afterward Anna and Ruth took Jess off to the living-room to relax and Hannah went upstairs to do some homework, saying something about an early test the next morning.

Mary announced it was time to take her boys home to bed and Chris quietly asked if she could get a ride to the Skytrain station.

'Nonsense. We'll drive you home,' Mary said, then took the boys to say goodbye to Anna.

Daniel and Chris leaned on the porch railing.

'I'm glad you finally told me who you are. I wish I'd known you all these years.'

'I wish I'd tried to find you sooner, but I had to grow up before I could separate the truth from Vince's lies. I've known where you were for a few years but was afraid to meet you. I couldn't face another disappointment.

'Last summer I saw your firm's advertisement for an office manager and did some research. I decided if I worked for you, I could get to know you. If necessary, I could quit and you'd never know about me.'

'I'm glad I passed muster. Not to mention you're the best office manager I've ever had. I used to wonder how you seemed to be able to make decisions in my absence, exactly the way I would.'

'Shouldn't I resign? Once the staff finds out I'm your sister, things could get awkward.'

'Who cares? My office has never run more smoothly –' his eyebrows twitched into a frown, '– except for that blasted School-Work Project.'

She laughed. 'Daniel, you'll have to lighten up about those kids. I should tell you, though, that Gwen quit today. She'd going to work for Finders Keepers.'

'Better Jess than me.' He laughed. 'She'll probably enjoy herself there.' He heard the boys thundering toward them. 'Here they come.'

'I guess I'll see you tomorrow,' she said and squeezed his hand.

'Better get lots of sleep.' He bent to kiss her cheek. 'We're going to be really busy for the next while. I'm going to be dividing my time between Concept House and the Institute.'

Ruth left at the same time as Mary and, after he waved them off, Daniel wandered into the living-room where Jess was sitting with Anna.

'Are they gone, dear?'

'Yes.'

Jess was sitting on the stool beside Anna's rocking chair, staring into the fire, and didn't look up when he came into the room. Nora was curled up in her lap and Nick stretched out at her side.

Daniel crouched nearby and stirred the logs with the poker.

'I like Chris, we all do,' Anna said. 'The girls enrolled her into the Sisters before dinner.'

'I appreciate you taking care of her tonight, Anna. I didn't want to leave her alone when she'd been so upset, but Jess and I had to go.' He stretched out on the floor at her feet.

'You did the right thing, bringing her here. She's your sister, Daniel, and that means she's part of the family. I shudder to think what might have happened if you hadn't gone back with Jess.'

'Me, too,' he said.

'I'm so glad you're both safe. When Tom called to tell us what was happening and said to lock the doors, I was scared for you both.'

'Jess calls these exciting interludes "adventures".'

'No more adventures tonight, okay? This old lady needs her sleep. Speaking of which, it's past my bedtime.'

'Can you stay a minute?' Daniel asked. 'I need to talk to you about something.'

'Sounds serious.'

'Yes, it is. Warren will go to jail. Before the police took him away tonight he agreed to sell me all his shares in Concept House for one dollar each. I will do my best to save the company but, if it does fail, you will lose your entire investment.'

'You are going to manage the company?'

'Yes.'

'Then I don't see any problem. My investment is safe.'

Jess chuckled. 'Now that's faith.'

'Yes, dear, a mother's faith in her brilliant son. A very tired mother, so I'll say goodnight.'

Daniel went to help her to her feet.

'Now, I'm going to give you two an order and I don't want to hear any argument, you hear?' Anna shook her finger at them.

'Both of you are to sleep here tonight. Daniel, you can have your old room. Jess, you'll sleep in the guest room. It's at the top of the stairs, first door on the left.'

'I have to take my cats home.'

'No, you don't. Before they left, I asked the boys to run down to the corner store and pick up a bag of kitty litter. It's in the kitchen in a cardboard box; just show Nick and Nora where. And if they get hungry again, there's more of the tuna they liked.'

'Jess?' Daniel waited for her answer. Hoping she'd stay.

361

She watched the fire for a few minutes, then turned to Anna. 'Thank you.'

When Daniel came back downstairs alone, she was still sitting in front of the fire, watching the flames. He stretched out on the floor beside her again.

The rest of the house gradually settled into the cool stillness of night. The fire was dying and shadows crept closer, no longer held at bay by the warmth and light of flames.

Daniel decided he had to try. He wondered what Jess would think if she knew he felt more fear asking this question than he had tackling an armed criminal.

'Will you marry me, Jess?'

CHAPTER 17

'I love you.' His voice was low and she knew he was watching her.

Jess had thought she was prepared. But she wasn't! 'I can't marry you, Daniel.'

'You love me. I know you do.'

'Whether I love you or not doesn't matter.'

'It's all that matters!'

'I won't marry you when I can't be the wife you want and need.'

'You are exactly what I need. Do you have any idea how much I admire and respect you for what you've achieved? On your own, with only Harvey and Sophy to help you?'

'What about kids? What if they inherit it from me?'

'There are lots of people who achieved their dreams despite dyslexia. Heck, I have a friend at the university who has it and he's a teacher with a PhD. So don't try to tell me it will get in our kids' way.'

Jess put Nora down on the floor beside Nick.

'I won't marry you, Daniel.'

363

'You're afraid. I never thought I'd see it. Jess Phillips, letting fear stop her from going after what she wants.'

'I said no, Daniel.'

He sighed, then stood up and scooped her into his arms. 'Come here. I can see we need to take this to a higher authority.'

He walked over to the big chair opposite Anna's rocking chair and sat down with Jess in his lap. She could tell by the grip he had on her waist that he wasn't going to let her leave. Daniel tried to urge her back against his shoulder but she sat straight, determined not to let him coax her into a marriage she knew wouldn't work.

'This was Sam's chair.' He ran one hand down the arm. 'The Sisters always sit here when they have problems. They talk things over with him and usually figure out a pretty good answer.'

'And you think sitting in this chair will give us an answer that will change my mind?'

'I'm hoping so. I've never tried it myself but the Sisters swear by it. Do you want me to go first?'

She nodded, dazed.

He cleared his throat.

'Hello, Sam. It's Daniel. This gorgeous woman in my lap is Jess Phillips and I'm trying to convince her to marry me.' He ducked his head down and whispered in her ear, 'Say hi.'

Jess couldn't quite believe she was sitting here, listening to him talk to the air. He jiggled her and she wet her lips. 'Hi, Sam.'

'I don't know if you noticed, Sam, but I made a big fool of myself a while back. I made a list of all the things a woman needed to be a perfect wife, then I set out to find her. Needless to say, it all went wrong. Luckily Jess set me straight.'

'Daniel, this is silly,' Jess whispered.

'Shh.' He touched her lips, then her nose with one finger. 'It took me a while, but I finally realized Jess was the perfect wife for me. But now I've found her, she's turned stubborn. So I've come to you for advice.'

He cocked his head, as if he was listening to a ghost. 'You think that'll do the trick? Okay, I'll give it a try.

'Sam says you need to know me better and suggested I tell you a story. For that, we have to get more comfortable.'

Daniel held her waist in both hands and twisted his body beneath her so he was sitting at an angle, leaning against the chair's wide back. He slid his knee up against the back of the chair so she fell between his legs, resting sideways against his thigh, facing him. 'Now, relax.'

She did, reluctantly, and immediately felt cradled by both his warmth and the comfortable chair. When she nestled into the cradle of his thighs, her hip rubbed against him and he hardened in response.

He groaned. 'Not now, Jess.'

She smiled. 'I thought you were going to tell me a story?'

'I am, if you'll sit still.' He gave her a stern look.

Jess did her best to look apologetic.

'Once upon a time there was a boy who found himself plucked out of hell and set down in heaven. For a long time he believed the moment he did something wrong, he'd have to go back to hell. And since he was afraid and angry, he tested the man and woman who'd brought him to heaven.'

He laughed and looked up. 'I heard that, Sam.'

'Finish the story,' she said.

'He showed them, over and over, that he didn't belong in heaven, but their patience was stronger than his anger. Even the two little girl angels who lived in heaven wanted him to stay. After the third little girl angel was born, the woman asked if he would watch out for them, be their big brother.'

'How many years is he going to wait before he lets himself call her Mom?'

Daniel's eyes opened wide, and then narrowed as he stared at Jess. 'He was afraid.'

'She wants to be his mother. I think the woman has proved herself enough, don't you, Daniel?'

He smiled. 'Yes, she has.'

'Now finish the story. What happened after the mother asked him to be the little angels' guardian?'

'She made him feel as if he had an important job in heaven and eventually he started to believe that he would be able to stay.'

'This house is your heaven?'

'No, Jess. This family.' He'd been half-smiling the whole time he pretended he was talking to Sam, but now his expression grew serious. He touched her cheek. 'Heaven isn't perfect, though. I've been lonely, Jess. And if you won't marry me, I'll always be lonely.'

'Daniel, I –'

'And you've been lonely, too, even with Harvey and Sophy. Do you really think a little thing like whether or not you can read is important enough to keep us apart and lonely for the rest of our lives?'

Jess slid her arms around his neck and rested her head on his shoulder. 'No, Daniel, I don't.'

'Good morning, Daniel.'

He opened his eyes and stared up at the ceiling, aware of Jess's weight on his chest as she stirred. He squinted at the light and realized it was morning. He and Jess must have fallen asleep in the chair while they planned their wedding.

Jess wanted a small ceremony, preferably in Anna's backyard and that was fine with him. As long as it was *soon* and legal and binding, with no way for her to wriggle out of it, he would be happy. Though he imagined the Sisters would put up a vigorous fight for a wedding spectacle.

'Daniel?' He turned his head and saw Anna standing in the doorway. She was smiling at him, her hands clasped at her waist. The leopard brooch glinted, seeming to move as she breathed.

'Hi, Mom.'

Anna's eyes filled. She pressed one hand to her chest.

Jess kissed him and they both stood up.

Daniel crossed the room in three quick strides, and wrapped his arms around his mother. 'Thank you, Mom. For everything.'

He held her as she wept. Eventually she wiped her eyes with a tissue from her pocket and patted him on the chest as she stepped away. 'Thank you, Daniel.'

She held out her hand to Jess, who'd been standing aside, watching. Anna grasped her hand and drew her close so the three of them formed a circle.

'When I found you both here, in Sam's chair, I wondered . . . I hoped . . .'

'Last night I asked Jess to marry me and, with Sam's help, I finally convinced her to say yes.'

'Good.' She reached up and unpinned the leopard brooch. It sparkled as she cupped it in her hand. 'Sam gave me this the day he asked me to marry him. If it wasn't for this brooch, we wouldn't have been able to keep you for our son, Daniel.'

She took his hand in hers and placed the brooch on his palm. 'Now you must give it to Jess.'

'Oh, no, Anna.' Jess stepped back. 'I couldn't. One of your daughters should –'

Anna gave her a stern look. 'Jess, you are my daughter now and you *will* wear the leopard.'

Jess's throat felt thick and she experienced a strange tickle behind her eyes but knew she wouldn't cry, no matter how happy she felt at that moment.

Jess Phillips never cried, couldn't cry, hadn't cried since she was a child.

EPILOGUE

Daniel stood beside Jess, watching as she opened wedding presents. The battle over the wedding had gone about as he'd thought it would.

The afternoon wedding had been simple but beautiful and even the weather had cooperated with bright sunshine, a bright blue sky, and fluffy white clouds.

He'd stood at one end of the yard between Tom and the minister and watched as Harvey and Jess walked toward him across the grass. Her dress was white, her hair a dark cloud around her shoulders, and the leopard brooch sparkled on her breast. When she came close she'd held out her hand and smiled at him. Then, in front of God and witnesses, she promised to love him forever

He was a happy man.

Daniel noticed she was almost finished unwrapping the last wedding present and reached behind her chair for the parcel he'd stowed there earlier. He turned it nervously in his hands, wondering if he'd made a mistake, worrying that he should have gone with a more traditional gift like pearls.

When he was trying to decide what to give Jess for a wedding gift, he'd remembered her lecture the day he'd given her roses. It had been hard to find a sculptor who was willing to take on the job. He'd even rented the movie so he could get the wrapping just right.

Jess held up the crystal vase for everyone to see, then handed it to Chris who was recording the gifts and arranging them on the deck for everyone to admire. Thank heavens that was the last one, she thought.

This had all been a lot of fun, but she'd be glad when it was over. The Sisters had forbidden any contact with Daniel since the day before and she'd had enough.

She wanted to get her new husband alone.

When she turned back to scoop up the fancy wrapping paper and ribbons and hand it to the boys who were on garbage duty, she noticed someone had placed a parcel in the middle of the glitter.

It was wrapped in tattered newspaper bound with twine. How odd. She tried to pick it up in her hands, looking for a card. Nothing. It was very heavy. Chris handed her a pair of scissors and she snipped the twine.

She pulled apart the newspaper and found the next layer was a piece of wool cloth. As she unrolled the cloth, her hands began to shake. Underneath the cloth was a layer of batting and when she pulled that away there was a layer of thin white fabric.

She ran her hands over the cloth, feeling the hardness and shape of the item inside. She looked up at Daniel. He nodded.

The white cotton shredded easily in her hands, baring a black statue of a bird.

As soon as she saw it she realized it was from Daniel. He'd given her an ebony replica of the statue from *The Maltese Falcon*.

Jess smiled shakily at Daniel. When he knelt beside her and touched her cheek, she realized she was crying. Whatever was true about Jess Phillips, it seemed Jess St Clair could cry.

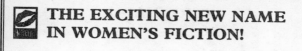

THE EXCITING NEW NAME
IN WOMEN'S FICTION!

PLEASE HELP ME TO HELP YOU!

Dear *Scarlet* Reader,

I have some wonderful news for you this month – we are beginning a super Prize Draw, which means that you *could win an exclusive sassy Scarlet T-shirt!* Just fill in your questionnaire and return it to us (see addresses at the end of the questionnaire) before 31 November 1998, and we'll do the rest! If you are lucky enough to be one of the first four names out of the hat each month, we will send you this exclusive prize.

So don't delay – return your form straight away!*

Looking forward to hearing from you,

Sally Cooper

Editor-in-Chief, *Scarlet*

QUESTIONNAIRE

Please tick the appropriate boxes to indicate your answers

1 Where did you get this Scarlet title?
Bought in supermarket ☐
Bought at my local bookstore ☐ Bought at chain bookstore ☐
Bought at book exchange or used bookstore ☐
Borrowed from a friend ☐
Other (please indicate) _____

2 Did you enjoy reading it?
A lot ☐   A little ☐   Not at all ☐

3 What did you particularly like about this book?
Believable characters ☐   Easy to read ☐
Good value for money ☐   Enjoyable locations ☐
Interesting story ☐   Modern setting ☐
Other _____

4 What did you particularly dislike about this book?
_____

5 Would you buy another Scarlet book?
Yes ☐   No ☐

6 What other kinds of book do you enjoy reading?
Horror ☐   Puzzle books ☐   Historical fiction ☐
General fiction ☐   Crime/Detective ☐   Cookery ☐
Other (please indicate) _____

7 Which magazines do you enjoy reading?
1. _____
2. _____
3. _____

And now a little about you –
8 How old are you?
Under 25 ☐   25–34 ☐   35–44 ☐
45–54 ☐   55–64 ☐   over 65 ☐

cont.

9 What is your marital status?
   Single ☐   Married/living with partner ☐
   Widowed ☐   Separated/divorced ☐

10 What is your current occupation?
    Employed full-time ☐   Employed part-time ☐
    Student ☐   Housewife full-time ☐
    Unemployed ☐   Retired ☐

11 Do you have children? If so, how many and how old are they?
    _____
    _____

12 What is your annual household income?
    under $15,000   ☐   or   £10,000   ☐
    $15–25,000   ☐   or   £10–20,000   ☐
    $25–35,000   ☐   or   £20–30,000   ☐
    $35–50,000   ☐   or   £30–40,000   ☐
    over $50,000   ☐   or   £40,000   ☐

Miss/Mrs/Ms _____
Address _____
_____
_____

Thank you for completing this questionnaire. Now tear it out – put
it in an envelope and send it, before 30 April 1999, to:

Sally Cooper, Editor-in-Chief

USA/Can. address   *UK address/No stamp required*
SCARLET c/o London Bridge   SCARLET
85 River Rock Drive   FREEPOST LON 3335
Suite 202   LONDON W8 4BR
Buffalo   *Please use block capitals for*
NY 14207   *address*
USA

FIHER/10/98

Scarlet titles coming next month:

TOO LATE FOR LOVE   Lisa Andrews

When Gemma Davenport hears that Blake Adams is going to buy her glass company, her heart sinks. He probably doesn't even remember her name, but ten years ago they had a passionate affair which left Gemma broken-hearted. As soon as she sees him again, though, it is clear that Blake does remember Gemma and makes it apparent that he has never forgiven her for what he sees as her 'betrayal' in marrying another man. Penniless after the take-over, Blake offers her a job as his housekeeper! Gemma has no choice but to accept, but she is soon wondering why, if Blake is so intent on getting his own back, he's trying to rekindle their once 'fatal attraction'.

ALL SHE WANTS   Karen Templeton-Berger

'He wasn't supposed to look better,' Gwyn thought when she met Alex Wainwright again. Alex has asked Gwyn to return home because her grandfather's inn is in trouble and, instead of the skinny boy next door she remembers, Alex is now a gorgeous hunk. Gwyn fell out with her grandfather over her desire to be an actress, and although she hasn't found fame yet, she definitely can't see a future for herself in a small town, married and helping run her grandfather's inn. However, she and Alex become lovers and he asks her to help organize the school pageant. Is Gwyn beginning to revise her ideas about marriage and children . . . what of her career? Then she is offered the acting break she's been waiting for . . . . Can she have it all?

WE ARE PROUD TO ANNOUNCE THE NOVEMBER PUBLICATION OF OUR THIRD _SCARLET_ HARDBACK:

MOON SHADOW   Julia Wild

Ellie Morrison is an actress by trade. So what's she doing on a ranch in Montana posing as a housekeeper and investigating the murky past of its good-looking owner, Declan Kelloway? And why does she find herself attracted to her new boss? After all she has a perfectly satisfactory man in her life. And Declan is just part of her job, isn't he?

JOIN THE CLUB!

Why not join the *Scarlet* Readers' Club – you can have four exciting new reads delivered to your door every other month for only £9.99, plus TWO FREE BOOKS WITH YOUR FIRST MONTH'S ORDER!

Fill in the form below and tick your two first books from those listed:

1. *Never Say Never* by Tina Leonard ☐
2. *The Sins of Sarah* by Anne Styles ☐
3. *Wicked in Silk* by Andrea Young ☐
4. *Wild Lady* by Liz Fielding ☐
5. *Starstruck* by Lianne Conway ☐
6. *This Time Forever* by Vickie Moore ☐
7. *It Takes Two* by Tina Leonard ☐
8. *The Mistress* by Angela Drake ☐
9. *Come Home Forever* by Jan McDaniel ☐
10. *Deception* by Sophie Weston ☐
11. *Fire and Ice* by Maxine Barry ☐
12. *Caribbean Flame* by Maxine Barry ☐

ORDER FORM

SEND NO MONEY NOW. Just complete and send to **SCARLET READERS' CLUB, FREEPOST, LON 3335, Salisbury SP5 5YW**

Yes, I want to join the ***SCARLET* READERS' CLUB*** and have the convenience of 4 exciting new novels delivered directly to my door every other month! Please send me my first shipment now for the unbelievable price of £9.99, plus my TWO special offer books absolutely free. I understand that I will be invoiced for this shipment and FOUR further *Scarlet* titles at £9.99 (including postage and packing) every other month unless I cancel my order in writing. I am over 18.

Signed ....

Name (IN BLOCK CAPITALS)..

Address (IN BLOCK CAPITALS)..

....

Town... Post Code...............................

Phone Number ....

As a result of this offer your name and address may be passed on to other carefully selected companies. If you do not wish this, please tick this box ☐.